THE BIBLE OF DIRTY JOKES

Also by Eileen Pollack:

Fiction:
A Perfect Life
Breaking and Entering
In the Mouth
Paradise, New York
The Rabbi in the Attic and Other Stories

Nonfiction:
The Only Woman in the Room: Why Science Is Still a Boys' Club
Woman Walking Ahead: In Search of Catherine Weldon and Sitting Bull

THE BIBLE OF DIRTY JOKES

A NOVEL

Eileen Pollack

Four Way Books
Tribeca

This is a work of fiction. Names, characters, places, and incidents are either the products of the author's imagination or are used fictitiously. Any resemblance to actual events or persons, living or dead, is entirely coincidental.

Library of Congress Cataloging-in-Publication Data

Names: Pollack, Eileen, 1956- author.
Title: The bible of dirty jokes : a novel / Eileen Pollack.
Description: New York : Four Way Books, [2018]
Identifiers: LCCN 2017029364 (print) | LCCN 2017031524 (ebook) | ISBN 9781945588150 (ebook) | ISBN 9781945588143 (softccover : acid-free paper)
Classification: LCC PS3566.O4795 (ebook) | LCC PS3566.O4795 B53 2018 (print) | DDC 813/.54--dc23
LC record available at https://lccn.loc.gov/2017029364

This book is manufactured in the United States of America and printed on acid-free paper.

Four Way Books is a not-for-profit literary press. We are grateful for the assistance we receive from individual donors, public arts agencies, and private foundations.

PROUD MEMBER

[clmp]

We are a proud member of the Community of Literary Magazines and Presses.

Distributed by University Press of New England
One Court Street, Lebanon, NH 03766

For Marian

THE BIBLE OF DIRTY JOKES

1.

My story begins last spring. I was sitting in this apartment, trying to make sense of the thousands of bits of paper, tape recordings, photographs, and erotic objets d'art that my dear late husband, Morty, managed to accumulate in his sixty-one years of research. I was doing this because the Department of Popular Culture at Columbia University had expressed such a fervent interest in acquiring this strange collection. And because I recently had come to realize what interesting, revealing clues to my husband's private life were scattered among these files.

As you might or might not know, Morty was a pioneer in the field of the dirty joke. The hubbub he created in the late 1950s, when he published his first few monographs on bawdy songs and jokes about farmers' daughters, was exceeded only by the furor created a decade earlier by his friend and colleague Alfred Kinsey. But in the area of organizational skills . . . let's just say dear Morty was deficient. By which I mean—if not for me—he couldn't have found a clean pair of socks to put on in the morning. Or, for that matter, found his feet.

In our twenty-nine years together, I helped him type up and organize nearly all the data he had amassed. But after Morty died, I found in his bureau drawer the key to a locker in New Jersey I hadn't known existed. Not only did I discover evidence that he had kept up a correspondence with a Playboy-bunny-turned-sociologist named Candace Cohen, the evidence seemed to indicate that Morty and Professor Cohen had carried on an affair until the day he died.

Nor was that all. In a small black leather book, Morty had recorded his visits to every strip club and bordello from Canada to the Rio Grande, with notations that seemed to indicate the names, ages, and identifying characteristics of the women with whom he had had encounters, along with receipts for the services they provided, charged to a credit card I hadn't known Morty owned.

Equally damning, the locker contained a trove of erotic artifacts dating back to Greek and Roman times. If Morty had sold only a few such treasures, I could have stopped working as a waitress. We could have afforded to take vacations. I could have accompanied him on his trips. We might even have had a child.

I was sorting through these mementos when I received a phone call from my mother. "Ketzel!" she said. "I know you didn't intend to come see us until next month. What with poor Morty dead, you have a lot of headaches on your hands. But your father and I could use your help. If it isn't too much trouble, could you possibly come today?"

A call from one's aged parents in which they politely request that one come that same day is not to be ignored. They were up to their necks in paperwork related to the sale of our old hotel. Not to mention I missed them terribly and was worried about their health. And, to be honest, I was tired of reading jokes.

I locked up our apartment and grabbed a taxi to the Port Authority, where I boarded the bus to Monticello, which we reached two hours later, the bus huffing past the soaped-up windows of what once had been the bakeries, delicatessens, kosher butchers, fish shops, and clothing stores of what once had been the Borscht Belt.

My bus pulled in and stopped.

"Ketzel!" Leo called. He waved and waddled over. "You got a suitcase, right?"

In Victorian times, Leo Bialik would have been known as our *family retainer.* By which I mean he thought everyone was out to get us and his primary job was to set those bastards straight. He was built like a bus himself—a bus that on this particular day was wearing green plaid shorts, a blue nylon shirt on which a regatta of sailboats raced around the considerable equator of his girth, and a red plastic cap from a batch we had given out as souvenirs to a convention of Teamsters from Teaneck, New Jersey, in 1962. Leo had worked for my family for more than sixty years. "Saved from a life of crime" was the way Leo liked to put it. "If not for your grandpa Joe, I would be floating at the bottom of Cuyahoga Lake."

Leo squinted at my bag and found the button to pop the handle. "Wonderful invention," he marveled, unable to get over that some genius had come up with the bright idea of putting wheels on one end of a suitcase and a handle on the other. He tugged it across the lot with the oddly prim waddle of a short, plump opera diva swishing on her heels in a tight, long skirt while leading a balky pug. When he got to my parents' car, he held the passenger door for me, then settled in the driver's seat, took off the plastic cap, and placed it on the dash.

"So how's the town look?" This being Leo, the question was pronounced *So howz duh town look?* Yet for all the indelicacy of his speech, his lips were lightly pursed, as if there were a necklace between his lips and he was letting it out one pearl at a time. If I imitate the way he talks, it's not to show disrespect. It's just that, given my inclinations as a mimic, it's too delicious to resist.

"Never mind," Leo said. "Lousy is how it looks. But maybe it's getting better? Two *faygelehs* from the city just bought the old movie theater. They're planning on getting it back in shape and showing, waddaya call, your classics. Your Bogart and Bacall, your Bette Davis and Edward G." He drove with his left hand on the wheel and his right hand on his knee, thumb and first two fingers pressed in an O, ring finger and pinky cocked, like a man holding a cigar, although I had never seen Leo smoke. He used this hand to burn home a point. "What is it with these *faygelehs*? They like all those tough broads. What's in it for them?" He scratched his warty neck. "Well, they wouldn't be doing it if they didn't think they couldn't pull in a buck. Same with Kaplan's Deli. A bunch of big shots from the city are pooling their resources and fixing it up. Not *faygelehs,* just regular businessmen. Speculators, you know?" This came out as *Speck-uh-latuhs, yuh know?* "Everybody's gambling on the casinos coming in." He fidgeted as if the mere idea of casinos made him itch. "Everybody's all excited. But if they knew what sort of riffraff gambling brought in the last time . . ."

I braced to hear the sentence I had been hearing all my life.

"If they knew how many bodies were buried around this town . . ."

There they were, those famous bodies. I had always assumed they were a metaphor for our family's acquaintance with Murder Inc. To be honest, I used to wish this acquaintance had been more intimate. The way I saw it, if those bodies had been real, they would have given off not the stench of shame but a certain perfume of glamour. Oh, come on, admit it. Don't your ears perk up when your oldest and toughest relatives tell and retell those stories of your great-great-great-uncle who hid Jesse James in his barn or hijacked booze for Al Capone? Why else would *The Sopranos* be the most popular show on TV?

So yes, my family had a romance with Murder Inc. My grandfather, Joseph Weinrach, came over from Galicia with everybody else's grandfathers. He bought a barbershop in the Bronx, where he earned a decent living cutting hair. But he was a very ambitious man. In the back of that steamy shop he invented a tonic that could restore a bald man's pride. Mar-Vel Hair Restorer, named as much to honor my grandma Marcia and their doted-on daughter, Velma, as to conjure up the miracle of hair sprouting on a head where there hadn't been hair before. The liquid was an appealing aqua blue and smelled sweetly of vanilla, which Marcia suggested he use for scent.

At first, Grandpa Joe sold this concoction from his shop. Then Prohibition came and distribution widened. The tonic was mostly alcohol. It smelled like something good to eat, and nothing in the ingredients made a person lame or blind. Women tended to wait until they got home to drink it. But men twisted off the cap and lifted the bottle to their lips before they left the store.

My grandfather made a mint. Rather than put his earnings in the bank—who could trust a bank?—he looked around for a sound investment. This was 1932. While Grandpa Joe was thinking, Grandma Marcia tried to book a room at Grossinger's, this being the first vacation she and her husband would ever take, and she was told the place was full. Full? Hundreds of rooms, each of which rented for fifty or sixty dollars a week, and all those rooms were full? Right then, Grandpa Joe decided to build his own hotel. Unlike the other immigrants who had colonized the Catskills, he didn't buy a crappy farm or start a rooming house and take in a few consumptives every spring. With a trunk of profits from Mar-Vel Hair Restorer, he bought an enormous expanse of land just east of Monticello. Then he built and built and built. Not for him the fake Tudor schmaltz or shabby stucco sprawl of most Borscht Belt resorts. He modeled the Hospitality House Hotel on the Fontainebleau in Miami Beach, all terrazzo, steel, and glass, floor after floor, with waterfalls in the lobby and balconies above the lake. Not only did Grandpa Joe build the world's largest indoor pool, he installed three outdoor pools as well, one for the kids and teens, another for the singles, and a third for the senior citizens, who liked to play pinochle and canasta without getting splashed. He flew in Bobby Jones to design a golf course. And when Bobby asked Grandpa Joe if he wanted eighteen holes to rival Grossinger's or an unheard-of thirty-six, my grandfather, who never had held a club, scoffed and said he figured an even fifty would do the trick.

"What do people want?" he liked to ask. "They want to feel special. So we make each and every guest feel more special than the rest. Also, what people want on their vacations is what they can't get at home. They live in the city? We give them the country. At home they got only one bathroom? At my hotel we give them two toilets for every bed!" This at a time when most Catskills resorts could offer no better than a bathroom down the hall. The Hospitality House provided not one but seven day camps, with a nighttime crew of counselors who went from room to room so the parents could enjoy the show. And what a show! The manager booked not only the usual array of Borscht Belt comics but headliners who had appeared the week before in Vegas or on *Ed Sullivan*. I grew up being pinched not only by Alan King, Red Buttons, Buddy Hackett, and Milton Berle but by Sammy Davis Jr., Dean Martin, Frank Sinatra, Judy Garland, and every Russian and Chinese acrobat who ever twirled across a stage. If Grossinger's was the oldest and most famous Catskills resort, the Hospitality House Hotel was the most luxurious and up to date.

But all this had its price.

"I hate to say this, Ketzel." Leo checked his blind spot, then passed a van of Hasids who were poking along the back road to our hotel at five miles an hour. "Gambling was the reason the Mob had your grandfather in its hip pocket."

That the thugs of Murder Inc. had considered my grandfather Joe to be their own private flask of whiskey from which they could take a nip when the need arose was hardly news to me. Given that Grandpa Joe had obtained Uncle Sam's permission to buy trainloads of alcohol to make his Mar-Vel tonic, he had plenty of alcohol left to sell to the likes of Louie Lepke. In return for such generosity, Lepke intervened in a labor dispute that otherwise might have doubled the cost of Grandpa Joe's hotel. But as so often happens when a person tries to keep accounts with a bunch of "businessmen" who can barely add, Grandpa Joe discovered he owed the Mob more than the Mob owed him. To pay off the debt, he allowed them to install slot machines in the lobby and promised to provide a complimentary Sabbath meal to any of Lepke's friends who happened to be vacationing in the Mountains.

It seemed a harmless enough concession. The idea of Kid Twist Reles, Tick-Tock Tannenbaum, Greenie Greenberg, and Gurrah Shapiro, their primly brushed kids and glitzily sequined wives enjoying matzo ball soup in our dining room struck me as more amusing than the dentists, furriers, and hosiery salesmen who sat consuming a similar meal in adjoining seats. If kosher hot dogs were purer than the pork-and-offal kind, then Jewish gangsters seemed less dangerous than the Irish or Italian brands.

Besides, how bad could Jewish gangsters be if they had names like Tick-Tock Tannenbaum (go ahead and say it, the tip of your tongue ticking against your palate, the burst of that final *baum*) or the wit to name their enterprise something as darkly funny as Murder Inc.? I assumed Leo had played the same role for Abe Reles as he played for my family, by which I mean he chauffeured the gang around, carried their bags, and, when a guest refused to pay, visited the deadbeat at his apartment and threatened to break a vase.

"Okay, kid, here we are." With one palm flexed suavely at ten o'clock—the watchband on his wrist and his big blue sapphire ring flashed sunlight around the car—Leo steered us past the guard booth, which was boarded and wrapped with vines. It made me sad to think there was nothing left to guard. Couples had fallen in love here. Babies had been conceived. So many guests from lesser resorts had wanted to row rowboats on our lake or attend our nighttime shows that we had needed to post a guard to keep them out.

The drive from the guardhouse to the lobby was half a mile. Once, the gardens on either side had been lovingly maintained. Who cared if the gardener's horticultural vocabulary had consisted only of the words *tulip* and *geranium*? Our guests were less impressed by variety than by statistics ("Imagine what it's like to get down on your hands and knees and plant fifty thousand bulbs!") and the sheer redness of all that *red*. Now, the road was so overgrown we could have been hacking through a jungle to reach a Mayan ruin. There seemed to be a law governing the decay of Borscht Belt resorts: hotels that had grown up slowly took longer to fall apart than upstarts like ours. Either that, or the Mob's involvement had guaranteed that shoddy materials and inferior construction techniques would be employed.

Leo drove around the back, where a tiered concrete deck rose above the empty pool like some abandoned coliseum; the place still echoed with the shrieks of teenagers who had climbed on each other's backs and fought watery raucous wars until one triumphant couple remained intact. Most of the facilities had deteriorated to the point where archaeologists would have scratched their heads as to what purpose these once had served. Who but me would know that the pulleys above the lake had provided the means for an entire generation of timid Jews to learn to ski before their children moved on to the death-defying slopes at Vail and Killington?

The golf course was the only facility still in operation—my parents leased it to a cartel of Russian businessmen who drove up from the city and played a leisurely fifty holes while their bodyguards held their drinks—but I couldn't bear to see the tennis courts. All those immaculate squares of fresh-raked clay, nets at regulation height, none with a droop or tear . . . nothing remained but fenced-in weeds.

It was hard for me to imagine how such a ruin could be rebuilt. But after fifty years of haggling, the lawmakers up in Albany seemed ready to legalize gambling in the Catskills. And the grounds of our old hotel, with its championship golf course, hundred-acre lake, and hookups for plumbing and electricity, would provide the perfect site for the first casino. To keep the Hospitality House afloat while the *chochems* in Albany had dithered about whether to bring in slots, my parents had been forced to take out a mortgage. In the late 1990s, they had given up and closed the hotel, but they still paid taxes and insurance. Unless they were able to cinch this deal, they would be saddled with all that debt. Or rather, my brother and I would bear the load.

Which reminds me of a joke. A cop is walking his beat when he sees a little boy running away with a suitcase. "Hey, sonny," the cop says, "where are you headed, a little tyke like you, alone at this hour?" And the boy says, "Let me go!" So the policeman says, "I'm not letting you go until you tell me why you aren't home in bed." And the boy says, "All right. This is what happened. I was listening at my parents' bedroom door. I hear my father scream, 'Here I go! Here I go!' Then I hear my mother yell, 'Wait for me! I'm coming, too!'" "Why, yes, my lad," the policeman says, "I understand all that. But why did you run away?" "Hell," the boy says, "you don't think I was gonna stick around and get stuck with the mortgage, do you?"

So you see, I had my reasons for wanting to help my parents. They were on their last legs—in my father's case, make that last leg—and I hoped they could use the proceeds to pay their debts and buy a few good years in Florida.

Leo parked and let me out. "Go on," he said. "Go see your mother. The poor woman has been counting the minutes until you get here."

The sun was already setting, but I was reluctant to go inside. Every time I saw my mother, she had gained another twenty pounds. *Oh, Mom,* I wanted to say, *you're killing yourself with all this eating. Come out, come out, wherever you are. Don't worry, I'll protect you.* Except I hadn't been able to protect her from all the losses she already had suffered, so how could I fend off whatever disaster was coming next?

First, my brother Ira had run away to fight in the Six-Day War. He was twelve years my senior, so I remember him mostly from the glossy graduation-photo that hangs above his bed (a portrait taken so long ago the paint the photographer used to airbrush Ira's zits has faded to reveal a lava field of boils) and the nearly life-size painting of my shirt-less, well-muscled brother that hangs in my parents' den. With its broad heroic strokes, the portrait could serve as a poster for the movie *Exodus*. Yet the snapshot from which the artist worked shows a slouchier, un-shaven Ira with a kaffiyeh on his head, a beer can at his feet, and a rifle projecting provocatively from his crotch.

To say my mother mourned Ira would be like saying Mary mourned Jesus, the agony of the loss offset only slightly by the hero each son became. Although the more appropriate analogy might be to the eldest Kennedy, who got shot down in World War II. And as happened with the Kennedys, the younger siblings in our clan were expected to honor their fallen brother by becoming heroes, too.

My second brother, Howie . . . Howie went into politics. From the mayor of Monticello he rose to become state senator. Then, like the family balloon he was, he kept rising until he hit the House of Repre-sentatives, where he grew so bloated with his own hot air he popped. By which I mean he got involved in some influence-peddling scheme it wearies me to explain. As often happens to Jews in jail, Howie became such a religious zealot he studied and prayed all day, allowed his beard to grow, and refused to see our parents on the grounds that their palsied observance of Jewish law had caused him to grow up with such a rot-ten soul that he committed the sins that landed him in jail, although I refrained from pointing out if he hadn't ended up in jail, he wouldn't have found the time to notice he even had a soul. Howie eventually was released, but instead of coming home, he entered a yeshiva in Rhode Island and refused to have anything to do with anyone who wasn't as observant, which included the rest of us.

I was never that fond of Howie. I barely knew him as a kid and, given the grief he caused my parents, he can go to hell for all I care.

The brothers I miss are Mike and Potsie. Mike was the kind of kid grown-ups liked to call "Mr. Personality." When Eddie Fisher married Debbie Reynolds at That Other Hotel in 1955, the women at *our* hotel laughed and said Debbie ought to have waited another ten years and married Mike, a statement that jolted me with the sort of jealousy only a younger sister can experience for a brother who has promised to marry her. (Sometimes I dream the StarLite Lounge has been set up for a wedding. Flowers line the aisle. A glorious chuppah awaits the bride and groom. But the seats for the guests remain vacant, and I keep glancing at the door and fighting my dread that the elegantly tuxedoed brother for whom I am waiting will never come.)

Mike had been working for my father since he was old enough to walk. But like the young crown prince he was, Mike was impatient to make the changes that would forestall the kingdom's fall. After a feud over whether to install Jacuzzis in every room, Mike went to work for Donald Trump, who promoted him until Mike was in charge of Trump's operations in Atlantic City.

If Ira was our Joe Junior, then Mike was our John-John. The two young men could have passed for twins. And they died the same way. Of course, John-John owned the plane in which he crashed off Martha's Vineyard, while the helicopter in which my brother plunged to his death off the Jersey Shore was owned by Donald Trump—Mike was scouting the best location in which to build a new convention center. But I think it's safe to say if I ever spend time with Caroline, it won't be these minor differences on which we dwell but the talented, charismatic brothers whose loss we mourn.

After Mike died, my mother refused to leave the house. She went directly from a life in which she bustled from building to building across 850 acres of one of the largest hotels in the world to a nearly comatose stupor in which she rarely left our den. A bunker it was. A hideout. In the middle of the room, my mother installed the kind of bed you see demonstrated on TV by a smiling older couple who show how easily they push a button and cause their heads to rise and their feet to fall, an image that never fails to disturb me since the couple in bed are watching an infomercial in which they watch themselves lying in bed watching themselves watch TV.

The only other furniture was a set of TV tables, two of which were being used for the purpose for which they were intended—holding my mother's snacks. But in some literalistic fit, she had put the other four tables to use holding the blocky RCAs my father had salvaged from the Hospitality's penthouse suites. My mother spent her days playing solitaire and nibbling chips while she shifted her gaze from one television to the next. Walking into that den, a person had the impression she was gaining access to Mission Control at NASA. But my mother was keeping track not of some space shot to the moon or Mars, but of any circumstance or event that could harm her surviving sons. Occasionally she flicked the channel to ESPN—she loved every kind of sport. But mostly she watched the news.

"Ketzel! Sweetheart!" She pushed a button so her pillow rose. She wore a muumuu so voluminous it might have been inherited from Totie Fields—Totie was a family friend, who, before she died, bequeathed her wardrobe to my mother. "I didn't hear the car drive up." She muted the four TVs: one screen showed a newscaster mouthing the narration to yet another bombing in Iraq; a second showed a fire in California, only a few hundred miles from my brother Potsie's home in Vegas, with nothing but dry brush in between; a third described a recall of Ford Explorers—thank God Potsie drove a Hummer; and the fourth, the semifinal round of a poker tournament in Cincinnati.

She motioned me to the bed, where she enveloped me in a hug. "Ketzel, I'm so worried. Most days I hear from Potsie every few hours.

I call him, or he calls me. This is the longest we've ever gone. And that idiot wife! I ask and I ask, but she won't tell me a thing."

"I'm sure Potsie is fine," I said, an assurance I did not deliver merely as a panacea to my mother. Back then, I refused to credit what every gambler in my family knew: the odds of each catastrophe are independent of every other. No matter how many misfortunes strike, the next accident, disease, or death has a fifty-fifty chance of also striking. "Potsie and Janis haven't been getting along. Maybe Potsie moved out and Janis doesn't want to discuss it. At least not with you."

"But even if he did move out, he would have called. It's not as if your brother keeps his marital difficulties to himself."

No, I thought, he didn't. Potsie might have been shy about confiding how much money he lost at poker, but he called me several times a week to ask my advice about his love life. He refused to understand that marrying a woman who loved him for his ability to provide fancy cars and jewels was not a good idea. Nor were his own criteria any sounder: he had fallen in love with Janis because she looked good in tight capris, was as feverish a gambler as he was, and allowed him to make love to her three or four times a day, no small allowance given that my brother weighed three hundred pounds and rarely wore anything but a Yankees jersey and nylon shorts.

"Did you check with Perry?" I asked, feeling as if I ought to wash my mouth out with soap for saying my cousin's name. "Maybe Potsie and Janis had a fight and Potsie went to stay with Perry."

I should take this opportunity to explain that my cousin Perry had come to live with my family when he was six. His father—my father's first cousin, Zig—had ended up in the Texas pen for committing his umpteenth scam, at which point Perry's mother found another man to supply her heroin and skipped off for parts unknown. My parents took Perry in. He was a sort of Eddie Haskell—handsome, clean cut, well groomed, and unctuously polite to grown-ups. "Oh, no," he used to say, "don't trouble yourself, Aunt Dolores. Uncle Len, please, I know how busy you are keeping this hotel running. I wouldn't want to put you to the inconvenience of attending a parent-teacher conference on my behalf." All of which fooled them into thinking they could trust Perry to pursue his own agenda. Which, for my cousin Perry, meant pursuing sex.

Every girl has a cousin Perry. He's the cousin who swims up to you underwater and tries to pull down your suit, the cousin who drops a salamander in your shorts in the hope you will tear off your clothes. For reasons I won't go into here—haven't we all grown weary of such stories?—I avoided my cousin Perry. But my brother Potsie saw him all the time. Perry ran a bar on the outskirts of Las Vegas, *outskirts* being the appropriate word for an establishment in which the women wore no clothes. My brother chose to ignore our cousin's failings in return for Perry's promise that any mug of beer Potsie ordered would be free, the TV would stay tuned to whatever athletic event Potsie wanted to watch, and a phone call from Janis demanding to know if my brother was on the premises would promptly be answered "No."

"Of course I called Perry," my mother said. "That girl who keeps the books at his bar ... she said Perry is not around. But something fishy is going on. It's like Perry knows something is wrong with Potsie, and Perry doesn't want to get on the phone because he knows I'll get it out of him. Oh, Ketzel, if anything happened to Potsie ..." She emitted a wail as chilling as the noise a television used to make when a station went off the air. The sound of that wail alarmed me. What if something bad *had* happened? What if, on top of losing Ira, Howie, and Mike, we lost Potsie? I loved my youngest brother so much that if even the slightest accident had befallen him, I would need to crawl in bed beside my mother and never leave. Except that losing another son would kill my mother. I threw my arms around her neck and promised I would do whatever she wanted me to do to assure that her one remaining son—and my one remaining brother—avoided the fates of the preceding three.

This seemed to be the promise she had been waiting to extract. "Good!" she said. "Now go and see your father. Leo wheeled him to the lake. There's something he wants to show you. Listen to what he says. Do what your father asks. Then wheel him back here for dinner."

"Are you sure?" I said. "I hate to leave you."

"Go, go." Already my mother's gaze had strayed back to the television set that showed the fire racing toward Las Vegas, although her interest also flickered toward a close-up of the players who had just earned their way into the final round of the poker tournament in Cincinnati.

I grabbed a suede coat that dated to my mother's thinner times, before Ira and Mike got killed, then took the back way to the lake. The woods were shadowy and full of ghosts. I am not a superstitious person, but the past had always been more present to me than it is to most people, as if I had been a passenger on the *Titanic* and continued to be haunted by the scrape of the hull against the ice, the band in the ballroom playing "Nearer, My God, to Thee," a chorus of cries for help echoing through the fog. No matter how hard I tried, everyone's pallid fingers kept slipping from my grasp.

Such an awareness is natural to a person who grew up hearing the word "heyday" as often as she heard "putz" and "schmuck." *Back in the Catskills' heyday,* everyone liked to sigh, which prodded me to imagine a bunch of burly guests, as muscled and inspired as the settlers on kibbutzim, frolicking in sunlit fields and forking hay into carts. I felt, as we say, *belated.* Then again, maybe everyone feels belated. By the time any of us are old enough to listen to the family stories, all the heroes and gods are dead. Or maybe we who live in this postmodern age truly were born too late. Whatever we dream of doing already has been accomplished. Every Promised Land—discovered and explored. The last great noble wars already have been fought and won. The geniuses who invented science and math are dead, the Newtons, the Freuds, the Einsteins. Gone are those ancestors who survived the Middle Passage and toiled as slaves; the immigrants who fled the famines and pogroms; the last real Indian braves; the last sweat-and-leather cowboys; the last real pioneers; the last farmers and inventors; and the last real politicians, by which I mean the guys who drafted the Constitution or helped us to conquer Fear Itself. Chaucer, Shakespeare, Dickens, even Virginia Woolf. The hoary old saints and graybeards who lived in the Age of Faith. Even the last great gangsters, the Bugsy Siegels and Al Capones, have been succeeded by a bunch of whiny punks who grew up modeling their behavior on Marlon Brando and now sit around bemoaning the old days and writing scripts about their lives in the hope of breaking into Hollywood, where they can play Mafia guys on TV.

It's not as if the old days were superior. But people back then weren't trying to imitate the people who had come before. The Borscht Belt created itself spontaneously, an entire loopy culture rising and coalescing from the wounded, self-serving impulses of a million vulgar Jews. The region developed its own traditions, its own humor, pastimes, food. Then, like the dinosaur it was, it died of its own ungainly weight. As much as I wanted gambling to be legalized so the people with whom I had grown up could find jobs and rebuild our town, I didn't want that rebirth to be orchestrated by a bunch of politicians and corporate planners. It's the difference between a raunchy country fair, with its clattering merry-go-rounds, penny-ante games of skill, and greasy frieddough delights, and a chain of Disney-orchestrated theme parks with nuclear-powered roller-coasters and quaint reproductions of American towns, each with its own "authentic" country fair.

I hurried through the woods to my family's lake. The path opened and the ghosts departed. Cuyahoga Lake isn't exactly Lake Superior, but the sight flooded my chest with pride. My grandfather had trucked in enough sand that the beach, in its heyday, had been able to accommodate several hundred children building castles, mothers asking their little boys to schmear lotion on their backs, fathers standing knee-deep in the sludgy waves, spinning their toddlers by their arms, and lovers propped sideways, admiring each other's tans. There had been a dock of such proportions it could have handled the *Queen Elizabeth*, with a corps of teenage boys in orange and green shirts inscribed with the Hospitality House logo handing out boats to men for whom it was an Olympic challenge to row a dozen yards without tipping said boat and drowning. Whenever I saw the decaying piers, I thought of the hormonally crazed waiters who had come up with the highly original idea of rowing me out to the middle of the lake, where I would be surrounded by so much water—as if I couldn't swim!—I wouldn't be able to refuse their advances. Not to be immodest, but even as a girl I had a figure that inspired many a teenage poet to compare me to the young Natalie Wood, who, as you might recall, made her name playing the leading role in that epic of Borscht Belt tragedy, *Marjorie Morningstar*. Although any such comparisons made me suspect the poet appreciated me less for my personality than for my bra size.

My father sat facing the lake. Unlike my mother, who had swaddled herself in fat to protect herself from whatever blows Fate might mete out next, my father had stood his ground and faced each battering clout and whack. He blamed himself for everything. He shouldn't have inflamed Ira's Zionist ardor by extolling the Jewish soldiers defending our homeland from Arab hordes. His own dealings with the Mob had corrupted Howie. And Mike! If only my father had allowed his favorite son to put in those Jacuzzis, Mike wouldn't have felt the need to work for Donald Trump. *Dad,* I wanted to say, *you're like Daedalus blaming himself for Icarus flying too near the sun.* But my father had no use for myths. *Ketzel,* he would have said, *a person cannot model his behavior on a fairy tale.*

I certainly understood my father's impulse toward self-reproach. There was nothing I could have done to prevent my brothers' disappearances. But a child's mind isn't logical. Do you know that Marx Brothers' movie in which Harpo is slouching against a wall, smoking a cigarette, when a cop comes up and punches him? *Hey,* the cops says, *what do you think you're doing, holding up that wall?* Harpo smiles and walks away, at which the building topples. That's how I felt, like Harpo, holding up all those walls.

Before my father took those blows, he was a powerful, craggy man. My brothers' deaths had shattered him the way a few well-placed sticks of dynamite might have blown apart one of the presidents' heads on Rushmore. Weakened by grief, he had offered no resistance to two strokes and diabetes. Seeing him in his wheelchair was like seeing the fragments of a statue of Teddy Roosevelt loaded in a shopping cart.

I bent and kissed the less damaged side of my father's face.

"Ketzel! How was the trip? Am I glad to see you, doll." My father still had that voice. There was something amplified about it, as if a loudspeaker had replaced his larynx. "Ketzel," he said again, and I ought to take this opportunity to explain that "Ketzel" is not my real name. My parents named me Kasia, after my mother's mother, but I was the youngest child and the only girl, so everyone called me "Ketzel," which in Yiddish means "little cat." I was everyone's pussycat, and the pleasure the grown-ups took in saying my name was the pleasure they might have gained from stroking a kitten's fur.

"Ketzel," my father said. He took my hand and lifted it to his lips. "There's so much I have to say." He sat for a while, holding my hand in his. "With this casino coming in . . . And now, with your brother . . ." He motioned toward the lake. "The water isn't deep enough for the aquatic amusements the new owners want to offer. And look at all those weeds! They plan to bring in backhoes and dredge the silt." His voice trembled. "When they dig up all the bodies . . ."

Those bodies again! What my father didn't understand was that even if the new owners drained the lake and a few skeletons should be revealed, our reputations would remain intact. "Dad," I said, "gangsters are in vogue. If people think anything, they'll think Grandpa Joe's connection to Murder Inc. was romantic."

My father sputtered. "Romantic! You think it's romantic, a bunch of goons hog-tie a man, they kick him and stab him, purely for the thrill? They slit his throat, maybe they chop him into little bits so he fits easier in the trunk? Or they stuff him in the trunk and drive him into the lake while he's still alive? This you call *romance*? All right, many of these victims were not upstanding citizens. But a human being is a human being. They had families—children, wives. And some of those men were innocent. Store owners, they wouldn't pay protection. Or they saw something they shouldn't have seen. A human being isn't meant to suffocate in a trunk at the bottom of a lake."

It occurred to me these were not metaphors we were discussing. "And Joe knew? Just how many bodies are down there?"

My father sat gazing across the shadowy waves like a boy attempting to calculate how many marbles are in a jar. If, on a summer day, the lake might have been the subject of a painting by Seurat, now, with the sun dipping behind the firs and the surface glommed with weeds, it brought to mind the dismal Scottish loch that harbored that elusive monster.

"Did you ever hear of Walter Sage?" my father asked. "King of the Slots. That's what they called him. That is, until he started skimming from the profits. They stabbed him so many times that even though they tied him to a rack for a pinball machine, the body filled with gas and floated to the surface." He motioned toward the water. "Not here, thank God. The bad publicity went to Swan Lake. But we escaped only by a fluke. Your grandfather and I looked the other way. They had us over a barrel. Better over a barrel than over a pinball machine, right? And even if they hadn't had plenty of dirt on us, what, we were going to say no to Abe Reles? They didn't call him Kid Twist for nothing. An arm around the throat and—" Here my father made a noise like a man getting the life twisted out of him. "Do you think we wanted those slot machines in our lobby? The guests put in coin after coin. Then, at summer's end, they couldn't pay the bill. Some of them couldn't even pay the hackie to the bus station. They screamed that it was our fault because we offered the temptation. They claimed we had bled them dry." He pretended to wring a sponge. "Farfel Schwartz ran a high-stakes poker game in the back room. One time, Sam Marks—he owned a plumbing-supply concern in Westchester County—the guy dropped ten, eleven grand. And this idiot brags he isn't about to pay his IOU! Next thing, we find him outside the front gate, a broken mess, a warning, everyone should see what happens to a man who doesn't pay. And to whom should we complain? Once, a new order of slot machines came in, and who should schlep the machines in from the truck but three state troopers, out of uniform, from the barracks down the road."

The sun, in its setting, did something peculiar to the lake. It became a glowing golden bowl, mist hovering above the broth. That bowl contained the most important memories of my life. And now, a bunch of gangsters had been added to the soup. It was like dipping in your spoon, expecting to find a bit of chicken or a noodle, and fishing out someone's thumb.

"If they start dredging this lake, there is going to be one big stink.

Leo is worried about the bad old days coming back. What worries me is how clean everyone connected with casinos needs to be. In Las Vegas and Atlantic City, the government cleared out the worst elements. The feds won't allow a man with even the whiff of crime to have anything to do with gambling. Which is why, if all those bodies in the lake turn up, not to mention the ones under the tennis courts . . ."

"Wait, wait," I said. "The tennis courts? What's wrong with the tennis courts?"

My father lifted one finger. "There was the body they buried under the first set of clay courts, back in '36." He held up a second finger. "And the one I saw them bury in '39, the night the new macadam courts went in."

Everyone in my family accuses me of being naive. But who wouldn't be unsettled to learn that in her younger days she had run back and forth, lobbing and chasing overheads, with a bunch of dead gangsters staring up her skirt? "You'll pardon me if I don't understand what you and Grandpa Joe got out of allowing Murder Inc. to dispose of their dirty work on our premises."

His laugh sounded like the fragments of Rushmore shifting. "First of all, we didn't have a choice. Second, who says we didn't get anything out of the deal? Your grandfather got protection from the unions. And I'm probably the only guy in the world who owes his marriage to the Mob."

"What did Mom have to do with—"

"Nothing! Your mother never had anything to do with those hoodlums! It's just . . . You know the story of how we met? There's more to it than you think."

My knees went weak. What could be more unsettling than finding out your understanding of how your parents met has been a lie? Changing one iota of that primal story derails the entire train of events that led to your becoming who you are.

"Such a night that was," my father said. "It was very late, but I couldn't sleep. A young man that age, I was always . . . stirred up. It was a beautiful summer's night. The clouds were rushing past the moon. It was, what would you call it, *moody*. It was a moody summer's night, and, stirred up as I was, I stopped to have a smoke near where the workmen had been digging to install the new tennis courts. I was leaning against a post, smoking my cigarette, watching the clouds blow across the moon, when what should I see but two men, clear as day, dragging a body. It was wrapped in a sheet. But a body is a body, even in a sheet. Another man was digging in the dirt where the courts were going in. This was a very deep hole the man was digging. I might have been the owner's son. Agreements might have been reached. But none of us, to my knowledge, had actually stood there watching a body be disposed of. And I couldn't be certain these particular men would know whose son I was. Maybe they would panic. Maybe they would bury me alongside their unfortunate comrade in his sheet."

I wish I could say this story seemed unlikely. *Not here! Not at our hotel! Not my father!* But it was like seeing an actor you have watched in a certain kind of movie play a similar role in a similar kind of movie. I had no trouble imagining my father leaning against that post, the hasty gesture with which he tossed down his cigarette and ground it beneath his shoe. I could hear the croaking of the frogs in Cuyahoga Lake, louder now, a crescendo of amphibian warning.

"In those days," my father said, "I was capable of great stealth. But it was inevitable I should be seen. Killers like that, with animal eyes and ears . . . They saw me, but I pretended I hadn't seen them. Do you remember when you were little, Ketzel, and you put your hands across your face and thought you were invisible? I began to walk away, but it was like knowing a tiger is behind you. Already I felt their claws digging in my neck.

"Then I saw your mother. Of course, I didn't know she was your mother. All I could tell was that a woman was walking across the lawn. Definitely a woman. Even a blind man could see that your mother was well endowed." Just thinking about my mother's silhouette as she crossed the moonlit lawn caused the droopy right side of my father's face to rise up and join its better half. "I assumed she was a local girl who had sneaked in to see the show, dance a little, maybe make contact with a professional Jewish man from the city, and now she was hurrying to get back to her car, which she had left parked behind the woods. But she had on very high-heeled shoes. It was difficult for her to walk. So I was able to catch up with her. I put my arm around her waist and swung her into the most passionate kiss, as if she were saving my life, which she was. And I whispered, 'Please, doll, whoever you are, don't make a *tsimmes*. This isn't what you think. Be quiet and just pretend.'"

To tell the truth, this part of the story wasn't hard to picture either. In the version I knew, my father had gone out for a smoke, seen a beautiful woman crossing the lawn, and, suspecting she might be a townie, used his authority to accost her. Nor was it difficult to imagine my mother slim and young. She was the sort of fat person whose thinner, younger self is still visible beneath her bloated skin.

In both versions, my father escorted her to her car. Then she drove him into town, where he decided he could trust her and offered an explanation. "Your mother, God bless her, wasn't the least bit flustered. Not that it was new to her, to be in contact with a rougher element than most girls would be accustomed to rubbing up against."

I started to laugh in agreement. Then I had to admit I didn't know what I was laughing about. "I thought Mom wasn't involved—"

"Not with the Mob. But that doesn't mean ... It's natural a girl like you would want to paint things as prettier than they are. And right from the start, your mother and I agreed to spare you the ugly truths. But you didn't want to know them, Ketzel."

Oh, I must say I was getting tired of my family poking me with that particular stick. *Ketzel with her head in the clouds. Ketzel who prefers not to see what's in front of her own two eyes.* My childhood was grittier than most. With the hotel going bankrupt and my brothers disappearing, I was left to amuse myself. Even as a child, I was allowed to hang around the kitchen, scratching the itchy backs of the dishwashers Grandpa Joe had plucked from the Bowery and imprisoned at our hotel with the promise that if they stayed sober for a month, they would be paid and allowed to leave. I lit their cigarettes and learned from their foul lips a dozen synonyms for *vagina*. I listened to the chambermaids tell bloody, frightening tales of miscarriages and abortions and men forcing them to perform acts that sounded to me then—and even today—to warrant jail sentences rather than the rueful head shakes and "amens" the women gave.

Sex was seething everywhere. For several summers in my teens, my job was to assign lounge chairs by the pool, where I made a fortune in tips from male guests who demanded I assign them seats beside women whose appearance they admired, and female guests who bribed me into letting them recline beside a widowed oncologist from New Rochelle or the pudgy but successful owner of an import-export business in Flushing, Queens. I understood that everything at our hotel—the rooms, the food, the ski lifts, the pools, the lake, the shows, even the bingo and Simon Sez—was merely an excuse for sex.

Unless it was an excuse for money. Conmen hustled their fellow guests into buying phony stocks; women showed off the minks they had connived to attain with carefully doled-out blow jobs. I once spied a gentleman in a tuxedo slip his manicured hand in the coats hanging outside the dining room, transferring the coins he found from their pockets into his.

If this wasn't sufficient to open my eyes to the realities of human nature, I hung around backstage at the StarLite Lounge and listened to the comedians practice their routines. Go ahead and ask how many variations of "The Aristocrats" I had heard before I even knew what an aristocrat might be.

So I wasn't as green as my family thought. *Oh Ketzel,* they used to say, *you have such a rosy disposition,* with the same cluck of the tongue they employed when heaping pity on a child who was born without eyes or hands. But a person can choose to be rosy. Why sniff the flowers if not because your nose is more sensitive than most to the stink rising from everything else?

"Ketzel," my father chided me, "do you really think Poppa Aaron supported himself and your mother by selling lollipops and Good & Plenty? Poppa Aaron was a bookie. I assumed you had that figured out. The cigarettes and candy were only a front for the book he made in back."

I tried to conjure Poppa Aaron, who died when I was ten. He was tall and brown, with a long neck and scratchy white stubble like the grains of kosher salt on the pretzel rods he kept in the glass cylinder beside the register. Despite his stiff demeanor, he was charming and warm, which didn't necessarily contradict my father's assertion that he ran a bookmaking operation in the back.

"So you see what I mean about those bodies turning up. The Weinrach name will be dragged through the mud. Your friends might shun you. This could even ruin your chances to remarry."

Having grown up in a time when a person's worth was judged by his or her moral stature, my father couldn't understand that we now gauge a person's worth by his or her nearness to celebrity. I tried to explain this.

"Celebrities! You consider gamblers to be celebrities?" He whistled in disbelief. A flock of ducks, attracted by his call, skidded across the lake, wings lifted, the way our guests awkwardly lifted their arms to slide in to home plate when playing the staff at softball. "Then again," my father said, "even in the old days, those goons would show up in the lobby and you would think a bunch of movie stars had arrived." He shook his head. "They were nothing but trouble. We had to give them the best rooms, even if it meant forcing another guest to move. We had to seat them at the best tables, then come running, running, with whatever food they wanted, alcohol, cigars, even girls. And that bum Reles! One look from that man and my balls shriveled up inside me. I am not easily frightened. But to see an animal like that . . . Believe me, the celebrity aspect soon wore thin."

He sat staring across the lake, no doubt remembering those unholy Sabbath meals when Abe Reles and his boys had shown up in our dining room, demanding my father allow him to fulfill their version of the Fourth Commandment—to wit, *Six days shalt thou murder, but on the seventh day, thou shalt show up at a Catskills hotel and demand a free meal.*

"One of these lugs, Sappy Appelnap, would leave his mother here all summer. Day in, day out, she lorded it over the other women. Wasn't her son a successful businessman? Wasn't he good to her, giving her all these displays of his affection—the fur stole, the tasteless jewels, a full summer stay at this magnificent resort? Once, a busboy spilled hot tea down this woman's back. We had to hustle the poor kid out the kitchen and hide him at my cousin Jenny's apartment in Philadelphia until the incident blew over."

As I listened, it occurred to me the members of Murder Inc. hadn't been characters in a storybook. My friends wouldn't shun me for finding out my family had skeletons in our closet, or, in this case, at the bottom of our lake. But if the developers who were buying our hotel uncovered said remains, questions might be asked. Licenses might be revoked.

"I think our best policy is to come clean," my father said. "I would hate to think of the slur against your grandfather's good name, but what the dead don't know can't harm them. The real sticking point is, what if the new owners say I foisted off the property without disclosing certain details? What if the deal falls through? Someone is going to need to face the music for the rest of us—talk to the press, take his place on the witness stand, represent the family. It's not as if Stuart can handle such disclosures. And I don't mean because of his lack of facility with public speaking."

My father had never liked my brother Stuart's nickname. Potsie had acquired the moniker not, as people think, because he had a pot belly as a child. Nor did he acquire it because of the relish he took in hauling in pot after pot when on a winning streak at poker, although that also was true. He had acquired the name because he loved to play a game most people call hopscotch but old-time New Yorkers remember as *potsie*. When strangers look at my brother now, they see a giant of a man who earns his living gambling. I see a sweaty little boy stooping to retrieve a rock, then crossing his pudgy legs and hopping back the way he came across a crudely numbered board. My father regarded hopscotch as a game for girls and thought the name diminished my brother's masculinity. When he couldn't get away with circumlocutions such as "your brother," he called him "Stuart," a name that drew blank looks from everyone, including Stuart's mother.

"I've told her . . . I've reassured her . . . I've said that your mother's fears for your brother are premature. But between you and me, Ketzel . . ." The wheelchair trembled beneath my hand. "If anything were to happen to that boy . . ."

I could no longer see his face, but the waves lapping the shore mingled sloppily with his sobs. I wanted to cry myself. If any of you have ever heard anything sadder than your poor crippled father weeping in his wheelchair beside a lake whose waters are washing over the violently ambushed dead, I don't want to know what that something is.

I wheeled him back to the house, our way eerily lit by the solar-powered torches that had been Mike's final innovation before he went to work for Trump. I pushed my father up the ramp Leo had built at the side of the house, and we ate dinner in the dining room, my parents, Leo, and I, served by the Polish cook, Hania, who had been the Hospitality's assistant chef and now helped Leo care for my parents. With her fair hair and broad, guileless face, Hania wasn't unattractive. Everyone knew Leo loved her. Something about her difficulty speaking English, her shy demeanor, and her reluctance to talk went with Leo's shady past, as if he could confide the terrible things he had done and his secrets would be safe with her. I had always wondered why they hadn't married, but it wasn't my place to ask.

Hania brought in her famous mushroom-barley soup, followed by a plate of potato-and-cheese *pierogin*, and a brisket so tender it fell apart in your mouth. With our anxiety about my brother, we wouldn't have been tempted to eat by a less outstanding meal. I tried not to be alarmed by the portions my mother shoveled in her mouth or the fact that my father's condition had deteriorated to the point Hania needed to cut his food. No one mentioned Potsie, but every time the grandfather clock in the hall ticked another tock, it emphasized my brother's failure to get in touch. *Tick-tock, tick-tock Tannenbaum,* the pendulum seemed to say.

When my mother could bear the suspense no longer, she retreated to the den, where we knew she was calling Potsie. Hania cleared the plates while my father tapped his knife in rhythm to the clock. Then my mother burst back in, so clearly distressed that if my father had been able, he would have leapt to his feet to comfort her.

"That's it! That's all the proof I need! I said to Janis, direct, 'Don't give me any more stories. Just tell me where he is.' So she says she *can't* tell me. And I ask, 'Why not?' And she says, 'They told me not to tell.' And I say, 'Who? Who told you not to tell?' And that idiot girl hung up! I called her back, but she won't pick up. Oh, Potsie, Potsie, Potsie!" my mother cried. "Whatever will we do?"

My father tried to calm her, but my mother would not be calmed. "Lennie," my mother said, "she has to go. There are no two ways about it."

I tried to ask who had to go where, but my father held up his hand. "Leo," he said, "we prefer to be alone." Leo set down his tea and went to help Hania in the kitchen. My father composed himself, the way the president of the United States might compose himself before addressing the nation on TV. "Your mother is right. I am sorry you should be dragged into such distressing matters. But there's no one else we can trust."

You can imagine my consternation. Dragged into what matters?

"Leo will drive you to LaGuardia. All we want is that you should look in on your precious niece Meryl and take her into your protection. We can't leave her in the care of your brother's wife. And you must file a missing person's report, something your sister-in-law hasn't seen fit to do. You are also to give a certain amount of money to Eberhard Salzman. You remember Ebby—his father maintained our golf course. Ebby is now a private investigator in Las Vegas. He already knows the basics—height and weight, distinguishing marks, and so forth. But a certain amount of personal contact might bolster his enthusiasm for the case."

My father's manner changed, as if the cameras in the Oval Office had stopped rolling and the president were now addressing a few off-the-cuff remarks to the makeup woman. "So tell me, doll, are you seeing anyone?"

My brother was in danger, and my father was taking this moment to inquire into my social life? My husband wasn't six months in his grave, and my parents had been nearly as crushed by Morty's death as I was. It wasn't as if I had told them that he died in a strip club in New Orleans, or that he had been cheating on me for years. "To be honest, Dad, it hadn't occurred to me to go out on a date." I was too dispirited to explain that a single woman in Manhattan, especially a woman of fifty-one, isn't exactly in high demand. "If we're finished discussing my prospects for remarriage, maybe we could get back to trying to ascertain my brother's whereabouts?"

My mother sighed. "We were hoping you could ask a friend to go with you. Your father would be happy to pay this person's airfare. Are you sure you don't know anyone who might enjoy a free vacation in Las Vegas?"

I didn't get it. Why were they so intent on my taking along a friend?

"It's just—" My father paused. "Who knows what unpleasantness might arise? Your sister-in-law—"

I could handle my sister-in-law, I said. She might not have been very smart, but—

My mother shushed us both. "It isn't a matter of intelligence. The first two wives were merely uneducated women who saw in your broth-er a way out of the lives they were leading. But Janis . . . Janis is all of the above and not a nice woman. That she wants your brother's money is no secret. That they weren't getting along and he would have divorced her and given her much less alimony than she might have wanted—"

"Mother! Are you trying to tell me that Janis had Potsie . . . Are you trying to say she had him . . ."

"See? You can't even say the word. You think only the best of people.

Besides, the person who knows your brother's habits most intimately is your cousin Perry. Tell me, are you going to pay Perry a call at that *farkokteh* bar of his? A woman like you, alone?"

"I've been in bars before," I reminded her. "Remember? I used to be a comic."

"That was a long time ago," my father said. "And I hope you didn't perform at bars where the girls shook their titties at the men and picked up money with their female underparts."

If my father had intended to shock me, he succeeded. Oh, he told dirty jokes all the time. But he never talked to me about *titties* and *female underparts*, especially when those titties and underparts were attached to real women.

"There's something else he's not telling you," my mother said. "Perry . . . your cousin . . . he runs a business in the back."

"A business?" I said. "What kind of business?" Given the addictions that had driven my cousin's father to carry out so many scams and caused his mother to abandon him, I doubted Perry would deal in drugs. Nor would he be a pimp, if only because he couldn't bring himself to allow any woman he knew to sleep with another man.

"Movies," my mother said. "He makes movies in the back."

"Perry makes pornography?" The hair on the back of my neck stood up.

"Yes," my father said. "And there's something else you need to know," as if he and my mother had divided these truths between them. "Your brother runs a betting operation."

I let this revelation settle in. Potsie, a bookie? What did that mean, to be a bookie in Las Vegas? And why had he never told me? "Anyone in Las Vegas can place a bet."

"To place a bet at a casino is legal," my father said. "And yes, when your brother first went out there, he worked for a legitimate sports-book operation. He helped them to set their lines. This is a very difficult thing to do, and your brother, strange as this may seem, was an expert in that field. He gained such a following he branched out on his own. Except, in Las Vegas, independence in such matters isn't to be applauded. Running a bookmaking operation that doesn't pay taxes and isn't subject to regulation is highly frowned upon by the authorities."

I was about to ask my parents if it didn't bother them that their son ran an illegal bookmaking operation. Then I remembered that a talent for making book ran in our family. Did any of this bother *me*? With all the evil in the world, could I really tsk-tsk about a man helping his friends place a wager on a horse? Was brutality required to accept a bet? Like the pretzel sticks he sold, my poppa Aaron seemed so frail he could be broken with a good hard snap. But what about my brother? Had he ever applied his excess weight to pressuring a deadbeat into paying? He didn't have a mean bone in his body. Not that I had ever conducted a detailed orthopedic dissection of his vast anatomy.

"You'll excuse me for asking, but how come you knew about Potsie's business and I didn't?"

"Well, dear," my mother said, "you always held such a high standard for your own behavior, it put a pressure on the rest of us."

This seemed a low blow, to insinuate that my family's illegal activities were my fault. According to this line of reasoning, my husband's infidelities were a result of my insistence that he remain faithful. Maybe I should have understood that in Morty's line of work, it was impossible not to stray. But I was foolish enough to think a husband and a wife should swear fidelity. And Morty believed it, too. At least, he pretended he believed it. Our agreement had been that Morty could go wherever he needed to go and read whatever he needed to read—even if, as the French so coyly put it, he was forced to *read with one hand*—as long as he came home to me. It was Morty who promised he would stop hanging around strip clubs. He hated the bald equation between money and sex, the sad lives the women led. Which must have made him feel twice as bad when he found himself paying for their wares.

"Your mother is too modest," my father said. "Your brother wouldn't be half the bookie he is if she hadn't taught him all she knew. Without her, Poppa Aaron couldn't have set the lines on a race between Seabiscuit and the nag that pulled the junk wagon."

My mother waved off the compliment. "When I married your father, I took a long hiatus. I had more than enough to do, running the hotel and raising you kids. But after Ira and Howie and Mike . . ." She drew a handkerchief from the sleeve of Totie's muumuu. "Potsie could run his business without me. All I do is watch the games on TV and read the opinions of various sportswriters. But Potsie wants me to feel needed. He wants that I should have something to keep me occupied."

So that was why Potsie and my mother talked so often! I wish I could say I was upset for reasons of immorality. But I would be lying if I said I wasn't jealous of their common bond.

"I bring this up only to prove I know your brother's routine. And that routine does not include his dropping out of sight and turning off his phone. I asked Owen—that's your brother's head clerk, Owen Dibble—if he noticed anything amiss about Potsie's behavior. Was Potsie in over his neck in his own gambling debts? But Owen is as mystified as we are."

"We've given all this information to Ebby Salzman," my father said. "Ebby will take care of the legwork. That's what we're paying him for— to assume the risks. But you can take the man out for a nice dinner. You can find out what he likes in terms of scotch. Grease the wheels of the investigation, so to speak."

It occurred to me that my parents were asking me to seduce Ebby Salzman into working overtime on my brother's behalf. Not that I minded. Ebby and his older brother, Goose, by virtue of their athletic prowess and raw good looks, had stood on the very highest rung of the social ladder at our high school. Which, sad to say, I had not. I might have been well endowed. My parents might have owned the largest business in the Catskills. But I was awkward and shy around people my own age. And many of my classmates came from families in which one or both parents worked at our hotel, which made the boys reluctant to ask me out. Bruce Salzman—whose honking laugh and beaky nose had earned him the nickname Goose—was four years my senior and out of reach. But Ebby had been the object of some very serious fantasies on my part, especially after I saw him lean forward on the football field one hot September day and raise the hem of his shirt to wipe his brow.

"Since when is Ebby a private eye?" I asked. "Wasn't he a cop? Didn't he marry a chorus girl and have some kids?"

"See?" my father said. "You know all about Ebby's romantic life, but you've blotted out what happened in his line of work."

I am ashamed to say he had a point. It came back to me that Ebby had beaten a man to death, then suffered a breakdown and quit or had been kicked off the force. "I'll go to Vegas," I said. "I'll make sure Meryl is all right. I'll meet with Ebby and grease his wheels. But I don't intend to take anyone as protection."

Even as I said this, I was struck by how Morty would have relished the opportunity to hang out at a Vegas bar and collect the latest jokes. Not that he approved of the way Disney and MGM had turned the casinos into theme parks. In the new Vegas, everything was patented and copyrighted and patrons were prohibited from telling jokes without a license. Until recently, I had been under the impression Morty hadn't been back to Vegas since the eighties. Then I found that leather notebook and discovered he had been back there many times. As bitter as this deception was, he would have known his way around.

"What about Leo?"

My parents exchanged a look, then my father explained that Leo had "a problem with gambling." As a young man, Leo had sunk himself into debt, at which time he had tried to clear his IOU by helping Abe Reles fulfill some contracts.

"Leo killed people?" I said—too loudly. Leo probably couldn't hear me over the racket Hania was making in the kitchen, but my father motioned me to keep down my voice.

"He didn't have the stomach for the job," my father said. "He told Reles he wanted out. But 'out' was not an option. Luckily for Leo, Reles owed a debt to Grandpa Joe. Some relative of Reles's wife knocked up your cousin Maeve, who was only fifteen. In return for clearing that debt, Joe agreed to accept Leo. That way, Leo would remain visible to Reles, and Reles could make sure Leo wasn't divulging what oughtn't be divulged."

"You got Leo as part of a debt?"

My father gave a one-shouldered shrug. "The man has few wants. Everything he needs is right here. And with Leo, the less money in his pocket, the better. One time, he got in trouble at the track and we needed to bail him out. On another occasion, Leo acquired some extra funds and made his way to Vegas. The result was not a happy one. At any rate, the point of Leo accompanying you is moot, seeing as how he is banned from entering the city limits."

That the lumpy, clownish man who, for my first sixteen years, had driven me to school each morning, had strangled or stabbed at least a few victims and dumped their carcasses in the lake was one more revelation than I could stand. I tottered outside to get some air. I thought of going for a walk, but what if I ran into Leo? I had never been afraid of wandering the grounds at night. But the patches of tattered, moonlit snow seemed sinister to me now, as if zombies from the lake sat huddled against the trees, waiting, just waiting, to wreak their vengeance on a descendant of the man who allowed Kid Twist Reles to use Cuyahoga Lake as their watery unmarked grave.

I had known my brother gambled. He had been driven to it as a kid by his insatiable need for candy. Candy, candy, candy, that's all my brother lived for. At first, he supplied his needs with handouts from Isaac Praise, the wizened black concessionaire who ran the snack booth off the game room. Not to mention our grandfather owned a candy shop. But by the time my brother turned a roly-poly ten, the grown-ups said, *No more!* Potsie understood that the only reliable way to provide himself with candy was to win it from the guests. Ping-pong, darts, Parcheesi—he wiped the staff kids clean. By the time he reached eleven, he could hold his own at pinochle, gin, and poker against men twice or three times his age. By fourteen, few of the adults could hold their own against him.

By then, he gambled purely for the thrill. He bet on which of two elderly guests would trip on the pavement first, or whether Buddy Hackett would use his Chinese restaurant routine when closing that night's show. Potsie started working as a bellhop and bet most of what he earned at the racetrack in Monticello. Since he wasn't yet eighteen, he funneled these wagers through his colleagues, who were smart enough to place their own hard-earned tips on whatever horse Potsie picked.

And even though my brother had no success at math—or any other subject—he gained an impressive following among his classmates—not to mention his teachers—because of the betting pool he ran. I was proud of his popularity. He was a generous, good-tempered boy. Unlike many of his peers, he didn't overindulge in alcohol—he said it made him do even dumber things than he usually did—and he was always sweet to girls. None of the girls he dated, or the women he later married, were what you would call quick witted. But until he married Janis, they were kind, warm-hearted women, grasping only for jewels and furs.

And he certainly loved his daughter. From everything I could tell, Meryl's father was as protective of her as he had been of me. That was why I loved him. With everyone else so occupied in keeping our ship afloat, only Potsie took the time to make sure I didn't slip overboard and drown. I mean this literally and metaphorically—he taught me to dive and swim, as well as how to ride a bike and dance the twist, how to drive a golf ball a hundred yards, then chip and putt in three. He taught me to spin on skates—for such a heavy man, he was grace itself on ice. Cushioned on my brother's ample lap, I hurtled down our toboggan run. He taught me to field and hit—I became such a skilled player I won Potsie many a bet from suckers who were too chauvinistic to predict my power at the plate. He taught me to ride the nags we kept for guests—with his imposing belly and massive thighs, he resembled a Union general spreading courage among his troops. And on more than one occasion, he appeared in the nick of time to release me from the clutches of some grabby slickster from Long Island, or our own cousin Perry.

If you still don't understand why I idolized my brother, one final example should do the trick. In the summer of 1969, when I wanted more than anything to attend the music festival that had erupted at Yasgur's dairy farm down the road, my parents decreed that I could go only if Potsie took me. And Potsie said yes. A boy of nineteen who could have gone to Woodstock on his own agreed to take his sister! We made it as far as Monticello, where the crowds grew even denser than they had appeared on the evening news. Rather than give up and walk, Potsie led me behind the racetrack. Everyone seemed to know him. *Hey there, Pot, old man! Potsie, what you up to?*

So here's what my brother did. One of the owners kept a retired thoroughbred in his stalls because her presence calmed the trotters. Potsie asked to borrow her for the day; the owner owed Potsie a favor, so he granted this request. And that's how I got to Woodstock, floating above the heads of all those stoned hippies, who patted the silky flanks of Everly's Pride and flashed the peace sign as we passed. That's us, if you've seen the pictures, the impressively heavy teenage boy and much smaller awestruck girl mounted on a horse above the muddy throng cheering Canned Heat and Janis Joplin.

So yes, I did close my eyes. I didn't want to know what my brother did to earn a living. When Potsie came east, he always spent a few nights with me before taking the Short Line north to see our parents. He and Morty stayed up late, two overweight men trading predictions about the Mets while I shuffled behind their backs, refilling their cups with tea. When I leaned in to put more cookies on the plate, Morty patted me on the tush, and Potsie smiled as if I were a cherished pet he could no longer afford to care for but was happy to have passed on to such a kind master.

But he never invited me out to Vegas, and when I hinted I would like to come, he put me off. I figured he had his reasons, the way Morty had his reasons for refusing to have a child. If Potsie didn't want me to come to Vegas, there must be some aspect of his life I would be better off not knowing. If Morty was reluctant to conceive a child, he probably shouldn't be a father. A person gives up her sight because there's something she doesn't want to see. She relinquishes her freedom because she prefers to be taken care of.

I went back inside and found my parents. My mother lay in her folding bed like an overweight Fay Wray reclining on King Kong's palm. My father sat beside her in his wheelchair. I stood and watched TV until I couldn't bear to hear another theory as to why my brother hadn't called, at which I said goodnight and climbed the stairs.

Since my parents slept in the den, the rooms on the upper floor were something of a museum. Or maybe a mausoleum. There was my parents' shrine to Ira, with its ageless if peeling portrait out of *Dorian Gray*. Then came Howie's room, with its grainy blowup of my brother playing shuffleboard with Nelson Rockefeller, and a similar shot of Howie shaking hands with Henry Kissinger, who spent a weekend at our hotel giving lectures and signing books. The decor in Mike's room was early sixties pinup—an entire wall of glossy PR stills of every female singer and chorine who ever graced the StarLite stage.

I hesitated outside the door to Potsie's room, then tiptoed in, running my hand along the Yankees and Giants pennants above his bed and the candid snaps of Mickey Mantle and Willie Mays playing a game of catch with a much younger Potsie, and the photo I loved most, which showed Muhammad Ali—who had trained at our hotel before his bout with Ken Norton—grinning that Ali grin and playfully punching Potsie in the head. Seeing that last photo, I was overcome by the possibility something might actually have hurt my brother—not Ali's oversized fist, but the brass-reinforced knuckles of a thug. A knife to my brother's throat. A bullet to his soft but loving brain. I thought of him swinging me onto that horse, the comforting, odoriferous bulk of him before me as we floated above that crowd at Woodstock, and I sank to his bed and prayed nothing worse had befallen him than that his grasping, unloving wife had ejected him from their house, then changed the locks.

Not wanting to fall asleep on my brother's bed, I staggered back to my own room, decorated as it was with charcoal caricatures of every stand-up comic on whose lap I had ever sat—Ketzel and Henny Youngman, Ketzel and Rodney Dangerfield, Ketzel and Danny Kaye. Grinning down from a life-size photo was the comic I loved the best, Zero Mostel, who, I had been told, was fanatically loyal to Grandpa Joe for allowing him to work the StarLite stage when the blacklist prevented him from performing elsewhere. Collapsing beneath Zero's photo, I dreamed a dream in which Frank Sinatra, Dean Martin, Sammy Davis

Jr., and Jerry Lewis were clowning in our lobby, waltzing with lamps and ash stands, jumping on the sofas and making faces for us kids. The problem was that Jerry—who, I now saw, resembled my cousin *Perry*—was molesting the female guests in such outrageous ways that even Frank and Dean advised him to cool it down.

"I'm telling you, cut the crap!" This, from an angry Dean.

"Yeah," Frank said. "These aren't some whorehouse broads. The management will get upset. What if that dame you're humping was your sister?"

But Jerry kept grabbing the women's breasts, slipping his hands beneath their gowns, and ramming them against the walls, until, in the dream's final moments, the lobby grew dim, and Frank walked down the staircase holding Jerry's head. Frank handed the head to Jerry, who cradled it against his chest. And the head in Jerry's arms began to blubber and wail, as the real comedian used to do.

"Wah!" he cried. "You guys! What's the matter, can't you take a *joke?*"

I awoke in a fevered sweat. Was I really getting on a plane in another few hours and flying to Las Vegas? Apparently, I was. I pulled on a pair of jeans and one of the dozens of Camp Hospitality T-shirts my parents had warehoused in my room, then descended to the kitchen, where Hania served me eggs. My mother walked me to the door. I could tell she wanted to escort me to the car but couldn't fight her inclination to stay inside. In her aqua-blue muumuu, she reminded me of a woman struggling to free herself from a jellyfish.

Leo carried my bag. My father rolled himself down the ramp and positioned his chair beside the car. I bent and kissed his cheek. "Please," he said. "Keep your eyes open. People aren't as nice as you think." I started to pull away, but he tugged me back. "And be careful about your genes."

I tugged my waistband. "What's wrong with my jeans?"

"Your *genes*. Your genetic makeup. Gambling runs in your blood."

"Dad, the only card game I know how to play is computer solitaire. I hate losing money. I've been poor my whole life. I might get a little something from Morty's estate—" I didn't think this was the time to tell him about the valuable objets d'art I had found. "But except for the cash you gave me last night, I don't have a cent to bet."

This worried him even more. "A woman like you, she puts her first quarter in a slot, and before she knows it, she has gambled away some very important items she didn't even know that she had to lose."

2.

AND THAT'S HOW I came to be flying to Las Vegas to search for my brother Potsie instead of sorting through my husband's voluminous and esoteric—and some would say disgusting—collection of dirty jokes. I am sorry if I've digressed. My life is of little interest except as it intersects with the life of Morty Tittelman. My intention is to shed light on the obsession that caused my husband to conduct his research and publish the sort of books that earned him notoriety in his youth and persecution by academics who refused to grant him the tiniest shred of authority or respect until Morty was too decrepit to shuffle across a stage and accept the honorary degrees they finally chose to give him after years of denying him funds because he lacked "the right credentials," "training in anthropology," "distance" and "objectivity," as if anyone can be objective about dirty jokes and sex!

And so I will leave myself sitting on that plane and explain how I came to be the person most responsible for pushing Morty Tittelman to write the books that brought him fame. The person who edited and typed those books. And—dare I say this?—the person who supported him while he wrote.

Not that I would claim the slightest credit for Morty's revolutionary theory that a culture's collective smut represents its pure unconscious and is therefore worthy of the respect of psychologists and anthropologists. Those collectors who came before didn't collect their smut to study it. They didn't publish what they found. The prim WASP musicologists who traipsed through Appalachia in search of bawdy songs bleached the lyrics free of sex. "Fakelorists," Morty called them, along with Columbia-trained ethnographers who pretended to be unshockable but treated their informants as if they were coated in inch-thick dreck.

Those few PhDs who preceded him in this field refused to publish jokes except in their tamest form and handled these few examples with metaphoric latex gloves, using dashes to replace the swear words and setting their jokes apart from the oh-so-scholarly text as if they were dangling a rodent by its tail. They offered no opinions, let alone the diatribes against Hollywood and Madison Avenue that cluttered Morty's work. They excoriated his lack of footnotes and his refusal to cite statistics to measure the creativity and depravity of the human mind. The only statistic Morty liked to quote was that among the millions of dirty jokes *Homo sapiens* had produced, not a single one presumes that a woman and a man—or a man and a man, or a woman and a woman—might copulate from love.

Even Alfred Kinsey took Morty to task for using the first-person pronoun, as if "I" were a greater obscenity than "shit" or "fuck." Kinsey lambasted Morty's "lack of rigor" in measuring the male erection, a job Morty accepted from Kinsey only because Morty was so hungry and desperate for paying work his hands shook when he held the ruler. Not to mention, like any two snowflakes, no two sets of human genitalia are in any way made alike. Would *you* care to measure a human male erection to the twentieth of an inch?

It was Morty's sharpest pain that his friend and hero Kinsey declined to acknowledge his contribution in measuring those erections. Nor did Kinsey credit Morty for tracking down the many rare volumes of erotica he had asked Morty to acquire, including the legendary *Codex of Abufillah*, reputed to be the repository of a single dirty joke whose telling required thirteen days and nights and whose punch line caused at least one listener to asphyxiate from laughter. Scholars had presumed the last remaining copy had been committed to the flames by angry mad Savonarola during the Inquisition, but Morty's sleuthing revealed a single extant copy in the library at the Vatican, don't ask me how he managed to smuggle that copy out.

And what did Morty get for finding Abufillah? Bupkes, that's what. Apparently, Kinsey had come to suspect Morty was skimming something extra from the finder's fees he was paid. Which, knowing Morty, he was. But if not for Morty Tittelman, Professor Alfred Kinsey's so-called encyclopedic knowledge of human sexual practices and perversions would have ranged from A to B.

That was the story of Morty's life. No one believed his claim to have invented the vibrating rubber dildo, a contribution he considered his most important gift to humankind. And yet, from various pieces of correspondence I discovered after Morty's death, I can prove this claim was true. I might have a few bones of my own to pick with Morty, but I wouldn't take away a jot or tittle from his achievement.

Tittle! That's a good one. Take a tittle away from Tittelman! Which, by the way, was the family's real name. People think "Tittelman" was a pseudonym, something Morty made up, as in "I'm a leg man" or "I'm a tit man." Which—this last—he was. A lover of female breasts. But Morty was born a Tittelman. Or rather he was born a Teitelman. *Teitel* meaning *fig*. When his father came over from Lithuania, he pronounced the name as *Tittel*man, which was how the officials at Ellis Island heard it. So Morty was both a fig man and a tit man. This being one of the games we played. He would reach out to touch my breast. "Oh, what a delicious, lovely fig!" He would smack his lips and coo, then lean down and kiss that fig and suck the sweetness from that fruit. Aren't those the moments that drive a widow mad? From now until I die, the mere mention of a fig will bring to mind the image of my husband's head as he nibbled and licked my breast.

So yes, you might detect a few mixed feelings in my voice. My husband and I enjoyed the happiest married life of any couple I know. But it seems he had other lovers. I am proud of my contribution to his work.

But I should have received credit for that contribution. The man was a genius and true original. Long before we met, when Morty's name was known only to the true cognoscenti of erotic literature, he already had amassed the bulk of what would come to be his astonishing *Bible of Dirty Jokes*. But he needed my encouragement to write up what he had. He needed my typing skills and talent for organization, not to mention my common sense and the money I brought home for food. What I am saying is: the man never would have achieved what modicum of fame he eventually did achieve if I hadn't saved him from despair, kept him happy, warm, well fed, put up with his shady visitors, and added to his oeuvre my own considerable collection of Borscht Belt lore.

Because that is what we shared. People scratch their heads as to why a sweet, shy girl of twenty-one would have chosen to devote her life to a rumpled satyr twice her age. But Morty and I were like Siamese twins born with one funny bone between us. What made Morty laugh made me laugh. If two people can bestow orgasms of comedic pleasure on each other, Morty and I were those two people. I had grown up in the Catskills, where I spent most of my time listening to the performers play can-you-top-this with stories so obscene even the connoisseurs in our audience jammed their fingers in their ears and groaned. It's not that the jokes were funny. Some were, but most were not. It's that I learned at an early age what Morty had figured out even younger: beneath the pleasant surface of respectable human life seethes a roiling pool of schmutz. I had trouble applying this observation to the people I loved. My brothers, say. Or my parents. But I suspected it was there. I knew, and I didn't know. I admitted, and I repressed. What we know and won't admit—isn't that the heart of the dirty joke, not to mention of life itself?

But all that came later. As a little girl, I understood only that the comics who performed at our hotel were heroes. When they strutted across a stage, everyone paid attention, while no matter what I did, no one seemed to see me. I started collecting jokes in a three-ring binder. I would transcribe a comedian's best routines, even his second best, or his third, then practice retelling them to the mirror until I had perfected each inflection, every eye-cross and pregnant pause. Back when I was ten and Rodney Dangerfield was still an aluminum-siding sales-man named Jack Roy who worked the Hospitality's stage for free, I could mimic that droopy lower lip, that heavenward gaze, and that sly self-mocking whine. *I tell ya, I get no respect. I was such an ugly kid, my mother breastfed me through a straw. My wife, her favorite position is fac-ing Bloomingdale's. And this girl I've been seeing? I say to her, "Come home with me, baby, and I'll show you where it's at," and she says, "You better show me, because last time I couldn't find it."* I could reel off twenty of Don Rickles's sharpest put-downs, then bug my eyes and puff my cheeks and do Buddy Hackett's little girl who looks up sweetly and asks her father what the word "degenerate" means, only to be told, "Shut up, kid, and just keep sucking!" (Not that I had any more notion than the little girl in the joke what the word "degenerate" meant, or what was "funny" about the punch line.) The next time these same performers came to play, I would treat them to my imitations of their own routines. Oh, how they hooted and how they howled. *Ketzel, you're such a natural! You've got the timing down pat. No one could teach a person to make the faces you make, to move the way you move. You'll carry on single-handed after all us old farts are dead.*

That is, until I revealed that I wanted to be a comic, too.

"We didn't think you were serious!" Buddy blubbered. "We didn't laugh because you were funny. We laughed because you were imitating us."

"They'll eat you alive, dear Ketzel." This from Alan King. "The Borscht Belt is dying. You're a hack if you tell a joke. Mort Sahl and

Lenny Bruce ruined it for the rest of us. You need to be 'topical' and 'observational.' Or you've got to be really blue, which isn't something an audience wants to hear from an innocent girl named Ketzel."

Then my father put down his feet—and these were the days when he still had two good feet to put down. "No daughter of mine is going to earn her living telling jokes!"

"Please," my mother begged, "could it hurt to go to college? Get your diploma, and maybe a nice teaching certificate, so you'll have something to fall back on when being a comedian doesn't pan out."

My father went so far as to phone a crony of his at Brandeis and hint that if the admissions committee would overlook my so-so grades, he might see his way to donate a wing to the library or gymnasium.

But I had no desire to go to college. And, for one brief and shining moment, I refused to do what my parents said. Where did I find the nerve? Perhaps I was too naive to be aware of the dangers I now would fear. I packed an old valise—no wise man had yet come up with the bright idea of putting it on wheels—and started dragging it along the road. It was a sunny autumn day, and since I wore my red wool coat, which otherwise would have taken up the entire case, I soon grew warm. I made it to the gate and was stunned that the guard did nothing to prevent my leaving. Hadn't my parents ordered him to call my bluff and bring me home?

On I walked, putting down that battered case every few yards to shift it from one aching arm to the other. A mile past the gate, Leo stopped and picked me up. "Come on, kid, get in. Your parents would kill me if they knew. But they wouldn't want some crazy person to offer you a ride instead."

He drove me to Monticello, then sat with me until the bus pulled in. "Knock 'em dead," he said, a suggestion that, coming from Leo, has a more sinister connotation than I realized.

I found a boarding house in the Village whose name I had heard performers mention as somewhere they had stayed—five or six decades earlier—before they had made it big on the vaudeville circuit. The heat was rarely on, and more than once I saw someone sitting in the stairwell pushing up the sleeve of an oily parka as a prelude to jamming a needle in. I kept a hot plate in my room and lived on Goodman's noodle soup until my savings ran out and I was forced to take a job waiting on tables at a deli where third-rate comics and entertainers liked to hang out and gripe. After I worked the dinner shift, I would hurry home and change and sit waiting in some grimy underground bar for my turn at the open mike, where I was allowed to do my shtick for the three inebriated, ill-tempered patrons who had nowhere else to go.

It's a story often told and I won't retell it here, except to say that the version you see in movies, a montage of flops in crappy clubs, after which the hero—it's always a hero—gets his big chance, is rarely true in life. My big chance never came. My jokes got no laughs, even when I realized no one understood the Yiddish punch lines and I translated them into English. If my impressions were more successful, it was only because people found it bizarre to see a teenage girl imitate Henny Youngman. My father's last name got me in to see the agents who handled comics, but only so they could tell me that he had forbidden them to get me work.

I tried making friends with the other comics, but I soon grew weary of the bitter rivalries and whiskey-soaked depressions, all the boasts and lies about the beautiful girls who had knocked at their dressing rooms and offered to suck their dicks, or their bitching about the women who refused to do the same. They dropped their pants and mooned the customers and made cracks about my breasts. If I had needed to listen one more time to the general wisdom that women can't be funny, I would have clouted someone over the head with a bottle of Dr. Brown's.

Occasionally, my dear friend Zero Mostel would take me out and buy me coffee. But he always ended these sessions by shaking his bulbous head and saying, "It's a tough business, Ketzel. If you want my opinion, you'll give it up and go back to school." Totie Fields and Phyllis Diller provided what tips they could, but Totie, like my father, already had lost her leg—it broke my heart to see another of my idols reduced to a broken state—and as much as I admired Phyllis, I wasn't about to put on a fright wig, wear ill-fitting schmattes, and pretend that I was so ugly and incompetent I could never be a threat to men. Bad enough the hecklers hurled insults about my breasts, did I need to insult them, too?

I did on occasion try. Once, when someone yelled, "Where did get those tits?," I looked down at my chest and said, "What? These? Funny you should ask. I stepped out for the *Times* one morning and there they were in a cardboard box." I went on about my breasts as if they were puppies I had adopted, as if I had given each breast a name and trained them to sit up and beg.

"No, seriously," I said, the way a comic does when she's about to give the lie to her entire life. I talked about what a riot it had been to develop big breasts at ten, how my mother had dragged me to the department store, where the only bras my size were contraptions with wires and straps so heavy a plough horse would have balked at wearing one. The other fifth-grade girls wore bras with pink roses on the rim and names like First Love and Kiss of Spring; the bra my mother held up for my consideration was called the Iron Maid. After a prolonged dispute, I allowed my mother to carry two Iron Maids to the checkout counter, which was manned by a female gnome so stunted and deformed she could barely reach the register. She had warts on her warts and chin hairs so long she could have braided them. "Oh, dearie!" she said. "You will simply adore these bras. They're the ones I wear myself!"

On I went, ad-libbing about the miseries of growing up in a part of the world where a man considered himself a wit if he went up to a woman and asked, "Hey, lady, can you spare two nipples for a dime?" The routine was such a success I considered giving in to the popular trend and switching from telling jokes to making humorous observations. But watching my life go by while panning for nuggets of witty insight gave me the unsettling impression that I was living in a sitcom. Life is hard enough without watching yourself and taking notes.

Or maybe I was just too soft. I hated waiting tables to support not only my breasts but my entire self, then staying up late in some smoky bar and fighting off the drunks who grabbed my ass. What if I became successful? I would need to travel to far-off cities and sleep in strange motels while forever hurling comebacks at hecklers, drunks, and pickup artists. By the time I turned twenty, I was so exhausted by the possibility of a life I hadn't yet achieved I was ready to give it up.

And that's when I met Morty.

He had come to the Rising Star early enough to score a table at the front, then sat frowning and wiggling those white Medusa brows while a young male comic with a scraggly goatee discussed the styles in which his girlfriends maintained their pubic hair. I didn't look forward to performing for this maniac. But when I told my first joke, the eyebrow wiggling stopped. That enormous round face tilted up at me like a bowl waiting to be heaped with borscht. I was gratified by this strange man's response . . . until I noticed he was jotting everything I said on a little pad. Well, that solved the mystery. He was stealing my best routines. True, I had stolen them from other comics, but that was a lesser crime; it was as if Ali Baba had gone to all the effort to brave those forty thieves, only to have the magic lamp he had stolen lifted from his pocket at a bar.

After the club closed, I went out the back door and found Morty in the alley. "Not to fear," he said. "I am neither a masher nor a kook." This did little to diminish my concern. He wore a grubby, unbelted coat such as a flasher might have worn, and when he unbuttoned the front to reach in his pocket, I averted my eyes. "My credentials," he said and held out a card, which, when I examined it, proved that Mordecai Tittelman was a member in good standing of the Friars Club and entitled to all the privileges and rights thereof.

Suddenly, he looked less like a homeless person than a wise and courtly Virgil. What a dashing moustache! What a distinguished halo of hair! He looked like a cross between Burt Lahr and Albert Einstein. He bowed stiffly and invited me for a meal at a cheap café, where we stayed up past dawn, laughing and trading jokes.

"My dear," he said, "you are to Borscht Belt culture what Homer was to the ancient Greeks." Most comics today, Morty said, were afraid of offending anyone for fear they wouldn't get invited on Johnny Carson. Instead of telling real jokes, they minced about the stage, kvetching about the small stuff, inquiring politely of the audience "Did you ever notice?" or "Do you know what happened to me today?" Even Lenny Bruce had tried to get a sitcom. And—Lenny's worst sin—he had addicted us all to the soul-destroying vice of irony. After Lenny Bruce, we all became *hipsters*—Morty spat out the word as if he had found a lemon seed in the whiskey sour he was guzzling.

Such discourse would have been intoxicating even if I hadn't been imbibing those same whiskey sours. I couldn't get enough of Morty. I drank in his philosophical meanderings as avidly as I drank in his compliments. "What do you need with college?" he said. "Those cacademics will only teach you how to think like everyone else."

As for Morty, he had cadged his education by sitting in on lectures at NYU and setting up camp in the reading room of the New York Public Library. So assiduous a pupil was he that by the mid-1960s, he was asked to teach a course in erotic folklore at CCNY, a position he accepted and then resigned because his students were so spaced out on marijuana and psychedelics they couldn't follow a coherent argument, let alone come up with their own ideas.

"Is that why we're fighting a revolution?" Morty asked. "So people can lie around gazing at their navels and acting cool? Who wants to be 'cool'? Being hot is where it's at!" As to the other professors, with their fine words and fine ideas about Marcuse and Reich, all they really wanted was to get inside their students' pants. Morty's biggest disappointment was that after fighting to bring the country free love, what he had achieved was the *Devil in Miss Jones* and *Screw*. He wanted his students to chase Nixon out of office, not organize a giant grope-fest. And allow me this opportunity to point out that Morty did as much as any Weatherman to bring home our boys merely by inventing the slogan "Make Love Not War." What? You don't believe that slogan was Morty's? Here, let me just find the clipping. Ah yes . . . I think you can clearly see that Morty is carrying a poster with those very words as he marches around the Pentagon in his one-man demonstration against the president's "incursion" into Vietnam in the autumn of '63.

Morty was a teacher to his core, and in me he had found his ideal pupil. After we met at the Rising Star, he sent me a list of books to read, museums to visit, lectures to attend, and plays to see. As Herman Melville might have put it, Morty Tittelman was my Harvard and Yale College. He tutored me not only in love and sex but in politics, economics, religion, literature, mythology, and psychology. No doubt you have read his essay "No Laughing Matter: The Selling of the American Soul." According to Morty, instead of inventing dirty stories to amuse each other, we now allow multinational corporations to produce our humor for us. Movies, radio shows, sitcoms, LPs, and tape recordings have become mechanical substitutes for authentic human communication.

What we have ended up with—and I quote—"is sexless, synthetic art and sadistic entertainments no normal human being would ever wish to see. When every line of dialogue has to be written and reviewed, censored and rehearsed beforehand, nothing remains but kitsch." In other words, what we get is safe, self-conscious "humor." Not the collective id, but one man's girlfriends' pubic hair.

You can imagine how heady such discussions were for a girl my age. And Morty treated me like a queen. He showed up at the deli where I worked, ordered coffee and a slice of cake, and, every time I stopped to refill his cup, he offered me another compliment. "Ketzel, you have the most winning smile of any woman I have ever met." Or: "This cheesecake is delicious, but it isn't as sweet as you."

One afternoon, he came in and ordered soup. "Will you join me in a bowl of chicken noodle?" Morty leered.

"The offer is tempting," I said, "but I doubt the bowl is big enough for the both of us."

Morty nodded in admiration. Then, each time I happened by, he tried to stump me with variations of this classic joke. "Waitress," he said, "is chicken soup good for your health?"

"Not if you're the chicken."

"What about the alphabet soup? Is *that* good for a person's health?"

"Sure it is. It will help you to move your vowels."

Then: "Waitress! I can't find any chicken in this chicken soup!"

"Yeah?" I said. "So what? There's no horse in the horseradish either."

"But what about all these foreign objects?"

"They're not *foreign,* sir. They're from right here on the kitchen floor."

On we went, until Morty hit me with a version of the gag I had never heard. "So tell me," Morty said. "When Marilyn Monroe was married to Arthur Miller, he demanded she learn to cook him matzo ball soup, the way his mother used to make. Why did Marilyn refuse?"

The entire clientele held its collective breath. The tray of sandwiches on my arm grew heavy. I knew I was near defeat.

Then the gods of humor smiled. The punch line came to me in a flash. I put my tray on the nearest table and struck a seductive pose. "Oh, Arthur," I said in my breathiest Marilyn imitation. "It just breaks my heart to think of all those poor little matzos running around without their balls."

The outburst of laughter from the regulars at the deli was a comedian's fondest dream, but not as gratifying as the sight of Morty bowing his head and gesturing in my direction and lifting his hands to clap.

After that, no matter what shift I worked, Morty was there reading his *Daily News*, pouring sugar in his tea, and attempting to impress me with his adoration. Generally, he sat apart from the other comics, but when any of them were foolish enough to make comments about my breasts, Morty made a show of getting up and knocking their heads together, the way Moe used to do when his fellow Stooges misbehaved. "Apologize!" he would command, and I was astonished when the Stooges did.

He dished out much the same punishment to any hecklers who interfered with my act at the Rising Star. After the bar had closed, he walked me home. One time, he showed up driving a horse and carriage he had borrowed from a friend who ran the concession at Central Park, then drove me down Broadway, where he lifted me from the carriage, swung me to the sidewalk, clicked his heels, and bowed goodnight.

So it wasn't all what I gave Morty and nothing of what Morty gave me. Thanks to Morty and his familiarity with the janitorial staff at Lincoln Center, we got in free to every opera the Met put on. He took me dancing at Harlem nightclubs, on cruises to Staten Island and outings to the Cloisters, Jones Beach, and Coney Island.

Then there was the night he took me to a performance of *Macbeth* in Central Park. "Hey, Morty!" someone called, waving from behind the stage. And who should it turn out to be but Joseph Papp, whom Morty knew from the old days, when Papp was Joseph Papirofsky and Morty filled out the cast of his impromptu Yiddish versions of *The Merchant of Venice*, *The Merry Wives of Windsor*, and *Henrys IV* and *V.*

"Morty!" Papp said. "You've got to help me out! Jerry Stiller just got hit by a bike messenger. I could get somebody in back to read the part. Hell, I could do it. But I can't forget the time you played the night porter—what was it, in '42?" He turned to me. "Fantastic. The man was absolutely fantastic. How about it, Mort? For old time's sake? You'd be doing me a colossal favor."

At which Morty said, "Yussel, I would like to help. But I brought this young lady to the show, and it wouldn't be gentlemanly to desert her."

At which I said, oh no, he had to. How could I object to Morty sharing the stage with Richard Burton, who was playing the title role?

"Well, then." Morty kissed my hand. "You will excuse me while I prepare."

Morty followed Joseph Papp behind the stage and refreshed his memory as to the several small comic bits the porter must recite. Morty's memory was prodigious. It had to be, in his line of work. He had passed many happy hours studying the bawdy bard for the earliest examples of iambic smut. And, to be safe, Morty wrote the porter's lines on the underside of his shirt.

Still, when Morty came onstage in the second act, I held my breath. A knock at the castle door and there he was, staggering to unlock the gate while buttoning his fly. MacDuff, that eternal straight man, asks the porter if he knows the three things that drink provokes. At which the porter provides his answer: *A red nose, my lord. A desire to sleep. And an unbearable urge to pee. As to lechery, drink both provokes and unprovokes it. Drink provokes the desire, but it takes away the performance. It sets the man on . . . and it takes him off. It persuades him . . . and it disheartens him. It makes him stand to*—Morty pretended to reach in his pants and pull out his cock—*and it makes him not stand to.* He smiled slyly and let his imaginary member droop.

Oh, you must excuse my tears. When I think of Morty saying the porter's lines, I miss him too much for words. You see, from that night on, whenever he imbibed too much, he acted out that bit about how drink makes a man's member stand to and not stand to. And how can I help but mourn someone who, when he took his bow, received an ovation second only to the applause the star received? Later, when Richard Burton came over to thank Morty for stepping in and saving the show, Morty told him a joke about two Welshmen in a whorehouse that made the actor laugh so hard he nearly choked, after which Morty pulled me over and introduced me as his fiancée—this being news to me—and the most famous actor in the world took me around and hugged me, which caused Morty to jab him in the gut and say, "Now, Dick, don't you go stealing my girl! Can I help it if poor Liz has only her looks to offer while Ketzel here has brains and a sense of humor, too?"

So you can see why, when Morty got down on his knees and asked me to make his lie come true, I agreed and I bade him rise.

And then, yes, Morty wooed me. Morty and I made love. Until then, he had never so much as invited me up to see his etchings. He was ashamed of the mess, he said. Every square inch of his grimy flat was covered with spools of recording tape, index cards, notebooks, fertility figures from the Congo, and cans of meatballs and cabbage soup. But after we became engaged, Morty escorted me up those five flights of stairs and unlocked the door. The apartment was still a mess, but Morty had cleared a path from the living room to the bedroom, where his mattress lay on the floor, the linens clean, the pillows plumped, and flowers he must have picked in Central Park strewn across the quilt.

He helped me remove my coat. "I haven't the slightest doubt that I would be happy making love to you—and no one but you—for the remainder of my life," Morty said. "But it wouldn't be fair to ask that you go through with our impending nuptials without having sampled the goods. Perhaps making love with a man so much your senior will turn out to be a disappointing experience. In short, I would be a cad to ask you to buy a pig in a poke. I suggest you allow me to make love to you now, while you still have the chance to break our engagement and walk away. Without the slightest ill will on my part, of course."

"Oh, Morty," I said, "I thought you would never ask." I put one palm to either side of his head and lifted his face to mine. "Morty Tittelman, there is no one I would rather make love to the first time than you."

He removed my garments one by one and laid me on his bed, after which he stood looking down at me, shaking his head and smiling. "Oh, Ketzel. On the one hand, the world is too full of this." He waved his arms to indicate the piles of smut. "But then, my love, there is this." He stretched his arms toward me. "And if the poor bastards who were responsible for all that muck had been lucky enough to catch even one glimpse of you, none of that would exist."

What nicer words could a woman hear? And you won't be surprised to learn that the wear and tear on an old man's body can be offset by his knowledge of the hows and whys of love. Morty Tittelman loved me in a way few men are capable of loving women. He knew all the ins and outs. He wrote the book on cunnilingus. No, literally, he wrote the book. A thousand copies of his masterpiece *The Pleasures and Techniques of Oral Love* were printed in the fifties. Nine hundred and ninety-eight copies were destroyed by the FBI, but I own the remaining two, each of which is worth ten or fifteen grand. I intend to bequeath the nine hundred and ninety-ninth copy to Columbia, but I am sure the archivists there will understand if I keep this one remaining copy of *Oral Love* to peruse on those nights I miss Morty the most. Reading this book and admiring the illustrations, which Morty drew, I can almost feel his tongue performing its magic you know where.

Oh, oh, oh, when I remember those early years! Morty's apartment wasn't much, but it was certainly a big improvement on my room at the Bedbug Inn. And even though I kept working part-time to support us, Morty treated me to a life I otherwise wouldn't have known, or enjoyed without Morty. Our apartment was always full. The jokes we studied were rarely funny, but Morty and his friends were dazzling raconteurs. How many people can say they have had the pleasure of listening to Margaret Mead discourse on the joke-telling habits of adolescent Samoan girls? Or turned down the comforter on their bed to find their portrait sketched on the sheet by that lunatic genius R. Crumb? Or heard Harpo Marx tell a joke?

I was Dorothea to Morty's Casaubon. I remember the first time I heard Morty explain Sigmund Freud's idea that if two men are telling a dirty joke, there is always a woman present, if not in actuality, then in each of the two men's minds, and they are forcing the woman in the room to do what the woman in the joke is doing, or to submit to what is being done to her.

"Ketzel," Morty said, "the reason you wanted to become a comic is that you preferred not to be the woman standing idly by while those two men told their jokes. You didn't want to be the woman they were stripping naked for their amusement. You thought if you were the one telling the dirty joke, you couldn't be pinched or mauled. But the truth is, none of us will be safe from such indignities unless we manage to understand the ugliness in the soul that makes anyone want to tell such a monstrosity in the first place."

Which, when Morty said it, I immediately knew was true.

3.

So LET ME see, where was I? I was sitting on that plane to Vegas, which was the first plane I had sat on in twenty years, Morty having preferred to travel solo, since this provided the opportunity to collect new jokes from the salesmen he held captive in their seats or found waiting to use the restroom. Not that salesmen these days know any new jokes except the ones forwarded to them in e-mail by other salesmen.

Morty took me traveling with him only once, when he was being knighted by *L'Académie de la Comédie-Française,* the first time an American had been awarded that honor since Jerry Lewis won it for *The Nutty Professor*—or, as the film is known in France, *Docteur Jerry et Mister Love*—in 1964. The academy pitched in my airfare and put us up at a posh hotel. The weather was so dreary and wet, and Morty was so busy being feted, I might as well have stayed in New York and taken a shower in our apartment for all I got to see of France. But it was a pleasure on the final night to dress up in one of Totie's old gowns, which my mother had taken in especially for that occasion, then sit on the dais and applaud as Morty bowed his shaggy head and allowed himself to be draped with a medal signifying that he was now a *Chevalier de la Table Erotique.*

That was the first and only time he allowed me to accompany him on such a trip, a mystery whose solution I now attribute to his need to take a tour of the strip clubs in any city to which he was invited. Although, to be honest, traveling makes me nervous. Not so much because the jet might go down but because there are so many details to attend to. For instance, as I was sitting on that plane to Vegas, I remembered a cantaloupe I had left out on the kitchen counter in my apartment. But what is a rotting fruit compared to a beloved brother? As sad as my mission was, I was glad to *have* a mission. And to be free of all that smut. It was a brilliant blue day, and there wasn't a cloud to block our view, although most of my fellow passengers had pulled down their shades so the light wouldn't interfere with their ability to read their computer screens. The businessman to my left was entering numbers in a spreadsheet, while the teenage boy to my right was furiously pushing buttons on a game whose *pings* and *pangs* reminded me of the noises we used to make when we shot each other with our hands, *p-khew, p-khew, p-khew,* except that my seatmate was using a bazooka to obliterate an army of trolls and well-stacked female aliens. It came to me that if I ever did start to date again, I would need to do so by computer, an innovation Morty would have jeered at as yet another sign of our dehumanized age. Not to mention that a man could lie online even easier than Morty had lied to me face-to-face.

In front of me, on a movie screen, an unflappable Asian man was using a laser to fend off his assailants. Limbs were sliced and torsos hacked. Hands and heads went flying. Strangest of all, the film seemed to be a comedy. The passengers around me laughed, but I hadn't shelled out three dollars to buy a headset, so I felt comedically disabled.

Which, in a way, I was. I hadn't laughed since Morty died, having buried my sense of humor with the *Bible of Dirty Jokes* Morty had requested be placed in his coffin with him, as if to supply him with an eternity's worth of stories with which to regale the residents of wherever he ended up. I was like a music reviewer who has lost her hearing, or an art critic who is going blind.

The pilot announced that if we looked to our left, we could see the Grand Canyon. I was afraid my fellow passengers would rush to the windows and tip the plane. But no one glanced up, leaving me to wonder how anything on a computer could compare to the sight of the Grand Canyon as viewed from thirty-five thousand feet on a spectacularly clear blue day. I leaned over my seatmate's lap to look. And it came to me why no one else seemed to bother. The enormity of the sight induced nothing but awe, and what could you do with that? There was no button you could push to interact with the scenery. The Grand Canyon was simply *there*.

At last, the attendants were instructed to prepare for landing. My heart began to pound. *Potsie!* I thought. Would I be able to find my brother? Would Ebby? Would we even know where to look? I was prepared to spend my life crawling around the Grand Canyon on my hands and knees if it meant I might find a clue, but even a man of my brother's size might vanish into a hole that big without leaving a trace.

Worse, I couldn't begin searching until we landed, and the runways, the pilot announced, were full.

"Guess people can't wait to lose their money," the pilot drawled, an airborne Will Rogers. Around and around we flew, like buzzards waiting for their prey to breathe its last. That my brother's body might be lying in the desert, his corpulent flesh providing a feast for crows, caused me to cry. The businessman to my left stared at me as though I were weeping in a movie for which he hadn't purchased headphones. For the rest of the flight, he occupied himself with fitting his laptop into its compartmentalized case, while the boy to my right focused on the upright tray table in front of him as if it were a computer gone suddenly blank.

The landing gear clunked down and the plane took an Esther Williams dive. But the closer we got to Vegas, the more disappointing the city seemed. The movies always show Las Vegas glittering at night, but by day, the city was dusty, barren, brown; it reminded me of the performers at our hotel when I took coffee to their rooms and found them sprawled on their beds, devoid of tuxedoes and toupees, faces haggard, complexions dull, or later by the pool, a towel across their eyes as they baked away a headache.

The plane taxied toward the gate and my fellow passengers stood from their seats and wrestled their bags from overhead. They seemed to have undergone a transformation from the drab New Yorkers who had boarded the plane four hours earlier. The men now sported cowboy hats and bolo ties, while the women had tugged down their necklines to expose more cleavage. The businessman to my left removed his suit jacket to reveal a silky blue shirt unbuttoned to his navel. I took my place behind a man whose shiny black hair was combed up in a ducktail. When I accidentally stepped on his heel, he turned and sneered, "Baby, do you mind? You mustn't crowd the King."

I couldn't wait to get off the plane. The reason the other passengers had come to Vegas seemed an affront to mine. My brother was out there dying! My niece was in the care of a crazy, unpleasant woman who, for all we knew, had murdered Meryl's dad. I had dined too long on lies not to be ravenous for the truth. That I had come to Las Vegas, of all places, seeking a good dose of reality didn't yet strike me as a deluded thing to do.

"Come on, let's get a move on," muttered a woman in a buckskin vest. She cupped one hand to her ear. "I can hear those slot machines calling my name."

The attendants let us off. We filed into the waiting area, where I was astonished to see a row of slots. As we bumped and jostled past them, the woman in the buckskin vest seemed to hesitate. She muttered a helpless "what the heck" and slumped in a chair to play.

I went out and found a cab. When the driver asked my destination, I told him the name of the only hotel I knew. "The Flamingo, please," I said, feeling like a member of Bugsy Siegel's gang, which is the way a law-abiding person like me is meant to feel in Vegas.

The driver said nothing. In New York, the easiest strategy for making small talk with a cabbie is to ask what country he was born in. But my driver looked as if he had come to Nevada in the 1920s panning for uranium, then watched everyone grow rich around him until he gave up and traded his donkey for a cab.

"So," I said, "do you know any good jokes?" This was something Morty used to do—his best informants were often cabbies—and I somehow felt compelled to speak up for the dead.

"A joke? You want to hear a joke? Best joke round here is how a working stiff like me can't afford a place to live. Used to be, a person could get a nice house for fifty, sixty grand. Same house today? Three or four hundred thousand. Even some crappy apartment on the West-side, where the colored used to live? We're talking a grand and a half a month. Working stiff, he makes minimum wage, maybe he lives off tips ... Huh. That's a pretty good joke right there."

After we had compared the relative difficulties of making ends meet in Las Vegas and New York, the driver peered in the mirror and said, "Lady, I hope you don't mind my butting in, but you don't seem the high-roller type. Might as well take your hard-earned cash and flush it down the john."

Oh, no, I said. I appreciated his concern, but I wasn't there to gamble. I had come looking for my brother, who had gone missing a few days before.

The cabby nodded. "Surprising how many folks come to this town and aren't ever heard from again." A brief silence followed, a period of mourning for all those poor schmucks who had vanished in the maelstrom of suckers and wise guys churning around our cab. Already we had reached the Strip—the airport was so close to town, the latter seemed an extension of the former—and I searched the pedestrians for a familiar face. But even though I saw a dozen overweight men wearing nylon shorts and jerseys, each with his long gray hair tied back in a ponytail, none of them was my brother.

To pass the time, the cabby said, he did know one joke. A passenger had told it to him years before, and he would tell it to me now, as long as I didn't object that the punch line was a bit risqué.

"Oh," I said, "I am more than a little accustomed to risqué humor."

"As long as you're sure." He cleared his throat. "There's this businessman, right? The guy flies to Vegas, and after a few days, he doesn't have anything left except the shirt on his back and his airline ticket home. He goes to catch a cab. But it's late, and there's only one driver, and the cabby doesn't look any too friendly.

"But what the heck, right? The guy gets in and explains his predicament. 'You take me to the airport, I swear I'll pay you back. I'll give you my address, my phone number. Not only that, I'll pay you ten times what I owe. What's the fare to the airport? Ten dollars? I'll pay you a hundred.'

"The cabby says, 'No dice. I'm not running a charity. Get out of my fucking cab.' Well, what can the guy do? He hitchhikes to the airport, barely makes it home.

"So a year goes by, and the businessman flies back to Vegas. This time, he knows when to quit. He's feeling good, his pockets are full of cash, he goes out to find a cab, and this time there's a line of twenty taxis, and who should be sitting at the back of the line but his old friend, the asshole who refused to give him a lift.

"So okay. The guy comes up with a plan on how he can get even with the jerk. He gets in the first cab and says, 'How much for a ride to the airport?' The cabby says, 'Ten bucks.' The guy says, 'And how much for a blow job on the way?' The cabby says, 'What are you, some kind of pervert? Get out of my fucking cab before I kill you.' So the businessman gets out of that cab and into the next cab, and he goes through the same routine—how much is it to the airport, how much if you give me a blow job, etcetera. Guy does this with each of the nineteen cabs, and every cabby says, 'Get out of my cab or I'll fucking kill you.'

"Finally, the businessman gets to his buddy in the back, and he says, 'How much for a ride to the airport?' And the cabby says, 'Ten bucks.' And the businessman says okay and off they go. Except, as they pull past the other cabs, the businessman gives this big shit-eating grin and flashes a thumbs-up sign to the other drivers."

I knew the joke was funny. I had laughed at it the first twenty times I had heard my husband tell it. But, as I might have already mentioned, I had lost my sense of humor.

"What? You didn't like it? I asked if it was okay to get risqué." The cabby threw up his hands, which might have gotten us killed if we hadn't been stuck in traffic. Off to one side, a blowzy Lady Liberty lifted her torch beside a thirty-story billboard on which a woman in nothing but a thong kicked her thirty-story legs. "Believe it or not," the cabby said, "I got that story from this guy who claimed he was a professor of dirty jokes."

As you might imagine, this information caused such a constriction in my lungs I could barely breathe. On the one hand, I missed Morty so much I was grateful for any reminder of his existence. On the other hand, if my recently departed husband had chosen that moment to open the door of the cab and slide inside, I would have slapped him across his face.

I leaned across the seat. "Really?" I said. "A professor of dirty jokes? What did this professor look like?"

The cabby stroked his grizzled chin. "Mostly, I don't recall what a passenger looks like five minutes after he steps out of my cab. But this guy looked like ... You know that actor who played the lion in *The Wizard of Oz*?"

Tears rose to my eyes. Morty used to say that jokes—the kind that make people laugh—form a chain of gifts that get passed along without getting used up or diminished. When Morty was alive, he had given this gift of humor to this cabby, who, all these years later, was giving that gift to me.

The question was, exactly how many years ago had this professor of dirty jokes been sitting in this cab? I opened my mouth to ask, but I lost my nerve and closed it. I hadn't come to Vegas to search for Morty's ghost. Instead, I asked my driver if he had ever heard of a bookie named Potsie Weinrach.

This time, he not only glanced over his shoulder, he turned around and stared. "Lady, I thought you said you were here to look for your brother. What would a respectable person like you want with a scumbag like Potsie Weinrach?" Then his face underwent a series of contortions that reminded me of that nice old man in *The Treasure of Sierra Madre* when Humphrey Bogart accuses him of trying to steal the gold.

"You know my brother?"

"A guy like me know a guy like Potsie Weinrach?" He faced the front and put both hands on the wheel, although he could just as soon have let the cars behind us push. "No offense, but a guy like me doesn't really want to know a guy like Potsie Weinrach. Someone asks where the action is, I might say the sports book at Harrah's, or maybe at the Luxor, and if the passenger says, 'Come on, I mean the real action,' I might mention your brother's name. But personally? Do I personally want to know Potsie Weinrach?"

It occurred to me that he was trying to express something more than my brother's tendency to move in social circles beyond the spheres a cabby moved in. "Then you haven't seen him?"

"No. And if other people haven't been seeing your brother, that might be something to worry about. Given, you know, his size." He took a card from the glove compartment. "A nice lady like you could get hurt, poking your nose where it isn't wanted. We're not supposed to pick up passengers from the street. But if you find yourself in a fix, call that number and I'll see what I can do."

I tucked the card in my jeans, then turned to look at the giant neon signs and the crowds surging along the walks. The casinos were newer than I had imagined—I'd had in mind the old days, when the Rat Pack called Vegas home. But the buildings seemed uninspired. With those bottomless pots of cash, this was the best they could come up with? I might have missed the Eiffel Tower when Morty took me to visit France, but here it was, reduced in size and devoid of charm. Same with the canals of Venice, the Forum, and Caesars Palace. I wouldn't have been surprised to see a replica of the Hospitality House Hotel squeezed in between Bellagio and Monte Carlo.

The driver dropped me off and wished me well. I'm not sure who I thought would be waiting for me in front of the Flamingo, but whoever it was, he wasn't there. I asked a young man in a uniform if he could direct me to registration, but all he did was lift a lackadaisical finger and motion me past several dozen shops and restaurants toward a casino floor so vast I wished for a camel and guide to help me cross it. On and on I schlepped, weaving my way among senior citizens hobbling from stool to stool with Styrofoam cups of quarters and waitresses in high-heeled shoes carrying trays amid rows of flashing slots and spinning wheels. Where were the smooth tycoons and their svelte, bejeweled mistresses? The clientele looked as if they had been airlifted in from a Wal-Mart in Ohio or a megachurch in Texas. Call me old-fashioned, but it struck me as odd that people wearing crosses as big as fists should be sitting around a table shooting craps. I remembered what my father had said about customers at our hotel who lost so much money they couldn't afford to pay their bills. Didn't the Flamingo worry that a guest might lose her savings before she had so much as checked in? Then again, if I already had lost my money, why would they care if I checked in or not?

The bored room-clerk didn't even look up when I paid for my room in cash. Morty claimed not to believe in credit cards. He considered the interest they charged to be more obscene than anything you would find in his *Bible of Dirty Jokes*. But this apparently hadn't stopped him from charging all those lap dances at clubs with names like the Full Moon Saloon, the Body Shop, and the Sugar Shack, in cities as widely spread as Saint Paul and Tuscaloosa.

I took an elevator up to the twenty-second floor, where the maze-like halls stretched for miles. The room was disappointing, no fancier, really, than the best rooms in the Catskills, although there were probably fancier suites for people who didn't choose their accommodations based on which hotels had once been associated with famous Jewish gangsters. Still, the room had a decent view. With the time difference, it was only late afternoon, and the mountains to the west were lit up from behind like the backdrops on a Broadway stage. I put away the stack of Camp Hospitality T-shirts I had taken from my parents' house and stashed my father's money in the safe. I wished I'd had time to take a nap, but I wanted to see my niece. And I needed to set up an appointment with Ebby Salzman.

I was surprised when he picked up his own phone. Didn't all private eyes employ sexy, wisecracking secretaries like Della Street?

"Ketzel, is that you?"

As you might assume, this made me think highly of his detection skills. That is, until he told me that my mother had called him fifty times to see if I had come in yet.

"Geez, Ebby, I'm sorry if she bothered you. This thing about my brother—"

"No, I was happy to talk to your mom. I wish Potsie hadn't gone missing. But it isn't every day I get to talk to . . . Growing up where we did, you and your family were royalty."

"Ebby, you were the homecoming king! If that's not royalty, what is?"

"I'm embarrassed to be talking to someone who knew me during that period of my youth."

"Embarrassed? You were everyone's hero! And you weren't stuck up like the other guys. I have only the best memories of watching you play football. That pass you caught in the last seconds of that championship game against Port Jervis . . . to this day, it remains a thing of beauty in my eyes."

But Ebby was having none of it. "Maybe I didn't seem stuck up to you. But I thought very well of myself. I did things I'm not proud of. I just want you to know that any memories you might have of the Eberhard Salzman you knew at school don't apply to the man who will be conducting the investigation into your brother's disappearance."

This struck me as a shame, seeing as how I had been looking forward to renewing my acquaintance with the Eberhard Salzman who had made that desperate catch and been carried off the field by his teammates, not to mention the Eberhard Salzman who had raised his jersey to wipe his brow on that hot September afternoon when we were in our teens. But then, if he had been that same Eberhard Salzman, he wouldn't have been speaking to me now.

I informed him of my plans to see my sister-in-law. Unless he thought I should stop by the police station first and file a missing person's report?

Nah, Ebby said, no rush on that account. The clock wasn't exactly running out on that play. Potsie was a grown man. A bookie. The cops weren't about to leap into action just because he hadn't come home for dinner one night. They would assume he had gone missing to slip a debt. There would be plenty of time to file a missing person's report the next morning. Oh, and when I did, there was no need to mention I had hired a private eye. The missing persons officer might not work as hard if a professional was on the case. In the meantime, we might as well get some dinner and discuss my brother. "The Flamingo has a pretty decent buffet," Ebby said. "Not that the food is anywhere near as good as it was at your parents' hotel."

"Oh, Ebby, please—"

"I mean that. My dad used to bring home leftovers in a doggie bag. You should have watched me chow down."

The image of Ebby Salzman eating food his father had brought home in a doggie bag from out hotel was not something I wanted to contemplate.

"What say I meet you in the courtyard at seven-fifteen? Where they keep the live flamingoes? That way, if I'm late, you'll have something to keep you occupied." I was about to hang up when he said, "Ketzel? I'm really looking forward to seeing you again. I'm glad we're having this chance to reconnect."

I hung up as flustered as I had been the day Ebby and I had been campers at my parents' hotel and he had picked me first to be on his team at kickball. Then I remembered Ebby had picked me because I had bribed him with a box of Popsicles I had stolen from Ike Praise's concession, just as my parents were bribing him now to be on our team and find my brother.

I went down and found a cab. This time, I had no intention of asking the driver if he knew any good jokes. We got to the edge of town, where yet another subdivision had been laid out on the desert like something a child might build with Legos. A hideous brown wall hid the development from the street—all you could see was a bunch of roofs made out of flowerpots. *LA MANCHA ESTATES*, a sign proclaimed.

DARE TO DREAM THE IMPOSSIBLE DREAM!

"You need the security code," the driver said. "Or you gotta call somebody to let you in."

I had to be the last person in America not to own a cell phone. Although even if I had owned one, my sister-in-law would have greeted my request by hanging up. "You can leave me here," I told the driver. "I'm supposed to wait for my brother's wife to come home from work."

I could see he didn't believe me. But if a customer says she wants to get out of your cab, you have to let her out. "Just be careful," the driver warned. "I don't mean to bad-mouth your family, but people who live behind walls like this, sometimes it's not clear who's protecting who from what."

After spending so many hours cooped up in the plane and wandering the Flamingo, it was nice to be outside. The temperature had dropped to a delicious seventy-five degrees. What I couldn't figure out was why, if people moved here for the weather, no one was on the street. Then again, people who put walls around their houses aren't the type to go out for an evening stroll. I studied the wall to see if I might scale it. But if an out-of-shape New Yorker in her fifties is able to climb a wall, it can't be much of a defense, now can it? Finally, a silver Volvo glided up. The driver punched a code in the security device and the gate retracted. The Volvo slid through (*VICKSGRL*, the license read), and I slipped in behind, smiling ruefully to convey I was just someone's frumpy aunt who had gone out for a walk and forgotten the code to get back in.

At the center of the development stood a tennis court and a pool bordered with flowering plants whose gaudy hues led me to wonder if the gardener at our hotel had retired to Las Vegas. Branching from this park were six cobbled dead-end streets; judging by the numbers, my brother had built his house on dead end number three. Given how reluctant he had been to have me visit, I had imagined him living in a one-room flat with a sofa for a bed and candy wrappers and racing forms strewn about the floor. But the house my brother lived in must have cost a million bucks.

Still, it was a house that faced a wall. All I could see was a three-car garage, in front of which were parked a blood-red Hummer, a tiny blue Porsche that must have belonged to Janis (*POTZ4ME*, the license read), and a yellow Volkswagen I deduced belonged to Meryl, although, like any aunt, I found it difficult to believe she was old enough to drive. Nothing else seemed amiss. But then, I had nothing to compare it to. I had the unsettling sense of being watched, but since slipping through the gate, I hadn't encountered another soul. The gates on either side of the house were locked, so I walked up to a door beside the garage and summoned my courage to ring the bell.

Which makes this the ideal time to tell you what you need to know about my brother's wife. For example, she has two names. My parents call her Janis, which was the name given to her by her father, an orthodontist named Myron Brite, and her mother, a world-class mah-jongg champion named Bibi Stern, who had raised her daughter on Long Island three or four decades earlier. But after Janis moved to Vegas, she changed her name to Sunshine Brite and flew into a rage whenever anyone called her "Janis," which my parents tended to do because, as my mother pointed out, if you gave in to the first demand presented by such a woman, she would have you carrying out her every whim, a possibility that seemed unlikely, given my mother's reluctance to leave our hotel and my brother's equal and opposite reluctance to bring his wife home to meet my mother.

Which is the second thing you need to know: Janis and I had never met. Potsie had married her three years earlier at a wedding in Vegas to which none of us had been invited. In the one photo he had seen fit to share, my brother wears his perpetual nylon shorts, a Thurman Munson jersey, and a pair of orange flip-flops, and Janis-Sunshine wears a shiny yellow dress with a neckline so low and a hemline so high she might have confused her wedding with an audition.

"You wouldn't see in this person what I see in this person," my brother had told me to explain why I hadn't been invited. "Besides, you tend to be judgmental," which, in my experience, is what people say when they are afraid you might put into words the same judgment they have made themselves.

I took a deep breath—having lived so long in New York, I was disoriented by the discovery that the air in Vegas had no smell—and rang the bell. No one answered. I rang again. I could hear dogs racing toward the door, then hurling themselves against it. Given his line of work, my brother probably kept a pack of pit bulls. I had no method of self-defense. If a pit bull clamped its jaws around my leg, my only hope would be to pull off a sneaker and thwap the monster on the nose.

I knelt to untie my shoe. The door opened, and I found myself face-to-face with five canine muzzles too narrow to belong to pit bulls. The dogs were struggling to get past a girl so plainly dressed, her hair done up in a rag, I took her to be the maid.

"Aunt Ketzel? What are you doing here?"

I hadn't seen my niece since my brother had brought her east the previous year, and Meryl had changed so much since then I could have passed her on the street without knowing her. Then again, if there was one unchanging characteristic about my niece, it was that she transformed herself into a completely new person every six months. The summer she was ten, she was a prissy ballerina. The next summer: a swimmer in training for the Olympics. Then a studious artiste, a tree-climbing tomboy, and, the last time I had seen her, a shyly sullen punk.

You didn't need to be Dr. Spock to figure out she was hoping to find some version of herself that her mother might come back and love.

Her mother, whose name was Amy, had left town when my niece was four. She sued Potsie for divorce and took half of everything he owned, including a gold Mercedes, then gave it all to a man named Jurgen, who was so obsessed with the ancient Anasazi he tried to replicate the way they lived, first by moving to some ruins at Mesa Verde, and, when this resulted in his eviction, by digging a kiva on a piece of government land so contaminated with radioactive waste no one bothered to chase him off.

"I hope she fucking glows," Potsie told me. "I hope they're in that hole in the ground, and she's giving Jurgen a blow job, and a fucking mutant coyote tears off the roof and eats them limb by limb."

For each of Meryl's first three birthdays after her mother left, Meryl had received a lopsided pot with a card signed "ValZorah." But then the pots stopped coming, and no one had any idea where Amy/ValZorah went. Potsie took up with a string of girlfriends, but he didn't allow any of these women to interfere with his raising Meryl. She seemed happy to be his little girl—that is, until she hit junior high and started wearing jeans so low they showed her *pupik,* which she had pierced with a diamond stud. She dyed her hair an unnatural shade of red and slathered her face with so much makeup her father said she looked like a whore, at which she ran away and tried to be one.

Then, just as suddenly, she took to wearing a long black coat, pierced her tongue, and shaved her head. The last time my niece had come east, my parents had been as frightened of their granddaughter as if she truly had been an invading Goth.

"Close that door!" a voice screamed from inside my brother's house. "If those dogs get out, I'm going to fucking strangle you!"

Meryl made a face. But even with her eyes crossed and that schmatte on her head, she reminded me of an actress who can't take out the trash without attracting the paparazzi.

"Meryl! I'm warning you!"

My niece pulled me in and slammed the door. Immediately, I was surrounded by a pack of dogs so mute and skeletal they seemed to have risen from their graves.

"They're greyhounds," Meryl said. "They hardly ever bark. I mean, they *can* bark. But they don't. Unless they're, like, trying to tell you something. The tan one, that's Donner. And that one's Prancer. And that one's Dancer. And these guys over here, that one's Blitzen and this one's Vixen."

Santa might not have found a complete set to pull his sled, but in their contemplative, long-legged way, the dogs seemed more like deer. Donner looked at me with such a doleful expression I was tempted to joke: *Why the long face?*

Meryl was on her knees, nuzzling the dogs and hugging them. "Sunshine rescued them from a track in Arizona. But I'm the one who takes care of them. There used to be two more, but Comet ran away, and Cupid ..." She teared up. "Cupid got run over." She rubbed her face against Donner's bony flank. "Dad and I named them. We got the idea from *The Simpsons*. You know, Bart and Homer own this greyhound? And they name him Santa's Little Helper and put antlers on his head. Dad and I used to watch that show *obsessively*. We had all these inside jokes. And Dad looks exactly like Comic Book Guy, don't you think?"

I had to admit he did. Morty railed against *The Simpsons* for its knowing, postmodern air. But I admired the way, after so many years of marriage, Homer still loved Marge. And both of them loved their kids. And, well, the kids loved them.

Meryl led me to the living room, which looked like a gym combined with a video arcade. There were machines that allowed a person to walk without getting anywhere or climb stairs without getting higher, two pinball machines from our old hotel, an air-hockey game, a slot-car racing track, and a wood table you iced with salt so the puck would glide down the alley and cause bowling pins to fly up if you knocked them down. In one corner stood a virtual-reality center, which, Meryl said, allowed her father to pretend he was a quarterback in the Super Bowl or a jockey whipping his horse down the home stretch in the Kentucky Derby.

"Meryl! I told you not to let anyone in!"

Janis had come partway down the stairs. I probably should describe her. But if someone is born as Janis Brite in Mamaroneck, Long Island, then moves to Las Vegas, changes her name to Sunshine Brite, and gives up her career as an exotic dancer to marry a three-hundred-pound bookie who falls for her because she is willing to have sex with him three or four times a day, do you really need anyone to tell you what she looks like?

"We're leaving in fifteen minutes, young lady, and if there's nothing in your suitcase by then, you can wear those awful sweat-things for the rest of your stinking life."

I didn't know much about raising children, and I had never met a murderer—except Leo, I guess—but from the expression on Meryl's face, if my sister-in-law ever went missing, the prime suspect would be my niece.

"We happen to have a *guest*. She happens to be my *aunt*."

"I don't care if she's the queen of Spain, you're coming with me."

"I am *not* coming."

"If I say you're coming, you're coming. I'm only telling you to do what your father would have wanted you to do."

"My father would have wanted me to stay right here until he got back!"

"You can't stay in this house alone."

The phone rang, but Janis wouldn't let Meryl answer it. Probably it was my mother. But what if it was whoever kidnapped Potsie?

Janis noticed me eyeing the receiver. "Don't you even think of it. This is my house, and if I say not to answer the fucking phone, you don't answer the fucking phone!" She wore a shimmery sequin top and tight white pants. She was trying to keep up a bright facade, but every few seconds the veneer gave way to panic. "How did you get in? The gate wasn't stuck open again, was it?" She rushed to the adjoining room. Like my mother's command center, my brother's den in Vegas was decorated with ceiling-to-floor TVs, each of which could be used to watch the view from any of a dozen cameras he had hooked up around his house. Two of these cameras showed the front and back yards—one of them was trained on the exact spot on which I had been standing a few moments earlier—and another showed Janis and me standing in the den watching the other nine.

"Sunshine," I said, careful to use the name my sister-in-law preferred, "I can see where you have been through a very difficult time. Please, I am not your enemy. Having lost my own companion of many years, I have some inkling what you are going through. "

I was astonished when she burst out crying. "You have no idea!" There was no place to sit—the La-Z-Boy and sofa had been used to store cardboard cartons—so she sagged on a nearby box. "Everyone thinks, just because Potsie and I had our differences of opinion—"

Meryl, who was standing in the door, made a gagging noise. "Spare me. You and Dad hate each other's guts."

"That is so not true! You think you know everything, Miss Meryl, but you don't!" At which my sister-in-law shocked me by pushing my niece out the door and slamming it in her face. "I can't stand it! I've got to tell someone! I will die if I don't tell someone! Meryl wasn't home. She was sleeping at her friend Davia's house. Potsie . . . Potsie had gone to bed. I was taking a shower, and I heard people coming up the stairs, so I poked my head out of the shower—I still had conditioner on my hair. You know how you're supposed to wait with the conditioner on your hair? Or maybe you don't know. You don't use conditioner, do you? Well, you should. It would help you tame that frizz.

"Anyway, I poked out my head, and these two guys just *burst* in the bathroom and ... They were these Mafia types, you know? They wore suits and ties and hats—the old-fashioned kind?—and they had these big white handkerchiefs across their faces. And one of them had a gun! And before I knew it, the other guy had taped my arms behind my back. I didn't have a stitch on! I was wet and cold and, like, totally naked, with the conditioner in my hair, and these two guys . . . these two guys . . . one of them put the gun to my head! He said to shut up and sit there. So I just sat there, naked, with the conditioner on my hair, and I heard people fighting in the other room, then someone went thumping down the stairs.

"Then I heard a shot. I mean, it sounded like a shot. Except maybe it came while Potsie was upstairs? I'm all confused! But I heard something go thumping down the stairs, and the other guy came back in and said, 'Okay, it's done.' And the other one, the one who was holding the gun to my head, he said some really nasty things about Potsie—how Potsie ought to pay what he owed, and he shouldn't be selling drugs to little kids, and what was a pretty girl like me doing with a mean tub of guts like Potsie Weinrach? And then . . ." She coughed a hiccuppy kind of gasp. "He put his gun—he put it in my pussy! And he said I had such a nice pussy it would be a shame to mess it up. But then he said he wouldn't mess it up if I did what he told me. He said the Mob doesn't kill women and kids if they can help it, and if I just cleaned up the house and left town and never came back to Vegas, they wouldn't kill me or Potsie's kid. Then he untied my hands and the two guys left."

She rubbed her wrists as if she even now felt the tape. I didn't know what to think. Only a person who was pretending to be afraid would have carried on that dramatically. It didn't help that my eyes kept straying to the monitor above our heads. Viewed in real life, my sister-in-law seemed to be telling the truth, but if you viewed her on the screen, her performance was less compelling.

"It took me forever to stop shaking," the Janis on the screen complained. "I couldn't get myself to leave the bathroom. And when I did go out, the bedroom was a mess. You know, sheets on the floor? Papers everywhere? Someone had ripped out the safe, and all the money and chips were gone. I ran downstairs and there was, like, blood on the stairs? I remembered they said to clean it up and pretend nothing bad had happened, so I made the bed and scrubbed the steps. And while I was doing it, the phone rang, and a man's voice said, 'We told you to get out of town. Why aren't you gone yet, cunt? Get in that fucking Porsche and drive!'"

It occurred to me this was my brother's blood we were talking about. The Mob had shot my brother. Or maybe this woman had shot my brother and made the story up. I didn't know whether to join her in grieving for the husband and brother we both had lost or grab her by the throat and shake her until she confessed. The dogs were scratching at the door. Meryl was pounding and shouting, "Don't talk behind my back! If you have anything to say about my dad, I have a right to know!"

I couldn't hear myself think. The last thing I needed was to let my sister-in-law leave town. If she had killed my brother, I would be allowing a murderer to escape. But if she was telling the truth and I didn't let her leave, the Mob might come back and kill her. Then they might kill my niece.

The Ketzel in the den couldn't decide what to do. But something must have occurred to the Ketzel on the screen because I saw her ask

Janis if the surveillance tapes showed the night the Mafia guys broke in.

Janis used the back of her hand to wipe her nose. "They must have disabled the cameras. The tapes from that night are blank."

You didn't need to be Woodward and Bernstein to be suspicious of how neat that seemed. But what was I supposed to do, come right out and accuse my sister-in-law of committing murder?

"Janis," I said, "you can't leave town. You're the only witness to a crime. And, if you do leave, the police might think you did it."

The lack of options with which I had presented my sister-in-law set off a display of histrionics so unsettling I wished I could reach up and turn off the soap opera on which she was playing a starring role. "I don't want anyone to shoot me in my pussy! They said they don't kill kids, but what if they come back to kill me and Meryl? I haven't told her anything. It would serve her right, knowing the truth. She thinks that father of hers is so wonderful . . ."

"Let me in!" Meryl rattled the door. "Let me in or I'll call the cops!"

I asked why she hadn't just taken Meryl and left town.

"It's the dogs!" Janis sobbed. "Who's going to take care of five neurotic greyhounds? They're very high-strung creatures. If you put them in a kennel, they think they'll have to race again and it retraumatizes them. Besides, I don't have any cash. What must have happened is Potsie got into some very bad debts, and he cleared out everything we had, but it wasn't enough, so the Mob came and took *him*. All I have is my car and this one credit card Potsie let me use, but it's already maxed out." She motioned toward the boxes. "I have this thing about buying and selling things on eBay. Except I bought a bunch of things I haven't been able to sell. Potsie said that until I got rid of the stuff, the card would stay maxed out. I didn't have money for a plane. But the longer

I stayed, the more scared I got. I figured I could just get in the car with Meryl and the dogs and drive."

There was a banging and scraping that made me think my niece had started using tools other than her fists.

"I'm going to go to the police station and file a missing person's report," I told Janis. "I'm his sister. It's perfectly natural for me to—"

"You won't tell them about the Mob!"

"Not if you don't want me to," I lied. "But if I do tell them, they can protect you. They can send someone out to watch."

"No! Or, I don't know. Maybe it would be better . . . I don't know! I don't know anything! I just want to get out of town!"

I was trying to think what to do when the door fell off. Meryl stood there holding a hammer and screwdriver. "I told you to stop talking about my dad! Aunt Ketzel, don't believe a word she says. She *hates* my father. She only wants his money. I'm not going anywhere with that stupid bitch. She's not my mother. You can't make me go anywhere I don't want to go!"

I reached out. "Sweetheart, I know how upset you must be. Why don't you come stay with me at—"

Meryl pushed me away. "I won't go with either of you! I'm staying right here!" She ran back in the living room, threw herself down, and sat huddled with her knees beneath her sweatshirt, her chin to her chest and the hood pulled below her eyes. I hated to leave my niece with such a terrible woman. But how could I force a teenage girl to come with me? The dogs sniffed her hands and licked her face, and even though they seemed to be good-tempered dogs, who knew but they might turn savage to protect her? If Ebby thought Meryl was in danger, I would come right back with him and get her. In the meantime, she and Janis had all these cameras and alarms and a pack of dogs to protect them. Although the cameras, alarms, and dogs hadn't protected my brother, had they?

"Meryl, honey," I said, "I'll come see you again very soon. We'll talk about it then."

To which I received the muffled reply "I'm not going anywhere."

"I know, sweetie. You've had a lot of unpleasant shocks. I promise you won't need to do anything you don't want to do."

I stepped over the dogs, and with a queasy foreboding at leaving my niece with a woman who clearly wouldn't hesitate to throw her stepdaughter in front of a bus if by doing so she saved herself, I let myself out. I was walking down the drive when it came to me that I hadn't asked Janis to raise the gate or call a cab. What if the Mob was out to get us? As empty as La Mancha Estates had been before, it now was that populated by jowly men in velour jogging suits who stood watering their lawns and watching me as I passed. The driver of a black BMW rolled down his window to reveal the sort of unshaven Robert De Niro face that might have belonged to a successful lawyer, or a hit man.

"Anything I can do for you there, ma'am?" He lowered his sunglasses. "You seem in need of orientation."

"Yes!" I said. "Orientation! That's exactly what I need. I'm staying with my sister-in-law. Janis Weinrach? She sent me out to get some milk. And cigarettes." I added the cigarettes since it seemed more in keeping with what people in Las Vegas went out to get. "But she forgot to give me the combination to the gate. And she forgot to tell me where to find a store."

The man reached across the seat, opened the glove compartment, and took out a device that caused the two halves of the gate to slide apart. "Three blocks, turn left. Walk another mile. Can't miss it. And next time, tell that lazy cunt of a sister-in-law of yours to get off that little green lizard tattooed on her ass and drive you."

4.

WHAT WITH WAITING at the minimart for a taxi—I didn't call the driver from the airport, thinking his Get-out-of-Jail-Free card would serve me only once—I made it to the Flamingo with less than an hour to spare before my date with Ebby.

Just enough time to take a shower. The hotel provided not only free shampoo but a bottle of conditioner, which, as my sister-in-law had been correct in assuming, I had never seen fit to use. I was astonished at my own reflection: if I had been performing as a stand-up comic, my hair would have gotten me no extra laughs, but the sleeker, softer look might not be detrimental to the performance I hoped to give with my former classmate. I only wished I had brought something nicer to put on than a fresh Camp Hospitality T-shirt, with its distinctive orange and green design and the hotel logo of two people shaking hands across the chest.

I was about to go downstairs when I noticed the pulsing red light on the phone. Morty had viewed answering machines as yet one more mechanical contrivance that intervened between a human mouth and ear, but it made me sad to think I had no recording of his voice, that outrageous bellow and high-pitched squeal, not to mention a final message: *Pussycat, where are you? Your Morty is lonely in this hotel room. You know how much I miss you. Wait until you hear this joke!*

Even sadder, the first message on the hotel phone was from a woman who was trying to inform the man who had stayed in the room before me that she had been mistaken to break up with him and would he please, *please* forgive all the horrible things she said? Had the man, whose name was Dwayne, ever received the message? Or had he checked out brokenhearted and failed to learn that Sonia regretted her part in their last dispute? I tried to get a forwarding address for Dwayne, but it was against the hotel's policy, and I would be forced to live forever with Sonia's tearful voice pleading in my head to call her back.

Then the mechanical voice announced I had a second message. Was Ebby calling off our date? No, but a disagreement between him and his former wife as to who should pick up their daughter would delay our meeting until 8:15.

Which meant I now had no excuse not to relieve my parents' anxieties by giving them a full report. "Mom," I said, "it's me, Ketzel." For a moment, I thought of lying. How could I tell a woman who already had lost so many sons that her youngest and most beloved had been abducted by the Mob? But I was too recent a convert to Grim Reality to do anything but relate the truth. Or rather, my sister-in-law's version of the truth. Leaving out the part about the blood.

My mother was having none of it. "The Mob? That's what she said? Handkerchiefs over faces! Fedora hats! Where would anyone even know to buy a fedora these days? Your brother was too smart to get involved with gangsters. If he made some miscalculation and got deeper in debt than he intended, he would have told your father and me, and we would have bailed him out." She called to the other room. "Lennie! Come and listen to what that *klippe* Janis said. She said the Mob doesn't kill women and children!" She directed her comments back to me. "Believe me, Ketzel, if mobsters had come to kill your brother and found your sister-in-law at home, they wouldn't have hesitated to kill her. That's only a *bubbe mayse*, that gangsters obey a code of honor. You're too easily taken in. Obviously Miss Sunshine Brite was putting on a show."

I had considered that possibility. My sister-in-law was the type of woman who, when walking down the staircase in her living room, was in her mind's eye Ruby Keeler walking down the revolving flight of stairs in a Busby Berkeley musical. But I was a performer, too, and I prided myself on being able to recognize a performance when I saw one. "Mom," I said, "I'm meeting Ebby. I'll call again soon." And I hung up before she could ask why I hadn't demanded Meryl stay here, in the safety of my hotel. My mother is no one's fool. She would have guessed I wanted to dine alone with Ebby. And even though she ordinarily would have been in favor of such a plan, she wouldn't have wanted any romance to occur at the expense of her only grandchild. Oh, why hadn't I grabbed Meryl by the arm and dragged her out! Would her step-mother have bothered to drag her back? Then again, what if my niece had bitten and kicked and run back inside? I needed Ebby, not only for romance or advice, but muscle. If we decided my niece truly was in danger from the Mob, he could drive us out to La Mancha Estates, throw my unwilling niece over his sky-high shoulder, and carry her to the Flamingo, where we could stand guard and protect her.

I went down to the casino to kill some time. Like anyone who has waited tables, I saw in every coin a hard-earned tip. I might have tried video poker, but for all the times my brother had drilled into my brain which hand beats which hand, I was no match for a computer whose memory banks could inform it as to the right move to make for every bet; besides, I was convinced the computer could see my cards. After searching for a machine that would allow me to play solitaire—the only game at which I could boast an expertise—I found myself standing in a corner of the casino where a baseball game and a horse race were showing on giant screens. The numbers on the board described a system so esoteric that only the finest minds could beat the odds. How could my straight-D brother be a genius at such a forbidding field of math? I couldn't have been more surprised if Potsie had been summoned to advise our nation's nuclear engineers as to the best way to build a bomb.

"Ketzel Weinrach! Oh my goodness! What are you doing at the Flamingo?"

I might have said the same at finding my weak-chinned childhood friend Harvey Blatt wearing the most beautifully tailored suit I had ever seen and sporting an artfully shaved goatee. Harvey's father, Phil, had been the booking agent at our hotel. The last time I had seen Harve, he had been a timid teenage boy trailing after Potsie and Perry and begging to join their schemes. His father had died young, and despite the general wisdom that Harvey had not inherited enough of the old man's balls to succeed in such a cutthroat line of work, he had moved to New York and cut enough throats to make himself an even bigger and ballsier agent than his dad. I had begged Harvey to represent me. But like the other agents to whom I spoke, Harvey had apologized because my father had threatened never to hire any of his other acts if he took me on.

To show I harbored no ill will, I indulged in some wistful reminiscence. "That father of yours, Harve, he sure was some character, smoking those cigars, pinching Leslie Uggams on the tush, trying to get Lena Horne into bed with him. He had a thing for black women, didn't he? How did your mother put up with it, a fancy Jewish lady like that?"

"Oh, dearie." Harvey giggled. "I thought everyone knew. My mother was one of the black women he had a thing for! Don't tell me you believed that cock-'n'-bull story that my mom was a Spanish Jew. She came to clean the first office my father opened, up in Harlem. He did her on his desk, she got pregnant, and he married her. He bought her furs and jewels and let her pass as white. Do you think she was in any position to complain when he pinched Leslie Uggams? For that matter, do you think Leslie was in a position to complain? Now Lena . . . Many a time Lena Horne slapped the cigar right out of my father's mouth. Trouble was, my father enjoyed nothing more than getting the cigar slapped out of his mouth by a hot black momma like Lena Horne."

Harvey had worked himself into such a state of indignation, or maybe such high spirits, he was balancing on the tips of his Italian shoes. The curlicues of his hair shot up like exclamation points, which led me to believe this might indeed be the hair of someone whose mother might be black.

Harvey patted down his head and tucked back in the electric-blue silk handkerchief that had risen from his pocket. "Unfortunately, Daddy didn't confine his advances to classy singers who were used to having talent agents pinch their bottoms. He made a pass at a pretty black girl who had just gotten off the night shift at the hotel bakery. What he didn't know was the woman's husband was waiting for her in his car. My mother told everyone Dad died of lung failure. Which was true. But that failure was not, as everyone assumed, brought about solely by those terrible cigars he smoked. The collapse of dear Daddy's lungs also had something to do with his getting punched and kicked repeatedly in the chest by an angry husband. My father died—" He took out his handkerchief and began dabbing at his eyes. "My father died because he couldn't keep his hands off a nice black tush!"

Harvey wiped his eyes and blew his nose, laughing and crying as only a man who mourns a much-beloved bastard of a father can laugh and cry. "And dear Daddy did not leave us the proverbial chamber pot to piss in. Nothing in the bank. Not a dime of insurance. He must have spent every penny buying minks and jewels for all those black mistresses and all those mulatto children, my dear little black half-brothers and half-sisters, who even now are wandering Monticello, searching for the man who promised their mothers an audition for a spot in a backup group for the Supremes." He waved at someone across the room. *Later*, Harvey mouthed, pointing to the upper floors. "Then again, he left me perfectly situated to take over the family business. Gay. Jewish. Black. Occasionally I lose a straight white *goyishe* actor to a straight white *goyishe* agent. But honey, they're hardly the clientele one cares about losing. I don't mean to put on airs, but you are looking at one of the biggest talent representatives on either coast. Harvey Blatt Enterprises, with offices in Beverly Hills, Chicago, and Manhattan. And I owe it all to my wicked black-booty-obsessed old man."

I looked at Harvey and blinked and saw the underdeveloped youth he once had been, a stunted sapling languishing in his father's many-branched and thick-trunked shadow. Then the father tree was hacked down with an ax, and in a sort of time-lapse photography, the sapling looked up and saw the sun, rubbed his eyes with his spindly arms, then sprouted his own exuberant foliage and brilliant blooms. Still, I had loved Harvey's colorful but not-bad-hearted dad. "Come on, Harve, your father had some good points. If nothing else, he hired Zero Mostel when no one else would touch him with a ten-foot pole."

"Oh, honey. Don't tell me you fell for that crock of shit. Hired poor Commie Zero when no one else would hire him? You know what really happened? My father offered Zero five hundred dollars to headline at the Hospitality, and Zero said, 'Five hundred bucks? Philly, you used to give me two or three thousand dollars for a show.' But Philly knew no one else was offering Zero *anything* for a show, and Zero would have no choice but to take the five hundred, which Zero did. So Zero drives up to Monticello, it's an hour before the show, and my father hands him a check, only it's made out for two-fifty. 'Two-fifty?' Zero screams. 'Philly, you promised me five hundred!' But what's Zero supposed to do, drive back to Manhattan empty-handed? He would have *lost* money on the gig. He would have been out the price of gas. 'Two-fifty, my friend, take it or leave it,' so what can Zero do but go on for two-fifty?

"But you should have heard the show. Boy, did Zero tear into the guests! He insulted my father. He insulted your parents. He insulted everyone who had ever stiffed a waiter or talked down to a chamber-maid or griped about a caddy. Then he started in on Joe McCarthy,

Dwight Eisenhower, Tricky Dick Nixon, then Golda Meir and Abba Eban, then the entire Jewish race back to Abey, Ike, and Moe. And the guests ate it up! They loved it! They thought it was part of the act. After all, who could tell when Zero was serious? After he'd hurled his last insult, he came barreling offstage, grabbed the check and a bottle of expensive scotch from the bar, got rip-roaring drunk, nearly killed himself driving home, then he called my dad and screamed, 'You fucking kike! If I ever see you again, I'll kill you! If I have to, I'll come back from hell and shove that cigar up your ass and squeeze your guts until smoke rings come out your *pupik*!' That's how kind and considerate my old man was to your pal Zero Mostel."

That such an injustice had been perpetrated at my family's hotel caused me to bow my head. "How could that be? Zero acted as if he loved your father." Although even as I said this, I knew the word *acted* had given away what I always knew—that Zero's smothering affection for Philly Blatt had been the pretense of a man who would have preferred to smother him with a pillow.

Harvey shrugged. "Zero needed to feed his family. Maybe he couldn't bring himself to name names to Joe McCarthy, but planting kisses on my father's backside . . . Once the blacklist was over and Zero got the lead in *Fiddler,* you should have heard what he had to say about conniving sons of bitches like my dad."

It must have shown on my face that if Zero had feigned fondness for Harvey's father, he might have feigned fondness for me.

Harvey lifted my hand and kissed it. "I will always regret that I didn't take you on as a client. I thought you were a scream, imitating those old guys the way you did. Retro Borscht Belt humor! You were so far ahead of your time everyone else is only catching up to you now. None of us could figure out why you let that old guy—what was his name, Feebleman?—talk you out of doing stand-up. Now there was a man who couldn't keep his hands off the ladies. You had to have known that, didn't you? It burns me up the way you think so highly of people who played you low."

He was trying to boost my confidence, but I was tired of people thinking I was a fool. If I was a fool, then I was a fool like the hero of that story "Gimpel," the original draft of which Morty helped Isaac Singer write. Singer trusted no one but Morty to advise him on his work. With whom else could he share his love of bawdy Yiddish folktales? So yes, if Gimpel was a fool, then I was a fool. But as Singer's story proves, there is no shame in being a fool who *chooses* to be a fool. Oh, I could have peed in the dough and baked it into bread and sold it to my enemies, the way the devil urges Gimpel to do to get even with the townspeople who cuckolded him and laughed about his gullibility behind his back. But I took to heart what happened to Gimpel's wife— at least in the version Morty helped Singer write. Gimpel is about to pee in the dough when his wife comes back from the dead, covered with soot, and scolds him: *Gimpel, just because I was false, is everything false? I never deceived anyone but myself. I'm paying for it all. Here in hell they spare you nothing.*

"Listen," Harvey said, "I don't suppose I could persuade you to audition for this new reality show I'm producing. You've seen *American Idol?* We're doing the same for comics. We go around holding auditions, then we bring the best ten comics to LA, and the last few rounds are broadcast on Comedy Central. The winner gets a gig on Letterman and a contract with yours truly."

A shot at Letterman? Me? I couldn't have been more suspicious if a dealer had winked me over to his table and promised if I placed a chip on a certain number, I was sure to win the pot. I reminded Harvey that I hadn't done my act in years. And never before a camera.

He pointed slyly above our heads. "You're on a camera right now. Eye in the sky. Big Brother is watching. Everyone in Vegas is on some kind of camera twenty-four seven." I looked up, and sure enough, a beady lens swiveled my way. Didn't people mind being spied on? Maybe everyone in Vegas harbored a secret wish to be a star. Maybe I had more in common with them than I had thought.

"Really, Ketzel. I'd like to do something to make up for the shabby way all of us treated you way back when. And you would be doing me a favor. Everywhere we go, we get hundreds of cocky jerkoffs who think they're the next Chris Rock or Andrew Dice Clay. The audience gets tired of seeing the same old same old. But a woman. A *mature* woman. A recent widow to boot. The audience would be rooting for the underdog. Even if you bombed ... The only thing the home-viewing audience appreciates more than a funny comic is an amateur who stinks up the place."

I admit I am only human. The temptation to say yes was very great. Morty might have taught me that it was wiser and nobler to collect jokes and study them than to hurl them at an audience. But Morty was no longer there to stop me. Or maybe what I wanted was to hurl a few jokes at Morty.

"Harve," I said, "I appreciate the confidence. But I'm preoccupied with other matters." I explained about my brother.

"Darling, that is the all-time worst reason I have ever heard for anyone coming to Vegas. I shouldn't say this, seeing as he's your brother, but Potsie never was particularly astute in the company he chose to keep. That cousin of yours! Talk about a bad seed. I know, I know, a gay boy like me trailing after a hoodlum like your cousin Perry was begging to be shat upon. It is no mystery that a man of your cousin's sexual proclivities should have taken it as a personal affront that I wasn't interested in hiding in the women's locker room. But the things he did to get even!" Harvey put his manicured fingers to either side of his temples. "I don't suppose your cousin has died a terrible death since then? Perhaps Perry is on death row? Perhaps I could pull the switch?"

I was genuinely sorry I couldn't answer in the affirmative, although I thought it might please Harvey to know that my cousin had grown up to be the proprietor of a sleazy bar. I asked if it didn't strike him as odd that so many of us from such a small town had ended up here in Vegas.

But he didn't share my incredulity. "Show biz, dearie. It's in our blood." Harvey flicked open a silver case, slid out a business card, and jotted the time and day I should turn up at Harrah's. "Usually I make people audition for the audition. I'm reserving a slot for you, sight unseen. That's how much faith I have." He waggled a finger. "But you better show up. Don't leave me standing there looking foolish in front of the bigwigs from LA." He reached out and touched my hair. "Speaking of big wigs, you're not going to get many laughs with your hair looking so nice. Wear it frizzed out, the way you used to. For me? For old time's sake?"

I felt flattered and insulted. Could a woman be funny only if she looked like someone you would never ask on a date? Or, if you did ask, couldn't afford to turn you down? "It's been wonderful talking to you, Harve. But I have to meet someone for dinner." I couldn't resist mentioning who that someone was.

He covered his face in mock horror and backed away. "You're kidding, right? Your brother and your cousin aren't bad enough? At least they didn't tear apart someone with their own bare hands. A *black* someone, I might add."

"Come on, Harve. Ebby is nothing like my cousin Perry."

He peeked out between his fingers. "Maybe I am being a tad harsh. Maybe he had a reason for beating that man to death. A *black* man, I think I mentioned? Let's just say I won't be going out of my way to crash your dinner party with Goose Salzman's brother."

I put Harvey's card with the other business cards I had acquired. The phrase *play your cards right* kept running through my mind, as if life had become a poker game whose success depended upon how wisely I played my hand. We pecked each other's cheeks. I promised not to stand him up, then I went to wait for Ebby. I was still a few minutes early, which gave me time to ponder the information that he had beaten a man to death. Maybe his brother had been a brute. But Ebby? Hadn't there always been something sweet about his face? Then again, I hadn't seen him in thirty years. All that time as a Vegas cop might have turned him bitter to the core.

I wandered the groves and grottoes, but the only guests I saw were the members of a Japanese wedding party posing for photos on a bridge beside a lake writhing with carp so big I feared for the safety of the flower girl, who leaned over the rail to toss them bread. Penguins waddled along the shore like miniature groomsmen, their flamboyantly attired escorts the long-legged, long-necked flamingoes, stunningly aloof in pink.

The sight of the bride and groom brought to mind my own wedding, which had been the last occasion at which my family had been together. Ira was already dead, but Mike was still alive, and he had brought as his guest a young actress named Meryl Streep, who hugged me and said my brother was the only man who made her laugh, after which Mike took me around and whispered, "You promised you would wait for me!" Even Howie was there. He was running for reelection and was pleasant to all the guests in a glad-handing sort of way. I'm sure Potsie felt outclassed. He had yet to make his name setting lines for the big casinos. He didn't even have a date. But Morty persuaded him to be his groomsman, and for the first time in his adult life, my brother put on a tux. He accompanied my mother down the aisle—she was crying so hard that even though she hadn't yet gained the weight she gained after Mike died, it took all of Potsie's strength to hold her up. My father walked me to the chuppah—he still had both legs—and, as we passed, Zero stuck out his tongue. Alan King tipped his cigar in my direction and mouthed a kiss. And there on the StarLite's stage stood our rabbi, Jackie Mason, who interspersed the ceremony with so many jokes Morty and I were buoyed aloft on the laughter of our guests, although I was so stupefied by love I don't recall a single one.

Morty stomped the glass and crushed it. Everyone wished us *mazel tov*, then we marched back down the aisle to an aria sung by Jan Peerce, who, when he wasn't singing at the Met, led the services at our hotel. We served a banquet in the dining room. The guests hoisted us on chairs, which was easier for me than Morty, who required not only Potsie and Mike to loft his bulk, but Howie and Zero. When I think of us all that day, then wipe from the scene everyone who has passed away or lost the legs or the will to dance, the world seems so full of loss that anyone who gambles and risks losing even more has to be *meshuggeh*.

The Japanese wedding party yelled "Banzai!," as if marriage were a suicide mission from which neither party would emerge alive. Flashbulbs popped, and I wandered back to wait for Ebby. As far as I could tell, this was the only cool, green, watery spot in town. But the gardens were enclosed on all four sides, so the penguins and flamingoes seemed as artificial as their stuffed and ceramic counterparts in the gift shop. Everything inside the park—the river, the fish, the waterfall, the flora and all the fauna—seemed to be the invention of Las Vegas Casinos Inc.

That's where Ebby found me. "Ketzel," he said, "hello."

"Oh!" I said, startled by an Eberhard Salzman who was thirty-two years older and fifty or sixty pounds heavier than the last time I had seen him. He still had all his hair, and though it was considerably shorter than he had worn it in the sixties, it was still nicely thick and black.

On the other hand, he had gone doughy. A man never looks as rugged in Dockers and a polo shirt as he looks in shoulder pads and a helmet. And there was something dull about his face. Gone the bright star of confidence. In high school, Ebby's face had been like a scratch card, the shiny circle radiant with the promise of a million-dollar prize. But time had scratched off the sheen to reveal the disappointing words SORRY PLEASE TRY AGAIN.

Then again, he hadn't given up. You could mail in that scratched-off ticket and enter it in the drawing for a year's supply of shakes and fries.

"Ebby! My parents were right. I feel much better knowing you're handling my brother's case."

He scuffed a loafer across the path. "You haven't changed a bit. That shirt! I spent the best summers of my life at the camp at your hotel. My dad used to drop me off in the mornings. Then he picked me up after work." His eyes misted over. "I ran. I climbed. I swam. Sure, I played ball. But it wasn't a matter of life and death. It wasn't about getting paid and getting laid. You don't have any more of those T-shirts, do you?"

"Oh, Ebby," I said, "I have plenty of shirts, only none of them would fit you." I hoped he didn't take this as an insult. "The shirts were meant for kids."

"Yeah," he said, "I can't even get one for my son. He's nearly as tall as I am. And my daughter ... she wouldn't be caught dead wearing a T-shirt. Unless it said, I don't know, LITTLE MISS SEXPOT. Maybe I could get one as a keepsake? I can't tell you the feeling I get just looking at that shirt."

Who would have thought that a Camp Hospitality T-shirt could have aroused in a hardened private eye a sentiment such as this?

"I guess you're shocked, seeing me this way." He grabbed the excess flesh above his waist. "But you! You haven't put on an ounce. And you still look so . . . I used to love how innocent you looked. I was tempted to ask you out. But even if my father hadn't been the guy who cut the grass on your father's golf course, you weren't the sort of girl . . . A guy like me didn't go out with a girl who wasn't going to, how should I put this, let him get to third base."

This was news to me, that Ebby Salzman had noticed I existed, let alone considered how many bases I would let him get to. This erased the years and pounds. If you knew a man when he was your high-school football hero, your heart will always pound to the stomping of the crowd as the cheerleaders trill his name: *EH-BEE! EH-BEE!*

A penguin waddled between our legs. "You must be starving," Ebby said. "My ex signs up our kid for all these classes, then she conveniently forgets that one of us has to drive her." He assumed the look of outrage that comes over most men when they talk about their exes, a look that asks, *What did I do to deserve what she did to me?* Human nature being what it is, a waitress like me usually requires only five minutes to provide her customer with such a list. "Would you tell me why a kid needs to tap dance? I say, Nikki, you might find this hard to believe, but there are careers to which a young girl might aspire other than to be a show-girl. You do not need to enter a twelve-year-old child in a beauty contest. You do not need to try to get her a modeling contract." He waved an arm so thick I could have hung it with a tire swing. "Sorry. Have to remind myself not to ride that particular hobbyhorse. My divorce. My custody woes. Oh woe, woe is me. Here I am, jabbering about myself, and you're too polite to say you're dying for a meal. Not to say we have your brother's disappearance to discuss."

I might have denied his analysis of the situation, but his mention of Potsie's predicament made me guilty to be sizing him up in any regard other than his capacity to complete the case. I let Ebby run interference as I followed him through the casino. We stood in line at the buffet a long time. It was a very long line, not only because there were so many people standing in it, but because each person took up so much space. Gluttony is nothing new. The guests at our hotel packed away as much food as possible for the all-inclusive rate they paid. But back then, human beings hadn't wanted to be so big. Larger than life. Celebrities in size if not in talent. Come to Las Vegas and win a jackpot, eat all you can eat, buy all you can buy, be the last comic standing and win a spot on Letterman.

We reached the cashier. I pulled out my wad of bills.

"Whoa," Ebby said. "Would you look at that. Five twenties, folded over and fastened with a rubber band, then another five twenties, folded the other way. I used to see these stacks of bills by my father's bed, and I'd ask, 'Dad, why do you fold your money that way?' and he'd say, 'Because Mr. Joe Weinrach, he fold *his* money this way. Mr. Joe say, you want to have idea how much money you spend, you fold with rubber band. With rubber band, you spend another hundred, you know another hundred is kaput, you think hard about starting to spend with another stack.' A few months ago, I'm in Florida with my old man—this is a week before he died. We're waiting in line at Publix, he pulls out his cash, it's folded in half and wrapped with a rubber band."

I started to tear up, too. "My father folds his money the same way. So do my brothers. I mean, Ira and Mike did, when they were alive. *I* fold it that way, too. The money I get from tips."

The four young men ahead of us traded stories about some nursing students who had flashed them in the elevator, and who, amazingly enough, had agreed to come to their room and play strip poker.

"Can you believe the dumb cunts thought they could just call it quits when they got down to their bra and panties?"

"Yeah, like we're going to let them get up and walk away just when the stakes get interesting."

"You should have seen the look on the redhead's face when I locked the door! You flash some guys you don't even know, you go up to their room and play strip poker, and you're, like—" His voice went falsetto, which was as unsettling as if an elephant had raised his trunk and let out a squeak. "'You unlock that door right now! We were just having fun! We're not that kind of girls!'"

I could hear Ebby mutter "assholes." To distract him from the conversation—while Ebby was larger than any of these men alone, he might not have been a match for all four—I asked about his mother, who had been the masseuse at our hotel before she and Ebby's father had retired and moved to Florida.

"Retired? That's a good one. 'Mom,' I say, 'in this country, you get to be seventy-nine, you're entitled to sleep past five-thirty. You're entitled to sit around all day and enjoy your husband's company.' But that whole generation . . . What if their savings get wiped out? What if the social security checks stop coming?"

It turned out Ebby's mother had kept working as a masseuse in Delray Beach. She was just saggy enough that the women didn't feel self-conscious letting her see them naked, but still attractive enough that the men enjoyed kibitzing with her about the good times they might have had if they were young. As for Ebby's dad, he so badly missed caring for the Monster, which was what everyone called the fifty-hole golf course my grandfather had commissioned from Bobby Jones, he had taken a job maintaining the modest par-three across from the development in which he and Ebby's mother lived.

"He was raking a sand trap and he keeled over from an aneurysm in his brain. They ought to have buried him in the trap. It would have been Pop's idea of heaven." Ebby was smiling and crying. "You'll get a laugh out of this one. I'm a kid, right? I hear him talk about 'grooming the Monster,' 'watering the Monster,' 'fertilizing the Monster.' And I think this is a real monster we're talking about. It's like a lion at a zoo, something to amuse the guests? And my dad is in charge of grooming it." Here Ebby smiled, and it was like seeing a rainbow. "What I couldn't figure out was the fertilizing part. 'What's fertilizer, Pop?' I ask. And after he tells me, I'm more confused than ever."

"Oh, Ebby," I said, "I used to hear my parents talk about paying off the Mortgage. The Mortgage this, the Mortgage that. If we didn't pay off the Mortgage, we would lose our hotel. Our lives would be destroyed. I thought the Mortgage was a fat, hairy ogre, and if we didn't pay him enough, he would come clomping in and destroy us all."

"Boy oh boy," Ebby said. "My mom is going to think it's something, my working for your family."

We might have followed this reminiscence with others in a similar vein, but we had reached the buffet, and such a mode of dining does not lend itself to sustained conversation. We made our way past chafing dishes of Swedish meatballs, glimmering mounds of sweet-and-sour chicken, platters of beef and fish, carving boards of fatty prime rib, batter-dipped breasts and thighs, the oil iridescent beneath the lights, onion rings, baked potatoes, potatoes au gratin, mashed potatoes, French fried potatoes, scalloped potatoes, and candied yams. The four men ahead of us abandoned their debate as to which nurse had given the best head and piled their plates with pyramids of the major food groups, as well as groups of food that seemed to exist only in Las Vegas.

I didn't do too badly myself. I hadn't eaten anything except a pack of peanuts on the plane. And I have a weakness for shellfish, which we didn't serve at our hotel and which Morty and I hadn't been able to afford. I scooped on my plate a larcenous quantity of shrimp and crab and a pool of scarlet sauce in which to dip them.

Ebby had found a table. I carried my plate across the room and joined him. With our eyes at the same level, I saw details I hadn't seen before. Furrows ran across his brow, as if he had been pushed face-first along several yards of Astroturf. Still, he remained an impressive example of our species. The salad on his plate looked like the inadequate offering of a tropical people to their giant god.

"You don't eat meat?" I asked.

Ebby looked embarrassed. "After I left the force, I just sat around all day stuffing my face. One night, I got, you know, pains." He patted his chest. "The doctor said I was a coronary waiting to happen."

I tried not to show how disillusioned I was that between the sturdy, high-spirited linebacker and the middle-aged private eye there had been an obese and brokenhearted former cop.

"Besides, my son is a vegetarian. The stuff doesn't even appeal to me anymore." He took out his wallet and showed me a photo of a boy who was as young and lean as his father had been at the same age. The boy, whose name was Nate, stood precariously atop a rock, a bandana around his head and a backpack on his back, arms flailing as he mimed tumbling backward off a cliff. He wanted to be an archaeologist, Ebby said. He already had been accepted to the University of Arizona. On a free ride. And not because he could throw a football. The kid spent his weekends working at a historical site outside of town, and he would be spending the coming summer at a dig in Chaco Canyon.

"We get along pretty well," Ebby said. "At least, since I stopped being a cop."

I could tell he was hoping I would ask why he had left the force. A waitress sees this all the time, a customer who wants to divulge the worst about himself. He wears this story around his neck like the albatross in that poem. Or maybe it's like a badge. Or the opposite of a badge: *You think I'm a good guy, but I'm not. Don't trust me. Don't let me in.*

I patted Ebby's hand. "You can tell me what happened. But you don't have to."

He slumped back. "I tend to think everyone already knows. But that's another symptom of what my therapist calls my narciss . . . narcissis . . . My tendency to think only about myself."

That Ebby Salzman had been to see a therapist and that this therapist had convinced him that he was a narcissist was almost as depressing as his having beaten a man to death.

"Some sleazebag was renting hookers," Ebby started. "He took them to cheap motels, tied them to the bed. Then he left them there until they starved." Apparently, this had happened four times, until a chambermaid disobeyed the man's directive not to come in and clean and found the fifth victim before she died. Ebby, who had been a cop for twenty years, had never seen anything like the prostitute who had been tied to that bed and subject to that madman's whims.

"Oh, look at the big man cry," the perpetrator had taunted Ebby when Ebby had tracked him down. "As if you really could give a fuck about some dirty crackhead whore." The man made a few more comments about what cops liked to do with whores, how worthless the women were.

"He was just mouthing off," Ebby said. "I don't know why it got to me the way it did. It wasn't because the guy was black. Some of the douche bags on the force were slapping me on the back for ridding the world of . . . you know the word they used. Me, I'd been hanging around with black guys my entire life. It was just, what he'd done to those girls . . . What they looked like on those beds . . ."

"Ebby, that's the most terrible story I ever heard." I looked down at my plate, and maybe it was the glare from the lights, but the remnants of the shellfish and cocktail sauce reminded me of arms and legs in a pool of blood.

"Are you all right? Ketzel? What's wrong?" The voice sounded hollow and far away. "Ketzel? You don't look so good."

I was glad when one of the women whose job it was to clear our dirty plates stopped by and took mine. She pointed at Ebby's half-eaten salad, at which he patted his belly and replied in perfect Spanish that he needed to watch his weight. I doubted he had acquired this fluency from our teacher, Miss Wayne, who had been so frightened of the athletes she didn't correct their pronunciation even when they said *show me your maracas* instead of *muchas gracias*.

The woman giggled and hid her smile and took away Ebby's plate. I tried to see him as someone who had beaten a man to death, but I lacked the imagination. Maybe, as my family claimed, I saw only the good in people and refused to see the bad.

"I could have kept my job," Ebby said. "This was not a man whose fate anyone seemed anxious to inquire into. It just didn't seem we were doing anything to stop the bad from happening. I kept thinking about those women . . . I sat in my house and ate. If Nate hadn't decided he couldn't stand living with his mom, I'd be sitting there still. Even if the kid only eats beans and rice, I still had to feed him. Which meant I needed a job. It wasn't as if I had a lot of skills. If I wasn't going to be a cop, I could be a PI. That was the extent of it. At least I could pick my cases. If something interested me, I could—"

"Eberhard, my friend!" A man stopped by our table. His earlobes were enormous. "I don't mean to interfere, but I thought you would want to be apprised that I came upon that young woman in whom you expressed so much concern. She was in the parking lot of that Chinese place on East Fremont. I was going to take my turn, but hey, I figured I could save the five bucks and pick up another hundred from you. Which is why, as I say, I am interrupting your heart-to-heart." He tipped an imaginary hat in my direction. "Besides, if I'd let the kid suck my dick, you'd have torn the fucking thing off."

The way Ebby squirmed, you would have thought he had been the one caught with his pants down. He took out his wallet and handed the man a bill whose worth was twenty times what the girl got paid for blow jobs. "If that's really the kid I'm looking for, and if she's still there when I go to look, and if she confirms that you didn't avail yourself of her services, you get another of the same."

"You'll find her." The man laughed a rubbery laugh. "It was an awfully long line. She probably hasn't gotten to the end of it yet." He put one finger to the rim of his imaginary hat, winked at me, and left.

"See?" Ebby said. "This nice girl runs away from her family in Toledo, Ohio, she ends up in Vegas, and what does she become?" He put on the overly sincere expression of an addict or alcoholic who is reciting his sins to a meeting of fellow sinners. "I admit it. I bought into the system as bad as anyone. From the time I was a kid, where did I hang out except the clubhouse with my old man? All those naked golfers, yukking it up about how they had just done some piece of ass, her knockers were out to here." He made a motion to show how big her knockers were, at which he recalled the size of my knockers and put down his hands. "Then in high school . . . in the locker rooms and on the buses . . . Then four more years at Syracuse. Do you have any idea what it's like to be a starting linebacker for a top team? The parties you go to? The girls who . . . they'll do just about anything you want them to do. And things you *don't* want them to do." He shook his head to clear an image the average man would have treasured all his life. "Then all those years on the force . . . The topless dancers, the topless waitresses, the topless anything you can think of. Flesh and more flesh. Then being married to Nikki." He made a motion as if he were pushing away plates of repulsive food, although there weren't any plates left to push.

"Underneath it all, there were other things I wanted to do. But I wasn't sure how to go about doing those things. What if I wasn't as good at those other things as I was at throwing tackles? In college, I took this art course. More than one, actually. I told the guys I was doing it for the chance to see naked pussy. Or I wanted to make it with the horny artistic hippie-chicks. But what I wanted to do was paint."

He looked at me as if I might make light of this information. But I was hardly in a position to look down on anyone for pursuing an unconventional career. Not to mention it's difficult to look down on someone who is a foot and a half taller than you are. I tried to imagine Ebby in a beret, dabbing at an easel, but this was as difficult to imagine as Pablo Picasso—who, by the way, Morty had gotten to know when he bummed around France in his teenage years—strapping on a helmet and tackling an opposing lineman. "Ebby, if you hate it here so much, why don't you leave?"

Wouldn't he love to do just that! But he was in a custody dispute with his ex-wife. The minute that dispute got settled, he would take his daughter to live in whatever city had an art school that let him in.

He seemed embarrassed by any further discussion of his artistic aspirations. Having gotten off his chest what he needed to get off his chest, he took out a notebook. "Okay," he said, "tell me everything that might be relevant. What your brother's wife said. What you saw inside the house. Anything strange about your niece."

I told him everything I had seen, the strange and stranger still—Janis and the TV monitors, the conditioner in her hair, the Mafia guy with his gun up her vagina, the greyhounds and angry Meryl, who refused to leave her house.

With a flourish, Ebby underlined the last few words and snapped shut his pen. "You'll excuse me for saying this, but your sister-in-law is serving you a crock of you-know-what. Your brother is no Boy Scout. But Potsie isn't the type to do business with the Mob. In fact, and this is probably something you oughtn't to spread around, he used to give us the inside dope on those individuals. He and I were acquainted from the old days, when he hung around with Goose. Potsie would let me know which wise guys were in town. Who was doing business with whom. Not that we want illegal bookmaking going on. But better it should be a clean, family-type bookmaking operation like your brother's than the Mob getting its hands back in.

"So Potsie let me know what was going on. And we cut the guy some slack. Sure, we busted him now and then. But he got a fine. A suspended sentence. Abducted by the Mob!" He snorted. "Your mother is right. That's a fairy story, that they don't hurt women and kids. Your brother occasionally dropped a bigger load than he intended playing poker at the Mirage. But he was too smart to get into the sort of obligation you pay for with your life. He never dealt in drugs. He didn't even smoke cigarettes."

Still, I said, a bookie had his enemies.

"Nah. Today everything is a business. A client refuses to pay, the bookmaker writes it off as a loss. Maybe he will try to intimidate the individual. Certainly, if this trend keeps up, he won't accept another bet from the guy. He'll place the deadbeat's name on a blacklist so no one accepts his bets. Which, for a certain type of gambler, is worse than getting his kneecaps blown out. But a man like Potsie doesn't show up at your door with a baseball bat. Your brother might not have a stellar personality. But in comparison to the real slimeballs out here ... Besides, I've already paid a call on your brother's clerk, Owen Dibble. Owen let me nose around, talk to the guys who helped your brother run his operation. They all agreed on one thing: your brother's only enemy was his wife. Unless you count his ex-wife. And several irate former girlfriends."

"So you think Janis is lying? Geez, Ebby, I don't know. I thought she was telling the truth. At least, so far as she knows it."

He shrugged. "Your brother wanted to dump his wife. But she didn't want to be dumped. And he wasn't too keen on dividing up his wealth.

Hence, she got rid of him before he could get rid of her."

I was shocked that Ebby would so casually impart the opinion that my brother had been gotten rid of. He must have been so engrossed in dissecting the details of the case he had forgotten that the victim we were dissecting was my relative. But something wouldn't allow me to believe that my brother was dead. How can I explain this? I seemed to have transformed myself overnight from someone who believed everything I was told to someone who rebelled against believing anything. If my parents and Ebby thought my brother had been done away with, I would assume the opposite.

"It doesn't make sense," I told Ebby. "Are you saying my sister-in-law hired fake Mob guys to do away with my brother?"

"Maybe they were better actors than she anticipated. They got carried away. Made it look and feel too real. One of the guys, he realizes they've caught their employer in the shower, he takes advantage of the situation. The mere memory of which can bring your sister-in-law to genuine tears of fright. She's fooled herself with her own illusions. A lot of people do that. Look at O.J. Simpson."

I had to admit this was a plausible explanation for my sister-in-law's better-than-expected acting skills. And it allowed me to believe my niece was safe. Until it occurred to me that Meryl's stepmother, if she had done away with Meryl's dad, might not want to take on the responsibility of caring for his daughter.

"I should never have left Meryl at that house. What if Janis has my niece bumped off, too?"

Ebby reached down to scratch his calf. Unless he was checking to make sure he had his gun? "Not a pleasant thought. Girl that age, living in an environment of that nature. But if your sister-in-law harbored any ill intent toward your niece, she would have gotten rid of her at the same time as your brother. Besides, until a body has materialized, no crime has been committed. The authorities have no grounds to take away your niece. *You* have no grounds." He must have seen how agitated I had become. "But I can keep an eye on her. If that will give you peace of mind."

I asked him how he intended to get inside the gate.

"You got inside, didn't you?"

I didn't want to say he hardly looked like someone's frumpy aunt.

"Don't worry, I have my ways. Even if I can't get inside, I can keep a watch on who goes in and who comes out."

"Would you, Ebby? That would take a lot of pressure off my mind."

"No problem. First thing after I leave here, I'll stop by your cousin Perry's bar to ask a few questions. Then I'll nose around Fremont Street and make a few inquiries about that runaway. After that, I'll spend the rest of the night keeping surveillance on your sister-in-law. After your niece gets safely off to school tomorrow, I'll tail her stepmom and get a better idea of how she spends her days."

That was a wonderful plan. Except I was going with him to Perry's bar.

"What? No way. Do you have any idea as to the nature of the establishment your cousin Perry runs? You know the Bada Bing on *The Sopranos*? The Bada Bing is twenty steps higher on the ladder of evolution from slime to human life than the Schoolhouse Lounge. And we won't even discuss what goes on in the back. What goes on in front would be enough to disqualify a girl like you from stepping in."

I wasn't sure why I insisted, unless, at fifty-one, I didn't appreciate being thought of as a girl who needed to be protected. Besides, I had a few questions of my own to ask my cousin, many of which would be easier to ask with a six-foot-six former police officer and linebacker as my bodyguard. "If you don't take me, I'll call a cab and go alone."

Ebby considered this alternative. "Fine. But this is not something your parents can ever find out about."

I didn't find it difficult to swear that if Ebby did not impart this information to my parents, I wouldn't be the one to do so.

"Just one other thing. That cousin of yours? If Perry is around, you leave that jerk to me."

I allowed him to believe my silence implied consent.

He took his napkin from his lap. "You really ought to check out the dessert table. I used to think there couldn't be any more desserts than the desserts on the dessert table at your hotel. But the Flamingo, well—" He stopped and looked embarrassed, as if I might take offense.

"I'm pretty stuffed," I said. And I hardly wanted to be gorging on rich desserts while my brother needed to be saved from a bunch of thugs.

"Yeah," Ebby said. "Besides. My favorite dessert isn't on that table."

"No?" I said, sensing he wanted me to play his straight man. "And what dessert might that be?"

"A Popsicle," Ebby said, color rising to his cheeks until they matched the Flamingo's bright-pink decor. "You know, you didn't need to bribe me. I would have picked you for my team anyway."

I felt my own cheeks growing hot. "Really?"

"Sure. I just never picked you first because that would have been too obvious."

Not knowing what else to do, I left a few dollars for the women who cleared the tables. Ebby pulled out my chair, then I followed him across the lobby to the garage, steeling myself for my journey to my own private Heart of Darkness, where I could settle my long-held grudge against my own private Mister Kurtz.

5.

IF I AM going to tell you the details of that trip to my cousin's bar, I suppose you will need to hear what my cousin did to me when we were kids that made me so determined to confront him now. As I've said, that story isn't new. And, like its counterpart, the dirty joke, with each successive telling it loses its power to surprise or shock. What my cousin persuaded me to do that August afternoon when he was fifteen and I was an understandably naive but prematurely developed ten would be sadly unremarkable if he hadn't made a film of my performance and played it for the young male members of our staff. What makes me squirm—the reason I told no grown-ups at the time and I never confessed to Morty—is that I was captured by my own vanity. Until that afternoon, my cousin had been forced to rely on the usual tactics teenage boys employ to persuade younger girls to endure their fondling. Then he stumbled on me practicing a mambo routine I had seen Mitzi Gaynor and Tito Puente perform the night before.

"You want to be a performer?" Perry asked. "Not to worry, my little Shirley Temple. Your cousin Perry is here to help. See, what you need is a manager. The way things in Hollywood work, your manager gives you a screen test. If it turns out okay, he sends copies to all the studio heads, and if they like what they see, voilà! They fly you out and audition you for a part. What we've got to do is show them what you've got. You run and put on that swimsuit I saw you in at the pool the other day. That jazzy two-piece number with the little bow here and the little skirt there and the red-white-and-blue dots all over it? You put on that bathing suit, you tie your hair behind your ears, then you meet me in the pump house behind the pool."

I am ashamed to say I kept the date. I believed my cousin had the power to bring my talent to the attention of the men in Hollywood who made the movies I loved to see in the theater in Monticello. I imagined my family gathering around the television in our den—in those days, we had only that one set—watching me clown and dance the way we had gathered to watch Lucille Ball, Carol Burnett, or our own dear Totie Fields.

And this girlish faith seemed justified. My cousin showed up for our rendezvous with the most impressive movie-making equipment I had ever seen. This was 1964. Hardly anyone owned that kind of camera. How could I have known Perry had "borrowed" the equipment from the hotel's PR department, which had acquired it for the purposes of documenting my father shaking hands with visiting politicians, or second-rate celebrities getting married in our club, or the children of those same celebrities blowing out the candles on their cakes? What my cousin directed me to do made me queasy. But my discomfort had less to do with the nature of his request than my premonition that my parents wouldn't approve of my moving to California and performing in grown-up films. I was nervous about my ability to shake my hips and kick my heels as gracefully as Mitzi Gaynor. But as Perry informed me, any child who hoped to become a star needed to ignore such fears. And everything I had seen or heard, from the comedians' sly innuendoes to the boasts of ten-percenters like Philly Blatt, had prepared me to expect that any girl who hoped to make it in show business needed to take off her clothes.

Perhaps it would be more dramatic if I told you that I was plagued by amnesia whose traumatic source I needed a therapist to recall. But I remember with painful clarity the hum of the pump—*whoosh, mmm, mmm, whoosh,* like a backup group moaning to keep the rhythm—and the tang of chlorine in my nose, and the darker, funkier odor of the mildew on the cushions some lazy cabana-boy had neglected to dry before he stored them in the shed. I remember what Perry wore—blue-

and-white cotton trunks and a seersucker jacket that hung open to expose his chest, which was as rich and smooth as butterscotch. He was a clean-cut, handsome kid. He wore his hair crested in front but short and slicked back at the sides, so his ears stood out in an all-American kind of way. And he had the most dizzying smile of any boy I had ever seen. I remember how polite he was, how he complimented me on how pretty I looked, then got down on one bare knee to direct me. I remember the textured gray metal camera and the rack of lights he held above his head like a moose's antlers. I felt the glare of those bulbs like sunburn on my chest even before I took off the suit.

"Wow," Perry said, "Ketzel, that's great. Now just slip off the straps. That's great! Keep dancing! What a good girl! Now pull down the top. That's it, now turn to the other side and put your fingers in the, what's it called, the waistband. Tug it down a little. And now a little more."

I never would have told. At most, I would have waited a few days and asked if he had heard from the men in Hollywood, at which he could have said they wanted to see me perform another number before they decided to fly me out. He could have watched and rewound that film, getting off on it for years until he found a wife who could put on a better show than a ten-year-old girl.

But my cousin made one mistake. He showed my "screen test" to the other guys. For all I know, he charged admission. Still, that wasn't what did him in. Not a single member of that audience—an audience composed of boys who professed to be my friends and who owed their lucrative summer jobs to my father—would have turned him in. No, the mistake my cousin made was not taking enough precautions to prevent the star of the film from wandering by the door and catching a glimpse of yet another screening of *Ketzel Does the Mambo*.

I was halfway through the room before I understood what I was seeing. The end of the spool unwound and flicked against the lens. No one moved or turned on a light. The projector seemed to burn a hole in the screen. I can't remember what happened next. I only remember the cool, slick linoleum beneath my feet as I wandered down the hall, and the fact that no one in that room came after me to apologize.

Of course I didn't tell a soul. If no one knew, I could pretend the incident had never happened. And I was afraid if my father or Potsie or Mike found out, one of them would kill my cousin. Instead, I avoided Perry. And he must have felt a modicum of guilt about what he had done, because he avoided me. When Potsie turned twenty-one and drifted west, Perry drove the car. After that, I encountered him only at family funerals. I wished my brother hadn't stayed friends with Perry, but I couldn't tell him why he shouldn't. Potsie already had lost so many brothers he wasn't willing to give up a cousin. And, as I've said, after Perry bought the bar, he let Potsie drink there for free. As to the movies Perry directed, I only can assume my brother had nothing against people making porn, as long as his sister wasn't in it.

So you can understand why I was determined to accompany Ebby to the bar and tell off my cousin. You might also understand why, as I followed Ebby through the garage attached to the Flamingo and saw the security monitors on every post, I realized I had lied to Harvey Blatt about never having performed on camera. Not that my memory of that first experience would make it easier to perform a second time.

"Here we are." Ebby slapped a truck so wide I wasn't sure how he had gotten it in the garage. A few minutes later, spiraling down the ramp, I felt as if I were traveling with my considerably larger twin down a birth canal too narrow to allow our passage. I was relieved when we burst out on the Strip, although after the dim garage, the pulsing neon signs were as disorienting as the lights in an operating room might have been to a newborn's eyes.

"I can't believe I used to get excited going to joints like this," Ebby said. "What was I thinking? I guess I *wasn't* thinking. It was just what all the guys did." He steered us down an alley only an insider would have known. "You know the Kit-Kat Lounge? Across from the raceway in Monticello? No matter when you went, that place was packed. Doctors, lawyers, your friends' parents ... Heck, I used to run into teachers we knew from school. You remember Mr. McClatchy? Or Fuzzy Magandanz? No matter when I went, those slobs were there." Ebby shook his head. "And then, all those recruitment trips ... The coaches would hook you up with the fellas on the team. And that's where they would take you. That is, if they didn't hire a stripper for your own private amusement."

We turned on the Boulder Highway and headed out of town.

"Out here, they don't even charge the cops for drinks. I admit, I used to take advantage of that perk. But then I had Saffron. Here's what I don't get. A lot of the guys hooting it up at strip joints have daughters. How can they not think ... Ah, who am I to judge. Mr. Morality, right?"

Interspersed among the used-car lots and gun and ammo shops were shabby bars where a patron apparently could be served a drink by women pretending to be librarians, nurses, lion tamers, or flight attendants. At an establishment called Rodeo Drive, a customer could buy his drinks from *SEXY COWGIRLS!*—after which he could watch these same cowgirls ride a mechanical bull.

I suppose I had always known what the name of my cousin's bar implied. But I had never gone so far as to imagine what the Schoolhouse looked like. When Ebby pulled in the lot, I saw a windowless bunker with a plaster bell in a fake cupola on the roof and a poorly drawn billboard of a skimpily attired "schoolgirl" leaning across a desk with a yardstick above her bottom as she smiled guiltily and licked her lips.

Ebby parked beside a van with a fiery desert sunset painted across the sides and a plate that read *VNTSTC*. At least no one was demented enough to own a car with a vanity plate that read *PRRY4ME*. Ebby shot me a look to say *I warned you*, then came around and let me out. The air stank of gasoline and the exhaust from the In-N-Out Burger joint next door. *THE GIRLS HERE ARE HORABLE* someone had sprayed across the Dumpster, leading me to wonder if the artist had misspelled "horrible" or left a *w* off the front.

Ebby held the door and I stepped inside, and all I could think was, if I were searching for my lost sense of humor, the Schoolhouse Lounge seemed to be where every dirty joke had gone to die. It was so dark I was afraid to take a step for fear of bumping into something. Ebby led me to some version of a desk, complete with graffiti gouged by bored students. As to what the graffiti said, let me just point out that *TITS* and *ASS* are among the only words certain students know how to spell. Luckily, the dancers were taking a break and I had the chance to look around. Only the barest effort had been made to give the impression of a classroom—a chalkboard scrawled with some ABCs, a clock perpetually set at 3:15, doors labeled *GIRLS LOCKERS*, *PRINCIPLES OFFICE*, and *LITTLE GIRLS ROOM*. If this was what little boys thought about all day at school, it was a wonder any of them learned to read.

Most of the customers were drinking at their desks. But a pair of older men sat at the bar watching a ball game and joking with a bartender who, given his beer-keg build and beefy, tattooed arms, must have doubled as the bouncer. His head was shaved, but to make up for the lack of the ponytail all the other men in Vegas wore, he had a ropy Fu Manchu. An overweight girl in a pleated skirt, bobby sox, and Mary Janes—she seemed to have forgotten to put on a shirt when she left for school that morning—patted the customers' knees and flirted. At the table next to ours, a redhead in a yellow slicker with nothing underneath eased herself onto the lap of a man so old that the last time he had been in school they must have used quill pens.

Then the music began to thud from loudspeakers shaped like megaphones, and a woman dressed in a schoolmarmish suit, her hair done up in a bun, thick glasses on her nose, appeared from behind the stage.

"Hey, teach!" a patron called. "I've been a naughty boy. Whatcha gonna do about it? Hey, teach! Over here! Whatcha gonna do?"

The teacher thwapped her yardstick on the padded rail that ran around the perimeter of the stage.

"Ooh, teach! Did I get you mad? Huh, teach?," at which she rebuked him further by taking off all her clothes.

After she had danced a second dance and used what my father so delicately had referred to as her *female underparts* to pick up the five- and ten-dollar bills her "students" had placed on the leather rail, she flounced behind a door, presumably to offer her knowledge to the students in another room. The next number started, this time with a majorette in a red sequined suit awkwardly twirling a baton. Need I describe the rest? There are only so many ways for women to take off their clothes, a process made more depressing by most of the dancers being far past their prime, with stretch marks, bruises, scars, varicose veins, and sagging breasts. That the naked female form, which should have been the source of so much joy, could create such despair seemed the dirtiest joke of all.

Still, such is the power of watching amateurs that I couldn't help but think how much better I would be taking off my clothes than any of these women. I saw myself slipping off a strap, putting my fingers in the waistband of a bikini, tugging it down, jutting my hips back and forth to the Latin beat my cousin was tapping with his foot. I got dizzy and hot and cold. I looked to Ebby for reassurance, but he was gripping the desk the way a passenger might grip the rail of a ship going down in a storm.

At last the music stopped. Ebby unclenched the desk. The dancers came out, twirling satchels and purses and asking in lisping drawls if the nice big strong men would carry their books home from school.

"Hey! You!" one of the customers yelled. "You, in the little skirt! Bring your little purse and come on over here. Get it? Bring your *little purse?* My friend here has got a little something to put in your little purse! And when I say *little*, I do mean *little!*"

While our fellow patrons were yukking it up with such clever repartee, a waitress sauntered over. Her hair seemed to shimmer and float behind her. In her long, tight denim skirt, she reminded me of a mermaid, albeit a tattered, world-weary mermaid making her way through a dark and polluted sea.

"Hi there." She smiled as if to acknowledge she knew I was only there because my goofy boyfriend wanted me to watch him get off on watching other women take off their clothes. "What will you nice folks have to drink?"

"Hi, Miranda," Ebby said.

"Ebby?" She touched his arm. "You haven't been here in ages." She laughed a watery laugh. "Not that you missed anything."

Ebby pulled out a chair. She looked around to see if she could take a break, and the bartender shrugged. She sat carefully, knees together, ankles to one side, like a mermaid perching on a rock.

"Any chance you've seen Potsie?" Ebby asked.

"A few nights ago. Why?"

Hearing that someone had seen my brother alive a few nights earlier gladdened my heart, as if this information proved Potsie hadn't yet had time to die. I turned to Ebby, expecting him to grab Miranda's arm and pump her for every detail about her last sighting of my brother. But he must have decided it was better to feign nonchalance. "Family dropped by and can't seem to find him. Any idea where he went?"

"No," the woman said. "But I bet he didn't go on a happy cruise with the little wife. Not unless he planned to throw her overboard."

Ebby laughed in an encouraging way. What about Perry? Had Perry been around? He wasn't in back by any chance?

I thought she would say, *No, I haven't seen the prick, and it's a good thing I haven't!* But Miranda looked concerned. "He's gone away before, but not without telling us how to reach him." She hadn't seen my cousin since the evening before. No, it was the night before *that.* Perry had told the bartender, Chickie, to cut off some asshole who wouldn't stop bothering a dancer named Summer Storme, then Perry grabbed his coat and hat and slipped out. When Miranda showed up to open the bar the next morning, Perry wasn't there, which, considering he slept in back, struck Miranda as odd. As did the disappearance of the bearskin rug he used for a blanket on his bed.

"No note?" Ebby said. "No call? Chickie doesn't know where Perry is?"

She shook her head. No one knew anything. Not Chickie. Not the other girls. "I'm worried," Miranda said again.

"Worried?" I said. "You're worried about my cousin?"

"Sure," she said. "Aren't you?" I could see her do a genealogical calculation. "I know who you are. You're Potsie's kid sister. He talks about you all the time. You're lucky, having an older brother to look out for you. Me, all I've got is Perry."

Even in that gloom, she must have sensed my disbelief.

"He's not a bad guy. He gave me a job when no one in his right mind would have given me the time of day. I was so stoned I could barely carry a drink without spilling it. Perry helped me clean up my act. He used to tap me on the head—believe me, that's not the part of my body most guys touch. 'You owe it to yourself to go back to school.

More than that, you owe it to your daughter.' He even let me manage the Schoolhouse books. All I'd had was an accounting course in high school. Then my boyfriend kicked me out, and Perry let Kalindi and me live in the van."

The van with the sunset on the side?

"Sure. You should see it—wall-to-wall carpet, stereo, queen-size bed. Once in a while, Chickie uses it to run some errands. But most of the time, Perry uses it as a set. You know, the Vantastic series? *Vantastic Journey I, Vantastic Journey II.* Perry films most of his movies here." She waved to indicate the props and fixtures in the Schoolhouse Lounge. "But when he gets tired of the whole schoolgirl thing, he takes the crew on the road. A guy he knows lets us use a room at some casino. Or we shoot right out on the street. Or we end up in the desert."

Miranda and her daughter hadn't had to live in the van for very long, but she appreciated Perry's generosity while it lasted. And Perry did her other favors—like, he gave her afternoons off to take business classes at the community college, and when Miranda's mother couldn't babysit for Kalindi, he let Kalindi hang out in back and do her homework. He did all the dancers favors, Miranda said.

"Favors," I repeated in a tone that implied I knew what sort of gratitude my cousin would expect.

"Perry doesn't need to force anyone to have sex with him," Miranda said. Between dancing at the bar and performing in the Vantastic Journey films, the girls earned a lot more here than they could have earned at a normal job. Some of them were hoping to use an appearance in Perry's films as an entrée to the professional adult-film industry. Besides, he wasn't bad looking. He didn't have to twist anyone's arm to sleep with him. If one of the male actors didn't show up, Perry took the guy's place on the set. But most of the time, he worked the cameras and directed.

It occurred to me that my cousin could afford to be generous: he was like a shark in a big aquarium, so well-fed he needn't bother to snap a victim from the smaller fish swimming by.

"Anything else?" Ebby asked. "Anything unusual going on?"

Miranda snorted. "In a place like this?"

If she was looking for sympathy, Ebby wasn't about to give it. "You could get out. I keep telling you, there are other places to work besides a strip joint."

She patted Ebby's cheek. "We've been through this. The hours here are right. I get the tips from waitressing on top of what Perry pays me for keeping the books. Until I get my degree, there isn't anywhere that's going to come close to what I'm making here."

"Suit yourself. Only remember, you have a kid."

"Huh," Miranda said. "If I didn't have a kid, why would I be working in a shit hole like this and going to school the few hours I have left to sleep? If it was only me, I'd be home smoking dope and screwing around and sleeping late instead of getting Kalindi off to school and trying to do my statistics homework before catching the fucking bus to class." She stood wearily and smoothed her skirt. "I didn't mean to take it out on you."

"Nothing else you can think of?" Ebby said. "Just the missing rug?"

She cocked her head. "The van. I forgot about the van."

The van?

"Someone must have borrowed it. It wasn't here when I came to work. Perry wasn't here either, like I said, so I assumed he was the one who took it. The van was gone the whole day. Then whoever took it put it back. But it wasn't Perry. I mean, the van came back but Perry didn't. And it wasn't in the same space. The key was under the mat, so somebody probably took it for a joyride. It's a pretty famous van."

"This the van we were discussing before? Who had copies of the keys?"

"Perry," she said. "He had one key. And the other key was hanging behind the bar. It's still there. As far as I know, no one took it. How could they, with Chickie tending bar? That would have to be one slinky thief, because as everybody knows—" Miranda and Ebby laughed and said in unison, "Chickie has eyes in the back of his head."

"Literally," Ebby said. "The man literally has a second set of eyes."

I glanced toward the bar, but Chickie was frightening enough from the front, I wasn't about to ask him to turn around.

"Anyone driven the van since then? Anyone notice anything, you know, amiss?"

"You mean, is Perry dead in the back?"

I expected her to laugh. Instead, she said, "No bodies. No blood." She might have said more, but a man at the next table began waving an empty glass, and Chickie made a motion that Miranda get back to work.

"You're family," she said, "so we'll waive the two-drink minimum. But don't forget to leave a nice big tip for all the hard-working girls entertaining you here tonight."

Ebby said he would. Miranda smiled at him so tenderly I realized I was jealous. Then the music started up, and just as I was wondering how I could make it through another long day at school, Ebby pulled out his wallet and tossed a few twenties on the desk. I was impressed with his generosity, until I remembered my parents would be reimbursing him. He made his way to the stage and left another twenty on the rail. And maybe it was then, as he tripped over the book bag belonging to the schoolgirl who was straddling the man at the table next to ours, that I started to fall for the clumsy lug. As any woman will tell you, tripping over a stripper's purse is a far more attractive thing to do than slipping a ten-spot in her G-string with savoir faire.

Even so, I shouldn't have laughed.

"Okay," he said, pointing at me as if I were a puppy learning a new command, "you stay here while I snoop around outside."

He started for the door. I jumped up to go with him.

"Ha! Big talker. You really think I would leave you alone in a place like this? Come on, I'll introduce you to Chickie. Believe me, you're at the bar with Chickie Kurek, no one's going to mess with you."

"What if it's Chickie I'm afraid of?"

"Chickie is a very religious man. Very old-school Polish. Not one but two of Chickie's brothers grew up to be priests. Only difference is, Chickie is more into the high life than his siblings. He moved to Vegas in the fifties. Owned his own club. It was doing okay, too. But Chickie here gets to thinking he needs to increase his clientele. Know how Catholics love raffles? Take my word, they do. So Chickie thinks up this scheme where you come in and you get a ticket. You stay until closing, Chickie picks a few numbers from a hat. Grand prize, you get the dancer of your choice. You can even use Chickie's room upstairs. The rest of the numbers, the prize is, I don't know, a wallet, a watch. Maybe a portable TV, a transistor radio.

"Well, this raffle gimmick brings in the customers. Three, four months, and Chickie's is the place to be. Then it turns out the watches and radios are hot. Chickie's getting them from some fence who's getting them from people's hotel rooms. The law comes down hard on poor Chickie. He loses the bar, spends six months in the can. He gets out, there's no way he can support himself. Can't run his own bar because he can't get back his license. Hence, your cousin Perry gets him to tend his bar. Chickie keeps an eye on the girls, doubles when needed as the cameraman or the soundman, everyone scratches everyone else's back . . ."

If this was meant to increase my eagerness to spend an evening with Chickie Kurek, the strategy failed. What was to say I wouldn't end up as the grand prize in that night's drawing? But Ebby had started tugging me toward the bar.

"Chickie. You know who this lady is?"

Chickie uncrossed his arms and held them out, a gesture that had the effect of showing off his art. On the right upper bicep hung Jesus on his cross, with Mary below Him, mourning. On the other arm was a well-endowed naked man whose member projected down in such a way that when Chickie bent his elbow, the voluptuous girl on his lower arm received that member in her mouth.

"This is Potsie's sister," Ebby said. "I have some business to take care of. I trust you'll entertain her until I get back?"

Chickie joined his palms and bowed, like the genie he appeared to be, or maybe like Mr. Clean. Then—my heart sank to see this—Ebby went out the door.

Chickie pointed to a video-poker game on the bar. "Your brother puts a quarter in that thing and it does whatever the fuckola he wants it to do. He's got the touch, the lucky bastard. No matter what game he plays, the sucker can't lose."

"Oh," I sighed, "Potsie got all the luck in our family. Me, I couldn't win a candy bar from a vending machine."

"Ha! That's a good one! I remember now, you're the sister that's the comedian. The professor's wife, am I right? I always thought that guy was putting me on. He got paid to study dirty jokes? I'll tell you, if he got paid a fucking dime for every joke I told him, he owes me a shit load of money."

Chickie knew Morty? Morty had visited the Schoolhouse Lounge? I had never been able to bring myself to tell my husband what Perry had done to me when we were kids. And if Morty had come to Vegas searching for dirty jokes, it stood to reason my brother would bring him here. But the news that Morty had been sitting at this very bar, trading jokes with

Chickie Kurek and flirting with a bunch of women dressed to resemble schoolgirls, while I went around New York thinking he was giving a lecture in North Dakota or receiving an honorary degree in New Orleans, caused me to wobble on my stool. I was so preoccupied I didn't manage to correct Chickie's faulty assumption that Morty got paid for what he did. That Morty supported *me*.

"Funny guy. Haven't seen him for a while. The professor all right?"

"No," I said. "The professor is dead."

"Dead!" He stroked his Fu Manchu. "Reminds me of a joke the professor used to tell. There are these two guys, right? One guy says to the other, 'You hear what happened?' And the other guy says, 'No, what happened?' And the first guy says, 'Moe just passed away. Terrible, isn't it? Dropped dead, just like that.'" Chickie snapped his fingers. "'Gee,' the other guy says, 'that's a shame. But it could have been worse.' 'Worse!' the first guy says. 'What do you mean? The guy is dead!' At which the other guy says, 'Sure it could be worse! It could have been me instead of Moe!'"

Ordinarily, hearing Morty's favorite joke would have caused me grief. The reason he liked telling that joke was if you were the one telling the joke about the man telling the joke to celebrate that the worst thing that can happen to anyone hadn't yet happened to him, the worst was even less likely to happen to you. But the worst had happened to Morty anyway. And the fact that my husband had told *this* joke to *this* bartender at *this* bar limited my tears. I looked around at the women squirming on their customers' laps and wondered which of them had wiggled and squirmed for Morty. Had he paid to take the stripper dressed as a field-hockey player into the so-called SHOWER ROOM? Or had he paid the "schoolgirl" in the slicker to bend over so he could spank her? The possibility that my husband might have spent time at a bar like this and not accepted the favors the girls were handing out was as unlikely as a man who loved chocolate taking a tour of the Hershey factory and not accepting a single free chocolate kiss.

"What a cutup that guy was," Chickie said. "And smart! What did he call this shit hole? The smithy of the human race? Smithy, says I? What the fuck is a smithy? And the professor starts in about anvils and forges and a bunch of intelligent crap like that. I couldn't follow half of what he said."

But I knew what Morty must have said. Clubs like the School-house Lounge were the smithy of the human subconscious upon whose sooty anvil all true dirty jokes were forged. As bars like the School-house closed, the last authentic sources of dirty jokes were drying up. But if losing the Schoolhouse Lounge meant no new dirty jokes were invented, I supposed I could endure the loss.

Chickie rubbed a glass with a dirty cloth. "Can I stand you a little pick-me-up, on the house?"

I could have used a glass of wine, but I had been up since dawn and crossed two time-zones. The last thing a woman wants is to pass out at a topless bar. "Thanks," I said. "I'll just have Seven-Up."

Chickie scooped ice cubes in the glass. "Sure I can't upgrade that to a Seven and Seven?"

Not to seem ungrateful, I said, "All right."

That was my first mistake. Because when Chickie turned to pick up the Seagram's, I saw the eyes tattooed on the back of his skull. I nearly toppled from my stool. Given what happened later, Chickie must have made the drink a Seven and Fourteen, or a Seven and Twenty-one. He slid the glass across the bar, and because I didn't know what to say, or because that second set of eyes had peered in my soul and knew what I was thinking, I asked if he had any idea where my brother might have gone.

"Not the foggiest," he replied, and I thought that would be the end of that, but he mumbled a little coda. "Now, if the bitch had been the one to turn up missing."

I swayed a little more. "The bitch being?"

"Like I told your friend Big Dick Tracy out there, your brother wasn't exactly subtle in conveying how much he wanted his wife out of the picture."

"Out of the picture as in . . ."

"As in not giving the cunt half of all he owned. Not supporting her fucking eBay habit, her coke habit, those fucking spooky dogs. As in asking me to pay some guys to get rid of her without the services of a goddamn flesh-eating lawyer."

The stool was not the spinning kind, but I felt as if I had done a complete three-sixty. "My brother asked you to hire someone to kill his wife? You can't be serious."

"Serious as a heart attack. I did not see fit to comply with your brother's request. But we had done previous business of a similar nature. You remember that dancer who came out dressed like little Mary who had the lamb?"

Unlike the other dancers, most of whom were in their forties, the dancer dressed as Mary had been in her teens. She had sashayed across the stage, nestling in her arms a dirty stuffed lamb, which, according to the story she performed, she not only had brought to school but tutored in the ways of carnal knowledge to such an advanced degree both of them got expelled.

"Mary's boyfriend wasn't treating her with what you might call respect. She used to come in here looking like a punching bag. Your brother might have his faults, but he is not a man to sit idly by while a young woman is mistreated. For that matter, neither is your cousin. You want to fuck a woman, fine, that doesn't mean you get to hurt her. So, with Perry's blessing, Potsie pays for my friends to teach the guy a lesson."

"They killed the guy?"

"You can't teach a lesson to a dead guy. They just tied him to a chair and pulled down his pants and went at him with a knife." Chickie bent beneath the sink and brought out a jar of what seemed to be human testicles.

I must have keeled over, because when I awoke, I was lying in someone's bed with a wet rag across my brow to minimize a lump the size of the pickled testicles in that jar. At first I thought—I hoped—I was back in my hotel room. But the *turra-turra-BOOM* thudding through the wall informed me that I merely had been transferred to my cousin's bed behind the bar. A bright light shone down on the mattress.

I jumped up, knocking over the video recorder that was perched on a tripod beside the bed. As shaken as I was, I had to give my cousin credit. How clever to combine one's place of residence with the set on which one also filmed one's porn. I imagined various scenes that must have taken place on and around that bed. Had Potsie stood here watching? What about Morty?

Morty hated porn! I am sure people who read his books assume he approved of kinky antics. And Morty could be creative. But my husband's true obsession was the integration of love and sex. The trouble with pornography, Morty said, was that after you had seen a porn flick, you couldn't make love without imagining you were in a porn film, too. Porn made the real seem fake and the fake seem real. You felt the need to dress up and act out roles, which, though Morty and I were not above a little playacting, separated the self who was making love from the self who was dressing up and acting. Or from the self who was watching the self dress up and act. Not that Morty found anything wrong with what any couple did. If you wanted to hold parties at which the men pretended to be the masters of Roissy and the women vied for the honor of being O, Morty wouldn't say you couldn't. It's just not what he and I were into. What we were into was having fun. What we were into was making love as our own naked and laughing selves.

But more pressing than any such questions was what had happened to my brother. I admit I snooped around. My cousin was not a man whose privacy I felt a constitutional need to respect. Most of what I saw was as impersonal as the fake apartment in a sitcom. But off to one side I found a desk on which there stood a mug of cold coffee layered with mold, a pile of Tootsie Roll wrappers, a cheerleading pom-pom, and the computer on which my cousin must have edited his works of art. I was tempted to turn it on, but the monitor wasn't there. And did I really need to see Mary and her lamb being chased by a paddle-wielding teacher played by my cousin Perry?

I heard someone come in and jumped.

"Ketzel!" Ebby cried. "What was I thinking? You didn't really black out, did you? Let me see … Jesus, would you look at that lump? How could I have been such an idiot? Bringing you to a place like this, then leaving you with Chickie Kurek … It was just, you and I would have attracted too much attention, snooping around back together. I figured I would leave you at the bar as, well, a decoy. A distraction." He took my hand. "Come on, I'm taking you to a hospital."

"Please," I said, "don't make an embarrassing situation even more so. If you take me to a hospital, how are we going to explain how I came to fall off a stool at a topless bar?"

"Are you sure?" He touched my head. "That's really some egg." He brushed his fingers across the lump.

"I'm fine," I said, "really." And then, because I wanted Ebby to think bringing me to the bar had been to some advantage, I asked if he knew that my brother had tried to hire a hit man to kill his wife.

The lack of surprise on Ebby's face reminded me that he already had talked to Chickie. "Ketzel, your brother is not the worst person in Las Vegas. But neither is he the best. I hate to be the one to make you give up your illusions, your illusions having always been your most attractive feature. But if there's one thing a private investigator knows, it's that illusions blind us to the facts."

True enough, I said. I used to be very poor in money and very rich in illusions. Then Morty passed away, and I found out that we had been wealthy in money all along. All Morty needed to do was sell his priceless knickknacks or one of his dirty books. Now, I said, those knickknacks and books were mine, and I had plenty of financial assets, but not a single illusion left.

Ebby shook his head. That was no good either. A person needed a few illusions. Otherwise, how could you be a parent? How could you fall in love? As for Ebby, he was trying to get his illusions back.

But never mind the philosophy. He asked: Was I sure he couldn't take me to the emergency room? With a lump like that, complications might develop later. And things were complicated enough as they were.

"I know!" I said. "I'm trying to figure out if my brother put out a hit on Janis and it somehow went bad and the hit got put on him. Or if Janis put out a hit on Potsie. Maybe the two sets of hit men ran into each other on the stairs and rubbed each other out."

Ebby picked up a trash bag he must have brought in from the Dumpster. "There's one thing your sister-in-law did get right." He took out two big cotton handkerchiefs and two fedora hats.

"Are these clues?" I asked.

"Sure. Except we don't know what they're clues *to*. I'll just hold onto them until your brother turns up. I'm beginning to think Potsie and your cousin are off sunning themselves in the Caribbean until this mess blows over."

"Oh, Ebby! Really? You think Potsie isn't dead?" The hope went rushing to my head and caused the lump above my eye to pound from joy. "Should I still fill out a missing person's report? What about a report for Perry?"

"I think it's to everyone's advantage that the police should be looking for your brother. I'm just not sure your cousin qualifies."

"Qualifies?"

"Do you miss him? Do I? Does anyone but Miranda?"

I told Ebby how much it surprised me that the women at the lounge seemed genuinely concerned about my cousin's whereabouts. At which Ebby reprised his comment about my brother—as bad as Perry was, he wasn't the worst strip-joint owner in Las Vegas. If the Schoolhouse closed, the dancers would need to work for someone who paid even lower wages, took an even bigger percentage of their tips, and didn't look out for their welfare. Naturally, it chilled me to learn there were worse denizens of this city than Perry Weinrach. And it didn't do me much good to think that my brother could be described under the same general rubric as my cousin.

"I'll hand you this," Ebby said. "Passing out was the smartest thing you could have done. Chickie puts you back here, it entitles me to come in and make sure you're all right. And what's to stop me, while I'm here, from taking a quick tour of your cousin's taste in interior decor?"

Ebby conducted his own reconnaissance around the room. He stopped by the computer. "I guess your cousin got a little frustrated while he was editing his latest masterpiece. I found the monitor in the Dumpster. Looks as if he put his fist through the screen and drop kicked it down the field. Can't say I'm sorry. If your cousin is into making snuff films, I don't want to know." He motioned me to follow him out the back door. "If there's ever an actual crime to investigate, I'll get my buddies to hightail it out here with a warrant and look around. For now, I just want to get you to your hotel."

How could I object? It seemed rude not to say goodbye to Chickie and Miranda, but neither Ebby nor I was eager to interrupt whatever class was being taught in the Schoolhouse Lounge that period, so we exited by the rear. The air outside, even with the fizz of exhaust from the nearby highway, might have been the elixir of youth for how restorative it felt to breathe.

Ebby pointed to the van. "Quite the bachelor pad. Shag rug. Wet bar. Built-in stereo and DVD. But Miranda was right. No blood-stained knife. No smoking gun." He tapped his head. "Sometimes you've just got to put the pieces in storage until you know what picture the puzzle is meant to be."

This struck me as good advice. Although the word "storage" made me wonder if I was being fair to Morty. Did the items in that locker in New Jersey mean what I thought they meant? What if there was a picture into which those pieces fit and I didn't know what it was?

Ebby hoisted himself into his truck. I settled in the passenger seat and we started back to Vegas, each of us trying to figure out who had put a hit on whom, who had stolen the van, and why he or she had put it back. After the pounding music of the Schoolhouse Lounge, the hushed safety of Ebby's Silverado seemed refreshing. I had never felt safer, not even when I was sitting on that horse at Woodstock, wrapped in my brother's arms.

We pulled up to the Flamingo, then lingered in a silence as awkward as if we had come home from the date we had never gone on in high school. Ebby turned to me behind the wheel, a difficult maneuver for a man that size. "I'm glad you came. It's hard for me to go places like that alone. When a case requires I go, I go. But seeing women that way . . . it gives me flashbacks."

His confession enabled me to admit that I hadn't enjoyed the trip myself. For all my bravado, I had passed out and conked my head.

"Yeah," he said. "That was my fault, too. Are you sure you're all right? I could see you to your room."

I wanted to say he could. I felt like a kid who falls asleep on the car ride home and wants to be carried up to bed. Then I remembered all the nights I had fallen asleep backstage and someone—my father, Potsie, an unknown employee—would carry me to my room, and I would wake the next morning unsettled because I had no idea in whose arms I had been transported.

I thanked Ebby, then told him I wanted him to catch that runaway, then go and watch my niece.

"If you're sure," he said. "But if you need anything in the meantime, you call me."

I climbed down from the truck and went inside. After five or six wrong turns, I made it to my room, where I fell on the bed in all my clothes and dreamed a terrible dream in which Ebby and I were in a cage with a menagerie of tigers, bears, lambs, penguins, and flamingoes. I wanted Ebby to . . . what? Get me out of the cage? Protect me? But he seemed as powerless as I was. The lambs were as ferocious as the tigers. I looked at Ebby. He looked at me. Neither of was wearing clothes. I reached out to touch his chest. But he flinched, drew back, and pointed. And that's when I realized that my cousin and Chickie Kurek were standing outside the cage, filming our every move.

6.

A PERSON DOESN'T need to have trained with Sigmund Freud to inter-pret a nightmare as obvious as the one I have just described. Nor does it take a genius to understand that when the phone rang next morning, so close to my pounding head I thought my skull was the cupola above the Schoolhouse Lounge and my brain was the bell inside, tolling, toll-ing, if not for the students, then for me, I was reluctant to pick it up. If my parents could keep so many shady truths from me, I could keep a few from them.

"Hello, Mom," I said. "Yes, yes, I'm sorry. It was wrong of me not to call. I came in very late and didn't see that I had a message. I was exhausted and went to bed. Ebby's keeping an eye on Meryl. Yes, yes, I promise. I'll call you then. No, really, I'm fine. Goodbye!"

I examined the lump above my eye, which was twice as large as the night before, with the addition of a very impressive shiner. I showered and shampooed my hair—what a blessed life in which a person could use up a bottle of conditioner and find a fresh one to replace it! Having discovered what an aphrodisiac a Camp Hospitality T-shirt could be, I chose a fresh one. Then, stifling the urge to explore the Flamingo's buf-fet for breakfast, I grabbed an overpriced muffin and a cup of coffee and went out to hail a cab, hoping for a silent and uneventful ride.

Unfortunately, I underestimated the curiosity that would be aroused by a female passenger with a visibly lumpy head and a Technicolor eye asking to be driven to the police station.

"Good for you," the driver said. "Nail that son of a bitch. Then again, forget the cops. I know some guys, you tell them your boyfriend's name, they'll teach that asshole a lesson he'll remember every time he looks between his legs."

Naturally, this made me think of that jar of pickled testicles, which caused my head to spin. What a town! It was socially acceptable to pay a naked woman to gyrate on your lap, but if you punched your girlfriend in the eye, every man in town vied for the honor of cutting off your dick.

Oh, I said, I hadn't been beaten up. I didn't even have a boyfriend to whom a lesson might be taught. But that didn't satisfy the driver. He was the sort of angular man whose every visible part—the prominent chin, the bumpy nose, the long, curly black hair, the prodigious bulge of his Adam's apple—reminded you of the body part he was forced by etiquette to conceal but thought about all the time.

I volunteered that I was visiting the police station to file a missing person's report. And no, the swollen eye had nothing to do with the person who had disappeared.

You would have thought that would end the matter. But my driver saw himself not only as the protector of Las Vegas womanhood, but his own private missing person's bureau. "No one goes missing in this town that the Rock doesn't get wind of his whereabouts. If I haven't seen the dude, I can put out the word to my colleagues. You want to find somebody in Vegas, you get the Rock on the case."

And so on, until I couldn't stand the man's prying any longer. And who knew? Maybe he had seen my brother.

"Weinrach?" he said. "I know a Perry Weinrach. But not a Potsie. Perry I saw last week. Great guy. Much defamed in certain circles, but in my book, the guy is very talented. Everything I am I owe to Perry. Discovered me, what, two years ago? Right in this cab. Saw potentialities I didn't see myself. 'Rock,' he says—that's me, Daryl Rokowski, although for professional reasons I go by the Rock—'Rock,' he says, 'you could be big. I mean, *very* big.' One day I'm a cab driver; next day, I'm an actor in the crew of Mr. Perry Weinrach's Vantastic Venture Films." He glanced in the mirror. "It isn't Perry that's gone missing? As I say, I saw Perry last week. You want next time I see Perry I give him your number? Endowments such as yours do not grow on trees. I'm sure my man Perry would be eager to give you, what do you call it, a screen test."

Thank God he had pulled up to the station and I could open the door and lose what little of my muffin I had managed to eat, although it would have served Daryl Rokowski right if I had left him that mess instead of the fare he asked for.

"You all right? You want me to take you to see a doctor?"

I got out and closed the door, although not before the Rock had promised that if he saw this Potsie Weinrach dude, he would tell him I was looking for him. And was I sure I didn't want the Rock to mention my name to Perry? No? Well, as Perry and the rest of the crew liked to say, have a Vantastic day!

I needed to sit and take a few good breaths to calm a stomach so unstable that the mere sight of the Hot Tamales in the machine beside the bench made me retch. Except for the palm trees down the median, this could have been any suburb in America. How could such normality surround a town in which nearly everyone made his or her money selling sin?

I got up and wobbled inside the missing persons bureau, which was as dingy and nondescript as the sort of establishment a person might visit to get her shoe heels fixed.

"May I help you, dear?" asked the blue-haired lady behind the glass. She leaned forward and peered up at my eye. "That didn't just happen, did it?"

I assured her that I was fine.

"You take a seat and I'll buzz one of the detectives to come out and get you."

I sat in a plastic chair. On the wall behind the receptionist, amid the photos of the employees' kids, hung a poster-size reproduction of the mug shot of one Francis Albert Sinatra, taken in 1938 in the Bergen County Sheriff's Office, as if to say that Old Blue Eyes was one of the family, too.

"Mrs. Weinrach?"

A man with the thickest glasses I had ever seen emerged from the inner office and stood peering around the room. One of his sneakers was minus a lace, the belt loops on his trousers could have used a belt, his shirt was missing the top two buttons, and his hairpiece was slipping off. There were only three chairs, but he couldn't seem to locate me until I had risen from my seat and entered his line of sight.

"There you are." He held out his hand, less as a gesture of greeting than a way of making sure he didn't lose me again. "I'm Sergeant Maguire. Although for obvious reasons, people call me Sergeant Magoo."

He led me to the door, only to discover that his key card was gone. Sheepishly, he motioned to the woman behind the desk. "Janette? Sorry, would you mind?" Clucking with mock exasperation, Janette buzzed us in. Sergeant Magoo noticed my eye. "My goodness!" he said. "We'll get you to see a doctor right away. Then we'll have you speak to an officer who handles domestic violence."

I found myself wishing what everyone thought was true. There's so much misery in the world, so little of which is visible. Maybe if people with nowhere to live, terrible diseases, or broken hearts punched themselves in the eye, they might attract more compassion.

I told the sergeant I appreciated his concern, but no one had hit me. I had fainted and hit my head.

I could see that he didn't believe me. But then, I wouldn't have believed me either. He steered me into an industrial-colored room barely large enough to hold four desks and four chairs. The other officers sat joking and teasing. A fan in a dusty cage rotated this way, then that. Across the front of the room, a dry-erase board listed all the John and Jane Does who had been found in and around Las Vegas, with the locations where they had been discovered and such identifying characteristics as "cowboy boots," "jawless skull," "no face," "no arms," "no feet."

The other three detectives were talking on their phones or typing at their computers, their clothing neat, their desks devoid of clutter. Sergeant Magoo's desk was piled so high with newspapers, file folders, candy wrappers, sneakers, hats, and dozens of barely identifiable objects that half the missing persons currently being sought by the Las Vegas PD could have been hiding beneath the mess.

Still, he seemed a man who let the minor details slide so he could focus on what was vital. A photo of his wife was nailed to the wall, as were his diploma from the University of Minnesota and a citation for exceptional service to the force. It took him a while to locate his bifocals, which had ended up in an empty mug, but then the sergeant wasted no time in getting down the facts of my brother's case: that his name was Stuart Weinrach but everyone called him Potsie; that his date of birth was October 22, 1950; that my mother had last spoken to her son some sixty hours earlier and that she and my brother rarely went more than a few hours without communicating. I had no problem informing Sergeant Magoo as to my brother's address, but when I got to his occupation, I stammered and stumbled until the sergeant uttered a sympathetic, "How about if we just put down 'gambler, self-employed'?" I described my brother's height—five-foot eleven; his weight—three hundred pounds; race—Caucasian; hair— long and silver gray, pulled back in a rubber band; eyes—hazel; last seen wearing ... well, the only shoes that fit my brother's feet were flip-flops, and, as I've said, his wardrobe consisted entirely of Yankees jerseys and nylon shorts.

The sergeant doodled on his pad as if he had another question he needed to ask but lacked the nerve. "I don't suppose there's anything else that could help us make a positive identification. In case there's any doubt."

I admit this question stumped me. How many grossly overweight Caucasian men with hazel eyes and a silver ponytail were likely to turn up dead in a given week? Then I looked up at the board and saw the list of John Does who hadn't been found until they had been reduced to "skeletal remains."

"Maybe your brother was carrying something only he would carry? Other than a wallet. Which someone might have taken. Or which might have decomposed by the time we find him."

Most people, if asked this question, would need a moment to think. "A lanyard," I said. An orange and green plastic lanyard key-chain I had fashioned for my brother when I was a camper at our hotel. *What a great gift!* Potsie had said when he unwrapped it. *I can use this for all my keys.* Later, when he took to hanging around the track, he added a stopwatch to the hook. *Ketzel,* he said, *other guys have their rabbits' feet, their pair of lucky socks, their crucifix or their mezuzah. Me, the only good-luck piece I need is this.*

"A lanyard!" Magoo repeated the word, rolling it around his mouth as if "lanyard" were a candy. "A lanyard, you say?" He took off his glasses and rubbed his eyes, which seemed as watery and soft as snails. "My parents sent me to a Christian youth camp in the UP—that's the Upper Peninsula, in northern Michigan. I wasn't much for the Christian part. And nature . . . I got lost trying to find the dining hall. But I did love arts and crafts. I still have one of the billfolds I tooled that year." He took it out, the brittle leather stitched around the edge and etched with horses. "And those wooden plaques we used to burn? You remember that wonderful smell the soldering iron gave off?" We reminisced about that smell. "But lanyards! I was quite the master lanyard-maker. There was the square stitch, of course. The butterfly stitch. The diamond braid. The Chinese staircase—now there was a challenge. The twisted triangle. And the tornado."

I sat there with Magoo, our lips moving in silent prayer, repeating *lanyard, lanyard, lanyard,* fingers moving as we tried to recall how to stitch a Chinese staircase. Then I saw my brother's skeleton with that lanyard in the sand where his pockets once had been, and I must have started crying, because the sergeant reached inside his desk and handed me a linty tissue. "I hate to mention this," he said, "but is there any possibility your brother wants to be missing?"

I wasn't about to tell this nice nearsighted man that my brother had asked the bartender at the Schoolhouse Lounge to kill his wife, so I merely retold the story my sister-in-law had related about the Mafia men in their disguises, although for reasons of delicacy, I omitted the part about their holding a gun to her vagina.

The sergeant whistled. "That's quite a tale." Then, like my mother, he disabused me of the notion that Mafia hit men act in the compassionate manner my sister-in-law seemed to think. As per Ebby's instructions, I didn't mention I had hired a private eye. But Sergeant Magoo suggested I should. "It's not that we won't try our utmost. Your brother being a professional gambler doesn't make his disappearance any less of a priority. It's just that even if this were a homicide, which I'm not saying it is, we have a hundred and fifty murders in Las Vegas every year and only twenty detectives to solve them." He found a business card in his drawer. "Best PI in town. Twenty years on the force—Patrol Division, Narcotics, Homicide, you name it. The only reason he retired was . . . let's just say there was an incident. And this officer, he decided to take matters into his own hands."

I read the name on the card and smiled. "Yes," I said, "thank you. I will certainly consider getting in touch with Mr. Salzman."

"You tell him if he finds anything, he should give Magoo a call. And if we discover anything, we will share our information with Mr. Salzman. We'll be making a few inquiries. But if anything suspicious happens ... for example, if any inexplicable charges appear on your brother's credit-card statement or on his phone bill, you be sure to get in touch with me."

I supposed it was time to leave. But I couldn't help looking one last time at the board across the front, with its list of missing persons, all of whom seemed to be the offspring of the absent-minded Mr. and Mrs. Doe. I wanted to ask this nice man to help me find the other people who had gone missing from my life. Not only Potsie, but Howie, Ira, Mike, and my beloved husband, Morty. Not the Morty who had keeled over in a dressing room in a strip joint in New Orleans. But my faithful, adoring husband of twenty-seven years.

"I don't suppose you could give me a ride back to my hotel."

The sergeant looked abashed. "I'm afraid we aren't allowed to do that. But you could use my phone to call a cab."

I took the business cards from my pocket and shuffled through them until I found the number of the cabbie who had driven me from the airport. Sergeant Magoo and I shook hands and—with only one wrong turn—he led me to the reception area, where he realized he had left his key card in his office and needed to ask Janette to buzz him back inside.

By now, the sun was so bright it inspired me to dart across the street and buy a pair of tinted glasses and a hat whose brim I could pull down to cover my lumpy head. When the taxi pulled up, I tried to slip in back without the driver noticing what I looked like.

"Jiminy H. Cricket! Didn't I tell you not to go messing around with your brother's friends? You haven't been in town twenty-four hours and you're already in trouble with the cops and running around in a disguise? You got a shiner? That what you hiding? Listen here, little lady. You get out of this place before anything worse than what already hit you hits you again."

And right at that moment, I wished I could take his advice and leave.

As you might suspect, I wasn't eager to return to my hotel room and wait for my mother's call. I found the only pay phone in Las Vegas and managed to reach Ebby on his cell.

"Salzman," he said, and I realized what I needed wasn't so much a private eye as a private ear.

"Ebby," I said, "it's Ketzel." I started to tell him about my encounter with his friend Magoo, but I was cut off by a blaring horn.

"Damn semis. Think they own the road."

"What road? Where are you?"

"Just crossed back into Nevada from Arizona. I'm on Route 15 heading west."

His voice kept fading in and out, but I managed to understand he had maintained surveillance on my brother's house the night before. Nothing of significance had transpired. He had waited until my niece had walked to school that morning, then followed her in his car, after which he had driven back to La Mancha Estates to see what my sister-in-law was up to. And damned if her little Porsche didn't come tearing out the gate. He followed her, and sure enough, she got on the highway and headed east.

"My apologies," Ebby said. "I didn't have a full tank. I was thinking 'stakeout' not 'high-speed cross-country chase.' I made it ninety miles, then I needed to stop for gas. Still, it's not as if we could have pulled her over. What would we have charged her with? A body turns up, we call in the big guns. My guess is she's not going to be giving up that car, and a blue Porsche with vanity plates isn't hard to find."

Ebby's signal faded out, and when it faded back in he was telling me that in his opinion, my sister-in-law hadn't been blessed with the strongest of maternal instincts. "Maybe she's better off this way. Your niece, I mean."

"Better off? How?" But I knew what Ebby meant: *Better off with you.*

"I ought to make it back to Vegas inside the hour. Why don't we grab a bite, then I'll drive you to Meryl's school? We can wait for her and break the news. If she's agreeable, you can move in with her right away. Save paying for that hotel room."

Move in and take care of Meryl? What did I know about raising a teenager? I entertained the notion of taking her back to live with my parents. But it hardly seemed ideal to coop up a teenage girl with two elderly eccentric shut-ins. And if she refused to leave town with her stepmother, why would she leave with me?

Ebby and I made plans to meet for lunch. He started to say good-bye, but I asked him about the girl.

"Which girl?"

"The runaway. The one giving blow jobs behind the restaurant."

Another truck horn blared. Ebby cursed.

"Ebby?" I said. "The runaway?"

He cleared his throat. "I found her. She wasn't the girl I thought. She was another one. Another runaway. But I was looking for that one, too."

I had an hour to kill in Vegas, but I'd had my fill of gambling. And I wasn't in the mood to be a tourist. It occurred to me that if my brother was hiding nearby, he might not be able to resist the temptation to place a bet. I'm not saying I believed I would find him sitting at a table at the Mirage playing Texas hold 'em. But checking out such a hunch would give me a way to pass the time. And it might make up for all the years I had willfully stayed ignorant of anything to do with my brother's world.

What I hadn't considered was how far apart the casinos were, how bright the light, how hot the sun. My dark glasses and hat provided some relief, but pushing through the throngs along the Strip was as exhausting as if I had been traversing the blazing sands from Pharaoh's Egypt to Caesar's Rome. As is true in any imperial city, the daunting distances and inhuman scale were meant to dwarf mere mortals; in the case of Vegas, these also provided a rationale for entering the cool interiors of the casinos and never leaving.

Around the world I wandered, from the Barbary Coast to Mandalay, from Casino Royale to the Stardust Lounge. I slogged past waterfalls. Volcanoes. Lions pacing in glassed-in dens. Finally, I reached the poker room at the Mirage—a bunch of tables surrounded by fake rocks in a tropical expanse designed to convey the illusion that while hacking through the bush, you had happened to stumble on a friendly game of five-card stud. It was barely past noon but the tables were filled with players, one of whom so closely resembled Potsie that I needed to stop and stare.

Like Potsie, the man was overweight. His gray hair was tied back in a ponytail, and his moustache and beard looked as if they had been scribbled with a crayon on his upper lip and chin. His aviator glasses resembled Potsie's, with a pair of shades attached to the regular frames but flipped up so he could see his cards. I felt as if I had been holding a hand in which a king of spades would complete a royal flush, but I had drawn the king of clubs, and I kept staring at the card, hoping the suit would change.

The man pushed back his chair. "Whadda ya lookin' at? You never seen a fat man lose at poker? What's with that getup? Who sent you here? Domino? Domino sent you, didn't he? Or Butchie Bear? Butcher said, 'Go over there and stare at that fat guy with the glasses until you get him rattled'? Well, bitch, I have a message you can give to Butchie."

He staggered up and lumbered toward me—I could hear his flip-flops slapping at his heels—but an off-duty dealer intervened. "Whoa there, big guy. The lady just got lost. She got confused. Didn't you, lady? You don't know Butchie, do you? Domino? No, see, she don't know anyone. She's leaving now. She's coming over to sit with me. And you're going to go back to your seat and play out your hand. Something tells me you're going to be getting some good cards anytime now."

The dealer put a hand on my elbow and guided me behind the rocks. He was Native American, I surmised, with shiny black hair fanning across his back, a stiff white shirt, and a bolo tie. He had a leathery face, with bags under his eyes so pouchy they each could have held a roll of coins. You could tell he had never been dealt any spectacularly good hands in life, but he had done as well as anyone could with what cards he got.

"Thanks," I said. "I didn't intend to start a fuss. I was looking for my brother. That man looked just like him."

"You thought that fat dude was your bro? Whoa. You got to be Potsie Weinrach's sister. Am I right? You the Pot-man's sister?"

I wished I'd had a brother who, when someone asked if you were related to him, you weren't afraid to say you were. "You haven't seen him, have you?"

"Nah. Been wondering where the Pot-man went myself. He usually stops by after his phones stop ringing for the night. He tallies up, comes over, plays a few hands to unwind." He slid the bolo up and down. "Probably fed up with *turistas* like Four-Eye Fats over there. Man, it sure ain't the old days. These new guys, they watch a few episodes of tournament poker on ESPN, they think they got all the moves. Fly out here from Scarsdale or Cheboygan, stake out a spot at one of my tables, don't know shit from Shinola, just like to make these big dramatic moves. All they want is to push in their chips the way the pros do on TV and say, 'I'm all in.' In the old days, you had to earn a nickname. You didn't just show up and say, 'I'm Tennessee This' or 'Texas That.' You played a few years, earned some respect. Now everybody and his grandma got monikers right off the bat." He waved his hand toward the players—there was a bear claw tattooed on his wrist. "More than once I heard your bro say he was going to blow Vegas and set up shop on some nice little island offshore, run his business tax-free from there."

"You think that's where he went? An island in the Caribbean? Did he ever mention which one?"

"*No se.* But the man sure does love the easy life."

By which I assumed he meant my brother loved to lie around naked in the sun, popping Baby Ruths and M&Ms. "Thanks," I said. "If he does turn up, could you tell him his family is worried sick? Could you ask him to please call home?"

By now, I was late for my date with Ebby. I had to run to meet him, and when I got there, I was so sweaty and drained, I almost asked him to carry me to the restaurant. It wasn't that far, he said. We only had to make it from Treasure Island to New York, New York. Although that was easy for him to say—I needed to walk twice as fast to keep up with his Goliath stride. We passed through a gauntlet of Hispanic boys hissing enticements for escort services. They must have taken Ebby to be a tourist—he was wearing Bermuda shorts and a gaudy shirt—because they tried particularly hard to get him to take a flier. He held up his hands, but one of the boys succeeded in getting him to accept a photo of a naked blonde, at which Ebby ripped up the card and showered the confetti on the young pimp's head.

It was a relief to reach the restaurant, although it turned out to be such an authentic replica of the deli where I used to work in New York, I could barely resist the urge to pick up a tray and start taking orders.

"This is the only place in Vegas you can get a decent pastrami on rye," Ebby said. "Not that I eat pastrami. But their cottage cheese and fruit plate is pretty good, too."

My sandwich, when it came, was so ridiculously overstuffed I could barely lift it. At the next table, a toothpick-thin old man looked at my plate and sighed. "Who can eat so much food! When my wife was alive, we used to come here and share a meal." He winked. "Maybe you want to split your sandwich?"

He was kidding, but only to the extent that he wished his wife were sitting across from him at their booth, remarking on the dimensions of the food and agreeing that yes, one pastrami on rye would be more than enough to feed them both.

Not that a widower in Las Vegas needed to remain alone. As Ebby filled me in on my sister-in-law's flight across the border, two men slid into a booth across the aisle, accompanied by two much younger Asian girls. The women were nicely dressed and well made-up, but the men reminded me of the dumpy balding clerk who worked at the post office near my apartment, a veteran of the Korean war who, if an Asian woman came to his window, engaged her in a conversation so lengthy the rest of us would grumble and check our watches. ("Fetish," the woman behind me muttered. "He probably had a thing for a Korean whore.")

The women in the restaurant made a show of leaning over their boyfriends' arms to study their menus, tapping them on their hands and patting their balding heads in such a stagy way I felt too uncomfortable to eat my lunch.

"Are they mail-order brides?" I asked Ebby. "Or are they prostitutes?"

He took a forkful of cottage cheese. "Could be either, or both. You want Asian, you order Asian. You want Chinese, Korean, Japanese, or Thai, you order those. You prefer your women dark, you ask for Mexican or black. You got your Nordic, your barely legal, your handicapped, your blind, you name it. Know how many pages in the phone book the escort services here take up? One hundred and thirty. Know how many women's bodies turn up in the desert every year? Know how many *Asian* women's bodies turn up? Year before last, three Chinese hookers turned up dead in one month."

He finished his cottage cheese, then pulled out his notebook and filled me in on all the pawnshops, gun suppliers, hotels, hospitals, casinos, airline companies, buses, and car-rental agencies he had visited or called to find clues to my brother's whereabouts. "Nada. Zip. Like I said, everything points to his staging this fake kidnapping scenario to scare his wife into leaving town. Which it looks like she's done. Your brother lays low for a while, then he cashes in his chips and opens a new bookmaking operation offshore. Only thing I can't figure out is how he left his kid with no one to look after her. Or how he thinks his wife is going to give up her claim on that expensive house. Most assets you can hide. But you can't hide a house. He comes back and lives there with your niece. Or he puts the house on the market. Either way, his wife's going to catch wind of what's going on. She gets a lawyer, she sues his ass to get her share."

Something came to me then, a piece of information I had overheard and not known what to do with. "The house is in my mother's name," I said. Ebby's silence proved this to be the final piece of evidence in favor of his theory that my brother had engineered his own disappearance.

But how could I present that theory to my parents? How would they excuse such behavior in their son?

Then again, they had excused his being a bookie. They had excused his hanging around my cousin, who, even if they hadn't been aware of what Perry had done to me when we were kids, they knew to be a pornographer. I would call to reassure them I was staying with my niece. But after that, they were on their own.

We still had an hour until Meryl's school let out, so after I had paid our bill, Ebby drove us to a neighborhood where he wanted to check a hunch. We parked and entered a grimy door between an establishment that sold venetian blinds and an outlet for imperfect linens. Ebby put his finger to his lips and led me upstairs. DOLLY-LEN ENTERPRISES read the yellowing index card thumbtacked beside the door.

There was a combination lock, but the door swung open when Ebby nudged it. I followed him inside and found myself standing in a room devoid of furniture. A ray of dusty light filtered in through a set of blinds so cheap they must have been the rejects not even the store below could sell. A door led to an inner office, which turned out to be as empty as the first. But a thin strip of light leaked from the office beyond that. Ebby didn't need to warn me to be quiet. Would I be happy to see my brother? Or furious he had been hiding so close to home?

Except it wasn't my brother we found in that final office; it was a man so wispy and pale that when Ebby called out "Smoke!," I knew this wasn't a command but the person's name. It was two in the afternoon but he still had on a nightshirt, and his nearly transparent hair was as disheveled as if he had just gotten up from bed.

Which he probably had. An inflatable mattress lay on the floor, with a paint-spattered tarpaulin for a blanket and a pair of rolled-up jeans for a pillow. I looked at the man again and saw he wasn't wearing anything but boxers beneath his shirt.

"Don't tell me you've been living here since Potsie went away. What, Potsie disappeared and the bets stopped coming in and you lost your room at the Roach Motel?"

The man drifted behind the desk, where he stood trailing his fingers across a laptop computer and a box of gingersnap cookies. I had the impression if Ebby made a move toward either item, Smoke would defend them with his life.

"What'd Potsie do, tell you to wait here until he turned up or gave the word?"

"He told me—" The man's voice was so reedy I had to close my eyes to make out what he was saying. "He told me if he didn't show up for a few days, I should hang around anyway, because even if the front office shut down, he might phone in bets from . . . somewhere."

"He didn't say where? Didn't say how long he intended to be away?"

"I don't—" He looked around the room. "I don't know what to do with myself."

Ebby handed Smoke his card. "You hear from Potsie, you give me a call. You going to be all right here in the meantime?"

The man hugged himself, although the room was so stuffy I could barely breathe. "I never was much good at knowing what to do with myself unless somebody told me."

"Yeah. That can be a problem. You want me to leave the front door open? Sure you don't want it locked?"

The poor man twitched his head. "Delivery boys," he whispered. "Takeout."

Ebby smacked his head. "Sure. Takeout. You got all the bases covered. You okay on the cash? Need a few bucks to tide you over?" He unfolded five twenties from his wallet.

Relief washed over Smoke's face. "Thanks." He took the money and

Ebby's card, but, since he wasn't wearing pants, he seemed at a loss as to where to put these.

We went back through the first two rooms—Ebby left the door ajar—and were out on the street before I could bring myself to ask if that was my brother's office.

"Back office. The clerks downtown take the bets and tote up the lines. Every so often, someone in that office phones the vital statistics to Smoke back here. At which point, the clerks in the front office destroy the hard copies. Cops stage a raid, poof, no evidence. Meanwhile, Smoke here has all the statistics on his computer. He gets a call the cops are on his tail, he hits one button and bam, *delete*."

I glanced at the window above the store. What if the delivery boys stopped coming? How long would my brother's clerk lie moldering on that bed before anyone smelled his smell? There were missing persons so lost that no one even knew to go looking for them.

We got back in Ebby's truck and drove a few sun-parched blocks to Meryl's school. I couldn't help but think that as heartbroken as my parents and I would be if my brother turned up dead, it would be the end of my niece's life. Who knew where either of her "mothers" went? My parents could take her in, but if my brother died, my mother would be even crazier than she already was.

Ebby hadn't wanted to summon Meryl from class, fearing she might assume worse news than that her stepmother had flown the coop. But the bell had already rung and a swarm of students was pouring out the doors. It was one of those cinder-block campuses that are about as attractive as an auto factory, baking in a sun so harsh it seemed a miracle the students didn't vaporize when they hit the air. Nearly everyone had a car, and the roar of all those engines made me think we had stumbled on the track at Indianapolis. I saw no hope of finding Meryl, but Ebby said if we followed the route she had walked to school that morning, we were likely to intercept her.

We drove slowly along the curb, the students glancing in our direction before dismissing us as too old to be important.

"I'm sorry I ignored you," Ebby said.

I had no idea what he meant. In the space of twelve hours he had taken me out for two meals and was helping me to find my niece and break the news that the one adult who was supposed to be taking care of her had fled the state.

"It kills me I was so mean to you. Just because you weren't the cheerleader type. I hate to admit it, but I made some comments about your . . . you know. Your figure. To fit in with the other guys."

Like most women, I wasn't sure if I should be angry or flattered that a man had discussed my breast size with his friends. "Ebby, you and I existed on different planets. You didn't ignore me any more than a Martian ignores an earthling. It was an embarrassing situation, your parents working for my parents. Besides, there's a statute of limitations on anything that goes on in high school. We were Meryl's age! Who knows anything at sixteen? You think you know, but you don't. That's what makes being a teenager so dangerous."

He inched along the curb. "It's a mystery how anyone makes it through high school alive."

By the looks of it, surviving high school in Las Vegas in 2005 was even more precarious than it had been in upstate New York thirty years earlier. The girls looked like hookers, the boys like reedier, less heavily bearded versions of the men with gold chains and gelled hair playing blackjack at the casinos. The only kids who didn't resemble younger versions of the employees or clientele at the Schoolhouse Lounge were a bunch of Goth kids—maybe the same ones my niece used to hang around with—who clustered at the corner of a construction lot adjacent to the school, their black coats and heavy boots so absurdly out of place it was as if someone had punched a hole through the fabric of the universe and all the light was pouring out.

That's when I noticed the three girls in loose-fitting jeans and baggy shirts, wearing kerchiefs around their heads. They approached a group of heavily made-up and scantily attired girls who were leaning against a bulldozer. The girls in kerchiefs tried to pass out fliers, but the other girls refused to take these, turning their backs and laughing, except for the girls who made a show of crumpling the fliers and tossing them to the ground.

One of the girls in kerchiefs bent and picked these up. "That one's Meryl," I said.

Ebby peered through the windshield. "Some private investigator. I followed her to school, she was wearing that same outfit, and you had to point her out. Maybe I'm not as oblivious to teenage flesh as I thought. Was it my imagination or was one of those girls wearing a bra and nothing over it?"

Ebby pulled up beside my niece and her friends. He powered down his window.

"Go fuck yourself," the shortest girl said, giving him the finger.

"Pervert," muttered the second girl, who, beneath her baggy clothes, was model thin.

"Doesn't it even bother you that we're only, like, sixteen?" Meryl said.

"Meryl," I called, "honey, it's your aunt."

Her face, which was the only visible part of her body, pale and innocent as the moon, flushed red. She told her friends goodbye, then trotted over to the pickup, although she came around to the passenger side rather than talk to Ebby.

"Sweetheart, this is Mr. Salzman. He's a friend of your father. From the old days? In Monticello? Where Nanny and Pop-pop live? He used to be a police officer, but now he's a private investigator, and we've hired him to find your dad. He's a very nice man. Ebby, this is Meryl, my niece."

Meryl peered in the window and squinted across the seat. "You're really a private eye? My Nanny and Pop-pop hired you?"

I turned and unlocked the door. Meryl slid in cautiously. I twisted around to face her. "Darling, I have some news. No, it isn't that. It isn't about your father. Your stepmother ... Janis ... Sunshine ... she ran away."

Meryl leaned back with an unreadable expression. "Like, with another guy? She left my dad?"

I told her what Ebby had observed, namely, that her stepmother had crossed the state line to Arizona and, as far as we knew, had no intention of coming back. But I wasn't sure if I should share that her stepmother thought her father had been abducted by the Mob. Or Ebby's theory that her father had engineered his own abduction.

"Sweetie? Do you have any thoughts about any of this? Where your father might have gone? Or why your stepmother left?"

A stray twizzle of hair had freed itself from her scarf and she sat sucking on the tip. "Um. I'm not sure I should say." She glanced at Ebby.

"This is someone your father and I grew up with."

She smoothed the flier on her lap. "I'm not supposed to tell." She chewed her hair while Ebby and I waited. "But I'm kind of worried. And I think it was only Janis I wasn't supposed to tell."

I was getting a pain in my neck from twisting to face my niece. It occurred to me that caring for a child required that you disregard your own comfort in favor of hers.

She looked out the window, but the other two girls were gone. "About a week before my dad disappeared, he said that if he ever went away and didn't come home, I should just wait for him in the house and he'd eventually come back to get me." She seemed on the verge of tears. "He is coming back, isn't he? When he said he'd be away a while, I thought he meant a few days. He ought to show up pretty soon. Shouldn't he? Isn't 'a while,' like, two days?"

Ebby and I exchanged a look. "Sweetheart," I said, "I have to be honest. We think maybe your dad planned this whole thing to get away from your stepmother. Or to get her to go away. And the plan got screwed up."

She scrunched her face. "He planned what? What are you saying?"

My parents had hidden so much from me, I had decided that if I ever had a child, I wouldn't keep the truth from her. I told my niece we suspected that her father had hired someone to show up at his house while she was away and pretend to kidnap him and threaten Janis so she would get scared and leave town.

Meryl sat there trying to make sense of what I had said. *Oh, sweetheart,* I wanted to say. *Trying to figure out the workings of such a tangled mind is a good way of tying your own beautiful mind in knots.*

"But what about me? If my dad comes back, won't Janis know? You can't just divorce somebody and not give them *anything.* But if he doesn't come back ... So, what, he'll be off gambling somewhere, and I'm living here on my own? I get a check in the mail, a birthday card, he calls me once a year to ask if I fed the dogs? Where do you think he went? I wouldn't mind leaving this stupid place, but he might have, like, consulted me." She rolled her eyes. "Aunt Ketzel, I know my dad is your brother, and you worship him and all, but I hope you don't mind my saying he isn't very smart."

I patted her knee. "That's all right. You can love someone even if he isn't smart."

She snorted. "Yeah. The philosophy of life according to *The Simpsons.* That's another reason my dad likes that show. Homer is a total dufus, but Maggie and Bart love him anyway."

By this time, we had driven to the development. Meryl hesitated, then told Ebby the code for the gate, which he punched in the cobra's head. "So, like, what are we going to do? Are you going to look for my dad?" *You* meaning Ebby.

"I can look," he said. "But it's not so easy finding someone who doesn't want to be found. It's easy on TV. But in real life . . ."

"Yeah, okay, thanks for the ride." She grabbed her backpack and the stack of leaflets and jumped out.

I hurried after her. "Wait!" I said. "You don't think you can stay here alone!"

She turned to face me, and with that handkerchief on her head and that backpack in her arms, she reminded me of Patty Hearst cradling the machine gun against her chest as she helped to rob that bank.

"Aunt Ketzel? To be honest? I've had my fill of grown-ups. I can take care of myself. At least as well as Janis took care of me. I bet I can concentrate a whole lot better without that crazy bitch screaming at me all the time to help her sell her stupid shit on eBay."

She fumbled to get out her key, at which the backpack began to slip, at which she started to lose the fliers, at which she dropped to her knees to catch them, then gave up and put her head in her hands and made no effort to stand back up.

I sat beside her on the pavement, where her stepmother's sports car used to be. "Meryl, honey, I'm sure you could do an A-double-plus job of taking care of yourself. But it isn't much fun to live alone. I'm sure your dad will come back soon. In the meantime, I could move in and keep you company."

She looked at me with the skeptical expression of a revolutionary who has been told if she lays down her weapon, she won't be shot. "You would do that? Move in here? Until my dad gets back? What about your life in New York?"

"Oh, that," I said, not wanting to admit my life in New York consisted of a few boxes of dirty jokes and some expensive marble phalluses. "Let's just say I could use some company myself."

A pained expression crossed her face. "Geez. I forgot about Uncle Morty. Here I am going on about me, me, me, and the guy you were married to, like, *forever* ..." In a gesture that literally took away my breath she threw her arms around my neck. When I managed to inhale, I smelled incense and patchouli, fragrances I hadn't smelled since I had hung around with the waiters at our hotel, who, in the 1960s, used these scents to camouflage that they were getting high. Did my niece smoke marijuana? Did she take worse drugs than pot?

"Sweetie, where did you get this scarf? No offense, but it looks like something that was very chic in 1968."

"Isn't it great? There's this vintage shop my friend Davia and I found, and we're, like, can you believe the cool stuff people give away? Everyone else brags how their jeans cost two hundred and fifty bucks, and we're like, 'I found this really cool pair with a peace sign hand-stitched on the butt and they were only fifty cents!'"

It occurred to me that the way to my niece's heart might be through her politically well-developed head. I nodded toward the VW bug beside us. "How come you walk to school when the other kids drive?"

"Ugh." She jumped to her feet. "All that pollution! And the oil companies getting rich! Someday I'll need to drive. But for now? Just to get a few crappy blocks to school?"

If there's one thing that can make a person feel old, it's watching a younger relative leap straight up from a sitting position without using her hands. By the time I had managed to achieve a similarly vertical state, Meryl had gotten out her key to the house and was inserting it in the door. I glanced back at Ebby, who motioned me to go in after her.

Meryl punched some buttons and disarmed the security system. Still, a different kind of alarm went off—the greyhounds whipped their tails against their crates, which made it sound as if we were being greeted by a band of steel percussionists. Meryl ran from cage to cage, setting each dog free. They skittered across the floor. She sank to her knees and let them lick her. To give my niece time to greet her pets and let them out in the fenced-in yard to do their business, I read one of the leaflets she and her girl guerrillas had been handing out at school.

HAVE SOME SELF RESPECT!!!

DON'T WALK AROUND WITH YOUR TITS AND BUTT HANGING OUT!!!

DON'T GIVE A GUY A BLOW JOB UNLESS YOU LOVE HIM

AND HE GIVES YOU ONE!!!

THERE'S MORE TO LIFE THAN GETTING

A CUTE GUY TO WANT TO FUCK YOU!!!

DON'T BUY INTO THE WHOLE CAPITALIST SEXIST IDEA

THAT THE ONLY THING A WOMAN CAN BE IS A WHORE!!!

Where, oh where, do children come from? My niece looked nothing like my brother. Or anyone else in Vegas. If Morty and I had had a child, would he or she have been anything like either one of us? This is a question I suspect bothered Morty, too. But watching my niece lavish her affection on a flock of dogs begging for food and love, all I could do was curse. *Damn you, Morty Tittelman! Why didn't I argue until you got tired of all my nagging and agreed to have a child? And if you refused, why didn't I find someone else who would?*

I wanted to tell my niece how much I admired her for writing that flier and having the courage to hand it out, but I was afraid she would think I was corny. Instead, I sank down with her on the floor, wrapped my arms around her, and let that pack of skinny dogs wash over us both with their sloppy, loving tongues.

That's when Ebby came in, walking so softly not even the dogs seemed upset by a strange man's presence. Then again, if a real Mafia hit man had managed to get inside, these poor creatures would have tiptoed away and hidden.

Ebby motioned me out of earshot. My niece and I would be perfectly fine alone, he said. But to be on the safe side, he proceeded to show me how to use the alarms and monitors. First thing next morning, after Meryl had left for school, he would come back and examine the house for clues. A private investigator didn't need a warrant to search a house, as long as someone with legal access let him in. Then he said goodbye, and I let him out.

At which I found myself responsible for another person's life, not to mention five canine victims of posttraumatic stress. What was I supposed to say to make conversation with someone who wasn't studying the latest cycle of dead-baby jokes going around the playgrounds of Manhattan? And what was I supposed to cook to nourish a growing but health-conscious teenage girl?

The latter question seemed easier to answer than the former. Scrounging through the beautifully crafted cabinets and up-to-date refrigerator in my sister-in-law's kitchen, I found a loaf of bread, of which all but the innermost pieces were blue with mold, a plate of cheese with colored toothpicks protruding from the cubes, and a can of Campbell's tomato soup. I did what I could with these sad ingredients.

"Meryl?" I called. "Honey? Do you want to come in and eat?"

When my niece shuffled in with the dogs behind her, I felt the panic I used to feel when a horde of tourists showed up at the deli and we were three waitresses and a line cook short. The dogs whined and sniffed expectantly.

Meryl rubbed their snouts. "Were you worried no one was going to come back and take care of you?" I watched her fill each of five bowls with water and shovel kibble from a vat beneath the sink. We stood listening to five eager tongues lap water from those bowls and five sets of canines' canines crunch their pellets of lamb and rice. Then I put my niece's bowl of tomato soup and her grilled cheese sandwich on the table, and, as an afterthought, a glass of milk.

She picked up the sandwich. "What's this?"

"What do you mean? What is what?"

"It's a sandwich, but what's inside?"

She had never eaten a grilled cheese sandwich? She took a tentative bite. "It's good." She began to spoon up the tomato soup, gobble the sandwich, and drink the milk.

"Didn't your parents ever cook for you?" I asked this, knowing that as much as my brother loved to eat, he never had learned to cook. How could he, growing up at a hotel? Then again, hadn't I learned to cook for Morty?

"Janis always sends out for takeout." She ran her finger through a grease spot on her plate, licked her finger, sucked it, then picked up her spoon and scraped the last drops of tomato soup from her bowl.

"There's another sandwich," I said. "There's more soup in the pot."

She couldn't hide her wish to eat it. "What about you?"

"Me? I had this really enormous lunch. And there are still a bunch of these." I put the last few cheese-cubes on my plate.

"You're sure?"

I popped a cube in my mouth. Should I bring up her father's disappearance? Her stepmother's flight from town? Was there anything to say on either topic that hadn't already been said? "So," I said, "how was school?"

Meryl rolled her eyes. "You saw what those kids are like. Everybody thinks they're on some kind of reality show. The boys all want to grow up to be Steve Wynn, and the girls want to grow up to be Steve Wynn's wife. So, like, it's not as if anyone is particularly interested in learning anything." She finished the second bowl of soup and picked up the second half of the second sandwich. "Pop-pop once told me that all Jews go to college. But *he* didn't go, right? And neither did my dad. Or you. You didn't go to college."

I hated to admit I hadn't. I had pursued an education with Morty Tittelman. But what an education that turned out to be! And studying with Morty Tittelman, even if he had been alive, was hardly a course of action I could recommend to my niece. "Sweetie, I don't think you should take our family's educational history as a model for your own."

"But what would I want to study? Just watching *ER* makes me want to puke. And who wants to be a lawyer? What am I going to do, spend my life helping slimeballs stay out of jail? Given what my dad and his friends do to earn a living, it's not as if I want to spend my life putting slimeballs *into* jail, either."

Oh, I said, there are all sorts of possibilities about which a person knows nothing until she enters the gates of higher knowledge. Although not having entered such gates myself, I was hard pressed to reveal what they are.

She had finished her meal by then and said she needed to study for a test on the mammalian reproductive system. She stepped over Blitzen and Donner, who were lying across the threshold. "Thanks for the sandwich," she said. "It was, like, the best thing I ever ate."

As exhausted as if I had tried to entertain an audience for an hour and a half with five minutes of material, I took a can of macadamia nuts and went to recuperate in the living room. It was difficult to ignore the TV, which was the size of the screen at a drive-in theater. After flicking through several hundred stations, I found a *Seinfeld* rerun. Morty had considered Jerry Seinfeld to be the king of observational humor, and, as such, one of the main contributors to the demise of classic Borscht Belt shtick. But I was homesick for New York. And they were playing my favorite episode.

Meryl heard me laughing and drifted in—she carried a biology book thick enough to fill any adult with dread. She slumped against the armrest at the opposite end of the couch, and even though there's nothing more pathetic than a middle-aged person dropping the only famous name she knows to impress a teenage relative, I couldn't help but impart that I had gotten my start at the same comedy club where Jerry Seinfeld had gotten his start, or rather, he had gotten his start at the comedy club at which I earlier had gotten mine. Although either way you looked at it, I had reached the end of my beginning much sooner than Jerry Seinfeld had reached the end of his.

"Really?" Meryl said, although I could see she didn't know what to make of this information. "I don't mean to hurt your feelings," she said, which is what people say before they go ahead and hurt them, "but, like, aren't you kind of shy? I can't see you getting up on a stage and telling jokes."

I patted myself up and down to see where the wound might be, but my ego had escaped unscathed. "Most comics are shy. At least, when they aren't performing. What a comic does on stage is pretend to be someone else. Or a louder, crazier version of himself."

"But why?" she said. "Why would you want to get up onstage and pretend to be someone you're not?"

How could I explain what it had felt like to sit through all those performances by Zero Mostel and Buddy Hackett, mouthing their routines, moving my hands and face the same way they moved theirs, emptying myself of *me* and letting those men take me over? "I guess I thought if I tried being someone else, people might pay more attention. My parents might love me more."

I looked at my niece to see if she would acknowledge she was doing much the same thing. But if she got my drift, she didn't trust me enough to admit she did.

"Yeah," she said. "Whatever." Another commercial came on, this one for constipation. "So," she said, "who else can you imitate? Besides this Hackett guy, I mean. Or Zero whoever."

Most of the people I could imitate had been dead so long my niece wouldn't know who they were. "Do you know who Jerry Lewis is?" When she shook her head no, I tried to explain how Dean Martin and Jerry Lewis had once been the most popular comedic duo in the world. But she had never heard of Dean Martin either.

By then, *Seinfeld* had come back on. "Can you do Kramer?" Meryl asked.

I felt my stage fright ease. "Sure." I fluffed my hair and bugged my eyes and did my best version of Kramer sliding into Jerry's living room.

"That's pretty good," Meryl said. "Who else can you do? How about Elaine and Jerry?"

I ran through the scene we had just watched in which Jerry and Elaine are called upon to perform a baby's bris. You will have to take my word, but I did a passable imitation of Jerry and Elaine discussing the human male member in its uncircumcised state. "You ever seen one?" Elaine asks Jerry. "No," Jerry says. "Have you?" At which Elaine does that thing where she nods and hums and grins. "Ya," she says. So Jerry asks, "What'd you think?" And Elaine makes an expression like this and says, "Noooo." And Jerry says, "Not good?" And Elaine tells him, "No. It had no face. It had, I don't know, no personality. The penis was very dull. It was, I don't know, like a Martian. But hey, that's only me."

As humble as my performance was, my niece seemed dutifully impressed. "Wow! You're like some human Xerox machine! Can you imitate anyone else? How about my mother? I don't mean Sunshine. I mean my real mother."

Sadly, I had never had the pleasure of meeting Amy/ValZorah. But I was able to climb halfway up the stairs and do Sunshine coming down. Then I went over to the Superman pinball machine my brother had salvaged from our hotel and did my best imitation of Potsie as a teenage boy trying to score a free game.

"That's my dad! That's *exactly* how he jerks his butt when he works the flippers! And that's how he curses and kicks the wall when he makes it tilt!"

Buoyed by her good reviews, I did her father dancing to "Satisfaction" and playing "Stairway to Heaven" on air guitar. I did him eating a Baby Ruth and diving from the high dive into a swimming pool.

"That's totally amazing!" Meryl laughed and laughed, until her laughter had turned to tears. "What if he never comes back? What if I never see my dad again?" And, what she didn't say, *If my father never comes back, is this the best I'll have? My crazy Aunt Ketzel, pretending that she's him?*

I spent the rest of the night assuring my niece that her father would be all right. In the meantime, here I was, a responsible adult who would see to her every need. After she went to bed, I treated myself to a drink from my sister-in-law's poorly hidden stash of sweet liqueurs, then went up to my brother's guest room to sleep. Although, judging by the candy wrappers, sports magazines, and issues of *Playboy* and *Hustler* scattered beside the bed, I guessed my brother's guest room was used less as a site of hospitality than a refuge for my brother when my sister-in-law was unwilling to grant her favors even once in a given night, let alone the three or four times for which he married her.

I'm not what you would call a snoop. But I felt more than the usual dispensation to hunt for a cloth to wash my face and a brush to brush my teeth, which is how I came to find, beneath a pillow and an extra quilt, the sort of metal box in which people keep their financial documents. I would never have dared to open it, except the key was in the lock. And wasn't I amazed to find—instead of my brother's taxes—a curl of my niece's hair, the first baby shoes she had ever worn, six tiny glassine envelopes, each of which contained a tooth no bigger than a seed, labeled with the date it had dropped from my niece's gums, every drawing she had ever drawn and every card she had ever crayoned to wish my brother a *HAPE FATTERS DAY,* every report card she had ever brought home from school, and stacks of snapshots showing Meryl at every stage, from tiny child to teenage girl—you could have flipped these with your thumb and watched my niece develop like the kids they used to show on those Wonder Bread commercials, the children's bodies growing in a dozen ways.

I might not have bothered to open the scrapbook at the bottom, assuming it contained more mementos of my niece, but I saw protruding from the book a fraction of my brother Ira. And there they all were, my dear departed loved ones, reunited and in their prime at a place as close to heaven as anywhere on earth could be. First came Grandpa Joe, if not young, then not so old. Beside him stood my father, healthy, unbent and whole, with a jaw so firmly cleft that if, instead of the golf club in his hand, he had been holding a sword, he might have been Kirk Douglas inciting his fellow slaves to march on Rome. To my father's right stood Arnold Palmer, fresh from his latest triumph, sexy, relaxed, and slim. All three men were laughing, and each man held his club so the heads of their irons met in that Three Musketeerish way men use to pledge their loyalty to whatever ideals they see fit to pledge to.

Kneeling before the grown-ups were my four buzz-cutted brothers—Ira, who must have been seventeen; Howie, two years younger;

Mike, a scrawny but handsome ten; and Potsie, a balloon-cheeked and chubby nine. The occasion—which I guessed from the gaily festooned golf carts and the impressively large floral arrangement in the shape of a ball and tee—was the grand opening of the clubhouse my father had ordered to replace the quaint but outdated locker rooms and woefully puny bar that had served golfers at our hotel before the Monster became a venue for tournaments on the PGA.

It came to me how difficult it must have been for Potsie to be the youngest brother in a family of overachievers such as ours. How could a boy whose only skill was winning candy bars hope to join a club that included Grandpa Joe, who had built the Hospitality House from scratch, or our father, who had promoted it until it was the second-most famous Jewish resort in the world, or Ira, who had died a hero, or Mike, who forever would be remembered as Donald Trump's right-hand man? Even Howie had been sent to Congress before he had been sent to jail. I felt I had found the diary in which my youngest brother recorded his struggle to prove himself worthy to be a Weinrach. He had pasted in his scrapbook Ira's obit from the *Times,* an account of Howie's trial, the search for poor Mike's remains, a photo of Donald Trump with a yarmulke on his head, bowed in grief by my brother's grave, and, at the very end, a ragged notice about Stuart "Potsie" Weinrach placing first in a poker tournament, and another item about that same Stuart Weinrach having been arrested in a sting—*BIGGEST BOOKIE EVER NETTED* ran the cutline beneath a shot of Potsie pinioned between two cops like a record-breaking tuna—and a story about a plodder that had won the Belmont Stakes against the longest odds ever offered—the article didn't mention my brother's name, but he must have been among the lucky few who had bet on that nag to win.

Oh, I thought, *poor Potsie.* He had spent his life trying to impress our parents and older brothers. And who was left to bear witness to his title as Biggest Bookie in Las Vegas, to the Hummer and the Porsche, to his million-dollar house and his sexy showgirl wife? Who else was there now but me? He must have assumed I would disapprove. If I ever had any doubt as to the overly ideal reverence in which my brother held me, that doubt was laid to rest by the final item in the box—a laminated reproduction of a photo in which a zaftig teenage boy and a much smaller teenage girl sit astride a thoroughbred horse amid the ragged throng at Woodstock. I hope you will understand if I went to bed that night with that photo against my chest. The rumpled nature of the sheets and their odors of chocolate and Old Spice led me to believe they hadn't been changed since my brother slept there. I buried my nose in the pillow and inhaled the scent I used to smell when he took me sledding, my face pressed against his back as we went screaming down that toboggan run, and I offered a prayer that whatever trouble he had gotten into, whether by his own hand or the hands of others, he would manage to get out of it.

I barely slept. But I rose happily at dawn to get Meryl off to school—scrambling the last pair of eggs I had found rolling around my sister-in-law's Frigidaire, squeezing a glass of lemonade from the shriveled lemon beside her gin, giving Meryl money to buy some lunch, then helping her to hoist a backpack so heavy a well-conditioned marine might have had trouble lifting it, before sending her out the door with a kiss and hug.

Why had I thought being a mother must be so difficult? My own parents had found it hard only because they were taking care of twenty-five hundred other people at the same time they were meant to be taking care of me. For all Morty's high-flown rhetoric about not wanting to raise a child in an inauthentic postmodern world, he probably was just afraid that a man so obsessed with sex wasn't fit to be a father. Or maybe the fault was mine. Unlike the brotherhood of stand-up comics, motherhood was a club that society expected me to join. As Groucho Marx so famously said, none of us wants to join a club that is eager for us to join it. Yet here I was in my fifties, discovering that caring for a child made me happier than anything I had ever done. And—surprise!—I did it well. It was like waking in an operating room with your hands in a stranger's chest and, wonder of wonder, repairing that stranger's heart.

I fed the dogs—five other souls that needed me!—then took a taxi to the Flamingo, where I packed my jeans and shirts, resisted the temptation to steal the fresh bottle of conditioner the chambermaid had left, and with a sigh of relief checked out. When the cabbie dropped me at La Mancha Estates, I caught myself enjoying the proprietary thrill of knowing the secret code to get inside. I nodded in a friendly and, I hoped, noncondescending way to the Hispanic men weeding the flower beds around the pool. Unlocking my brother's house, I disarmed the alarm, and, as soon as I had stepped inside, rearmed it. The greyhounds beat their tails against their crates and, after I had let them out, nosed me as gratefully as if I had been the one to rescue them from the track. Precisely at 10:15, Ebby knocked and I let him in.

"Good morning, Ketzel," he said.

"Good morning, Ebby," as formally as if an inspector from the Bureau of Proper Conduct for Private Investigators had been observing us from the camera above his head. Ebby wore another pair of Dockers and a yellow shirt that seemed to come from the same pack of Lifesavers as the first two shirts he had worn. I was dying to ask why he dressed like an insurance salesman, but who was I to take anyone to task for a lack of sartorial splendor? Also, I found it difficult to think of anything except my being alone with a man upon whom I once had had a sizeable teenage crush.

He snapped on a pair of latex gloves, an act that made me feel as if I were about to receive a gynecological exam. Then Ebby led me from room to room, rifling through stacks of mail, browsing the last few sites my brother had visited on the Web, reading the expiration dates on the prescriptions above the sink, peering under sofas, flipping up the corners of my brother's Persian rugs. As far as I could tell, the only real discovery either of us made concerned the boxes in the den, which, when I accidentally peeled back the tape and burrowed through the Styrofoam pellets, turned out to hold dolls from around the world. Dolls! The kind that came in plastic bells and were meant to be admired for the costumes they modeled and the exotic cultures they represented. Was this how my sister-in-law saw herself? As a perfectly costumed Las Vegas doll in a glass-and-marble house?

I followed Ebby up the stairs, thinking that even from the rear he still had many attributes to appreciate. We entered the master bedroom and stood beside the bed. And what a big bed it was! What size comes after king? Emperor size? A bed expansive enough to fit a pope? Ebby tossed the pillows to the floor and yanked off the covers, an act that seemed as cruel as if he had caught my sister-in-law having sex and ripped off her clothes. But the sheets were spotless white. My sister-in-law was quite the *baleboste*. Even in a house this big, with a teenage girl and five dogs to care for, everything was clean and in its place. Although why this made me think she couldn't also be a murderer wasn't clear. Maybe the crime was the house itself, given that she had married my brother to acquire it and he had hired a bunch of thugs to scare her from claiming half.

The mattress was too heavy for us to flip, but Ebby crawled under it far enough to satisfy himself that the underside wasn't stained with my brother's blood. Then he pulled open the nightstand drawer to reveal a box that, according to its label, once had held a gross of condoms, although now it held only five, as well as a brochure that advertised a dude ranch in Montana at which the guests were encouraged to ride horses not only barebacked, but bare from head to toe.

"Your brother into this kind of thing?" Ebby held the brochure by an edge, either because he didn't want to mar the evidence or was reluctant to lay his hand on the riders' breasts. I explained that one of my brother's gripes about his wife was that even though she had been willing to dance naked in front of strangers, she refused to take a vacation at a resort where she could engage in such innocent pastimes as playing tennis or swimming in the company of perfectly normal men to whom it was not a matter of sexual interest to see other people in the buff, to which my sister-in-law had replied that if a man was paying money to be within visual distance of a woman whose tits and pussy were on display, he was getting off on what he saw, and if she was to be the one taking off her clothes, she damn well ought to be the one getting paid instead of paying.

My brother's wallet wasn't there. Nor was the lanyard key-chain I had made for him at camp. Did that mean he had left the house of his own accord? Or that his credit cards, cash, and keys had been in his pockets when the goons surprised him? My brother never went anywhere without his cell phone, but it lay beside the lamp.

Like some ghost of Christmas past, Ebby pointed a white-gloved finger.

"What?" I said. "You want me to . . ."

Ebby nodded.

The idea of touching my brother's phone, let alone listening to his messages, seemed such a violation of his privacy I would have preferred to spy on Potsie and my sister-in-law making love.

I shook my head.

Ebby pointed to the phone again. "The messages might be the

171

only real lead we have."

I closed my hand around the phone and was startled at how heavy and warm it was. I could have sworn I felt it beat.

"Go ahead. Push that green button. Okay, now punch in one."

The mechanical woman spoke. She seemed to be the same woman who had taken the message from lovelorn Sonia to her jilted boyfriend Dwayne. How could anyone hear such heartbreak day after day and maintain such calm? And how, in the four days since my brother had gone missing, had he managed to accumulate sixty-seven messages?

The answer should have been obvious: all but a few were from my mother.

"Potsie!" she cried. "Why won't you pick up? Potsie, dear, please, God, not you, too!" Then: "You idiot! You promised you wouldn't take any risks!" Then: "My baby, my baby. Where are you? What's going on? It's all my fault! I never should have taught you this terrible business. As you sow, so shall you reap!" And finally: "Potsie, darling, please, everything is forgiven, please just call home. Whatever it is, whatever you've done, your father and I will do everything we can to help. Please, darling, just call home!" I felt I was listening to my mother's heart speak directly to my brother's, a connection I had never been granted with either one.

I sank on Potsie's bed and listened to the rest of the messages while Ebby tapped his foot. Finally, I heard a message from one of my brother's poker friends, wondering where he was, and six curse-filled calls from a man whose name seemed to be Pickles Pinkowski. "Pot? You there, man? Come on, pick up. What the fuck's going on? You fucking owe me, man. All this time, my ship comes in, and what, you don't pick up the phone? Word's out you skipped town. What, you don't have forty grand? Forty large ones break the bank? What is this bullshit? Pot, this is the last fucking time I'm calling. I'm getting pretty pissed off here. I'm getting pissed off to the point I fucking do something about being so pissed off. You may be bigger than I am, you fat fuck, but I come up behind you some night on a dark street, your being big just means you provide a bigger target."

I handed the phone to Ebby, who pushed some buttons and replayed the last few messages while I watched his face.

"Huh," he said. "That's interesting."

"Just 'interesting'? That was a death threat! That man threatened to kill my brother!"

"Yeah," he said, "but it sounds as if this Pickles character went apeshit *after* Potsie disappeared. The guy just wants his money. I'll talk to Owen and check it out. But it doesn't sound as if Mr. Pinkowski here is out to get anyone but your brother. He just wants his forty grand."

I said I wasn't convinced.

"Look, I'm sure your parents would kick in for you and Meryl to stay at a hotel. But if you ask me, your niece isn't all that eager to leave this house. The kid's lost her father. Her stepmother ran off. Living here is the only constant in her life. Even if Owen doesn't know how I can get in touch with this Pinkowski, I can keep your brother's phone and talk to Pinkowski the next time he calls. Anybody calls you on the landline, you let the machine pick up. Anyone comes to the door, you don't let him in, call me right away. You got the gate, the fence, the cameras. You've got locks and alarms on every door. And the dogs . . . don't underestimate the power of a pack of five big dogs to scare off an intruder. No one has to know these particular dogs are a bunch of powder puffs. Guy takes a look at five dogs, he's not about to bust down the door and start messing with their owner."

He snapped the cell phone shut, then motioned me to follow him to my brother's closet, which was larger than the entire bedroom Morty and I had shared. A pair of black tuxedo pants hung upside down like the lower half of my brother's torso. In cubbies along the wall lay stacks of nylon shorts; hanging from a rod was a collection of jerseys so complete that if my brother had built his own field of dreams, every Yankee who had ever held a bat, from Babe Ruth to Derek Jeter, could have found his old shirt, taken it down, and played.

"Any idea who's missing from the lineup?"

I wished I had been able to perform some impressive feat of memory and astonish Ebby with my detecting skills. But I knew that my brother owned multiple copies of MARIS, MAYS, and JACKSON, and every now and then he wore a shirt that honored a Knick or Met.

Ebby knelt to inspect a pair of dress shoes that seemed never to have been worn, and five pairs of flip-flops, each of which could have served as a raft for a good-sized cat. A Giants banner hung opposite my brother's shirts; Ebby pushed it aside to reveal a square of drywall that had been cut out and fit back to form a door.

"What's that?" I said. "What kind of safe has no lock?"

"Any decent thief can get past a lock. But if a safe doesn't have any metal, it's harder to detect." He grabbed the plastic handle and tugged out the door, then reached in up to his armpit and fished around. Personally, I would have been afraid of some sort of trap. But Ebby suffered no worse injury than a splinter, for which he was rewarded by three blue poker chips and a single pea-size pearl. "My guess is, this hidey-hole held a shitload of chips and cash before your brother cleared it out."

Ebby replaced the drywall and covered it with the banner, then he backed out of the closet and replaced the covers on the bed. I almost expected to see him walk backward down the stairs and out the door, as if to erase his presence in the house, after which he would keep moving backward until he and I had never met.

He waved me to join him at the mate of my brother's closet. My sister-in-law must have taken several suitcases, but you could have stocked a small department store with the clothes she had left behind. I counted eighty-nine pairs of shoes and fifty-six or -seven handbags, depending on how you classified the Louis Vuitton duffel on the floor. I stopped counting at a hundred belts.

In the bathroom, every square inch was occupied by cosmetics, lotions, perfumes, facial treatments, plastic fingernails, fake eyelashes, contact lenses, swatches of hair, and wigs. By the time I had finished reading the labels on the hair-care products, Ebby had left the room.

"Ketzel? You want to come take a look?"

I found him crawling up the stairs, sniffing like a dog. He had taken off one glove and was pressing his palm against the shag. "Feel how the carpet is still damp? It stinks of cleaning fluid. And here's a stain she couldn't get out. Or maybe she didn't bother to take the time."

I felt queasy and had to sit. "No," I said. "No! Are you saying he really did get shot?"

"Not unless he had cranberry juice in his veins."

Perhaps, as I've said, I had lost my sense of humor, but this was my brother's blood we were discussing. "How can you joke about something like that?"

"Sorry. But I wasn't kidding. If you don't believe me, we can call in the guys from *CSI*." He pointed to a shiny red splatter on the rail. "Or you could just taste the stuff."

"You want me to taste my brother's blood?"

"Trust me, it isn't blood." He put his thumb to his mouth and wet it, then reached out and rubbed the stain. I tried to turn away, but he put the thumb to my tongue.

The taste was bright and sweet. My conclusion differed from Ebby's only in that I suspected the juice had come from a jar of maraschino cherries.

Ebby got up and massaged his back. From where I sat, he seemed ten feet tall. "No bullet holes. No empty casings. If your sister-in-law did hear shots, they must have come from blanks. Or a paper bag being popped."

He beckoned me downstairs, through the kitchen, and into my brother's garage, where, if nothing else, we solved the mystery as to why all three cars were parked outside: namely, the garage, which could have held a 747, was filled with cardboard boxes like the boxes that filled the den.

"As someone who recently found himself in a similar marital situation, I have to say that getting abducted by the Mob might be preferable to hiring lawyers and dividing all this crap."

We walked to the side of the house, where Ebby used his football-player's arms to vault the fence. By hopping up and down, I could glimpse his head. Then he clumsily swung back over. "Nada." He turned up his heel and sniffed. "Unless you count the dog shit." He rubbed his soles on the scrubby grass. "Come on. Let's take a walk."

I followed him down the driveway, out the front gate, and around the brick wall until we reached the back side of the development. It was like stepping off a movie set.

"Anything strike you as out of the ordinary?"

I had to admit it didn't. "There isn't a grain of sand out of place."

His face lit up the way Sherlock Holmes would have shown approval of Dr. Watson. "My guess is, the construction company finished building Don Quixote-ville, then graded the place and replanted the vegetation. If a bunch of thugs had driven up to your brother's house and dragged him out the back, it would have messed things up. If they'd dragged him out the front, one of your neighbors would have seen or heard. Which they didn't. I went around and asked. They're a shifty bunch, but I'm pretty sure they were telling the truth on this. I'll keep my eyes and ears open. But honestly, all we can do is wait."

My relief that my brother wasn't dead was so enormous I sank to the sand and wept. "Oh, Ebby," I said, "how can any of us ever thank you? It was like I had a boulder on my chest and you took it off."

Embarrassed, he helped me to my feet. We walked back to the front of my brother's house, where Ebby and I compared ideas as to what party or parties might have spattered cherry juice on the stairs, after which Ebby presented me with our options for making contact with my brother, most of which entailed waiting for Potsie to get in touch with us.

Ebby took off the remaining glove. "I know this isn't great timing," he said, "but I hate thinking of you sitting here alone, not knowing a soul in Vegas. I thought maybe you and your niece would like to come for dinner tomorrow night."

"You want to cook for us?"

"Are you implying I can't? I'll make some vegetarian thing for the kids, and you and I can bore them with stories about what a dickhead I was growing up."

This was nothing but a friendly gesture. He was sorry I was here alone. "You don't need to go to all that trouble on my account. Meryl probably has a million social obligations. You know how teenagers are."

"Sure. But you and I are no longer teenagers. Do you have a million invitations for tomorrow night? I hope I'm not letting the cat out of the bag, but I, for one, do not. Honestly, you would be doing me a big favor. Can you drive? Or do you want me to pick you up?"

Not wanting to appear a helpless dolt, I said I would drive my brother's car. Then I remembered that my brother didn't own a car, he owned a tank.

"Great," Ebby said. "Then it's a deal." He opened the door to his Silverado; you could see waves of superheated air come blasting out. "Expect you around six-thirty?"

"Sure," I said, "thanks." Then I watched the truck drive off, wishing I weren't wishing he had said "date" instead of "deal."

I had nothing to do until Meryl got home except walk the dogs. All well and good that we had been invited to dinner at Ebby's house the next night; I had nothing to feed her in the meantime. The keys to my brother's Hummer lay by the door. I had barely driven in thirty years. And I hadn't been a good driver even then. But I still had a valid license—how else to cash a check?—and it wasn't as if a person forgets how to turn a wheel.

Like everything else in Vegas, my brother's Humvee had been built on an inhuman scale. Walking around it took as long as walking around an elephant. The tires were as big as Ferris wheels. I needed to take a running jump and fling myself in the seat. I could sense the Hummer's shock that such an innocuous human being would dare to drive it. But the Hummer didn't buck me off. In fact, the ride was surprisingly smooth. Just backing out of the driveway consumed a quarter of a tank of gas. But I loved how invincible driving a Hummer made me feel. It was all I could do not to drive to the Schoolhouse Lounge and run it down. And what a relief that I no longer needed to rely on cabs.

No wonder I had never seen anyone outside walking; they were all walking around the air-conditioned grocery store to which I drove. If I ignored the women's miniscule shorts, I could almost fool myself into thinking I was shopping at my dearly missed Gristedes on Ninety-Sixth. I bought organic this and whole wheat that, then hedged my bets by piling in my cart an assortment of Ben & Jerry's, Entenmann's cakes, and Pop-Tarts.

That left only the question of what to bring Ebby as a gift. I knew he avoided sweets. And considering what had happened the last time I'd had a drink, I nixed the idea of alcohol. Then I entered the produce department, and the answer presented itself in the shape of a pineapple so ripe it glowed, along with mangoes and papayas, citrus from California, and fruits in shapes like stars. How could I go wrong? If Ebby didn't want to eat my gift, he could arrange it in a bowl and paint it.

I loaded the groceries in the Hummer, then made a quick detour to the public library, which seemed the only building in town in which a person couldn't play the slots. I wasn't sure that the effect of growing up in such a place could be counteracted by *Jane Eyre* or *Pride and Prejudice*, but it couldn't hurt to try.

I got home just in time to pop the Pop-Tarts in the cupboard and the vegetables in the vegetable bin and bake a box of brownies before Meryl got home from school. She patted the dogs and kissed their heads while I fought the urge to thank her for giving me someone to be there to greet.

She dropped her backpack and sniffed the air. "What's that incredible smell?" She ran to the kitchen. "You *made* these? For me?" She opened the fridge and sniffed the milk. "Fresh milk! Janis never went shopping, except for stuff *she* liked. Which mostly was, you know ..." She raised an imaginary bottle to her mouth, and even though I couldn't read the label, I knew it didn't say MILK.

She settled happily on a stool, nibbled a gooey still-warm brownie, sipped from a glass of milk, and told me how absolutely blown away she had been dissecting a worm in biology class. "They're fucking hermaphrodites! But they can't, you know, have sex with themselves. They have to find another worm to mate with. And—this fucking blows my mind—each itty-bitty worm has five even itty-bittier hearts!"

After she had provided a detailed description of the innards of a worm, she asked why English teachers assigned these crappy frustrating stories about ridiculous situations like a woman cutting off her hair and selling it to buy a present for her husband, who had been saving up to buy her a comb, or these people drawing straws to see which of them gets stoned by the rest of the village. "Life isn't fucked up enough? How many times does somebody tell you that you've got to stone somebody? Or hunt or be hunted? Or choose the lady or the tiger?"

I couldn't have asked for a better introduction to *Pride and Prejudice*. I wasn't sure the marital situation women faced in Jane Austen's time would seem any more relevant to my niece than the plots manufactured by O. Henry or Shirley Jackson, but she would see that people who lived in other places didn't live the way they lived in Vegas. Or, until recently, they hadn't.

Meryl caressed the book as if I had bestowed a priceless scroll from the archives in Alexandria. "I always wanted to go to the library. I did go, a few times. But there were so many books! How does anybody know which are good and which are crap?"

"It helps if someone can get you started," I said, thinking of Morty, who, despite his flaws, had informed me about what to read.

Things seemed to be going so well I decided to broach that Ebby had invited us to dinner. At which my niece seemed underwhelmed. Even a girl who doesn't want to walk around looking like a hooker might not want to waste a perfectly good Saturday night in the company of a middle-aged aunt and an overweight detective she barely knows.

Then her expression changed. "Aunt Ketzel! That's so sweet! You knew this guy when you were, like, my age? And now he's divorced and you're both, like, available? I can see where he was once a good-looking person. He doesn't have the best taste in clothes. But for an older guy he's cute. And he was a friend of my dad's, right? Of course I'll go! How could you think I wouldn't?"

Overjoyed at this new success, I asked my niece what she might like for dinner. She got a wistful look and said, "You know the stuff that nice Polish woman cooks when Dad and I go to visit Nan-nan and Pop-pop? That chicken with the crispy skin? And, what's it called, that noodle thing?" She noticed a bunch of asparagus standing on the counter, held together by a rubber band so they resembled prisoners awaiting execution. "Wow. I had some of these when I stayed with Davia's dad in Tahoe and they were delicious. And maybe we could have more brownies for dessert?"

Let me tell you, if you are someone's Jewish aunt and your niece asks you to roast a chicken and prepare a noodle kugel and asparagus for her dinner, you feel as if your entire life, which until that moment has seemed a waste, suddenly has proved worthwhile.

"Are you sure that's okay?" Meryl asked. "You could just call out for pizza. I don't want you to spend your time shopping and cooking and stuff for me." She fingered the asparagus. A tip broke off and she popped it in her mouth, closing her eyes and smiling. "I don't mean to pry, but what are you going to do with yourself all day? Janis spent her life shopping. Or she worked out at the gym. Or she bought and sold those stupid dolls on eBay. But you don't do any of that junk. What's to keep you from going nuts?"

My niece, whose mother had run off when she was four and whose father had disappeared and whose stepmother had abandoned her, was worried about her aunt being left to her own devices from eight to three. Unless she was worried about herself. If her aunt grew bored and left, what would become of her?

"Sweetheart," I said, "don't you worry about your aunt Ketzel. I have the dogs to keep me company. And I need to practice for this audition that's coming up."

"Audition? For what?"

Oh, I said, I was supposed to get up on the stage at Harrah's Improv and do an eleven-minute monologue. Whoever won, the people who ran the contest would fly you to LA and make you jump through a few more hoops, after which you got to do your act on Comedy Central and maybe appear on David Letterman.

"You're kidding. Right? You *aren't* kidding? This is for real? And you didn't, like, tell anyone? Aunt Ketzel, I can't believe you!" She was so excited the dogs came skittering across the floor see if this meant they might get petted or made a fuss of. "I can be your test audience!" She sat straighter on her stool. "Go ahead, make me laugh."

I protested, but in truth I was more than a little worried that in the past twenty-nine years my material had gotten stale, especially since it had been stale to being with. A few aficionados like Harvey Blatt might appreciate my retro Borscht Belt shtick. But who else would even know who Henny Youngman was? And Morty would roll over in his grave if I gave in to the current trend and made pithy observations about bourgeois life. Yet here sat my niece, waiting to be made to laugh.

"All right," I said. "Here's something that happened to this guy I know, right here in Vegas. So I figured it's apropos." I proceeded to tell the joke Morty had told the cabbie, who had told it back to me. But when I came to the part about the guy getting in the cab and driving past the other cabbies and giving them the thumbs-up sign, Meryl rolled her eyes.

"Uh," she said, "I don't mean to hurt your feelings. I can see how that joke might make an older person laugh. But, like, it's homophobic."

This time, my feelings were mildly hurt. But I could see that she had a point. I raced through my mental Rolodex of all the stories under BETTING in Morty's *Bible of Dirty Jokes*, but all I could come up with was a joke about a boy who gambles so much that his father feels compelled to teach him a lesson. He calls the boy's teacher at school and tells her that if his son offers to make a bet, she should do everything she can to make him lose. The teacher agrees, and the next day the kid waits until the other kids have left, and he goes up to her and starts sniffing. The teacher says, "Bobby, what do you think you're doing?" And Bobby says, "I bet you a buck you've got your period." Ha! the teacher thinks. I've got the rascal now! She pulls up her skirt and proves he's wrong. "Okay," Bobby says. "I guess I lose." He pays her his dollar and leaves. The teacher is so excited she calls the father and tells him his son is cured. "Cured!" he says. "Just this morning the little shit bet me twenty bucks he could get you to show him your pussy!"

I admit, the first time I heard Morty tell that joke, I laughed. But I knew what my niece would say: the real story is that a little boy fools a grown woman into showing him her vagina. "Sweetheart," I said, "I don't think you would like any of the jokes I know."

Meryl was sitting with her knees drawn up so her feet wouldn't touch the floor. With that scarf around her hair, she looked like a scrub-woman who has just finished mopping the kitchen floor and is afraid she might leave footprints on the tiles. Or maybe she was afraid the world would dirty her.

"Aunt Ketzel, I know you and Uncle Morty spent your whole lives collecting dirty jokes. I can even see where that's kind of cool. Someone had to do it. But aren't dirty jokes, I don't know, obsolete? Who's going to go to all the trouble of getting revenge on some cabby who won't give him a ride to the airport? Couldn't the guy just use his ATM? Or take the hotel shuttle? I don't get why people need to make jokes about sex anyway."

I could have provided a defense of the dirty joke as an expression of human freedom in the face of oppression by tyrannical governments, religious fanatics, and our own repressive ids. But I couldn't get past the fact that I wouldn't have wanted to tell my beautiful bright-eyed niece a single one of the sixty thousand jokes in the two volumes of the encyclopedia Morty and I had spent our lives compiling.

"What's the worst joke you've ever heard?" Meryl asked. "I mean, you're the world's expert. What's the dirtiest joke in the whole history of dirty jokes?"

I looked at her on that stool, as innocent as a Kewpie doll, and asked her why on earth she would want to hear such a thing. Serious as death, she told me. "I want to know the worst that's out there. I want to know the absolute worst joke a guy could tell when a woman isn't around to hear it."

I still had my misgivings. But I could see my niece's point, which, after all, pretty much summed up my reasons for spending my life helping my husband collect his oeuvre. "Well," I said. "This isn't the world's *dirtiest* joke. Morty had a special section for those, and just typing them made me sick. But this other joke. . . it might not be the dirtiest, but it's the saddest." Preparing to tell that joke, I felt like a guy at a carnival booth picking up a baseball and winding up to throw. "There's this circus, okay? And the midget is accused of raping the fat lady. The cops find a bucket in the room, and they assume the midget stood on the bucket to commit the rape. But when the midget's being tried, his lawyer stands him on the bucket and shows how, first of all, even with the bucket, the midget isn't tall enough to rape the fat lady, and second, even if he were tall enough, the fat lady could have kicked the bucket out from under him.

"So the defense wins, the jury acquits the midget, but the judge calls the defendant into his chambers and says, 'Look, buddy, you can't be tried twice for the same crime, you might as well come clean and tell me how you did it.' The midget shrugs and says, 'Fine, I used the bucket.' 'The bucket!' the judge says. 'Your lawyer showed how the bucket doesn't make you tall enough to reach the fat woman's privates! Besides, even if you were standing on the bucket, she could have kicked it out from under you.' 'Well,' the midget says, 'I never said I *stood* on the bucket. I put it over her head, grabbed the handle, and did a chin-up.'"

Oof. My niece took the softball in her face. "Uck. Aunt Ketzel. You're right, that's the worst thing I ever heard. It's like, nobody really cares that the fat lady got raped! Just thinking about her with that bucket over her head . . . And the midget! He's . . . I don't know, I kind of feel sorry for him. Who wants to have sex with a midget? That's why he has to rape the fat lady in the first place." I thought she was going to cry. "Why would anyone make up a joke like that?"

I put my arms around her. How could I explain that men invented jokes to make women feel lucky to be having sex with anyone, even a nasty midget, and to show that no matter how big a woman thought she was, even the smallest, weakest man could find a way to rape her. Or—just as sad—most men secretly were afraid they might be the midget.

Meryl sat quietly with her hands between her knees. I touched her cheek, which was soft as the finest peach. "Don't feel bad. Your uncle Morty spent his whole life studying the subject, and he didn't understand it any better at the end than he did at the beginning."

"But how could you tell a joke like that? If there were dirty jokes that were just . . . funny, I guess that would be all right. But they're not funny, are they? Don't you know any good jokes that aren't about sex?"

Maybe Morty had been right that studying dirty jokes was one thing, but telling them was another (although he'd had it both ways, hadn't he?). And inventing a bunch of dirty jokes that insulted men didn't seem much of an improvement. But Morty also had been correct that making funny observations about my personal life seemed small. Perhaps, in the thirty years since I last had been on a stage, humor had become impossible. And yet, if my darling niece was right and telling jokes had become obsolete, why did I still so desperately want to make my fellow human beings laugh?

Well, who had time for academic navel-gazing such as this? I thought of doing my imitation of Zero Mostel doing his imitation of a percolator, one chubby hand on his even chubbier hip, the other hand curved delicately as the spout, his head the glass button on the top, eyes rolling this way and that way as the coffee began to perk. But my niece had no idea who Zero Mostel was. Worse, she had never seen a percolator.

Still, I couldn't help but ask what, in my situation, my poor martyred Zero would have done to get a laugh. And—strange as this might seem—I was visited by Zero's ghost. *Ketzel, my dumpling, in case you haven't figured this out, the Borscht Belt is dead. Kaput! It isn't coming back! Use your head! When in Vegas, do as they do in Vegas! If there are no percolators to imitate, what else might do the trick?*

The answer didn't take long to think of. I squatted and lifted one arm in a heil-Hitlerish salute. Then I enlarged my eyes until these were the windows in which symbols might appear to spin, and I stuck out my chest until it was the shelf on which a button could be pushed to stop them. "Yeah, yeah, over here, sweetheart. You know you want me. Come on, put your butt on that little stool. Put your cup right here. Ooh, you got a lotta quarters in that cup. You musta clipped a lot of coupons for Metamucil. Come on, you old bat, stick a quarter in my slot."

"Eech," Meryl said. "Isn't there anything you could imitate that won't freak me out?"

I tried to conjure something pleasant. But it was as if I had stuck a fork in an electric socket and images of the past few days kept shooting through my mind. I saw my father sitting in a wheelchair beside a lake in which uncountable dead men floated. I saw marble phalluses and grinning satyrs. I saw two overweight bald men who looked like retired postal clerks eating lunch with their much younger Asian escorts, followed by a gauntlet of teenage boys handing out cards for hookers. I considered imitating the customers at the Schoolhouse Lounge, but that was too much of a downer even for me.

Meryl sat on her stool, unmoved. I had to do something, so I tried a bit involving the poker guy at the Mirage who thought I had been sent by Butchie, and the other players at the table, the guys from Cincinnati who had watched too many tournaments on ESPN.

"Not bad," Meryl said. "That poker-playing dude reminds me of my dad. And the dealer who looked like Cochise, I think I met him."

"Really?" I said. "You didn't hate it?"

"It wasn't funny ha-ha. It was more like funny weird. But it was so weird it was pretty funny. Who knows, maybe you'll win. Can I be in the audience? I guess not, if you're playing at a nightclub. But how do they judge? Is it one of those clap-o-meter deals? You ought to get your friend the private eye to come. He has these really huge hands. If *he* clapped, the meter would go off the chart."

Given such tepid praise, I knew I stood little chance of avoiding a long, slow death at Harrah's. At least I could keep my niece from starving. I thanked her for her suggestions, then took out the ingredients I had bought and started to prepare the crispy-skinned roast chicken Hania liked to cook, along with her cinnamon-raisin kugel and a recipe for the asparagus vinaigrette our hotel served. We ate a cozy dinner, after which Meryl excused herself so she could go upstairs and draw pictures of an earthworm's organs and read *Jane Eyre*.

With nothing to keep me occupied, I couldn't escape the chore I had been putting off. No matter where I went, a phone in each room reproached me.

My mother answered before it rang. I explained about Janis fleeing town and my moving in with Meryl, then asked if either of my parents knew an individual named Pickles Pinkowski.

"Pinkowski?" my mother said. "Of course I know Pinkowski. His father used to be the handyman for your grandpa Joe. And the son, Pickles, ran numbers for your poppa Aaron. Except, in order to work in the numbers racket, a man must be able to count. I shouldn't say this, but this is a Polack so dumb that even if he decided to shoot your brother, he wouldn't be able to figure out which end of the gun to use. This is a man who once placed a wager on a horse because it reminded him of his *chocha* Basia back in Warsaw. If your brother owes Pickles Pinkowski forty thousand dollars, it's because even an ox, if you let it paw the racing form often enough, one day might pick a winner."

Annoyed at my mother's know-it-all tone, I described Ebby's search of Potsie's house for clues, the fake blood on the stairs, and our theory that my brother had staged his own abduction. I assumed she would admit this was the only possible conclusion to which the evidence seemed to point and reward me with a flood of grateful tears. *Oh, Ketzel! Do you mean he isn't really dead? I'm so sorry your father and I underestimated your powers to get things done! How can we ever thank you for giving us back our child!* But she couldn't accept that her youngest son would have staged such a wacky scheme, if only because Potsie knew faking his death would have killed her. I reminded her that she had winked at his wacky schemes for so long she had no business to deplore them now. For that matter, our family seemed to suffer a hereditary trait that caused us to shut our eyes to any immoral goings-on.

"I'm surprised at you," my mother said. "You used to be such a compassionate, loving person. What's gotten into you since Morty died?"

"What's gotten into me?" I repeated. "What's gotten into me since Morty died? Here's what's gotten into me. What's gotten into me is a little truth!"

7.

THE NEXT MORNING, after Meryl went to school, I practiced my routine in front of the greyhounds, who lay at my feet like five underweight sphinxes. They seemed the perfect stand-in for a bored and jaded audience of Las Vegas retirees. *You call that work? Now, chasing a rabbit around a track and never getting to catch and eat it, that's work. Standing on a stage and telling a joke? Sorry, sweetheart, you'll have to sweat harder than that to get a laugh from us.*

When Meryl came home, I performed the new—and, I hoped, improved—eleven-minute monologue. She clapped. She made suggestions. Then we noticed the time and hurried upstairs to dress, which in my niece's case consisted of putting on a baggy shirt with a picture of a blonde celebrity I didn't recognize circled in red and crossed out with a slash, and in my case meant succumbing to the temptation to explore my sister-in-law's closet for something more festive to wear than yet another Camp Hospitality T-shirt. As much as Ebby loved those shirts, nostalgia has its limits as an aphrodisiac. I settled on my sister-in-law's most modest dress, feminine but not too frilly, revealing but not obscene. I walked down the stairs to show my niece, but Meryl screwed up her face.

"I don't mean to hurt your feelings, but, like, you're starting to look like everyone else in Vegas."

As much as I love my niece, there are times the objections of anyone under twenty don't seem relevant to one's own assessment of what to wear. Besides, we were running late. We went out and I threw myself in the Hummer—a difficult thing to do in a short, tight dress—and followed the directions to Ebby's house. At one point, we saw another Hummer coming, and I was seized by the sensation that we were two tanks on a collision course to test whose army would win the war.

"Aunt Ketzel! Watch out!" Meryl snatched the wheel and jerked us back in the proper lane, after which we continued without further incident, which was safer for my niece but less fun for me. We pulled up at Ebby's house, which seemed smaller than the Hummer; it reminded me of the boxes Ebby and I used to fashion from Popsicle sticks at camp.

I took the basket of fruit, and we walked up and rang the bell. Ebby let us in, wearing shorts and a Hawaiian shirt.

"Don't you two ladies look beautiful?" he said, staring at me and not my niece.

He showed us around the house, the furnishings of which—the dusty tweed sofa, the cracked armchair, the coffee table with Olympic-circle beer stains—might have been classified as Early American Divorced Male. The walls were devoid of paintings, a detail I found confusing, given that the owner considered himself an artist.

Nate turned out to be even more boyishly attractive in three dimensions than he had been in two. He wore a red bandana around his head, and since Meryl had worn exactly the same bandana around her head, they seemed to be members of the same rebellious tribe. Except that the next time I saw my niece, she had slipped off her scarf and stuffed it in her pocket. I gasped when I saw her hair, so shiny, thick, and blonde I could see why she hid it from men whose attentions she didn't want to encourage.

Nate set out the silverware, and my heart expanded with the beauty of a teenage boy arranging a fork just so, folding a napkin, tonging ice cubes into a glass, pouring water from a yard-sale jug. The three of us sat awkwardly on mismatched chairs while Ebby went in the kitchen and brought out a cheese-and-broccoli casserole straight from the *Moosewood Cookbook*. He served a loaf of homemade whole-wheat bread and a salad bursting with so many vegetables its presence in the desert seemed a miracle. Not to mention I had never eaten a meal a man had cooked, although once, when I was rendered helpless by the flu, Morty had run down to a pushcart and brought me back a potato knish and ginger ale.

After Meryl and I had exclaimed at the deliciousness of this and that, we lapsed into silence until Ebby broke the ice by telling stories of our old hotel, which I could guess by Nate's forbearance he had heard a thousand times—how Ebby had assumed that his father's job was to tend a fire-breathing monster, how Ebby once had seen a bum peeing against a tree on the fourteenth hole and run to find his dad, only to be informed that the bum was my grandpa Joe. Ebby told funny stories about carrying golf bags for Bob Hope and Jackie Robinson, although I noticed he failed to mention the many female guests who had vied to have him for their caddy, a circumstance I knew to be the case from all the times I heard attractive young wives bragging about how they had contrived to steal a kiss or otherwise rub up against the handsome teenage boy who held their clubs. (*Eberhard?* I remember thinking. *What is it about that name that makes them smirk?*)

Meryl's uncharacteristic silence and her inability to look in Nate's direction prompted me to ask about his experience as an archaeologist. He finished chewing his home-baked bread, washed it down with milk, and launched into an eloquent if overly detailed monologue about the caves through which he had crawled and the artifacts he had unearthed as part of this program he was in at school. "It just seems totally cool there used to be this completely different civilization on the same spot of desert we're living on now. It's like those parallel universes you read about. They were human beings just like us, so we would probably understand a lot about their lives. But they also were completely different."

He took a bite of casserole, which was so gooey and dense it could have been used to build the pyramids. "I shouldn't bring this up at dinner, but there's this one cave . . . nobody ever lived there. They just used it to store tools and food. And there was this latrine in the cave? For the longest time, archaeologists couldn't figure out why it was up there. Who would climb all that way up a mountain and crawl through a dangerous tunnel to take a dump? But in the desert, human feces don't just disappear. They turn into rock. The fancy name is a coprolite. But all that means is petrified human shit.

"So the archaeologists found all these coprolites in the cave. And it turns out there are these cactus seeds in the coprolites. There's this cactus that people ate? And the cactus seeds, they just passed right through their digestive systems without being, well, digested. So the seeds just sat there in the cave. And if things got really bad, if there was no rain for a really long time and the people were really starving, they could go back up to the cave and collect the seeds and grind them up and eat them."

Meryl sat glowing at Nate as if he had just described a method to turn human feces into gold. I could tell she wanted to see with her own eyes those life-sustaining coprolites, so I asked the question for her.

"Sure!" Nate said. The site he was working now, the one on the Vegas Wash, wasn't nearly as cool as the site where the archaeologists had found those seeds, but there were these really neat Clovis points, and they had found the remains of a woolly mammoth, and there were these totally neat artifacts from the mid 1800s, when a bunch of Mormons tried to start a settlement in the desert. The professor who ran the dig was always looking for extra hands. Meryl could come out that weekend. If she didn't mind getting hot and dirty and squatting in the sun for hours, she could sign on as a volunteer.

"Cool!" Meryl said. "I mean, if that's all right with you, Aunt

Ketzel."

"Why shouldn't it be all right?" I said. "I'm interested in archaeology, too."

"Really?" Ebby said. I was hoping he would say we should go along on the outing, but he went back in the kitchen and after a strangely long time returned with the pineapple, which he had peeled and cored and sliced in thin, neat slices and arranged around a plate so the dish resembled an astronomical representation of a solar eclipse.

"What do you do when you're not at school?" Ebby asked my niece.

Meryl didn't seem to know. Three or four minutes passed. And even though I was aware that the only thing more humiliating than being unable to speak for yourself was to have your aunt speak for you, I took it upon myself to say that Meryl and her stepmother had rescued a pack of greyhounds from a track near Phoenix, and Meryl devoted herself to caring for the dogs. "You would expect greyhounds to want to run around all the time," I said. "But all they do is eat and sleep and try to get you to pet them."

"Sounds like you, Dad," Nate teased his father. And then, when Ebby blushed, Nate said, "No, seriously, greyhounds are totally beautiful when they run. For their own pleasure, I mean. I was reading Martin Buber. You know, the I-and-Thou guy? And I was, like, yeah! That's the whole deal! You've got to treat an animal as a Thou and not an It. If you race a greyhound to make money, you're using it as a means to an end. And if you get a pet because you need this big ego-boost—my pet thinks I'm so great, I really must *be* great—or if you need a watchdog, or whatever, then you're using another living creature as an It. But if you get a dog because you love him, and you have this real relationship with your dog, the way you probably have a relationship with your greyhounds, that's completely cool."

Meryl didn't say a word, but her eyes were shining as if the Lord God Jehovah were addressing her as a Thou.

Nate pushed back his chair. "Want to see the iguanas with whom I have a very close and personal I-and-Thou relationship?" He said this with a smile to indicate he was poking fun at his own pontification.

"Sure!" Meryl got up and followed him to his room.

This left Ebby and me alone. The last two slices of pineapple lay on the plate between us. Ebby took the first. I took the second. I sucked the sticky sweetness from my thumb.

"Want to see *my* iguanas?" Ebby said.

"You have iguanas?"

"No," he said. "But it's nice to know if I did, you would want to see them." He sat staring at the dirty dishes as if he had planned the evening this far and no farther. "I have something else I could show you."

I had a hunch what that something was. "If you're sure."

He got heavily to his feet like a murderer who knows he has to make that last stroll to the gallows, although he was granted a brief reprieve when we passed his son's room and I was summoned inside to meet Barney and Fred, the first of whom my niece was cuddling against her chest and the other of whom was curled on her shoulder. I couldn't tell the two apart, whether because all iguanas look alike or because Barney and Fred, as a practical joke, liked to change their colors to appear identical. The iguana on Meryl's neck seemed to be whispering opinions about the rest of us.

"Ack!" Meryl said. The iguana hissed. I reached out to protect her— for my niece's sake, I would have done battle with a *Tyrannosaurus rex*—but Nate had scooped his pet from Meryl's shoulder.

"Did it bite you?" I asked, wondering if we needed to rush her to the hospital to get a shot.

"Uh, no," Meryl said. "He just, like, frenched my ear."

Nate cradled both iguanas as if he were nursing twins. To show she bore them no ill will, Meryl stroked Barney's head—unless she was stroking Fred. It closed its eyes and offered its throat to be petted. "They're just so incredibly sweet," she cooed.

"Actually, they're not," Nate said. "Disney makes us think every animal in the world is a cute wise-cracking sidekick, when the reality is they're wild creatures. People buy baby iguanas and don't have the faintest clue how big the iguanas grow up to be. Or what they need to eat. Or how many hours a day they have to get UV light. Or calcium! People don't make sure their iguanas get enough calcium in their diet, so the iguanas fall off their branches and break their bones. That is, if people put in branches in the first place. No one would buy an iguana if the pet-store owners were honest enough to admit how much it costs to provide a proper habitat, or how much space a proper habitat takes up."

Which was true. Two-thirds of Nate's bedroom was taken up by the glassed-in enclosure for his pets. From the way Nate's bed and desk were squeezed against the wall, it seemed the iguanas were keeping him.

"Hey." Meryl pointed to a poster that showed a system of classification for Anasazi pots. "My mom used to send me pots like those. She made them herself. And she was, like, crazy. So the pots were all like this." She threw her body out of whack and hung out her tongue. "She had this boyfriend, Jurgen?" She pronounced it more like *Jerk-gun.* "He thought he was some Anasazi god come back to life." She tried to tell the story of her mother's desertion as a joke, but no one laughed.

"That sucks," Nate said. "It's one thing to not know what you're getting into with an iguana. But a kid? How do you just say, 'Sorry, this turned out to be more work than I thought it would be' and leave your kid?" He opened the door to the iguanas' habitat and, despite their attempt to cling to his shirt, peeled them off and shut the cage. "I swear, the only time my mom noticed I was alive was when she needed someone to zip up her dress. And my little sister . . . you want to see some-thing sick, just watch my mom getting my sister ready for a pageant. Dad says we need to wait and go through the courts. But if it was up to me, we'd stage a commando attack and steal her. The kid is so screwed up, she thinks she likes being in those pageants. She thinks it's fine for my mother to turn her into, I don't know, her prize poodle."

We left the two young people sitting on the bed, comparing their mothers' sins, and walked down the hall to what once had been a green-house but now held an easel and a pile of paint-stained rags. Even at that late hour, the room was awash in light.

"What a nice studio," I said. "It certainly is sunny."

"Yeah," Ebby said, "and hot. Sometimes I'm afraid those rags are going to spontaneously combust."

I walked over to a stack of canvases and began to flip through them. The paintings nearest the wall, which must have been the oldest, showed naked women splayed on beds, although they seemed less reminiscent of Parisian odalisques than brassy Vegas hookers. I thought it best not to comment on this period of Ebby's work. Nor did I see the need to offer my opinion on the violent expressionist blobs I flipped through next, angry, dark messes with a severed buttock here, a bared breast or penis there.

But the paintings after that . . . Who could have imagined the furi-ously blushing private detective in the Hawaiian shirt beside me could have created such art as this? The canvases were colorful and a bit car-toonish, in a primitive bawdy style. It was as if Grandma Moses had lived in a motel off the Strip and spent her time painting the gamblers, strippers, cops, hustlers, pimps, and whores she saw.

I was even more impressed by the next section of Ebby's work. "Oh, Ebby, these are sort of Georgia O'Keeffe meets Salvador Dalí." I held up a canvas that showed a cactus whose magenta blooms strained toward the viewer like the beaks and throats of baby birds. Every painting showed an object—a lizard, a snake, a weed—so intensely seen and felt it seemed to bring a message from the Great Beyond. The viewer felt tempted to reach in and pick it up. *Hello? Is anyone out there? Hello?*

Ebby shuffled his feet and coughed. "I know realism is dead. But I'm out there in the desert, and I feel like, if I can look at even one thing . . . Really look at it. Peel away the layers and see it the way the first human beings saw it . . ."

"Ebby, I'm sure any art school in the country would be thrilled to accept you. Except, do you really need to go? Maybe they'll just ruin you." I stopped myself, hearing the echo of Morty's advice to me. *What do you need with college? The professors will only teach you how to think like everyone else.* What if Morty had discouraged me from attending college because he never had the chance to attend himself? What if he was afraid I would win the academic accolades he pretended not to want? What if I didn't want Ebby to pursue his dream because I hadn't followed mine?

"Thanks for the vote of confidence. But you have no idea how much I need to learn."

He was standing very close. I was starting to wonder why when he leaned down and kissed me. It took me so long to understand what he was doing that by the time I had decided to kiss him back, he had given up and returned to his normal height. Let's just say that if that kiss had been a football, I would have fumbled the handoff.

"Um," Ebby said, in the manner of a man who has done something that needs explaining. "A person shouldn't start something he can't finish. But seeing as I did, I guess it's fair I warn you."

Warn me?

It wasn't that he wasn't attracted to me, he said. It was just, after all he'd been through as a cop . . . And the divorce. And all the women he had been with, before and after Nikki. He wasn't sure he knew how to be . . . that way with a woman. With a *normal* woman. A woman who wasn't, you know.

No, I said, I didn't know. I had no idea what he meant.

"It's just, those women in the motel rooms . . . And all the strippers. And all the porn. It's hard for such a man to separate the personal from the professional. I see a woman without her clothes and something goes screwy in my head. I wouldn't want to treat someone like you like the women we saw at your cousin's bar."

I needed time to connect the dots. "What we saw at my cousin's bar could put off anyone from having sex. Don't you just need to get away from Vegas?"

He shrugged. "Everywhere is Vegas these days. And with Nate here, and Saffron . . . My therapist says I'm not going to learn new ways to relate to women overnight. It's going to be a very long and drawn-out process. And I wouldn't want to subject a nice girl like you to being my guinea pig in the meantime."

I had to agree that a man who had been through a divorce as recently as Ebby, even if he hadn't seen three women tied to their beds and beaten and starved to death, could hardly be expected to start a new relationship. After learning my husband of twenty-nine years had been visiting prostitutes without my knowledge, I wasn't that eager to start a new relationship myself.

As you might imagine, this line of conversation left us feeling so ill at ease we went back and found the kids, who seemed to be in the same state of discomfort as we were. Which only goes to show that knowing what to do in the company of someone you like is no easier in one's fifties than in one's teens.

"Hey there!" Ebby said.

"Hey!" his son echoed.

The iguanas blinked down from their tree.

"So!" I said. "Meryl! We need to go!" Although it was only nine o'clock and I couldn't think of a single thing to do at home.

To my surprise, my niece hopped off the bed and said, "Yeah! Well! Thanks! Good night!," as if she were eager to escape the company of this boy she liked so she could talk about how much she liked him.

Which, it turned out, she did. As I maneuvered the Hummer home, and later, as we sat on my brother's couch and shared a pint of Ben & Jerry's Heath Bar Crunch, I heard about Nate and his iguanas, Nate and the hidden cave, Nate and the Vegas Wash. Did I know Nate had studied Sanskrit? Did I know Ebby had tried to homeschool Nate, only to find out he didn't know enough to keep up with his own son, after which Nate's dad found this really neat school for Nate where the kids didn't only care about getting laid? Did I think Meryl might apply to that school? Did I know Nate's father had found a bunch of prostitutes who had been murdered in this really gruesome way and he had beaten the guy to death and that's why he had quit his job? Did I notice the way he stared at me all the time? Didn't I think he looked a whole lot better wearing shorts and a Hawaiian shirt than those stupid Dockers and rip-off Ralph Laurens? Did I know Nate said his dad wore those dorky getups because if a criminal saw a really big dude following him down an alley he might think the guy was an undercover cop, but if the guy was wearing such dorky clothes, the criminal would assume he was some kind of tourist and not give him a second thought?

On and on she went, until I fell asleep right there on the couch, and when I woke the next morning, there she was, still talking about Nate. If any of you has ever lived with a lovesick child, you know how hard it is not to get caught up in her elation, even if you are afraid the bubble of euphoria might someday burst. But the days that followed Ebby's dinner were among the happiest of my life. My husband was dead and my brother missing, but I had my niece to shop and cook for and my new comedy routine to perfect. Meryl came home from school and we walked the dogs as she told me about her day, then she talked on the phone to Nate. After we had shared our dinner, she sprawled on her father's couch and read the books Nate had given her about the earliest inhabitants of Nevada.

"Aunt Ketzel, did you know human beings only used to live until they were, like, forty? If I lived back then, I would be, like, halfway through my life! And they built these cities and roads . . . And the cities and roads are still there! We could just go wandering around the desert and find a city the Anasazi built. I knew there were ruins in Egypt. But in America? These totally priceless artifacts are just lying around on the ground, and people come and steal them. The Anasazi built these cities, they got married and had kids and sat around gossiping and making baskets, and they didn't have a clue that in another thousand years this crazy city called Las Vegas would be sitting on the exact same spot. And *we* have no idea what kinds of crazy things are going to happen *here* in a thousand years."

She took a sip from a bottle of vitamin-enriched water that had set me back two bucks. "Not that their civilization was so much better than the one we have now. They didn't even have, like, aspirin. And the women had to do whatever the men told them to do. The women just ground the maize and popped out one kid after the next and carried them around strapped to these little boards. But a person knew what she was supposed to do. It was all about finding enough water to drink and food to eat and taking care of your kids. You didn't think that if you hadn't made a zillion dollars and married Brad Pitt by the time you were twenty, you were, like, a total loser."

I knew what she meant. But right then, I wouldn't have wanted to exist in any time or place but the here and now with her.

8.

UNFORTUNATELY, MERE MORTALS like us rarely are allowed more than a week of happiness before the gods grow jealous of our contentment—or maybe what they grow is bored—and send troubles to disrupt our lives. One afternoon, I took the greyhounds for a walk—I felt like Santa guiding his sled, except, instead of a sack of toys, I carried a plastic bag in which to scoop the reindeer's dreck. I had the impression my neighbors were spying from behind their blinds and if I so much as left a fecal smear on their pristine lawns, they would shoot the dogs and then shoot me. But the only neighbor I ever saw was the Robert De Niro look-alike, who spent his days watering his lawn, except when he was transporting packages in and out of his garage. A car would drive up, and the driver would get out and disappear into my neighbor's house, only to reappear carrying a box, unless he carried a box *into* the house, after which he came out patting the pocket where his wallet must have been. I guessed my neighbor was dealing drugs. Unless he was dealing weapons. But I had enough troubles without calling the FBI.

Then the postman left a package in our mailbox that was addressed to the house next door. The box seemed surprisingly heavy, given that it barely was large enough to fit the recipient's name across the front. Which name, I might add, was Innocenzio Incognito. *Innocenzio Incognito?*

Still, the neighborly thing to do was to take the package to its owner, and, after a day or two of hesitation, I walked over and set the package on the stoop. The door opened, and Mr. Incognito discovered me with my head at a level with his crotch.

"Hello," I said.

"Hey, thanks," my neighbor said. "I've been wondering what happened to that particular item. I called the seller and gave him shit. But he said he tracked it and it got delivered."

"Sorry," I said, "I've been—"

"Hey. Not your problem." He took the box and weighed it in his palm, then flexed his hairy wrist as if he intended to pitch it down the block. "Want to see the rest of my collection? Not really supposed to run a business from the house, but I doubt you'll be ratting me out to the zoning commission."

Oh no, I said, I certainly wasn't one to rat anyone out to the zoning commission.

"Good. Didn't think you would. It's just, in my line of work, a person needs to take precautions." He stepped back inside the house, where he must have hit a button because the garage door squealed up. When he stepped back on the stoop, he recoiled from the blinding sun. "Sensitive," he explained, lifting to his eyes the dark glasses that had been dangling against his chest. "I moved here to get away from the fucking Michigan winters, and damned if I don't get headaches from the sun."

The garage door finished complaining on its tracks, and I saw that, like my brother's garage, Mr. Incognito's was filled with merchandise. From the shelf nearest the door, he pulled down a cardboard sheath from which he withdrew a poster-size advertisement for the original version of *Ocean's Eleven*. "I would be pleased if you would accept this as a token of gratitude."

"Oh no," I said. "A poster like that must be very expensive."

"Nah," he said. "Nine ninety-five plus shipping. Now this one—" He pulled down a photo that showed Sammy Davis Jr., Frank Sinatra, Dean Martin, and Peter Lawford shooting pool, and a photo of the four aforementioned celebrities—plus poor tag-along Joey Bishop—standing in front of the Sands with their names on the marquee behind them. "The matched set goes for . . . let's say we're talking five figures."

I whistled to be polite . . . and because I was amazed that anyone would pay anything for a photo of these five men. "These aren't all posters?" I said, indicating the rest of the merchandise.

He rocked back on his heels and smiled. "You bet your sweet bippy they're not. You've got your vintage vinyl, your signed headshots, your pins and pens and schlock like that." He moved to another row. "Face it, the posters are crap. Anyone on the Internet has posters. But this other shit . . ." He pulled down a plastic box the size and shape of the container in which my grandma Marcia used to keep her false teeth, then flicked it open just long enough to allow me to catch a glimpse of what resembled a turd one of the greyhounds might have left on his lawn. "Know what this is?"

I shook my head.

"Butt end of the cigar John Fucking Fitzgerald Kennedy left in the ashtray the night he showed up at the Sands, watched his pals perform, then went back to his room and boffed Marilyn." He dragged his sunglasses down his nose. "And this . . ." He showed me an envelope, inside of which was a Ziploc bag, inside of which—so my neighbor claimed—was a condom found by a chambermaid in the wastebasket of the penthouse suite that had been occupied by Frank Sinatra. "The genuine spunk of the Chairman of the Board. Theoretically, some dame could clone the DNA and use it to get herself knocked up. Kinda makes you stop and think."

Oh! I said. Yes! I had no doubt I would be thinking about that condom for the rest of my life.

After showing me a lipstick-stained pillowcase that had been slept on by Shirley MacLaine, and a towel that had been used to dry the nether regions of Sam Giancana's moll, who also had slept with JFK, my neighbor produced a box that held a jar—he unscrewed the lid—that held something round and white with two concentric circles on the front.

I screamed and backed away.

"Take it easy. It isn't real."

I laughed nervously and tried to simulate admiration. "You've got Sammy Davis Jr.'s glass eye? How can you be sure it's his?" I peered in at the eye, which was peering back at me.

A frown clouded my neighbor's face. "I wouldn't be in this business if I couldn't guarantee the provenance of what I sell. You want papers, I got papers. These days, with the Internet, you get caught once selling something that isn't one hundred percent absolutely bona fide," he pronounced this *bona fi-day,* "you're ruined from here to Tokyo."

I tried to apologize, but apparently I had tapped a sore spot.

"A lot of guys, they don't give a royal fuck if they can authenticate. That's why I stay away from Elvis. You wouldn't believe what some people . . . If Elvis had actually wiped his sweat with every handkerchief . . . Jesus Fucking Christ. Let's just say the guy would have needed to get up in the morning and wipe himself with hankies all day. Besides, you start dealing in the King, it takes over your entire stock. Sort of like crabgrass. And I don't do the Mob. That, to my way of thinking, is not in good taste. I cannot, in good conscience, perpetuate the stereotype that Las Vegas was dreamed up by Italians. Benjamin Siegel is not an Italian name. Am I right? Don't get me started on all the idiots who think Italians are responsible for every piece of evil that ever went down in Vegas."

Rather than discuss the relative contributions made by Italians and Jews to the festering corruption that is Las Vegas, I asked Mr. Incognito what was in the box that had been delivered to my house.

"This?" He picked it up and shook it. "How about we make a friendly wager. You guess what's inside and you get your pick of any of the items I just showed you. The eye, the cigar, the condom. But if you can't guess—" He held out his arms, as if guessing incorrectly meant I would have to surrender myself to their hairy embrace. "What happens is, you let me in your brother's house long enough that I am able to retrieve certain items of a compromising nature that, if an investigation into your brother's whereabouts were to materialize, might result in embarrassment for all concerned."

I might not have inherited my family's talents for winning bets, but even I could figure out that if Mr. Incognito was willing to risk Frank Sinatra's sperm for a chance to retrieve whatever incriminating items he might have left in my sister-in-law's safekeeping, this was a bet I hadn't a chance to win. As Sky Masterson told Nathan Detroit, if a guy shows you a brand-new deck on which the seal has not yet been broken, and he bets he can make the jack of spades jump out and spit cider in your ear, do not take that bet, because you are certainly going to come away with an earful of cider.

I held up my hand. "I appreciate your showing me your collection. But I need to be getting home to let out the dogs."

"Ah, don't be a spoilsport. I'll give you a hint. It's a kind of a pineapple."

From the sardonic way he said this, I knew the pineapple in question had little to do with the fruit I had brought Ebby as a gift. It crossed my mind that "pineapple" might be a euphemism for the genitals of a member of the Rat Pack. But I remembered how heavy the box had been and how it rattled when I shook it.

"A hand grenade?"

He pointed a finger and squeezed the trigger. "Bingo bango! See? You're already halfway home. But to win the prize, you need to specify to whom the grenade belonged."

At that point, the jack of spades was taking a gulp of cider as a prelude to spitting it in my ear. But in my other ear, I heard Morty whisper something to the effect that JFK had given the grenade to Frank Sinatra in the hopes that Sinatra would get close enough to his pal Fidel

Castro to stick it up his ass and pull the pin. I never would have uttered such a crude remark if Morty hadn't incited me to say it.

I could see my neighbor run the comment through his mind. "Hey. Good one. My pop always said, 'Innocenzio, be careful of the shy-looking ladies, because they're the ones who'll fool you.' Just for fun, I'll give you another hint. The item in this box is numero uno in what I like to refer to as my History Channel catalog."

"History Channel?"

He nudged me. "You know. History? Starts with *H*? As in, history of World War II?"

I must have looked blank.

"Hitler!" he said. "Adolf Fucking Hitler!" He shook the box the way a lawyer might indicate a piece of evidence to the jury. "This is the actual grenade with which the German High Command planned to frag *der Führer*. Unfortunately for the Allies, the grenade failed to detonate and the guy who planned the deal ended up in front of a firing squad. Fortunately for us, the grenade survived in a German vault, the English liberated it, and long story short, a guy I know managed to locate it and pass it on to me, so I, in turn, can pass it to a buyer who has a very keen interest in acquiring it. Trouble is, you send an item of this nature by special means, it attracts unwanted scrutiny. So you gotta pretend it's nothing, send it by parcel post, list it as something else. Most times, it comes through customs fine. But you can understand why, when it didn't appear on the day it was scheduled to appear . . ." He gestured to a vault as big as a meat locker in the back of the garage. "Happy to give you a tour. Once-in-a-lifetime opportunity. You did, after all, keep this precious little pineapple from going astray."

As tempting as it was to see the rest of the memorabilia from that fun-loving German Rat Pack, I passed on the opportunity. "Maybe another time. Dogs being dogs, you don't want to keep them waiting."

"Sure, sure. Some folks just aren't that into Hitler. Personally, I prefer Dino and Frank. Different strokes for different folks, right? Some people enjoy a nice mellow sip of Lambrusco. Other people prefer a needle of heroin in the vein." He grinned slyly. "And you? You're more the lemonade type, am I right? Listen, I don't mean to get nosy, but that sister-in-law of yours . . . What, she got tired of waiting for the big payoff and she cut out with whatever she could get her hands on? Or she and the big guy kissed and made up and she got him to take her on a second honeymoon to Bermuda?"

Maybe it was the lemonade remark, but I was tired of beating around the bush. "As a matter of fact, we don't know where either of them went. Personally, I think my sister-in-law might have had my brother whacked. Any theories? You seem to have known her more *intimately* than I did."

I thought this line of inquiry might upset him. But he smiled as broadly as if I had offered him a photo of the Chairman of the Board making love to JFK.

"What is this with everybody now? 'Whacked' this, 'whacked' that. As it happens, I do not think Little Miss Sunshine over there had it in her to have her hubby done away with. Marry the ugly mug for money? Check. Cheat on said hubby? Check. But hire a hit man to bump him off? More likely the other way around. Your sister-in-law might have been a cunt. But—you'll excuse me for saying this—your brother was an even bigger cunt."

With that, I took my leave, trying not to think what it meant that a man like Innocenzio Incognito thought my brother was a cunt. I hoped this was only a reflection of my brother's failed attempt to hide his pique that his neighbor was screwing his wife. Not to mention it might be a sign in a person's favor to be disparaged by a man who earned his living selling hairs from Hitler's mustache and monogrammed sets of

Hermann Göring's briefs.

As happens when one unsettling event sends out ripples of disturbance and upsets a second boat, the next afternoon I took the greyhounds to a nearby park so I wouldn't run the risk of walking them past Mr. Incognito's house, and what vehicle should I see but the Vantastic Ventures van. Not only might my cousin be back in town, the notion that his crew might be filming *Vantastic Adventures III* at a playground or public pool made me frantic to alert the cops. Even in Las Vegas there had to be a statute that forbade filming porn at a children's park.

I left the greyhounds in the Hummer, hoping that in the five minutes it took to find a phone, the dogs wouldn't suffocate from the heat. Just as I reached the restrooms, a girl of nine or ten came skipping out the door. She had an appealingly wide-cheeked face, a sleek brown pageboy cut, and the impishly androgynous look of a 1920s newsboy. I couldn't help but watch as she bent her fragile neck to sip water from a fountain. Then she waited for her mother, who backed out of the restroom with an armful of wadded towels, brushes, shampoos, laundry detergent, and what appeared to be clean wet clothes. Even in canvas pants and a man's white shirt, the woman seemed too pretty to be backing out of a public restroom with an armful of cleaning supplies. She motioned for her daughter to press the button on the fountain so she could get a drink, but her hair kept dangling across her face.

I had seen her before, but where? She gave up trying to get a drink and started walking toward the van, her movements so languid she seemed to be swimming through the shimmering waves of heat.

"Miranda?"

She looked up with an expression that seemed to say if anyone asked her to carry one more thing, she would cry.

"I'm Potsie Weinrach's sister." I hurried to open the back door of the van so she could dump in her burden. "I met you the other night? At the Schoolhouse Lounge? I was there with Ebby Salzman."

She put her hands to her lower back, a motion any waitress can recognize as a symptom of carrying too many trays. Her daughter came shuffling across the hot tar in a pair of transparent sandals so cheap they appeared in danger of melting. I was so focused on her feet it took me a while to realize the child's arm was wrapped in bright pink plaster.

"Mom?" she said. "I'm all sweaty again. Can I go run my head under the cold water one more time?"

Wearily, Miranda smoothed the child's hair. "Sure, honey, just be careful about the cast."

The girl turned and skated back. Her mother's gaze followed her across the lot, and then, after Kalindi had disappeared inside, remained fixed on the restroom door. Not knowing what else to say, I asked Miranda if she or Chickie had ever found that bearskin rug.

"What? Yeah. I mean, no. We figure Perry must have taken it. For this project he's doing? This film he's helping direct in Mexico?"

I did know. Ebby had heard the news from Chickie, who had received a postcard from his boss dated the week before, from Tijuana. Apparently, Perry had driven down to Mexico to finish filming a high-class erotic flick that had gone seriously over budget, its director having fallen ill from some parasite he had picked up eating food no one in his right mind would have touched.

After Ebby found out about the postcard, he had hurried to Mexico to look around. But he hadn't found anyone in Tijuana who resembled Perry or my brother. Nor was anyone from America filming any films. Like some Abbott-and-Costello version of Butch and Sundance, Perry and Potsie must have passed through Tijuana on their way to parts unknown, and we would need to wait and see where the next crime was committed by two suspicious-looking hombres fitting their rough descriptions. In the meantime, Miranda and Chickie were running the Schoolhouse Lounge. They couldn't keep it up forever, but for now, they were getting by.

Still, something must be wrong if Miranda and Kalindi were doing their wash in a public park. "I don't mean to pry," I said, "but are you living in the van again?"

She lifted her shoulders and let them fall. The dogs in the Hummer pawed at the glass. Miranda looked at them vaguely, as if she were supposed to be taking care of them, too. "It's just that Kalindi needed all this dental work. And some kid who didn't take his Ritalin pushed her off a swing and she broke her arm. If Perry was here, he would give me an advance. I could ask Chickie. But Chickie can be . . . You know how some people think if they do you a favor, you have to do a favor back? Which means it wasn't a favor to begin with."

Kalindi reappeared, her hair damp, her pink shirt flattened against her chest. "Mom, it's all sweaty inside the cast. It's just so *hot* in there. And it *itches*."

From another child, this might have come out a whine. But Kalindi seemed too tired and hot to whine.

Miranda laid her lips to her daughter's head. "Just a sec, okay? We'll drive around and cool off. Then we can go to the mall. We'll find one of those restrooms that have those blowers. You can blow air inside the cast and dry it out."

She glanced at me to see if I had anything more to say. I wanted to tell her to bring Kalindi to live in my brother's house with Meryl and me. But Miranda worked at a topless bar. She kept the books for my cousin Perry.

I pulled out my father's cash, but she motioned the bills away.

"Please," I said. "When you're on your feet again . . . when Perry comes back . . ."

She looked to see if Kalindi was watching, but Kalindi was using her toe to pop bubbles in the tar. Miranda touched my wrist. She whispered *thanks* and took the cash.

As anyone who has studied folklore knows, bad things come in threes. That same night, I was practicing my routine in the den when I heard Meryl let out the dogs. The greyhounds were getting on in years, but they took delight in racing each other around the fenced-in back yard. They ran so fast their paws kicked up clots of grass and they melded together into one many-legged blur. Occasionally, some two- or four-legged creature would make the mistake of settling on the fence to watch, and Donner or Vixen would launch himself in the air, surprising the startled crow or quail, who hadn't thought dogs could fly. The greyhounds' antics would have been pleasing to watch no matter what, but if a person knew their history, watching them play was like seeing five middle-aged black men who had come up the hard way kick back and relax and enjoy a friendly game of hoops.

I heard a tinny *pop-pop*, after which I heard the worst sound a person can possibly hear, by which I mean someone you love screaming your name and sobbing: "God! Oh God! Aunt Ketzel! Please, no!"

Needless to say, I didn't finish my performance. I ran out and found my niece kneeling with her arms protecting Donner. The other greyhounds clustered nervously like bystanders to whom a cop or EMT would need to shout, *Please, folks, give the victim room to breathe!*

"Meryl!" I screamed, and then, of all things, I shook her. "Meryl, honey, are you hurt?"

She was too upset to answer. But I could guess the blood staining her arms must be Donner's. Poor petite and loving Donner had taken a bullet to his head—think of a bottle of Coca-Cola shot through its widest part—while a second bullet had grazed his chest, revealing a cage of bones so delicate it might have belonged to a fish.

"Meryl, sweetheart, we need to get back inside." I pulled her by her arm, but she refused to go. "What about the other dogs?" I said. "Do you want them to get hurt, too? They won't go in if we're out here."

But she was sobbing and clutching Donner, and I knew I would never be able to persuade her to leave his side. I hated to think how dependent I had become on Ebby. But even a woman who is determined to prove she can get along without a man sometimes finds she can't—and vice versa. Ebby didn't take long to get there, but every second seemed an hour. I knelt by my niece, scanning the wall for an assassin's eyes or the barrel of a gun, while the dogs hovered around us like Secret Service agents who have failed to protect the president and now can only hope to protect whoever is protecting his fallen corpse.

Finally, the bell rang, and I ran to let Ebby in.

"What is it?" he said. "Are you okay?"

Nate pushed past us both. "Where's Meryl? What's going on?"

The three of us ran through the house and found Meryl in the back yard.

"Meryl!" My niece looked up. But even for the boy she loved, she wouldn't take her arms from around her dog.

Ebby ordered Nate to get a blanket from the truck. Then Ebby paced around the yard, looking at the ground. He stooped and found what turned out to be the casings from the two bullets that had killed the dog and another ten or twelve from bullets that must have missed.

"Not exactly Lee Harvey Oswald," Ebby said. "Talk about trying to hit fish in a barrel. It was totally by accident the guy hit anything."

Nate came back with a tattered white bedspread, which Ebby wrapped around the dog. He lifted Donner in his arms—by this point, the dog was stiff as a table—and carried him inside. I locked the door and followed Ebby to the kitchen, where he laid the dog on the floor.

Blood was seeping through the sheet, and it occurred to me how much it did resemble cherry juice.

I put my arms around my niece, but she pushed me off. I thought she was angry because I had allowed someone to shoot her pet. But she staggered to the sink and retched. She was shivering, so I ran to get a sweater, but by the time I got back, Nate was holding her as she huddled beside the pet whose loss she was experiencing with all the pain entailed in mourning a Thou and not an It. Who would do such a terrible thing? Did one of our neighbors hold a grudge because Donner had spoiled his lawn? If whoever had shot the dog had shot my brother, what could he be trying to accomplish now? Why intimidate a dead man? If Donner's death had been intended as a warning, who was being warned, of what?

"That bastard," Ebby said. "He told me we had a deal."

"You know who did this?"

"I have my suspicions. I won't be gone long. Nate? You stay here with the ladies."

Solemnly, Nate agreed. Meryl, still dazed, sat stroking the shrouded body on the floor while the other four greyhounds milled around them, sniffing.

I went to let Ebby out, then spent the next ninety minutes making sure every window and door was locked and no one was in the yard. I checked the monitors a thousand times. Then I went back and checked on Meryl.

You can imagine how relieved I was when Ebby's truck drove up. And how puzzled I was when he got out the driver's side and walked around to the other door. Even then, the passenger didn't get out until Ebby reached inside and dragged him. I wish I could say I felt sorry for the man as Ebby tugged him up the driveway by his wrists, which were duct-taped behind him, but I would be lying if I said I did.

Ebby twisted his victim's arms. "Meet Pickles Pinkowski. Pickles, say hello," a command Pickles couldn't obey because his mouth was duct-taped shut, although he made a noise behind the tape that sounded like *hello.*

"As you might recall, Pickles here, through no fault of his own, placed a lucky bet and was due to be paid forty thousand dollars. Which sum your brother was unable to pay because he disappeared. Mr. Pinkowski called your brother's establishment to arrange his payout, and you can understand his disappointment when he was told that only half the amount was on hand to be disbursed. Am I right so far?" Ebby gave the man a shake. "Am I giving your side a fair hearing?" Ebby did something with the man's arm that made Pickles Pinkowski grunt his assent. "Mr. Pinkowski here accepted the twenty thousand dollars your brother's head clerk gave him, and he promised to wait to receive the rest. But as you might recall from the rather heated messages he left on your brother's phone, Mr. Pinkowski is not a patient man. A week ago, I visited Mr. P. and provided him with a lesson on how to control his anger. I suggested meditation. To show I understood his point of view, I gave him, with your parents' approval, a few thousand dollars more, and Mr. P. swore on his beloved aunt Basha's grave that he would wait for the rest." Ebby shook his head. "Sadly, Mr. P. has gone back on his promise. He must not respect his beloved aunt's memory as much as he claims. Out of some misguided sense that killing your niece's pet would cause her father to come out of hiding and pay the remainder of what he's owed, Mr. P. dragged a ladder to the wall and waited for his chance. Through no talent of his own, he managed to kill a defenseless greyhound. Isn't that right, Mr. P.? I'm not accusing you unjustly? And you're here to apologize? And to promise you won't come within fifty miles of Mr. Weinrach's niece, or his sister, or his pets, unless you want me to turn you in for trespass and cruelty to animals, although not before I mete out a little punishment of my own."

Ebby told me to go get Meryl.

"Do you think that's a good idea?" I asked. "It won't upset her more?"

Ebby shrugged. "Nothing will bring back her dog. But at least she'll grow up knowing not all bad deeds go unpunished."

I still had my reservations about it calming my niece to see the man who had killed her dog bound and gagged and dangling from her boyfriend's father's arm, but who was I to judge?

"Meryl?" I said. "Sweetheart? Nate's father is here. He brought the man who shot Donner."

"What? He's here? At the *house?*" She glanced down at Donner one last time, patted Vixen, then, holding Nate's hand, accompanied me to the door.

Luckily, Ebby had ripped the duct tape from Pickles Pinkowski's mouth, and even though the rectangular shape of adhesive was still visible, the sight of the man was less disturbing. I had assumed his nickname came from a taste for that briny side dish so ubiquitous in the Catskills, but now I guessed it came from his diminutive size, warty complexion, and unhealthy pallor.

"This is Mr. Pinkowski. He has something he wants to say."

I thought Ebby would jerk the puppet's arms to make him talk, but the puppet spoke of its own volition. "Uh, I'm sorry I shot your dog."

"And what else?" Ebby demanded.

"Uh. I won't do it again? I won't come anywhere near your house?"

"Meryl, honey," Ebby said, "I thought it might help to know that Mr. Pinkowski is sorry for what he did. He won't bother you or your dogs again. It was just, your father owes him money, and Mr. Pinkowski got angry because your father isn't here to pay. But he's agreed to wait until your dad gets back. Isn't that right? Except Mr. Pinkowski here will be getting ten thousand dollars less than if he hadn't shot the dog. And five thousand less than that as—what should we call it?—an asshole tax. A tax on being the kind of man who would cause a nice girl like you to see her dog lying there with its head blown off. That's the deal, right? Isn't that the deal, Mr. Pinkowski?"

"Uh," Mr. Pinkowski said, clearly not happy to learn that now that his ship finally had come in, it was carrying fifteen thousand dollars less than he thought it would. "I'm going to wait, all right. I'm going to wait and bring this up with Potsie. I'm going to tell him . . . I'm going to tell the fucker he owes me the whole fucking forty grand! Never mind this bullshit about some 'asshole tax.' If anyone around here is an asshole, it's you, Salzman. No way I'm going to give up a single cent of what I'm owed. No way I'm not getting my—"

Ebby jerked his arms so violently Pickles Pinkowski screamed.

"Uh, right, sure," Mr. Pinkowski said. "I'm going to wait until Mr. Weinrach gets back and take whatever he thinks is fair. Seeing as I killed his dog."

"And you promise never to come near this house again? Never to bother Mr. Weinrach's daughter? Or his sister? Or any of these other dogs?"

Mr. Pinkowski mumbled something.

"You'll have to speak louder."

"Ow! I said, 'I promise.'"

"Meryl? I'm going to take Mr. Pinkowski here back home. Then I'll come straight back and bury Donner. I know that isn't much. But sometimes it's the best you can do. You bury your dead, you give them the nicest send-off you can give them, then you make sure you take good care of whoever you have left to love."

At that, Ebby dragged Mr. Pinkowski back to the truck, helped him up and in, and drove away. We stood there, Meryl and Nate and I, listening to the four remaining greyhounds whine in grief.

"I can't believe it," Meryl said, and I thought she meant she couldn't believe anyone would shoot a dog. "Aunt Ketzel, I love my dad. I really do. But what kind of a moral lightweight would do business with a prick like that?"

9.

I WILL OFFER a shorthand version of what happened next. Nate picked up Meryl in his father's truck and took her to the dig on the Vegas Wash, after which she came home and took a shower that lasted so long I knew she was not only washing off the sand and sweat but leaning against the tiles and nearly falling asleep with longing. The next afternoon, she drove to the Salzman residence so Nate could teach her how to differentiate among the types and styles of Anasazi pottery, after which Meryl broke down and confided that despite the hours she and Nate had spent together, he hadn't so much as kissed her. What was she supposed to do, start dressing like the other girls and, you know, seduce him?

As badly as it broke my heart to see my niece cry, and as fervently as I wished I knew the magic words that might entice the boy she liked to kiss her—although, to be honest, I didn't want him to do any more than that—I couldn't for the life of me think what those words might be. Luckily, on their next trip, Nate brought up the topic. Or rather, Meryl started the conversation by snatching the bandana off his head, at which Nate snatched it back, at which they started wrestling, at which he pinned her to the ground and kissed her, although just when things got interesting, he rolled away and stopped.

"It's that stupid Martin Buber!" Meryl told me. "It's that I-and-Thou crap!" Apparently, Nate had confessed he thought about sex so much he wasn't sure he could treat her as a person rather than as a means to his own sexual ends. "What am I supposed to say?" Meryl asked. "'I don't care if I'm just an It, go ahead and jump my bones?'"

To make the tension worse, there was my own mounting apprehension that my audition would be a dud. I hadn't told Ebby about running into Harvey Blatt. It had been my experience that most men don't want to date a comic for fear she will get up onstage and make jokes about the size of their genitalia. But Meryl spilled the beans to Nate, and Nate passed those beans to his father, who insisted on being told why I hadn't invited him to the show, all the while expressing such happiness on my behalf you might have thought I had won the lottery—and was giving the prize to him.

"Gee, Ketzel," Ebby said, "that's the kind of break a person waits for her entire life."

I was grateful for his enthusiasm. But the idea that Ebby would be in the audience to see me fail inspired a dread worse than if millions of strangers had been watching me on TV. Unfortunately, it was too late to back out. To hedge my bets, I planned to do a few classic jokes about gambling, followed by some observations about Vegas life. Already I could hear Morty railing against the ways in which hip, self-referential humor was destroying the authentic story-telling powers of the masses.

Shut up, I said. *You're dead!*

But he managed to come back and haunt me. The night before the show, I dreamed I was performing in the ruins of a Roman theater, which was empty except for Morty, who sat on the highest tier. He was cloaked in a light-blue toga. His hair had grown wild and white like a halo rising from his head. His expression was hard to read. Sorrowful? Scornful? Proud?

Then I uttered those awful words *Have you ever noticed?* and it became clear my audience disapproved. The jokes I told seemed hilarious—not that I could remember a single one—but Morty made a face and stood to leave. Heavily, he turned and climbed higher, at which I saw he wasn't wearing a toga but a light-blue cotton johnny such as hospital patients wear. It hung open in the back, and as he made his way higher, I saw tattooed on opposing cheeks of his baggy *tuchis* those frowning and grinning masks that grace opposite corners of the stage on which all human life is played.

As if Morty showing me his rear end weren't bad enough, I made the mistake of telling my mother about the show.

"Oy, Ketzel, I thought you gave up that crazy ambition long ago. A comeback I could understand. Even Judy Garland, may she rest in peace, went through her ups and downs. But to be down, a person must first have been up. And how can you even think of telling jokes at a time like this?"

I had no one to blame for my mother's admonition but myself. Usually, I didn't pick up the phone. Who wanted to hear my mother say that I was in no hurry to find my brother because I enjoyed living in his house and carrying on an affair with the detective we had hired to solve his case? She even put forth the theory that I was reluctant to find Potsie because I wanted to steal his child, an accusation so offensive—and no doubt true—I could react only by hanging up.

I had even less patience for my father's concerns that the developers would dredge our lake and unearth Jimmy Hoffa's bones. In my father's guilty mind, the corpses had multiplied until they were lying beneath every square inch of the Hospitality House Hotel. When I thought of my parents, I imagined the two Macbeths clutching at invisible daggers and rinsing their bloodstained hands in Cuyahoga Lake. If I listened to their messages at all, it was at a speed that made my mother sound like a chipmunk—the greyhounds cocked their heads in the hope she would escape and they could chase her.

Which is how I came to miss the message from Harvey Blatt that the audition would take place two nights earlier than planned, and not at Harrah's Improv. I only found this out because Harvey called my mother, who, when I didn't respond to the messages she had left, had the sense to call Ebby and ask that he pass the news to me.

"You've got to give her credit," Ebby said. "She could have kept the information to herself."

"Credit! You know what she would buy with that credit? She thinks you and I ought to be out there right now, knocking at every fleabag motel in Vegas, trying to find my brother." Although even as I said this, I felt a surge of shame I wasn't doing exactly that.

When I finally reached Harvey, he nearly sobbed with gratitude. Because of the change of date, he already had lost two of his top contenders. "Truth is, this is not turning out to be quite the high-class act I hoped it would be." The deal with Comedy Central had fallen through. He had negotiated a deal for the contest to run on a new cable-channel called Raunch. But the guys at Raunch didn't think Harrah's Improv was glitzy or big enough to provide the proper atmosphere. "They want to be able to pan the audience for reaction shots," Harvey said. "You know, people yukking it up? And if it's a topless joint, they have a good excuse to show the waitresses' tits. That's what keeps people watching. The viewer thinks of hitting the remote, then he thinks, 'Naah, if I sit here a while longer, maybe they'll show more tits.'"

"Are you telling me I'll be performing at a topless bar? You're kidding, right? I don't suppose first prize is still a shot at Letterman?"

"Ketzel, it is truly a thing of beauty when the dominoes fall in the right direction. But sometimes the first domino doesn't hit the second domino at exactly the right angle. And the domino after that . . ."

"Spare me the dominoes, Harve. What am I, the warm-up act for a stripper?"

"Relax, Ketzel. The winner at Nips still gets to go to LA. First prize is . . . well, we're negotiating with Letterman's people. But at the very least, the winner ought to get a shot at Howard Stern."

Bad enough to betray your principles for a chance to appear on Letterman. But to betray those same principles for an opportunity to be insulted by a foul-mouthed jerk like Howard Stern? What had my father said—I should be careful of losing something I didn't even know I had to lose? I wasn't sure if that something was my chance to appear on David Letterman, or my niece's respect.

I called Ebby and broke the news that I would be performing at a topless bar and therefore would understand if he preferred not to attend.

"Are you kidding?" he said. "I wouldn't miss your act for anything. I sat through the show at the Schoolhouse Lounge, didn't I? If you're not going to perform at a place where women show their breasts, you won't be able to perform anywhere in Vegas."

I was touched he would risk another round of flashbacks for my sake. And given the way Morty and I had spent our lives, who was I to object to performing in a topless bar? When had I become such a Puritan?

And so, the next night, I frizzed my hair, put on a fresh pair of jeans and a Camp Hospitality T-shirt, accepted a good-luck hug from my niece, then got in my brother's Hummer and drove to the address in Downtown Vegas that Harvey had spelled out on the phone. The billboard above the club showed two stylized women's breasts, with a flashing pink dollar-sign where each nipple should have been. How could I help but think of my father's joke about two nipples for a dime? Except if anyone had tried to tell me that joke right then, I would have hit him.

I hadn't wanted to arrive too early and get spooked by the competition, but Harvey had requested we assemble backstage an hour before the show so he could run through a few instructions and assign our order for going on. Nips was classier than the Schoolhouse Lounge. Judging by the posters, the dancers who ordinarily constituted the entertainment were younger and in better shape than the strippers at my cousin's bar. But the basic menu was the same. It reminded me of the way our chef used to describe the entrée as "Cornish game hen" or "French capon" when it was the same plate of roast chicken he had cooked the night before.

I handed the Hummer's keys to the valet—judging by his reaction, the keys to such a vehicle were the keys to being treated with respect in a town like this—and went in to find Harvey. As predicted, six of the eight contestants were scruffy young men, each of whom eyed me as if I were his girlfriend's mother. The only other female contestant was a black woman who, when I passed her in the hall, muttered, "Don't you go getting in my way, Campfire Girl, or I'll toast those big white marshmallows of yours, you hear?"

Harvey showed up in a frilly shirt and a purple tux and informed us of the rules. Namely, we could do or say anything, as long we didn't exceed our eleven-minute limit. The bouncers would take care of any drunks who turned violent, but ordinary hecklers were up to us. The judging panel would consist of the manager of the club, some sitcom star I had never heard of, and a top VIP from Raunch. I peeked out and was surprised to see that the club was full. Nor was it particularly calming to watch my fellow contestants pacing around backstage, mumbling like inmates at an asylum. I thought of all the nights Alan King or Red Buttons had been warming up at the StarLite Lounge. They must have been as nervous as I was now. No doubt they had endured my presence because I was the owners' child. Then again, my childish infatuation might have provided just the boost their egos needed before they bounded out onstage.

Harvey gave the thumbs-up sign and went out to start the show. In the Catskills, the emcees liked to introduce an act by saying it had arrived "direct from Vegas," which, with a New York inflection, sounded like "*dreck* from Vegas." Now that we were actually here, what could the emcee say? It was like using a compass while standing at the North Pole. I tried not to listen to the other acts or gauge how much applause they each received, but the black woman's voice was so loud I couldn't help but hear.

"If it wasn't for all that women's lib crap, we girls could still be hanging around at home, putting up our feet and shopping on QVC. Equal rights? You want the equal right to get up at six in the fucking morning and commute two hours to some crappy job and take shit from some asshole of a boss and then drag your sorry ass home and cook supper and take care of the kids and, oh yeah, throw in a wash and let your man fuck you before you get to sleep? You want the right to do all that? Fine with me, but don't you go messing with my right to sit home and watch Judge Judy."

Her act got a lot of laughs, as did the scruffily goateed young man who, I swear, told the same jokes about his girlfriends' pubic hair as the comic at the Rising Star told the night I met Morty. Then Harvey slapped me on the back, and there I was with the mike sticking straight up at my mouth, the lights shining in my eyes, and I couldn't think of a thing to say. I hadn't performed for anyone but my niece in twenty-seven years. Why had I given up? Maybe it had been easier to blame Morty for wasting my life than to admit I was afraid of coming up with my own material and making people laugh.

"Hey, how you all doing tonight?" I pointed to my hair. "Know what this is? This is what Jewish women look like *after* you fall for their JDate photos."

This got enough of a response that I lifted the microphone from the stand and walked to the edge of the stage. "I see a lot of you here are all dressed up, looking for a good time. Am I right? You're looking to sow some wild oats here in Vegas?" And here I stole a joke from an unsung pioneer of Borscht Belt humor, a comic named Rusty Warren, who, seeing as she had been dead for thirty years, couldn't complain about the theft. "You know, the sexes aren't really all that different. Everybody likes to go out on a Friday night and sow his or her wild oats. Am I right? The only difference is, come Saturday morning, the women hope for crop failure and the men don't give a shit."

I started to relax and tell the only joke I had been able to come up with that wouldn't offend my niece. "There was this friend of mine, right? She was going on this cruise? So she asks the doctor if he would give her an indoctrination. 'An indoctrination?' the doctor says. 'What, are you, crazy? You mean an *inoculation*!'" Here I made a face to express the woman's indifference to the doctor's scorn. "'Indoctrination, inoculation, what's the difference? I want a shot.' 'Okay,' the doctor says. 'Where do you want this shot?' 'Well, doctor, I'm planning on wearing a stripless gown, so don't give it to me on my arm.' 'A stripless gown? You mean *strapless* gown, don't you?' 'Stripless, strapless, just don't give it where it could show.' 'Okay,' the doctor says, 'so how about on your tush?' 'Oh no!' the woman says, 'I can't have it there. I plan on wearing a very revealing zucchini.' 'A zucchini!' the doctor says. 'You mean a *bikini*!' 'Bikini, zucchini, don't give it to me on my tush!' 'Okay,' the doctor says, 'so where *do* you want this shot?' 'Oh,' the woman says, 'I want it in my Virginia.' 'Your Virginia!' the doctor says. 'Don't you mean *vagina*?' 'Virginia, vagina, just give it to me already!' 'All right,' the doctor says, 'but what kind of an inoculation are we giving you today?' 'Oh,' the woman says, 'I want to be inoculated against smallcox.' 'Smallcox!' the doctor says. 'Don't you mean *smallpox*?'" And here I smiled my sweetest smile. "'Oh, doctor. You might have a very impressive vocabulary. You might even know a great deal about medical procedures. But you don't know the first thing about women, do you!'"

Judging by the audience's applause, reports of the demise of the Borscht Belt joke might have been premature. Quickly, before the audience's good will could evaporate, I launched into the story about the boy who tricks his teacher into showing him her female underparts, although I pretended my brother had been that boy and the story was true. Then my brother grew up to be the businessman who lost his shirt gambling at the Flamingo and asked the cabby for a free ride to the airport. I was in the homestretch by then. All I had to do was deliver my impression of the poker guy at the Mirage who thought I had been sent by Butchie, followed by the dealer with the bolo tie and the amateurs from Indiana who had watched too many tournaments on ESPN. I could sense Alan and Zero cheering me toward the finish line. *Ketzel, you really wowed them! Boy, did we have you wrong! You had it in you all the time!*

But who should I see just then except a guy who looked like Perry. Not Perry as he might have looked that night, a man of fifty-six, but as I remembered him from his youth. He even was wearing the same blue-and-white striped seersucker shirt my cousin had worn the day we made our movie behind the pool. A topless waitress put down his drink, and he tweaked her boob. She slapped away his hand. His girlfriend laughed. But something inside me snapped. I looked at all the leering men and their heavily made-up dates, the bare-breasted waitresses carrying trays above their heads while maneuvering between the aisles in their high-heeled shoes, and it came to me that I finally had gained admission to the club I had been trying all my life to enter. It was as if the boys had built a shack and put up a sign, *NO GIRLS ALLOWED.* I had tried for years to get inside, and when I did, I realized all I had missed was a bunch of pimply boys lying around belching and jerking off.

"So," I said, "what's with all the tits? This is, what, the twenty-first century? And we still get all *whoo-whoo-whoo* at the sight of a woman's breast? It's been hundreds of thousands of years since the first man climbed down from a coconut tree, and it's, like, 'Ohmigod, a nipple! I saw a nipple! Hey, Ogg! Get over here right now! Ogg, drop that spear! Forget about that mammoth! You have *got* to come see this.'" I reached out to poke a nipple—an imaginary one, I mean—squinting and poking and motioning for Ogg to join me. The audience tittered. The women turned to look at their dates and punched their arms.

"And we women are like, 'Sure, dear. That's nice. Just poke and tweak it all you want. Twist it, too, why don't you? What's that, honey? You want to go down to the strip club and watch a bunch of total strangers shake their hooters in your face? *Of course* I don't mind. I mean, it's the women's choice, right? They *like* shaking their tits in public. There are *lots* of high-paying jobs for women who don't have a college education. If those girls don't want to walk around with their titties hanging out, no one is forcing them. Really, if men's penises and balls weren't so damn ugly, *you* would be the ones serving the drinks to *us*.'"

I might have taken my bow and gotten off. But I noticed two overweight balding men with pretty, young Asian dates, and I couldn't help but get down off the stage and walk over to them and lean down and ask the men, "It's, what, a total accident these women are Asian? It's just that all the white girls were taken and you had to make do with these?" When I saw the expressions on those two men's faces, I figured I had crossed some kind of line. For all I knew, the women were the two men's wives. But I remembered what Ebby had said about all those Asian women getting tossed in the desert every year, and I couldn't make myself shut up. "What, if you pay these girls enough money, they won't notice the comb-over thing going on? They won't think you look like retired postal clerks? They'll think you're, what, Tom Cruise and Johnny Depp?"

I saw Harvey motioning from the wings, so frantic you might have thought a fire had broken out backstage, but he was only trying to tell me I had gone on too long and needed to stop or be disqualified. I muttered the obligatory refrain about what a terrific audience they had been, and I was amazed when the crowd applauded. Just as the audience at our hotel had thought Zero's insults about my father and Philly Blatt had been part of his act, so the customers at Nips assumed my rage had been rehearsed.

I managed to get offstage, then stood panting in the wings, my heart pounding so loud a cannon might have gone off and I wouldn't have heard it. Harvey brought all eight of us back onstage and made a big production of tallying the judges' votes and announcing that first prize went to the angry young male comic who had done a series of jokes about his insatiable need for anal sex and the tricks he used to get his girlfriends to allow him to enter them from the rear. The customers applauded a final time, and Harvey ushered us off the stage. I packed my bag and washed my face and was about to go out in front to find Ebby when Harvey grabbed my arm.

"Ketzel," he hissed, "you won't believe who's here." With that, he yanked me over to meet a man I knew I knew from somewhere—maybe he had been a guest at our hotel? He was lanky and tall, with a bald onion of a dome and glasses that distorted his eyes in such a way that you could see deep into his soul and tell he didn't believe anything good would come of meeting you. "Ketzel, this is Larry David."

The man held out his hand, and although my hand was slick with sweat, I shook it, at which Larry looked at his hand with an expression of disgust and wiped it on his pants. "That was quite some performance," he said in a New York twang that reminded me of Morty's. "I was just . . . I happened to be in the audience. One of the contestants is the son of a friend." Larry shrugged. "I had to be in Vegas anyway." He smiled a smile that was at least ninety percent a grimace. "What can I say, the kid sucked. But your act . . . pret-ty interesting. Pret-ty, pret-ty interesting."

"Larry here thinks you might be right for this new series he's producing," Harvey chimed in.

"Um, yeah," Larry said. "It's, you know, another show about nothing. Another show about a comic."

"He's being modest," Harvey said. "It's a brilliant idea. First there was *Seinfeld,* about this guy who's trying to make it big. Then there was *Curb Your Enthusiasm,* in which the guy is still in the business, but he's more of a producer type. And now this new one, it's like post-post-*Seinfeld.* One of the actors, a Jason Alexander type, can't get another hit. He's always being typecast as George. It's about, how do you live if you're famous and a flop at the same time? Everybody recognizes you, they stop you and ask for your autograph, they ask you to do your bits, but you can't get work, you're broke, you're going down the tubes." Harvey looked to Larry for confirmation. "Am I right, Larry? I hope I didn't butcher your idea." Larry held out his hands to show no harm had been done, at which Harvey turned back to me. "Larry thinks you'd be perfect for the part of the crazy middle-aged Jewish girl who lives next door."

"Yeah, well," Larry said. "Whatever. She's a bitter, aging feminist. She . . . I don't know, publishes a magazine called, who knows, *Bitch.* She rages against the patriarchy, but she is also a very lonely woman. She wants to find a boyfriend, so she does all this online dating. JDate, Sex.com, the whole schmear. She's always going out with these awful men and making jokes about them, putting them down, but she's very lonely and she has a crush on the Jerry/George guy." Larry lifted both hands in a splay-fingered gesture meant to imply that nothing would ever come of any of this. "At this point, it's just pie in the sky. Definitely in the planning stage. But if we get the green light from HBO, you need to come out and audition for the part."

I didn't know what to say. To Morty, Jerry Seinfeld and Larry David represented everything that spelled the ruin of the authentic folkloric joke as opposed to hip ironic "humor." Then again, Morty was dead. And I doubted I would have the strength to turn down a job on HBO.

"Gotta be going," Larry said. "Gotta be moving along here. I don't suppose you have, you know, a card?"

I shook my head.

"Ah, well, I can always get in touch with Harry here. Am I right? Harry is representing you? Is that right, Harry?"

"Harvey," Harvey said.

"Excuse me?" Larry cupped one hand to an oversized ear. "All the ambient noise. Getting deaf, getting old, what can I say, happens to the best of us."

"Harvey, not Harry. Harvey Blatt Enterprises."

"Right, right. Did I say Harry? I meant Harvey. Everyone knows Harvey Blatt. Like I said, great show, nice meeting you, I'll be in touch."

After Larry left, Harvey kept bouncing up and down, rubbing his hands and grinning, his hair standing straight up, as if he had grabbed the mike while standing in knee-deep water. "See! I knew you had it in you! Larry David, of all people!" He was so excited I thought he was going to rise from the stage and fly like Peter Pan. "You stay in touch." Harvey shook his finger in my face. "No more of this disappearing act. Make sure I have your contact information. And send a headshot. You never know who else might be out there looking for a middle-aged

Jewish female New York type."

What could I do but nod and smile and agree to whatever Harvey asked? I felt the excited dread a person feels when she has been presented with an opportunity she isn't sure she wants but would be crazy for turning down. Then I went out to look for Ebby, whom I found loitering in the lobby, his back to the posters of naked showgirls while he studied a diagram that described the proper way to perform the Heimlich maneuver. I wanted to imitate the figure in the diagram and reach around and squeeze his ribs. But I doubted my arms would stretch that far, especially with my breasts between us. And who knew how Ebby might react if someone came up and grabbed him.

Instead, I made a noise that sounded as if I were the one who needed to keep from choking.

He spun around. "Ketzel! I had no idea you were so . . . Those jokes you told! And those guys with the Asian escorts! I thought one of them was going to throw a punch. I was ready to get up there and . . . But then, you know, they laughed."

I waited for him to tell me that he liked the show.

"I couldn't believe that was you onstage."

This wasn't the praise I had in mind. "You don't need to lie, Ebby. If you didn't think my routine was funny . . ."

"No! Of course it was funny! It was only, I had this image of you the way you were when we were kids. I didn't think you were so . . . you know."

"Oh, Ebby, you can't keep dividing the world into innocent little girls and whores. Most of us are in between."

"Yeah," he said. "My therapist says the same thing. Really, you were great. I just need a little while to get used to . . . the new you. Have you eaten? Could I take you out for a meal? On my own dime, not your father's."

I had been too nervous to eat before the show. And I certainly didn't mind sharing a meal with Ebby. I hadn't told him about Larry David and my chance of appearing on HBO. On the other hand, it was already past one and I wanted to get home and see how Meryl and Nate were doing. Despite Pickles Pinkowski's vow not to come near our house, Meryl had been reluctant to stay home alone. Nate had been happy to keep her company, but that didn't erase my fears. When I voiced these concerns, Ebby assured me that Nate would never let anyone touch a hair on Meryl's head.

I was torn between saying the problem was Nate's own reluctance to touch a hair on my niece's head and revealing my fear that one day Nate would discover it was possible to take pleasure in a woman's body while relating to her as a Thou.

"This isn't a neighborhood known for fine dining," Ebby said. "But there's an Italian place that's pretty good. The lobster-tail Milanese is outstanding. And the waitresses keep on their clothes."

I inquired about his diet.

"Screw my diet. If this isn't something to celebrate, what is?"

I went out front to wait for Ebby to get his truck, trying to pretend I wasn't disappointed that the man I was falling in love with hadn't been more enthusiastic about my act. What did I want? Not only hadn't I disgraced myself, I might have won an audition for a show on HBO.

The truck pulled up, and Ebby drove us a few blocks west through a section of Vegas that seemed to have been preserved in mothballs, with casinos that weren't pretending to be anything but casinos and women who weren't pretending to be anything but the prostitutes they were. Ebby turned the Silverado into a lot behind a restaurant, and even though there were plenty of spaces near the front, some professional instinct caused him to explore the darkest corners.

Suddenly, he stopped the truck, jumped out, and ran toward a group of three men who were bent over the hood of a car, no doubt discussing why the engine wouldn't start. I wondered why Ebby would so violently object to their trying to fix their car, and why two of the men wore their trousers around their knees, and why they wouldn't stick around to fight but hobbled away as best they could, except for one man, who got shakily to his feet and offered a last comment to Ebby, who lifted him by his collar and slammed him headfirst into the side wall of the restaurant in which we had planned to dine. The man crumpled in a heap. Ebby picked up what seemed to be a pile of rags and carried it toward our truck, at which I cursed myself for not having noticed earlier that what he was carrying was a girl.

I hopped out, opened the back door, and helped Ebby slide her in. She was small and pale, her hair matted to her head by what appeared to be vomit. Her eyes were open but unfocused, and she was saying something that sounded like *Not what I . . . Not so many . . . Jack . . . Go tell them . . . Go tell Jack . . .*

"There's a blanket in the back of the truck," Ebby said. "Wait, no, we used it for the dog." He unbuttoned his Hawaiian shirt and laid it across the girl—it covered her from neck to knees—and I climbed in and held her head to make sure she didn't stop breathing while Ebby spun the truck and drove as fast as he could toward the hospital. "Honey," I kept saying, "you're safe now. It's okay."

She looked younger than my niece, the sort of vaguely attractive girl who wouldn't have gotten a place on the cheerleading squad but might have been allowed to twirl a baton with the majorettes.

"Tell Jack," she muttered. "This isn't what I . . . I'm not feeling so good." She coughed up some yellow liquid all over Ebby's shirt.

I wanted to ask Ebby if she was the runaway from Toledo, but he was driving at such a high speed I didn't want to interfere with his concentration. The big red sign for the emergency room flashed by, and

Ebby pulled in and braked. He didn't bother waiting for the EMTs but carried her through the doors. A security guard tried to stop him, possibly because Ebby looked so wild without his shirt, but Ebby shouldered past the long line of people waiting at the nurses' station.

"Gang rape," I heard him say. "I don't care how many winos and nut cases you've got ahead of her. She's fourteen, okay?" At which the nurse ran inside and returned with three women who removed the girl from Ebby's arms, laid her on a gurney, and wheeled her behind a set of forbidding metal doors.

Ebby picked up a soiled johnny from a wheelchair and used it to swab his chest.

"Mr. Salzman?" A nurse poked out her head. "We have a few questions. About what happened to the girl? Next of kin? What she might have ingested?"

Ebby told the nurse he would be right there, then said he hoped I wouldn't mind but the ER was so understaffed he would probably be there all night. Would I be okay taking a taxi back to the club and driving the Hummer home?

I wanted to keep him company. What if the girl needed a woman's touch? But the idea of those men crowding around that car made me want to get home to Meryl.

I went out and found a cab. The driver, I was thankful to note, had no interest in hearing yet another hard-luck story. And I, for one, did not want to be told that he had seen worse crimes than a fourte-year-old runaway high on who-knew-what being gang-raped in a parking lot.

I drove the Hummer home, let myself in, and tiptoed to the living room, where I found my niece on the floor with her head on Prancer's chest and Dancer and Blitzen coiled protectively around those two. Nate lay stretched out on the couch, his hand trailing along Meryl's

arm. I felt as if I were spying on Sleeping Beauty and her prince, protected by their four footmen, who had been bewitched into dogs. As I
stood and watched Meryl breathe, I understood why Ebby wanted to
put up a wall between innocence such as this and the depravity we had
witnessed at my cousin's bar. It was difficult to believe anyone could
exist anywhere in the middle without becoming tainted and corrupt
herself.

10.

IN FAIRY TALES, after the knight in shining armor has rescued the damsel in distress, she plants a chaste kiss on his brow and thanks him. Alas, in real life this rarely happens. When Ebby called the next morning, he told me the runaway had no memory of her attackers or how she had come to be splayed on that car. Because he was working for her parents and had informed them where she was, she refused to look in his direction. Her parents flew out from Ohio and were eager to take her back. But Ebby wasn't sure he had persuaded them that their daughter needed more than prayer sessions at their local church to heal.

Another aspect of such a rescue that often goes unremarked is the effect that breaking up a gang rape has on the knight who breaks it up. Ebby's armor remained untarnished, but the psyche inside grew dark. He took to combing the streets near where the rape had taken place in the hope he might recognize the girl's assailants. Whenever he closed his eyes, he saw a fourteen-year-old girl stretched out on a car with three grown men around her. With that image in his head, he could no more have made love to me than he could have visited a slaughterhouse in Chicago and gone home and eaten steak.

As much as I understood his state of mind, I wasn't in the market for a man who couldn't close his eyes without imagining a teenage girl getting gang-raped. At my age, I didn't need to make love as many times a day as when I had been married to Morty. But neither was I about to give up my inalienable human right to be touched and kissed.

Then again, if Ebby didn't want to make love to me, who would? A wave of despair crashed over me. Was Morty truly dead? How could his presence be so strong? Maybe my anger was what kept his ghost alive. But, strangely, it felt like love. How could I miss a man who had dealt me as many low blows as Morty? Twenty-seven years of marriage gone up in smoke. If only I hadn't opened that locker in New Jersey, I could have gone to my grave believing that the husband whose remains were lying in the plot beside me had been my one and only love. Or rather, that I had been his.

But I couldn't go back in time. I couldn't not find that key, or those letters to Professor Cohen, or the notebook and receipts for call girls, or the priceless works of art he hadn't sold. Not only had I lost my husband, I had lost my best memories of our life together. And a big chunk of my self-respect. Was I also going to lose the only other man my age I might hope to love?

School let out for the summer, a circumstance that allowed my niece to sit home and brood as to how she could possibly get through the next six weeks, while Nate was working on the dig at Chaco. She was too young to know that all a person really needs to do to survive is go to sleep each night and wake up the next morning and find some socially acceptable way to get through the day.

Then Ebby learned his former wife had eloped with another man, which was fine with him, except he needed to figure out how he could keep working as a private eye while caring for their daughter. He decided to drop Nate in Arizona, then continue driving south with Saffron so they could spend a few weeks in Florida with his mother. He hated to leave me alone in Vegas. But he was afraid that his daughter would insist on competing in the beauty contests her mother had signed her up for—and, what he didn't say, that she might end up like all those runaways. He hoped I would understand. There was nothing more he could do to find my brother, who, Ebby was sure, was hiding out in some town in Mexico. Unless Potsie made a dumb mistake like charging something to a credit card, we weren't about to find him. At least, not until he wanted to be found. With Pickles Pinkowski taken care of,

Meryl and I would be safe in the house alone.

Sure, I said, I understood. In a situation like that, does it ever help to say you *don't* understand? All I could do was take my own advice and find some socially acceptable way to get through the fourteen days and nights while the man I loved was gone and maintain a modicum of hope that when he got back, he might be cured of his inability to fall in love with a woman who was neither a Madonna nor a whore.

The day before he left, Ebby invited me to take his daughter, Saffron, to get a perm. From the way Ebby and Nate described her, I wasn't sure I wanted to meet the girl. But after all Ebby had done for me, not to mention my distant wish I might someday be more to Ebby's daughter than her father's friend, how could I say no?

You can imagine how relieved I was when I discovered that Saffron wasn't nearly as spoiled as I had been led to think. True, when we drove up in the truck, she was tapping her foot and looking at her watch. "Daddy," she said, "appointments at this salon are nearly *impossible* to get." I hated to see a girl of ten wearing lip gloss and a stretchy off-the-shoulder dress that looked as if it came from the Victoria's Secret catalog. But clearly she loved her dad.

"Are you upset Mommy got married again? Don't be jealous. Vince is a total loser compared to you."

And even if she was suspicious of my presence, she tried to be polite. "You are just *so* lucky your hair is naturally curly. If I had curls like that, I wouldn't need to get this stupid smelly perm."

After that, how could I help but like her? Ebby's daughter reminded me of a birthday cake that has been decorated with gaudy icing and those inedible silver beads, but if you manage to scrape off all that crap, there's plain vanilla cake underneath.

"Okay, button," Ebby said after she had gotten her hair permed and the nails on her feet and hands painted bright pink, "how about if we all go out for pizza?"

"Don't be silly, Daddy. If I ate pizza, how would I ever fit into those expensive new costumes Mommy bought?"

Seeing her eat her lunch—she picked at the undressed salad, disdaining to eat the croutons, which, with a theatrically wrinkled nose, she transferred to her father's plate—I could barely suppress the urge to carry her to McDonald's and force her to eat a Big Mac and fries.

A few days later, Meryl and I watched as all three Salzmans prodded and poked their duffel bags, backpacks, and pink lacquered cases into the back seat of the truck. Then we waved and smiled in a barely successful attempt to hide how bereft we felt.

Now, two women who miss their men can take out their frustrations on each other, or they can use their common misery to form a bond. Happily, my niece and I chose the latter course. We moped around the house, but we moped around together. When we could no longer bear the sight of those fake adobe walls, not to mention the sight of each other shuffling around the kitchen in the same T-shirt and sweatpants each of us had worn the day before, and the day before that, and the day before *that*, we decided to put our two good minds to better use and come up with a more inventive and productive way to pass the time.

First, we would acquaint my niece with art. Since the museums in Las Vegas turned out to be hidden inside casinos, this had the unsettling effect of reducing a painting by Rembrandt or Matisse to the same artistic grandeur as the prize that comes in a box of Cracker Jack. Undaunted, we took a tour of the Liberace Museum, but that establishment had been designed less as a tribute to the classical repertoire than as yet another showcase for Vegas glitz. Not even our excursion to the Boulder Dam turned out to be uplifting, given that in order to reach the dam, we needed to take the highway past the Schoolhouse Lounge.

"Do the women who work at these places actually pretend to be nurses and librarians?" Meryl asked. "Men like that? That turns them on?"

By the time we had reached the dam, the thermometer on the dash read 110 degrees. We sweated through the tour, and even though we were impressed by the skills of the engineers—although we would have been more impressed if a hundred workers hadn't died carrying out their plans—in the end, the Boulder Dam seemed just another example of Vegas pride in something oversized and artificial.

"Why do men always brag about how *big* everything is?" Meryl asked. "It's like Liberace's rings. Something might be the biggest rhinestone in the world, but it's still just a rhinestone."

We drove along Lake Mead, which seemed pretty but out of place.

"You know what I would really like?" Meryl said. "I would like to see something people haven't built."

This puzzled me until I realized that she lacked the word for *nature*. "Should we go on a camping trip?" I asked.

"Yeah. But not, you know, in a park. Dad took me to see the Grand Canyon. It was like the dam we just saw. I mean, it might not have been built by people, but with the parking lot and information center and all the restaurants and souvenir stands, it sort of seemed it was."

I asked if she wanted to see some wilderness.

A moment before, she had looked tired, hot, and bored. Now, she might have been the first human being who had gotten the idea of traveling to the moon. "We could visit Nate! I mean, that wouldn't be the *reason* we were going. We would just be taking a road trip. To see the Southwest? And visit the ruins I read about? It would be very educational, Aunt Ketzel. And then, when we got to Arizona, we could just, like, stop by and visit Nate."

I had to smile at her innocence in assuming the boy she liked would believe she had casually stopped to see him while traveling eight hundred miles from home and driving through the most remote and in-hospitable canyon in the country. His cell phone wouldn't work, and we had no way to warn him that we were coming. Even if we did, he might say we shouldn't come. And what if we couldn't find the site? What if—I hated to say this—Nate had taken up with another girl?

"Aunt Ketzel," Meryl said, as brave as any astronaut, "anything would be better than sitting around bored out of my fucking mind and missing him this bad."

I doubt she had any real hope I would consider such a scheme. If she did, she might not have proposed it. But what other way could we pass the time? Ebby was sure my brother was hiding out in Mexico. I admit now I had my doubts. Did I think I was keeping my niece safe by getting her out of town? Or did I think I was keeping her to myself? Of course I wanted my brother back. But I didn't want my idyllic time with his daughter to end. Why shouldn't Meryl and I travel around the West? I was one of those New Yorkers who saw nothing funny about the map that showed everything west of the Hudson to be blank. And my niece had seen even less of the world than I had.

"You're serious?" Meryl squealed. "You would take me to Arizona? We could stop and visit Nate?"

Sure, I said. The problem was, who would watch the dogs?

We sat pondering this dilemma until we drove past the School-house Lounge and the bare-bottomed girl leaning across her desk gave me an idea. I waited until we got home and called and asked Chickie to put on Miranda.

"Yeah?" she said. "Who is this?" It was only five in the afternoon but music was pounding in the background. "Oh, sure," she said. "Potsie's sister. You want your money back? I don't have it yet, but I could—"

No, I said, it wasn't about the money. I was just wondering if she and Kalindi wanted to stay in my brother's house and watch his dogs while his daughter and I went out of town.

She was silent so long I could hear one song end and another start. A man yelled, "Take it off!," which led me to wonder how many times a day Miranda heard those words. "Yeah," she said, "thanks. That would be really nice."

I decided to take the Hummer. Meryl's VW would have guzzled less gas. But who wants to be riding in a Beetle when an eighteen-wheeler goes hurtling past? Not to mention how much fun the Hummer was to drive.

We spent the next few days planning our expedition, shopping and packing with as much care as if we had been Coronado and de Soto setting off in search of the Seven Lost Cities of Gold. Every once in a while, Meryl would ask if I was sure her father was all right. But she didn't need much convincing. Like me, she was angry that he had betrayed her. She wanted to be free to obsess about the boy she loved rather than worry about her dad. And maybe, like me, she was enjoying our time together. Maybe it was a pleasant change to be cared for by an adult who knew how to make a grilled cheese sandwich, keep fresh milk in the fridge, and tell her which books to read.

And so, at the end of June, we said goodbye to Kalindi and Miranda and the dogs, left a note for Meryl's parents in the event either of them should come home and wonder where we had gone, climbed in the Hummer, and hit the road.

Although we didn't hit the road alone. I'm no expert on makes or models, but I couldn't help but notice that whenever I stopped or made a turn, a black Lincoln Town Car likewise stopped or turned. We merged on the freeway, and the Town Car also merged. An hour later, we stopped for gas—it truly was amazing how quickly the Hummer inhaled a tank—and after we had finished buying snacks and pulled back on the road, there the Lincoln was.

"Meryl?" I said. "Have you noticed we're being followed?"

She glanced back. "I figured he's just some asshole who's turned on by two women in a Hummer. You know, like that crazy redneck truck driver in *Thelma and Louise*?"

I can't say that allusion eased my fears. I was able to relax only after I had made an unplanned exit, then a sudden and unsignaled turn, then another turn, and another, until I was driving up a rocky, unmarked trail such as a person sees only in commercials for, well, a Hummer.

"Aunt Ketzel, you're too much!" Meryl swiveled in her seat. "We lost the guy! He's nowhere to be seen! Eat our dust, sucker!"

We had an anxious few miles before we found our way to another road. Even then, we had no idea where we might be and had to abandon our well-drawn plans. But this hardly spoiled our fun.

We stopped for lunch at a diner that had a jackalope on the roof and a gift shop that sold jackalope souvenirs, which allowed me to fool my niece into believing not only in the creature's existence but in its ability to mate with other jackalopes only when the moon is full. Old-timers, I said, used to leave cups of whiskey around their tents, which reduced the jackalopes' speed and made them easier to hunt. Meryl caught on to the joke only when I got to the part about the jackalope's talent for human speech, which allowed it to elude its pursuers by calling out in a human voice, "The varmint went that-a-way!"

We used the diner's restroom, giggling at the division between BUCKS and DOES, then went inside and took a booth. The waitress was a dazed and dreamy thing who hummed and smiled and sang to herself as she whirled around the dining room refilling cups and clearing plates. Her hair looked as if it had been dyed using the squeeze-bottle of ketchup on our table. She wore a ruffled skirt, a flowered blouse, and a ruby-encrusted pentangle around her neck.

"Aren't you the pretty one," she said, laying her hand to my niece's cheek. "Let me guess, you're feeling a little taco-and-Dr.-Pepper-ish this afternoon. And Mom here … Mom is feeling a little chicken-soup-and-mushroom-omelet-ish."

Her powers of divination might not have been accurate when it came to my relationship to my niece, but her ability to predict our culinary needs was downright spooky. She waltzed our orders to the kitchen, then came back out and pulled up a chair.

"You just drove out here from Vegas, am I right? I don't mean to offend you, but that place just about ate my heart. I went out there with a girlfriend. We were going to make it big as dancers. But I didn't have the competitive spirit enough. Some people just don't have that hustle and bustle? I ended up settling for waitressing. But heck, a girl can waitress anywhere. She doesn't need to live where it's so freaky expensive. I don't drink, I don't gamble, and I don't fool around more than is ordinary for a girl, so I figured I could waitress somewhere else just as good." She waved her arm to indicate the Jackalope's dining room and gift shop. "And somewhere else turned out to be here, I guess."

This gave my niece and me our first catchphrase of the trip. "I guess somewhere else turned out to be here," Meryl would say, studying the map to figure out where we had ended up and where we might find the next gas station for the Hummer and a restaurant and motel for us.

Later, when the waitress cleared away our plates and asked if we might be feeling "a little apple-pie-ish," she gave us our even more favorite phrase. "Aunt Ketzel, might you be feeling at all hamburger-ish today? How about ice-cream-ish? Or maybe what you're feeling is a touch liver-and-onion-ish this afternoon?"

"Meryl, darling," I might ask her back, "I don't suppose you happen to be feeling a bit bathroom-ish right now, do you?" Or, the time we passed a sign for the largest reptile zoo in Utah, "Might you be feeling a little zoo-ish?" Which led to an entirely new category of jokes about the rituals and beliefs of the Zoo-ish people ("I'm Zoo-ish. Are you by any chance Zoo-ish, too?"), until, by the end of that first week, we had developed an entire private language no one else understood.

Given my niece's tender age and the tacky roadside attractions at which we stopped, a description of our adventures might be more reminiscent of *Lolita* than *On the Road*. But our travels fulfilled the basic requirement of the genre, by which I mean we stopped wherever we took a whim and did absolutely nothing we didn't want to do. Occasionally, I tried to steer the conversation toward the sorts of questions a teenage girl might ask a mother. As ignorant as I was on some topics, I was an expert on some others. But it turned out my niece knew as much about those other topics as I did. Unless she knew even more.

"Aunt Ketzel, I can't believe you let your husband cheat on you. This one time, I heard Janis yelling at Uncle Morty that if he was going to stay at our house, he couldn't spend his time hanging around with whores. When my dad told her to mind her beeswax, she said what kind of brother takes his sister's husband to a strip club? I don't understand how you stayed married to such a douche bag. Why didn't you, like, tell him to get a job?"

After that, if any teaching was to be done, I allowed my niece to do it. We detoured hundreds of miles to see some Anasazi ruins she had read about in her book. After hiking down a canyon I was afraid I would never hike back out of, we found a cave whose walls were covered with a series of bright-red pictographs.

"Look! It's that guy who plays the flute! What's his name, Kokopelli? Nate taught me all about him. See? Kokopelli came to this village and played his flute, the winter went away, the sun came out and the corn grew tall and the women all got pregnant. See how fat this woman is? I bet she got pregnant because Kokopelli played his flute."

As proud as I was of my niece's erudition, I couldn't help but think that if I had hiked to these ruins with Morty—not that Morty had ever been in any shape to hike—he might have offered a different interpretation. "My dear," he would have said, "men do not as a rule use a flute to make a woman pregnant. This is yet another example of the tendency to whitewash the meaning of graffiti. Witness the seminal work on latrinalia by the brilliant F.S. Krauss in Vienna in the nineteen-oughts and -teens and the furor such work provoked. Ah! Do you see this figure here?" He would have pointed to the chubby stick-figure of a man to the right of Kokopelli, a figure with his genitals dangling down and his hands raised above his head, his hair standing out from his head like an Anasazi version of Bozo the Clown. "If this man isn't telling a dirty joke, I'll eat my hat."

I didn't want to spoil my niece's good mood by relaying the information I had received from Morty's ghost. Besides, she already had moved on to the next painting, and who would spoil a young person's first delight in finding a correspondence between what she has learned in books and what she is experiencing in the world?

We did not limit our discoveries to the educational. In our less scholarly moods, we weren't too proud to take the turn-off for every mystery spot, cowboy ghost-town, underground cave, mummy museum, LARGEST COLLECTION OF CORNCOB PIPES, historic fort, or birthplace that advertised its charms. We made the obligatory stop at Monument Valley, where we drove around a landscape of strangely shaped rocks that would have been impressive if they hadn't been enclosed in a park—they reminded me of the lions and giraffes wandering the grassy plains at some Safari World while tourists snapped their photos from zebra-painted jeeps. Besides, how awed could a person be by rocks that served as backdrops for every Western ever filmed, including *The Searchers*, in which John Wayne had circled these very same monuments for five long years as he tried to save Natalie Wood from the unspeakable fate of living with an Indian man she loved?

What Meryl and I preferred were landscapes where the mountains were free to roam. Once, we came across a rock in the shape of a hand giving the finger to passersby. Another time, we drove along a ridge with colossal rocks hanging above our heads in disturbing shapes. Up and up we drove along sharply curving switchbacks until we got out to enjoy the view.

"Aunt Ketzel?" Meryl pointed to a needle of rock so high not even the makers of a truck commercial could have airlifted a vehicle to the plateau on top. "Do you think anyone has ever been up there?"

I doubted anyone had.

"So, like, there are places no one has ever been?"

"Sure," I said. "Why?"

She was quiet for a while. "Do you really think my dad's all right? It's been, like, six weeks. You and Nate's dad, you're pretty sure he just pretended to be kidnapped. Right? To scare my stepmom?"

She looked at me with an emptiness in her eyes that seemed to be a product of the canyons below, and I didn't know how to fill it. "Your dad's having the time of his life, wherever he's hiding out." But Meryl must have heard the uncertainty in my voice, as if her father were out there among those twists and turns of rock, and even if he were alive, how could we hope to find him?

She leaned against me. "If he never comes back, do you promise I can live with you?"

My mother hadn't been far wrong in accusing me of wanting my brother to stay away so I could keep caring for his child. On the other hand, I loved my brother. I wanted Potsie back.

"Of course, sweetheart. But I'll bet your dad turns up before we get back to Vegas," a wager that, for all it calmed my niece, I had reason to regret.

After that, I avoided such scary views, not least because, taking a break at a scenic stop, I glimpsed a black Lincoln Town Car wending its way up the switchbacks toward us. I told myself there were probably thousands of people driving black Lincoln Town Cars, but I made sure to hustle my niece back in the Hummer before she could see the vehicle, or before it could overtake us.

Instead, we took to searching for what Meryl called "places people hadn't made," a pastime that involved steering the Hummer down the next dirt road we saw, parking, then getting out and walking. We fantasized about pitching a tent and surviving by sucking the milk from a cactus or catching one of the scorpions that skittered around our boots, cracking open its tiny claws, and prying out the meat. But even Meryl had to laugh at how dangerously close this brought us to the silliness that had led Jurgen and ValZorah to live like the Anasazi.

You can't go back in time. On a stretch of road so remote I wouldn't have been surprised to see a brontosaurus lumbering toward the Hummer, we passed a withered Navajo grandma in tribal dress minding a flock of sheep, a picture marred only by the Game Boy she was playing to pass the time.

We climbed to the top of Mesa Verde, where we crouched beneath the soot that had been left on a cave wall by a thousand-year-old cooking fire beside the ashy print of a toddler's hand. I felt we had found the beginnings of the human race. Yet the Anasazis' lives had been no realer than ours, and no freer from illusion. What about all the stories they had made up to explain why the sun rose in the morning or babies grew in their mothers' wombs? Didn't the Indians feel belated, too? Weaker and inferior to the first inhabitants of Mother Earth, who, according to Anasazi myths, had crawled up from underground, blinked and rubbed their eyes, then set out to find some food?

Finally, we filled our cooler with ice-cold drinks and headed south to Chaco Canyon. Meryl was quiet and pale, and when we saw a sign that announced the entrance to the park, she whispered, "I feel sick." I sent up a little prayer that whoever was in charge wouldn't disappoint my niece. And wonder of wonders, whoever was in charge complied. The ranger at the visitors' center, when we asked him to direct us to Nate's professor's camp, shook his head and said, "You would need a Humvee to get there," and when we said that a Humvee was exactly the vehicle we happened to be driving, he laughed and drew a map. The terrain was fractured by arroyos. We might as well have been driving across the moon. But the Hummer bounded happily up and down the obstacles in its path, and we managed to arrive unharmed.

Nate, once he got over his shock, seemed thrilled to see my niece. "Me? You came all this way to see me?"

"Sure," Meryl said, blushing. "And the ruins. We came to see the ruins."

"The ruins!" Nate said. "Of course!," relieved to play along that he hadn't been the object of our thousand-mile trip. The Hummer's engine had barely stopped humming before he had taken us on a tour of the abandoned city that was the center of a vanished world.

"See this?" Nate pointed to a thick pole that once held up a roof. "We're taking samples from all the logs to figure out where the trees came from and how old they were when the woodcutters cut them down." He pressed his palm to one beam. "These babies came all the way from the Chuska Mountains. The men would have had to hike fifty miles uphill, cut down these huge trees, then drag them back down here."

From the expression on my niece's face, Nate might have been the one who had cut down and hauled every one of those trees himself.

"Are there any people here?" Meryl asked. "Like, I mean, their skeletons?"

Nate lit up like any amateur who has been asked to display his knowledge. "That's a great question. But the thing is, nobody knows the answer. Thousands of people lived here. But there's no cemetery, no burial place, no nothing. So, where are all the bodies buried?"

I needed to bite my tongue to keep from saying *Maybe you should look at the bottom of my family's lake.*

Nate offered to show us this really neat pictograph the Anasazi had painted to commemorate the supernova of 1054, or maybe it was the passage of Halley's Comet a few years later. "It's got this star, right? And then there's this crescent moon, and a person's hand, and what looks like a comet or a burst of light. It's the coolest thing I've ever seen."

Pleading heat prostration—it would have been 115 degrees in the shade, if there had been shade in which to prostrate—I wished them bon voyage.

"Are you sure?" Meryl asked, unable to imagine a time of life in which the promise of a very neat pictograph might not be enough to make a person climb a cliff on a blazing day. I assured her that I was fine, and after she and Nate had scampered off, I was able to enjoy a cold drink and sit in the miniscule shade the Hummer threw and try to figure out why on God's green earth anyone would choose such a barren place to put a city. If the inhabitants of Chaco Canyon were going to go to all the trouble of climbing the mountains to cut their wood, why didn't they build their city there?

Then it came to me: No one had lived at Chaco. That's why no one was buried here. Chaco hadn't been a town like New York or Chicago, built near water or good green land. This wasn't a city where people *lived*. It was a city like Las Vegas, chosen by some Chacoan Bugsy Siegel, who had erected it not in the name of agriculture, commerce, or art but the more mysterious powers of sex and death.

The only troublesome moment in an otherwise perfect day came when Nate was showing us the largest kiva at the site. We looked down from the rim, the way people look down a well, and Meryl started crying. "I can't believe my mother preferred living in a fucking hole in the ground with that asshole Jurgen than living in a nice house with me and Dad."

Nate, bless his heart, took Meryl in his arms and held her. But the sun was going down, and it seemed to me, standing at that kiva, that each and every one of us had a mother in that hole.

The other workers came back for dinner. We shared their beer and stew, then sat around the fire, listening to our new companions turn that day's mishaps into funny anecdotes. I felt a pang for Morty, who would have loved to witness this example of exhausted human beings crouching around a fire, inventing new myths and jokes.

Then Nate and the other volunteers rubbed their limbs and yawned and crawled inside their tents. Meryl and I stayed up, marveling at how fresh and cool the desert air had turned, then we stretched out in the Hummer and tried to sleep. A coyote yipped. Beside me, Meryl snored. I thought of Miranda and Kalindi, and it seemed sleeping in a truck wasn't so unpleasant, as long as you had a real home to return to.

The next morning, Meryl and Nate went off to say goodbye in private, a leave-taking made only slightly less tragic by the fact that they would be reunited in eleven days. We climbed back in the Hummer, and as slowly as we had meandered from home to here, that's how quickly we headed back.

Home! Who could have guessed I would ever call Las Vegas home? But as we drove up to La Mancha Estates and the gate slid open before us, that was precisely how I felt. The greyhounds put their paws on our shoulders and danced us around the yard, berserk with joy. Miranda and Kalindi tried to act happy, too, but their enthusiasm was dampened by the fact that our return meant they would need to leave.

"Can we come back and use the pool?" Kalindi asked before Miranda could shush her. "I could only go in the shallow end. Because I still had my cast? But see? Yesterday I got it off?" She lifted an arm so frail and white I wanted to wrap it in the cast again to protect it.

I told Miranda that she and Kalindi were welcome to stay with us until they found a new place to live. "Thanks," she said, wiping away some tears. "If it's all right, I'll tell Chickie I'm not coming back. With Perry gone, the place has gone downhill. If you can imagine someplace that was already in the gutter going downhill. This way, I can put down a real address on my applications."

This quieted my conscience, but even with Miranda out searching for a job and Kalindi as quiet and well behaved as a ten-year-old can be, I was impatient and out of sorts. Rather than motion sickness, I seemed to be afflicted with staying still. Neither my niece nor I could bear to remain inside. But where did we need to go?

Then Meryl got a call from her friend Davia, who said she was being dragged to Tahoe with her father and his boyfriend, and would Meryl *please* come along? Meryl was bored and missed her friend, so I told her she should go.

"Are you sure?" she said. "What about my dad?"

Well, I said, her presence wouldn't bring him home any sooner. She worried I would be alone without her. I kissed her and said how lonely could I be with Miranda and Kalindi to keep me company?

All right, she said. If I was sure.

The next morning, Davia's father and his boyfriend picked her up, and when I saw the two girls hug, I was glad Meryl would be spending time with a friend her own age instead of a disappointed widow in her fifties. I babysat for Kalindi while her mother borrowed Meryl's car and drove to an interview with a company that supplied linens to the casinos. It was a pleasure to sit by the pool and watch Kalindi. She had borrowed one of Meryl's cast-off bathing suits, which she wore with a T-shirt to keep from burning.

"Look at me!" she called, running toward the pool and leaping in, after which she burst from the water and smoothed her waifish hair and hopped about dripping on the deck, as gold limbed and delicate as an elf. I considered telling Miranda she ought to let me mention Kalindi to Harvey Blatt, but I came to my senses just in time.

To keep from sitting by the phone, waiting for Harvey to call and tell me Larry David had chosen someone else to play the crazy Jewish neighbor, I manufactured things to do. I took the dogs for long walks, although they kept looking over their shoulders as if they were afraid of snipers. Once, I visited the office above the store that sold venetian blinds, to see if Smoke had heard from Potsie, but all traces of the man were gone. I stopped by the poker room at the Mirage, but the Native American dealer wasn't there and the other dealers seemed too busy to interrupt. I drove past Ebby's house, but all I saw was a friend of Nate's who was walking the iguanas so they got their daily dose of UV light.

As if the sight of two big lizards being walked on a leash wasn't unsettling enough, I noticed I was being followed, although this time the vehicle on my tail was a bright-white SUV.

Luckily, whoever was driving the SUV couldn't get past the gate. I hurried inside the house, not even pausing to exchange a wave with Innocenzio Incognito. I was so rattled that when I saw a note in Miranda's handwriting that "Sargent" Magoo from the missing persons bureau had called and please to call him back, I assumed he wanted to discuss my being followed. Even after I had gotten Sergeant Magoo on the phone and started describing my pursuer's car, I needed a few moments to understand that his purpose in calling had been to inform me a John Doe had turned up in the desert, and the sergeant was sorry to report but the remains might be my brother's.

It was like a joke I didn't get. How could my brother's remains have been found in the desert when Ebby and I had figured out Potsie had staged his own kidnapping and was hiding in Mexico until he could figure out how to dispose of his property without Janis claiming half? I asked the sergeant what had led him to believe this skeleton might be my brother's, but the only information he was prepared to divulge over the phone was that some teenagers had been out hunting jackrabbits (didn't he mean *jackalopes?*) a mile or so south of Bitter Springs Trail in something called Valley of Fire State Park when they smelled a godawful stink and noticed—he hated to say this—a leg bone sticking up. The two youths had hiked to the nearest trading post and called the police, who called the coroner's office, whose investigators examined the evidence and surmised—based on "circumstantial evidence"—that the John Doe might in fact be a missing person named Stuart "Potsie" Weinrach.

But the coroner wouldn't say more until a scientific identification could be performed. And to perform said identification, the coroner needed a copy of my brother's dental records, which meant he needed to know my brother's dentist's name. Sergeant Magoo wouldn't say another word, except, when I told him that even as an adult my brother had continued to rely on our childhood dentist, and that after that dentist had retired, Potsie had refused to see any dentist at all, Sergeant Magoo remarked, yes, well, if a person had perfect teeth like these, he wouldn't need to see a dentist, would he, unlike Magoo himself, who needed to go in for caps and crowns and murderously painful root canals every other week.

After I hung up, I stood dumb as a corpse myself. The dogs sniffed and licked my hands, then slunk back in their crates, as if my fingers stank of death. I was glad Meryl wasn't home. And I wasn't about to call my parents. It was after nine in Monticello, which was too late to get my brother's X-rays from whoever had taken over Dr. Rothstein's practice when he had retired to Boca Raton a few years earlier. Why should my mother spend the night wondering whether that leg bone was her son's? For that matter, why tell my parents anything until the results came back?

I called Ebby on his cell, praying he would answer.

"Salzman here," he said, at which I started crying and talking without making the slightest sense. "Whoa! Whoa, Ketzel, get hold of yourself." And then, after I had managed to convey the gist of what Magoo had said: "Okay. Right. That is a surprise. But there's no telling . . . Let me call my pals at the coroner's office, okay?"

I sat on my brother's couch and thought how lucky I was to have so many alarms and gates between me and the outside world, as if this would prevent the entrance of the messenger who was trying to bring the news of my brother's death. As stupid as this sounds, I was in no rush for Ebby to call me back.

Although finally he did. "I have to tell the truth, this situation does not look good. They found Potsie's wallet with the remains. And a pair of pink flip-flops in an extra-large size. And some strands of long gray hair wrapped around a cactus. And, well, that lanyard key-chain you made for him at camp."

With that, the intruder got in and shot me. How could that key chain be lying beside that skeleton if it hadn't been in the pocket of the person who had become the skeleton? My powers of coherent speech vanished and were replaced by the capacity to do nothing but cry *no, no, no, no,* until finally I seemed to lose even that ability. A long time went by, in which Ebby tried to comfort me. We didn't have all the facts, he said. There was no use believing the worst until we had gotten the report on my brother's dental records. In the meantime, I should just sit tight until Ebby got there. He was about to hang up, but I could sense he had something else to say.

"Ketzel? This is neither here nor there, but the coroner's office told me . . . The guys who found your brother? On the way to call the cops, they found another body. And this one was . . . it was fresh enough they could tell . . . It was another Asian woman."

"Ebby, I can't . . . This has nothing to do with my brother? It was just a coincidence? So many dead bodies get tossed in the desert every day people just trip over them?"

I could hear him compose his thoughts. "I'll start home first thing tomorrow morning. Nate called from the ranger station and said he decided to stay one more week at Chaco—he's getting a lift back to Vegas with another volunteer. I ought to be there the day after next. Call me if you need me in the meantime."

The line went dead and so did I. The last thing I wanted was to be sitting in the house when Miranda and Kalindi got back. What if Meryl called? It was one thing to be someone's mother when all that was required was shopping and cooking and taking her on a road trip. It was another thing to be the grown-up responsible for a child who has just been told that her one remaining parent has been found in the desert as a pile of bones.

I don't know how long I sat there. I only know that at a certain point, I couldn't sit a moment more. I'm not sure I had a plan. I only remember climbing in the Hummer and opening the glove compartment, hoping to find a map, then sobbing, "Oh, Potsie!," as if the packets of ketchup and mayonnaise, the flashlight, the Humvee manual, and yes, the gun that tumbled out were the relics of a saint. I remember driving out the gate and getting on the highway heading north. But I don't remember much else about the drive, except the ugliness matched my mood. I have seen some squalid highways in my life. But the roads that lead to Newark or New York don't pretend to be gateways to Paris or Mandalay. The area north of Vegas was a wasteland of construction rubble, warehouses, power plants, junkyards, construction companies, and storage trailers. Then all signs of the city vanished and there was desert on either side.

I exited at Valley of Fire Park. There was a minimart, a fireworks store, a small casino run by the Moapa Paiutes, and a launching area where customers could set off the rockets and flares they'd bought. A herd of scrawny cows grazed among the launching pads and trash barrels. A police car emblazoned with the blue and orange feathers of the Moapa tribal police sat beside a pushcart that sold tacos and REALLY GOOD BEEF JERKY; I was tempted to ask the officers if they could direct me to the site where my brother's body had been found, but I knew they would think it was stupid to go out in the desert alone at this hour—which, no doubt, it was—so I went inside and asked the girl behind the counter to point the way.

With the crazy state I was in, it seemed weirdly fortuitous that my brother's disappearance had made it possible for me to be driving the only vehicle that could navigate a road with a name like Bitter Springs Trail. A few miles past the minimart, I saw a spot where you didn't need to be Tonto to figure out that five or six vehicles had churned up the sand, so I pulled off and left the car.

The land was cracked and brown, with trees in distorted shapes like bonsai. The sky had turned an aquatic blue, with heavy-bodied clouds that reminded me of the swimmers I used to see when I sank to the bottom of the hotel's pool and watched the misshapen guests paddling above me. But I wasn't a little girl. I wasn't in a pool; I was in the desert. I had come to Las Vegas to find the truth, and even though I had been putting off that assignment for the past two months, I was going to face it now.

I walked south, hoping I might stumble on the site where those hunters had found my brother. Maybe it would be marked with yellow tape. The sky grew dimmer. I had to look down to see where I was putting my feet. I felt surrounded by so much loss I wanted to lift my face to the moon and howl. Ira was dead. And Mike. Howie was lost to us forever. Now Potsie was gone. How could I tell my parents? After this new grief killed them, I would be the only member of our family left. Only my niece and me.

I sat there a long time, trying to figure out who had killed my brother. Was my sister-in-law really as cunning and bloodthirsty as my mother thought? Or had Potsie gotten so deep in debt he had been ashamed to ask for help? Maybe he had been seduced into some shady deal backed by the Mob. Maybe our cousin Perry had been the one to do the seducing. Maybe Perry had gotten my brother into trouble, then left him to the wolves and run off to Tijuana to escape whatever fate my brother had been too fat and dumb to outrun himself.

I heard a coyote's chilling trills, like a bugler playing taps. A terrible peace set in, or maybe a state of shock. Something colorful caught my eye—the scrap of a rocket beside a beer can whose label was bleached bone white, and, to the side of those, a tiny white cactus with three luminous yellow blooms.

A rocket went whizzing overhead, where it burst into streamers that fizzled to the ground and popped. As the sulfurous glare died out, I saw that beyond the fireworks, the stars were shining in such profusion they made me gasp. Reality had been here all along. We were nothing. We were a miracle. Death was an illusion, and death was real. Everything we humans did in our pitiably brief time on earth was a magnificent and noble tragedy . . . and a ridiculous Borscht Belt joke.

But as happens when a person looks up at the sky too long, my neck ached, my head grew dizzy, and I had to look back down. That's when the fear set in. How had I come to be here? Not in an existential sense, but in the sense of finding myself alone in the desert in the dark.

For those of you who think I couldn't find my way back to my brother's Hummer, I was in danger but not from that. For all everyone in my family thinks I walk around in a fog, I actually have a keen sense of direction. I had walked south to find my brother; now I walked north to find his car. The Hummer was exactly where I had left it. I started the engine and turned around.

But since returning home from Chaco, I had neglected to fill the tank. After I had driven about a mile, the vehicle sputtered to a halt.

Even then, I wasn't scared. When a Hummer stops, it stops; you can't exactly push it. But I knew all I had to do was walk the four or five miles along Bitter Springs Trail and I would eventually reach the minimart. Just to be on the safe side, I took my brother's flashlight and gun. I was by no means a practiced marksman, but Leo used to take me behind the kitchen and teach me to shoot at the rats that scavenged amid the trash. "Good girl!" he used to say, thumping me on the back when I got a hit. Not that I had touched a gun in thirty years. But how hard could it be to shoot in the general direction of a coyote and scare it off?

I was starting to relax when I saw a pair of headlights. I considered flagging down the car, but something told me not to. It was coming in the wrong direction. And it was a large white SUV.

If my brother was dead, then maybe my sister-in-law's story about the Mob was true. I snapped off the flashlight and gripped the gun. No matter who had murdered whom, unless Ed McMahon was trying to inform me that I had won the Publishers Clearing House Sweepstakes, the driver of that SUV was unlikely to be bringing me good news.

I ran. Although even in sneakers, how far could I really go? Oh, why had I let Morty convince me working out in a gym was just another way corporations had convinced us to turn our bodies into salable commodities? Already I was out of breath. Glancing back, I saw that the SUV had stopped and the driver was hurrying toward me. I wasn't sure if I could shoot a man, even in self-defense. Then again, I wasn't about to go down without a fight.

I put my finger on the trigger and sighted as best I could. I was panting so hard the pistol shook. But something about my pursuer's square silhouette and waddling gait struck me as familiar.

"Ketzel! Don't shoot! It's Leo!"

Leo? *Our* Leo? Leo Bialik from Monticello, formerly of Murder Inc.? What was Leo doing here? Was he the hit man who killed my brother? Had he gone back to his murderous ways? Or had he never given those ways up?

"What's the matter?" *What's duh madduh?* "Can't you see? It's Leo! You need to put down that gun. Otherwise, you might shoot me accidentally. You wouldn't want that to happen, would you?"

I started to lower my arms, but I wasn't yet convinced.

A look of hurt came over Leo's face. "To think I scared you this bad! You don't even feel safe putting down the gun when you see it's me!" He turned, bowed his head, and started to walk away.

I dropped the gun and staggered forward. "Leo!" I shouted. "Wait!"

We fell into each other's arms. Not only was it a relief to discover that my pursuer wasn't trying to kill me, here was someone who—albeit he was eighty-three years old—was strong and savvy enough to protect me. That's when I started sobbing. Leo pulled out a handkerchief so big he could have used it to mask his face.

"Leo," I said, "it's not that I'm not glad to see you. But why have you been following me? I might have shot you!" The irony that I might have shot the man who had taught me to shoot didn't strike either of us as the least bit funny.

He doffed his cap and clasped it to his heart. "Ketzel, I'm sorry I scared you. But your parents and I were worried sick." He seemed to regain the upper hand. "Since when are you too important to return your mother's calls? She has a right to be frantic, not only about you and your brother, but about her only grandchild. No progress was being made. Someone needed to come out here and initiate such progress into occurring. Seeing your parents' debilitated circumstances, that someone could only be me."

"But I thought you were prohibited from stepping foot in Vegas!"

He pursed his lips in that parrotfish way he had. "For you, it was worth the risk."

"But wasn't it hard for you to avoid . . . you know, gambling?"

He held up his hands, which, for reasons I couldn't yet explain, didn't seem to belong to him. "Most of the time, I have been occupied in surveilling you and your niece. Admittedly, when you were tucked in for the night and no one was going anywheres, I gave in to my tendency to visit the casinos. The newer ones, at which my reputation has not yet preceded me. And, I am happy to say, I won a considerable amount at craps. It was only when you left town—I must compliment you, Ketzel, I was known in the business as a very difficult tail to lose—I had nothing to keep me out of trouble and so returned to the craps table and went seriously into debt."

By now, Leo had led me back to the SUV. By the light from the bulb inside, I saw what was missing from his hands. "Your watch! And that beautiful sapphire ring!"

He waved away my concern. "What is a ring?" he asked. "Ditto, what is a watch?" Albeit, the watch was a Rolex, but what were material possessions compared to a human life? The Rolex and ring had been what Leo called "ill and rotten gains," remnants of the bad old days when he worked for Abe Reles. The eye in the sapphire had given him nightmares about his role in certain individuals ending up at the bottom of Cuyahoga Lake.

"Come on," he said. "We'll get gas for your brother's truck. And perhaps you can explain why you were wandering in a place you ought never be wandering, at an hour such as this."

It occurred to me Leo knew nothing about my search to find John Doe. I explained about the call from Sergeant Magoo at the missing persons bureau, at which Leo was unashamed to cry. That was terrible news, he said. Terrible! He did not look forward to informing my parents that they had lost another son. Oh, that a member of the Weinrach family should have met such an ignominious end in a desolate place like this! Did the police have any idea as to who might have perpetrated such a crime?

Not as far as I knew.

Well, he said, we would just have to expend all our resources, financial and otherwise, to make certain the officials in charge of the case persisted in bringing the responsible parties to a fitting end. We started driving back to the minimart, each of us lost in our ruminations as to what it would do to my parents to learn that their youngest son had turned up as skeletal remains in a place called Valley of Fire Park, and, worst of all, what such news would do to Meryl. Leo waddled into the minimart to see about getting a can of gas. Wandering numbly past fireworks with names like Raptor, Rampage, Mine Shell Mayhem, and Air-otica, not to mention smoke grenades that looked as lethal as the item that nearly killed *der Führer,* I came upon bags of candy so large they could have fed an entire third-world nation. Oh, I thought, wouldn't Potsie have loved such outlandishly oversized bags of Mary Janes! How could I accept I would never again enjoy the light in my brother's eyes when he unwrapped a Baby Ruth?

That's when the real truth hit me. My brother had a cavity in every tooth. The reason he had never found a dentist he liked in Vegas was that the only practitioner of the art he trusted was kindly old Dr. Rothstein. What had the sergeant said? *If I had teeth that good, I wouldn't need to see a dentist either.*

The one with the perfect teeth was Perry. How could I forget? One afternoon, my brother needed to visit the dentist, and Perry said, "If you wouldn't eat all that crap, you wouldn't need to get your teeth drilled." Potsie shot back, "Yeah? You eat just as much crap as I do," and Perry said, "Yeah, but I've never had a cavity." Then Perry grinned and bared his teeth and said there was some chemical in the water in Texas, it was like kryptonite, which was why he had these Superman teeth. My brother pulled back his fist and would have shown Superman just how invincible his teeth really were if Perry hadn't ducked and run.

But if the skeleton belonged to Perry, the only person who could have put Potsie's key chain in his pocket would be my brother.

"Leo!" I called, hurrying outside to where he was pumping gas in a can. It took a while, but I made him understand what I was saying. What was more difficult to convey was why, after we had driven back to get the Hummer, we needed to stop at an all-night Wal-Mart, buy a computer monitor, and take it to the Schoolhouse Lounge.

There were barely any cars—the decline of my cousin's business was not a development that broke my heart—but I preferred not to attract the attention of the few remaining patrons by entering through the lounge. I waited while Leo got Chickie to unlock the back door. As far as I could tell, nothing in my cousin's apartment had been disturbed. The pile of Tootsie Roll wrappers still lay on Perry's desk beside the mug of coffee, upon which the layer of mold had grown even thicker. I hooked up the monitor and turned it on, at which I was treated to the sight of three naked women kneeling in front of an angular man with long, curly black hair whom I recognized as Eddy "the Rock" Rokowski. I couldn't figure out how my cousin had arranged for four naked people to be photographed in broad daylight in front of the WELCOME TO FABULOUS LAS VEGAS sign, but I supposed if you paid enough money to the right people, you could pose anywhere you wanted to pose in Vegas.

I began searching through my cousin's files, not knowing what I was searching for, but when I saw a folder named "kalindi," I knew with a sick chill I had found it, just as I knew my brother had seen these pictures—this must have been where Potsie had come to hide after Perry and his friends "abducted" him from his house. I could see everything in my mind. Perry had been working out in front, and my brother had gotten bored and decided to check a sports score, or maybe his cousin's porn, at which he had settled at this computer with a handful of Tootsie Rolls and a cup of coffee, and what should he find but clips of Miranda's daughter dancing naked around this room.

It could have been worse. There could have been naked men in those pictures with Kalindi. The men could have been having sex. But what my brother had seen was bad enough that when our cousin walked in the room, Potsie must have punched him.

Maybe those photos of Kalindi would have been enough to incite my brother to kill our cousin. But I knew beyond a doubt that the contents of the next file I opened—a file with the cryptic label "ketzel62"—was more than enough to do the job. Certainly, if my cousin had been standing behind me as I watched the dim image of my ten-year-old self dancing provocatively for the camera, then slipping my fingers in the waistband of my bikini and tugging down the bottom, then stepping out of the panties and twirling them around and tossing them out of sight in a manner that alternated between heartbreakingly reluctant and an unsettlingly confident imitation of Mitzi Gaynor, I would have beaten him to death myself. Even now, I can barely bring myself to describe what it was like to see my younger self dance a klutzy but touching mambo, following the silent orders of the man who held the camera, orders that must have instructed me to turn slowly in a circle while shimmying my childish hips. My blood ran hot, then cold. I thought, *Oh, no, God, don't let me pass out in this terrible place again!*

"Ketzel?" Leo said. "Ketzel, sweetheart, are you all right?"

A long time must have passed. Leo leaned down to look at the computer. "The fuggin' bastard!" He wobbled and closed his eyes and sat heavily on Perry's bed. It amazed me that a man who suffered no qualms about jamming ice picks in people's ears was so shaken by what my cousin had done to me that he turned green and could barely speak. "That fuggin' lousy ... I could tear off his fuggin' head! 'Mr. Bialik,' he used to say. 'If it isn't too much trouble, would you be so kind as to convey me into town?' The fuggin' two-faced pervert." Leo twisted his invisible cigar in the air. "If your cousin was here, old as I am, I'd gouge out the eyes that brought him any pleasure seeing those things he saw."

At some point, Leo realized such talk wasn't helping me to regain my equilibrium. He went off to get me water. I sat wondering how many times my cousin had watched this clip, how many people on the Web had seen it. I kept reaching for the computer as if to shield my younger self and cradle her in my palm and take her home.

And my brother? How long had it taken him to figure out he knew the little girl dancing in that bikini? And when he did realize what he was seeing, did Potsie become as angry at himself as he was at Perry? He had failed to protect me from a boy everyone knew to be a maniac. And for decades, he had turned a blind—and not-so-blind—eye to our cousin's profession as a pornographer. I learned most of these details later. But even on my own, I was able to fit together enough pieces of the puzzle that I got the picture. I would need to tell Magoo to look for a bearskin rug not far from where Perry's skeleton had been discovered, although only the bear's skull would be left by now. And they would need to go over the Vantastic van with a finer-toothed comb than the comb Ebby had used the night I was sitting at the bar with Chickie. After dumping our cousin in the desert, my brother must have driven Perry's van back to the Schoolhouse Lounge, left the key under the mat, then stuck out his thumb and hitched, barefoot, to the border. He wouldn't have risked flying to the Caribbean. And he wasn't stupid enough to have stayed in Tijuana.

When Leo came back, I showed him the photos of Kalindi, then mustered my courage to explain how the girl in the polka-dot bathing suit had come to be dancing the mambo.

"I never liked that jerk," Leo said. "From day one, when your parents took him in, I said, 'Lennie, Dolores, excuse me for casting aspersions on your relations, but this one is a bad seed. No one should be held responsible for his father's sins, but this one is a wiseguy all his own.'"

Given the child-pornography network my cousin Perry ran, with photos not only of Kalindi and me but the daughters of other strippers at his club, the term *wiseguy* seemed too tame. Not to mention this raised the question as to why, if everyone knew all along what a wiseguy my cousin was, they allowed him to hang around with me.

I couldn't bear to stay in my cousin's apartment a moment more, but there were questions I felt compelled to ask Chickie Kurek. Leo accompanied me to the bar and sat waiting for a signal to unleash the violence he had been tamping down for sixty years.

"Chickie?" I said. "Did you ever wonder why Perry was so generous about letting the dancers bring their kids to work? Or why he let Kalindi do her homework in the back?"

"I didn't wonder. I knew." Chickie picked up a glass and dried it. "He wanted to be nice to the kids so he could get in the mothers' pants. Not that they usually had any pants to get into."

I studied him as he said this. The events of the past six months had shaken my confidence to ferret out a lie. "What if I told you it wasn't the mothers he was after?"

He rubbed the towel inside the glass. Then something clicked, and he hurled the glass against the wall, where it struck a bottle of peach schnapps, exploding both. "You're telling me that son of a fucking bitch got Kalindi to . . ." Chickie picked up another glass and hurled it, this time shattering a bottle of a green liqueur that dripped down the counter in a sickening, sticky way. I would have allowed Chickie to continue using my cousin's expensive liquor as his private shooting gallery, but the stripper complained that Chickie was interfering with her act, and the five or six patrons watching the show added their complaints to hers, at which Chickie flipped a switch and the music groaned to a halt.

"That's it. Gigi, get some clothes on. Everyone else, get your fat asses out of here. Whoever was drinking what, that last drink was on the house."

The patrons needed a while to understand, but with Leo's help they found the door. When the lounge was empty—with all the vacant desks, it had the melancholy feel of a classroom after school has let out for the summer—Chickie stood looking around as if he couldn't believe that a man with two sets of eyes could have been so oblivious to what was going on beneath his nose.

"Your brother was right. You are one smart cookie." He brought up the jar he had shown me the night I had passed out at the lounge. "I was pulling your leg. You knew that, right? These are just pickled onions. Your brother really did put a scare into Mary's nutcase of a boyfriend. But Potsie only threatened to cut off his balls." Chickie handed me the onions so I could convince myself these were not human gonads we were discussing. "And that husband of yours? I didn't mean to leave the wrong impression. Morty Tittelman certainly did like the ladies. I cannot tell you otherwise. But all he wanted to do was talk. Or maybe what he liked to do was listen. He would pay them, you know, to talk."

"You mean talk dirty?" Why would Morty have flown all the way to Vegas to hear strippers talk dirty? Couldn't he have visited strip joints in New York? Was he studying regional variations in the jokes prostitutes liked to tell? And why, if he was conducting research, had my husband felt the need to lie to me?

Chickie led us to the door. "Don't look so glum. On more than one occasion the professor said—at this very bar—that he had never loved anyone except his wife." The three of us stepped outside. A flatbed truck with what appeared to be a missile on the back barreled past on the highway. "Or maybe what he said was he'd never *laughed* with anyone except his wife." Chickie stroked his Fu Manchu, trying to get the quote straight. "Or maybe it was loved *and* laughed? 'Chickie,' he said, 'I am a very lucky man. The world would be a far, far better place if everyone could find a woman like my Ketzel, with whom I am able to share not only terrific sex, but also a good laugh in bed.'"

I suppose I was relieved that the relationship to which I had devoted myself for twenty-seven years had not been a complete and utter sham. But my mind was already racing forward to the calls I would need to make the moment Leo and I got home, and how I would phrase what I had to say.

Leo insisted on staying at my brother's house, although, given that my brother was alive, and the only person who had ever posed a threat to any of us was dead, I'm not sure from whom he was protecting me.

By then it was after midnight. As reluctant as I was to rouse Ebby at the motel where he was staying with his daughter, I called him on his cell.

"Salzman," he said. "What? He what?," followed by a long and thoughtful pause during which he processed my convoluted account of the events that had transpired since we had spoken last. "I'm ashamed to say I didn't think of that myself. The only honorable thing would be for me to refund your parents' money. Tell them I said they should give it to you instead."

I was pleased to hear such praise. But I couldn't bear to hear Ebby berate himself. "If it weren't for you, I would still be sitting here thinking that was real blood on those steps."

Be that as it may, he knew his performance had been deficient. All he could do was to help me tie up as many loose ends as possible. He would be home the next day. Or rather, given how late it already was, he would be home that afternoon.

I hung up and fed the dogs, then spread an afghan over Leo, who had dozed off in a chair. I curled up on the sofa and tried to think. Since Nate was still at Chaco, it would be easy to persuade Meryl to stay another few days with Davia. I saw no reason to share my theories as to what crimes her father might have committed or what our cousin had done to poor Kalindi. The next morning, when I reached her at Davia's father's condo, all I said was that Ebby and I would be going out of town for the next few days and we hoped to find her father and bring him back.

"You think my dad's all right? I might get to see him soon? Aunt Ketzel, you're the best!," a compliment that made me squirm since I would be the one bringing her father back to face the repercussions of his deeds.

After that, I called my parents, harboring a vague hope they would thank me for discovering that their one remaining son was alive, albeit a murderer on the run. But I wasn't prepared for the satisfaction I would feel at hearing my mother scream, "Lennie! Come quick! Ketzel's found Potsie! She says it's Perry who's the corpse! I told you she'd solve the case! She's smarter than the rest of us put together! She's a regular Charlie Chan!"

11.

THE EVENTS OF the next few days remain muddled. I remember going up to my brother's guest room, tiptoeing in, careful not to wake Kalindi, who was sleeping in a sleeping bag on the floor, rousing Miranda, and motioning her out in the hall to talk. "I have some upsetting news," I said.

"Oh, no!" she said. "Perry isn't—"

Yes, well, I told her quietly, Perry *was* dead, but that wasn't the upsetting news. When I explained about the pictures on his computer, she broke down so badly I needed to reassure her the photos hadn't shown anything worse than Kalindi dancing nude, although that was bad enough.

"How could I have been so ..." Miranda sobbed. "How could I have taken my little girl ..."

I shushed her. My cousin was a monster, I said. And that's what monsters did. They seduced you into thinking it was your fault you had been their prey. She and Kalindi could stay with us as long as they needed. My parents and I would pay for counseling.

I considered going to see Magoo. But I decided to wait until Ebby was back. It would take at least a day for Dr. Rothstein's successor in Monticello to send my brother's and cousin's dental records.

I remember Ebby driving up in his truck, then jumping out and holding me. His daughter hopped down, freckled and tan, in sneakers and shorts and a blissfully filthy shirt that said MY GRANDMA LOVES ME. I remember picking up the phone and finding out that the John Doe in the desert was in fact my cousin Perry, after which I let Ebby drive me downtown to tell my story to a homicide detective named Jackson Vigor—Ebby pronounced it *Vy-gor*—with whom Ebby used to work when he was a detective, too.

The building in which Homicide was housed was even less impressive than the missing persons bureau. But it was the happiest workplace I had ever seen. We waited in the reception area while a heavyset detective carried in a bag of Styrofoam cups, a twelve-pack of ginger ale, and a rectangular cake with candles, plastic forks, and paper plates. Everyone bantered and joked, as if, given all the violence and death they had seen, they were deliriously grateful to be alive.

We had been waiting half an hour when Detective Vigor came out to get us. He seemed roughly Ebby's age, but shorter, as if Ebby had been crushed in a compacter and had come out twice as muscular and dense but half as tall. Vigor preceded us down the corridor, walking with the bowlegged walk of a man whose thighs are as thick as trees, elbows cocked, hands poised like a gunslinger's. He wore a pair of sunglasses pushed up to his forehead, so, like Chickie, he seemed to have four eyes instead of two, which allowed him to examine evidence with twice the shrewdness.

We sat opposite him at his desk. He put up his booted feet, balanced a legal pad on his legs and squinted suspiciously. But he never questioned a word I said. As Ebby told me later, anyone who has spent even one week working for the Las Vegas PD would have no trouble believing that a bookie tried to fake his own murder or that the owner of a strip club met a sorry end because he had been running a sideline in child pornography. If the interrogation lasted longer than I had hoped, it was only because Detective Vigor insisted on giving Ebby a hard time about his decision to leave the force.

"So, Salzman, you still think it's more important to send a few teenage hookers back to Mom and Pop in Oklahoma than put away the scum that ruin this city for the rest of us?"

I waited for Ebby to come back with a sharp retort, but he fidgeted and held his peace. Detective Vigor capped his pen and said that while he doubted any judge would impose a stringent sentence on a man who had killed a child pornographer, a murder had been committed, and the perpetrator of said crime would get off with a lighter sentence if he turned himself in. Oh, he said, and my brother would probably face some kind of charge for inviting his pals to tie up his wife and jam a gun up her vagina, an act that would not endear him to a jury. Unless, the detective added slyly, it was composed of a dozen men.

"He's an asshole," Ebby said as he drove me home. "But he's right about our needing to get your brother to turn himself in."

As if to make up for his earlier lack of prowess, Ebby called every nudist resort in Mexico until he was able to verify that Potsie was holed up at a "naturalist beach club" not far up the coast from Cancun. *Si, si, un norteamericano muy grande* was staying at the club. And no, the receptionist wouldn't alert *el norteamericano* that his sister and best friend were flying down to see him. She wouldn't want to ruin a surprise reunion, especially when, as Ebby said, we would be bringing *un regalo muy generoso* to repay her for her help.

Then Ebby took me to his office, which turned out to be as shabby and bare as the office above the store that sold venetian blinds, except that Ebby's office was above a shop that sold used appliances. I sat in the chair reserved for clients while Ebby went online and reserved two tickets so we could fly to Cancun the next day. We would have left that afternoon, but we needed to find someone to stay with Saffron. Since Nate was still at Chaco and Meryl was still with her friend Davia at Tahoe, that left only Miranda to watch the girls. It pleased me to think of Saffron and Kalindi playing in the pool at La Mancha Estates, but I could sense Ebby's apprehension. And when we dropped Saffron at the house and I saw the two young girls standing in the living room, surrounded by the dogs, I could understand why.

"You're pretty," Kalindi said, reaching out to pat Ebby's daughter's hair.

"You're pretty, too," Saffron said, stroking Kalindi's arm.

Ebby made a move to pull the girls apart, as if Kalindi were somehow tainted. "She's not the one who took the pictures," I reminded him. "Saffron will be okay."

We got on a plane and flew to Mexico, rented a car, and drove up the coast. But the nearer we drew to the resort where my brother was hiding, the weaker my belief that he still would be there. Potsie had seemed so solid when we were young, the fleshy bulk around whom I wrapped my arms while barreling down a toboggan run. Now he seemed as slippery as an eel. As excited as I had been to learn that he wasn't dead, I was furious at the terror he had caused my parents. True, he had needed to disappear to Mexico because he had killed our cousin in a rage at what Perry had done to Kalindi . . . and to me. But my brother wouldn't have been hiding in our cousin's bar and seen those clips if not for his idiotic scheme to scare his wife.

We turned off the highway at a sign for Playa Naturalista. Ebby rolled down his window. "Who knows, maybe it will desensitize me to my flashbacks. All these wholesome families without their clothes . . ."

I figured he might be right. And it wouldn't hurt that he would be witnessing those wholesome families playing amid the most beautiful setting I had ever seen. Ebby was wearing yet another of his Hawaiian shirts, and when we stepped out on the beach, it was as if we had entered the colorful, pristine paradise depicted on the cloth. The cottages were pink and white, with tropical vines and flowers. We seemed to have entered Eden before the Fall, and anyone who told a dirty joke would be escorted to the gate and expelled with a flaming sword.

We stopped at the registration hut and learned that *el norteameri-cano muy grande* was staying in cottage three. I told Ebby he needed to go in first and make sure my brother was presentable.

"Yeah," he said, "right," as if he were afraid that the sight of Potsie Weinrach nude might set back his desensitization therapy a good ten years. Still, he was brave enough to go in first, and a few minutes later he motioned me to follow him around the back, where we found my brother in a lounge chair beside a hot tub. Thank God he was wearing shorts. But Potsie had lost so many pounds, not to mention he had cut his hair and shaved his beard, I was shocked at how diminished and subdued he seemed. I felt the way Samson's family must have felt when they saw their son blinded and chained after the Philistines had done their worst.

"Hi, Potsie," I said, and my brother put down the sports magazine he had been reading. There was a pyramid of Diet Coke cans beside the chair. Despite the breeze, the sun was even stronger here than it had been in Vegas. I was dying for a cold drink. But the hand that held that Diet Coke recently had touched our cousin. True, it had punched Perry in the jaw, but that was too close for me.

"I really screwed up this time," my brother mumbled. He looked so miserable, I did what any sister would do: I wrapped my arms around his neck and reveled in the feel and smell of every sweaty square inch of him. Only when the chair began to give beneath our weight did I struggle to my feet.

"You have every right to be pissed off at me," Potsie said. "This was the fuckup of the century."

Although I appreciated his taking the responsibility for his fuckup, did he need to sound as if pulling off such a feat deserved a place in the Guinness Book of Records?

"I'm not surprised you were the one to find me, Ketzel. Salzman here is no slouch. But you're the real brains in this outfit. Even Morty used to say you were smarter than he was. And he was the smartest guy I knew."

I wasn't so easily mollified. "Potsie, how could you? Not the part about Perry. But everything else . . . How could you think you could get away with a fake kidnapping? And what about Meryl? After everything that kid already went through?"

My brother reached inside a bag of sugarless yellow candies, palmed a few, then swallowed them, as if he were popping Valium. "I know, I know. It seemed a good idea at the time. Janis was driving me nuts! All the time *hocking* that I didn't give her enough dough to buy more clothes. And those stupid dolls! It got where she wouldn't let me anywhere near her. She started talking divorce. And the idea that she would get half of everything I'd worked so hard to get . . ." He popped another handful of yellow candies. "Perry could have stopped me. But that bastard egged me on. The guy was always jealous that I was married. That I had a real house. A legit business. At least, more legit than his. I never let him anywhere near Janis. What guy in his right mind would let Perry near his wife? So he saw a way to get even. I was at the Schoolhouse one night, and we got talking. One thing led to another, and he came up with this fucking brilliant scheme. Anyway, it seemed brilliant at the time. That's why I stay away from alcohol. I'm stupid enough when I'm sober, but when I've had a few of those whiskey sours Chickie makes . . ."

Potsie wiped his sweat-soaked chest with a napkin printed with a cartoon of a Mexican boy wearing a sombrero and nothing else. I was sad to see that the hair on my brother's chest was white. He certainly looked better without that scraggly mustache. But he was so pitiful and forlorn, he only looked good in comparison to the pile of rotting bones I had been envisioning for the past few months.

"Even if I was drunk as a skunk, I should have known that any plan involving those 'actor' pals of Perry's—"

"Wait! Was one of the guys with a handkerchief around his face a cabbie named Rokowski?"

My brother looked at me as if I had just told him that I had been hanging around with, well, a porn star. "How do you know a shithead like Daryl Rokowski?"

I could see from Ebby's expression he was curious to hear the answer, too. "Never mind," I said. "The creep lied! I asked him straight out if he knew where you were, and he told me he had never even met you. Jesus. Doesn't anybody in Las Vegas tell the truth?"

My brother was nonplussed. "Of course he lied. What was he going to say, 'Sure, I saw Potsie the other night when I helped Perry fake his kidnapping'? Things had gone pretty far south by then. On the ride back to the bar, Daryl and Perry were whooping it up over how bad they scared Janis, and I'm, like, you put the gun *where*? This is my wife we're talking about! So I'm already fairly pissed off. Then I'm hiding in back of the lounge, and Perry's out in front, and I get bored and turn on his computer . . ."

As I had been able to deduce, Perry had come back in the room, and before he could offer an explanation, my brother knocked him out. Then, when Perry came to, my cousin had the nerve to ask Potsie what he had done wrong. So what if he had asked me to dance. I loved the attention, didn't I? I was asking for it, wasn't I, always wanting to be on-stage? At which Potsie picked up the monitor from the desk and ended this line of talk by bringing it down on our cousin's head.

My brother's only regret was that his cousin's predilection for little girls had caused him to mess up his life in ways it didn't need messing up right then. He had looked around Perry's apartment for something in which to wrap the body, noticed the bearskin rug, and wrapped the corpse in that. It struck me as more than a little fitting that my brother had used my cousin's own van to drive him to the desert, where he dug a hole and dumped him in.

Then, even though my brother wasn't what you might call a deep thinker, he got the bright idea that he would use our cousin's corpse to make his own disappearance more convincing. My cousin was thin and Potsie fat. But if you left a body in the desert, there soon would be nothing left of it but bones, which are as thin for a fat man as for a thin man. My cousin's hair was short and brown while Potsie's was long and gray, but by the time the remains were found, the skull would be bald, wouldn't it? How many skulls have you seen that aren't bald? To complete the trick, Potsie hacked off his own ponytail and tangled it in a cactus near the corpse. He might have gone further and outfitted our cousin in his shirt and shorts, but Potsie couldn't very well have fit in Perry's clothes. And Potsie couldn't have driven back to Vegas naked. Then again, clothing disintegrated at an even greater rate than skin and flesh. My brother decided he would leave Perry in Perry's own trousers, but Potsie put his flip-flops on Perry's feet and his wallet in Perry's pocket. To cinch the deal, he gave Perry the lanyard key-chain I had made at camp.

"About that key chain," Potsie said. "I hated leaving it there like that. I carried it around for years. You know that, Ketzel. But that key chain was the only thing that could convince the cops those bones were mine. And it was the only thing that would convince *you*. Like I said, I knew you would be the one who needed the most convincing."

As flattered as I was, I found it difficult to forgive my brother for having stuffed that gift in our cousin's pocket in a carefully thought-out scheme to convince me that he was dead. But I had a bigger bone to pick, so to speak. "How could you do that to your own daughter? How could you let her go around thinking her father was dead?"

Of all things, Potsie looked hurt. "What kind of father do you think I am?" Apparently, he had called Meryl from Tijuana, at which she informed him that her stepmother had flown the coop, at which he asked if she wanted him to come home, at which she said she couldn't bear to think of him going to jail and promised to find a way to sneak down to Mexico. And then, the next time he called, she said her aunt Ketzel had moved in with her, and she and my brother decided she should finish the school year there. I might have been angry at my niece for keeping this information to herself. But how could I fault a girl for trying to protect her father?

"Just one more thing," I said. "Don't you think it was a little disloyal to me to take Morty to Perry's bar? What kind of brother takes his sister's husband to a strip club?"

From the look on Potsie's face, I could see he would rather have stood trial for murder than the crime I had just alleged. His gaze darted toward the beach, as if he were contemplating swimming out to sea. He glanced imploringly at Ebby, but Ebby held out his hands to say that the question seemed fair to him.

"I don't want to defame a dead person's memory, but there's something you ought to know." He took a swig of Diet Coke. "Morty had a kid."

You can imagine my shock. The man who for so many years resisted my entreaties to have a child had a child with someone else? Even if that was true, why did my husband's having a child entitle him to visit strip clubs and make love to whores?

"He didn't make love to them," Potsie said. "As far as I know, the only time Morty was unfaithful to you was way back in the eighties. He met this woman in Chicago. He was doing research, and he met this bunny at Hugh Hefner's mansion. She was—no offense—pretty much drop-dead gorgeous. And smart. And what got Morty the most, she knew every joke he knew. He would start a joke and she would supply the punch line." Potsie shrugged. "That's not what I look for in a woman, but hey, who am I to judge? Not the best track record here, right?"

I wasn't about to contradict him.

"Turns out she was doing research of her own. She got her PhD in . . . I don't know what you would call the field. Morty would talk about stuff like this, and most of it would go shooting straight over my head. She had some cockeyed theory that stripping is a form of art. It expresses a woman's beauty, or her power over men, or some bullshit like that. That's how she paid for grad school—stripping at clubs, working as a bunny. Even after she got a fancy job at that university, she kept dancing. She used the stage name Candi Cone."

"This is supposed to excuse my husband from having an affair? Because she had a PhD and I didn't?" How was I supposed to feel, my husband discouraging me from pursuing a degree, then having an affair with a woman who had a doctorate? Was Morty afraid any child he conceived with me wouldn't have a high enough IQ?

"No, no, you've got Morty all wrong. He only slept with that professor a few times. To be frank, she scared the pants off him. She might have known all the jokes, but she didn't have any sense of humor. And the kind of sex she liked! Morty used to say he wanted to make the world safe for sex between people who loved each other. And her mission was to . . . how should I put this . . . make the world safe for people who wanted to tie each other up and beat the shit out of each other."

I knew I was a sap to feel pity for a husband who found himself involved with a woman who liked S and M, but that's what I felt for Morty. Not that he was in favor of banning any kind of sex. It was only that, as someone whose own parents had tied him up and beaten him, he was not interested in reliving such a punishment as a game or inflicting it on others.

Because that's the missing link to the psychology of Morty Tittelman. I could have told you straight out. But some facts about a person can only be understood within the context of his entire life. The reason Morty ran away from home at such a young age, the reason he became the scholar he became, is that he wanted to figure out if it was possible to tell a joke without anyone being hurt.

Apparently, the other key to my husband's psyche was that even though he had slept with Professor Cohen only those few nights at Hugh Hefner's mansion, the woman had borne his child. When I first heard this, I didn't accept the information with my live-and-let-live aplomb. I accused Potsie of lying to excuse his own behavior, not to mention Morty's. I said Morty should have known I would understand. I would have helped him to raise his child.

"Ketzel," Potsie said, "there are some things even a professor of dirty jokes is ashamed to tell his wife. He cheated on you! He was afraid if he told you the truth, you might leave him. He couldn't stand that possibility. And he was afraid if you knew he'd cheated, you wouldn't trust him to conduct his research."

But if Morty had slept with Professor Cohen only a few times, why did he keep visiting her in Chicago? Although even as I said this, I understood. "He was helping her bring up their daughter?"

"Trying to," Potsie said. "She wouldn't let him see the girl. The crazy bitch took the kid to meetings of some club of professional dominatrixes. And when Morty threatened to take her to court and prove she was an unfit mother, she said he wasn't fit himself. The pot calling the kettle black and all that."

But how could he be sure the child was his?

"Don't you think I asked? A woman like that must have had sex with a million guys. But Morty said only a heel would question a woman's claim that a child was his. After a while, I'm not sure it mattered. He couldn't bear to think of anyone's little girl growing up that way. Then the kid ran off. The thought that his daughter was out there turning tricks or stripping . . . And her mother didn't give a shit! In some crackpot, egghead way, she approved! Besides, I don't think she knew where the girl had run away to."

So Morty had been visiting all those strip clubs to find his child?

Sure, Potsie said. At first, Morty had gone looking for his daughter blindly. Then he had reason to think the girl had gone to Vegas. "After that, I don't know. He kind of gave up hope. He just talked to the girls in bars to see if he could figure out where they'd come from and why they were doing what they were doing. He talked about some kind of study on the subject. But I think he got too sad to write the book. He took to hanging around the Schoolhouse because it was easier hanging out there than places where he didn't know the bartender. I felt bad taking him. You don't need to tell me that's not what a brother does. But it wasn't as if he was sleeping with the girls. He just bought them drinks and asked them questions."

Did Potsie expect me to believe that my husband had spent all that time with strippers and hadn't had sex with a single one?

The sun must have been shining in Potsie's eyes because he lifted his hand to block the light. "Look, I can't swear Morty never had sex with any of those girls. All I can say is, that wasn't why he hung around them. That notebook . . . Maybe he was keeping track of who he'd talked to, where they'd come from, to see if any of them might know his kid."

I'm not saying I believed Morty was completely innocent. But at least I could explain his behavior. A memory came back to me from that trip we took to France. We were driving home from the ceremony at which he had been knighted a chevalier when Morty asked if I minded if we took a detour. Mind? How could I mind anything that would prolong my time outside the hotel room?

"Thank you, my dear." He kissed me. "I knew I could count on you." He leaned forward and asked the driver in perfect French if he would drive us to the Moulin Rouge. I thought Morty didn't want me to miss the most renowned strip club in the world. The driver let us out and we stood looking up at the brightly lit-up bar with the famous red windmill at the top.

"The Moulin Rouge," Morty marveled. "Who would have thought that a butcher's son from Wilkes-Barre, Pennsylvania, would be driven in a chauffeured limousine to the Moulin Rouge?"

I marveled that same thing about myself. To think I was about to enter an establishment upon whose unholy ground had trod the likes of Toulouse-Lautrec, Josephine Baker, Edith Piaf, and countless cancan dancers! But my husband, the recently knighted chevalier, surprised me by leading me not inside the club but down the street. He pointed to a window above a bar. "That's where Pablo kept his studio. And there, across the way, Señor Dalí had *his* studio. I barely had the funds to buy a baguette and a few slices of good French cheese. I earned my money . . . well, no need to go into that. But weren't those the days!"

I gripped his arm tighter, and we turned down an alley that ran between an establishment called Le Sex-o-dome and a decrepit hotel that probably had been a brothel since the French were known as Gauls. The young and not-so-young women loitering in the alley came swaggering toward us, assuming the fat American in his tuxedo and his much younger wife in her flowing silver muumuu were looking to find a bedmate so they could enjoy that triple pleasure to which the French have given the name *ménage à trois*. Not being as fluent in French as Morty, I lost the thread of their conversation. I took for granted he was conducting research. Such occurrences weren't rare in my married life. But reexamining the evidence now, I couldn't help but think Morty was looking for his daughter—if not in fact, then metaphorically.

That must also have been why he took out a stack of francs and paid the girls, then ushered me back to the limousine, and, when we were safely ensconced inside, wrapped me in his arms and said, "I don't deserve a wife like you. Everything I am today, you made me. And I have given you nothing in return. I only hope you will find it in that generous heart of yours to forgive your undeserving Morty."

Which, standing beside my brother at Playa Naturalista, I found it in my heart to do. What could I lose? It wasn't as if I stood in any danger of being betrayed by him again.

What was harder to accept was that Potsie had taken Morty's side. There are some things a person can forgive a brother, and other things she can't.

Although this didn't mean I wanted to see Potsie live in a permanent state of exile. Not to mention a permanent state of undress.

"Come on," I said. "Let's get you back where you belong."

A change came over my brother's face. No, not his face. It came over his entire body. Despite the drooping skin, which hung on him the way a suit of clothes from his fatter days might have hung, I could see his every nerve go tense. He popped more candies in his mouth and took another swig of Diet Coke.

"Uh, no can do. I'm sorry I dragged you and Salzman down here. But I can't go back. Listen, Ketzel, there's Janis. There's Mom and Dad. There are guys like Owen and Smoke I left holding the bag. I would have to start over from scratch. And I can't see myself . . . Ketzel, do you want me to go to jail?"

Of course I didn't! The mere idea of Potsie sitting in a jail cell made me ill. But given that his victim was a child pornographer, his sentence might not be that long. How could he chicken out and abandon us? In all the time Ebby and I had been searching for my brother, it never occurred to me that he wouldn't want to come home. It was as if we had found the spot on the map marked by the big red X, except, when we tried to move the treasure chest, we discovered that whoever had buried it had cemented it to the ground. "You can't mean that. What about your parents? What about your daughter?"

"She's better off," he muttered.

"Better off? How could your daughter be better off without her father?"

He mumbled so softly I could barely hear. "Yeah? Look at everything I exposed her to. She was, what, nine years old? We were shopping at Toys 'R' Us and we ran into that fucking creep Perry. He was probably buying toys to use . . . to use for . . . He got down to her level, he patted her on the head, and . . . I let that fuckface touch her! And you! Look at what I let that bastard do to you!"

I could see where a brother might regret having palled around with a man who filmed his sister naked and distributed the video on the Web. Not to mention the damage this so-called friend had done to other little girls my brother knew.

"Not to interfere in a family conversation," Ebby said. "But I am here to say I know what it's like to do away with a really bad fucker, and then feel bad you killed the guy, except you feel worse that you didn't do away with the prick a lot sooner. But I'm also here to say you can't spend the rest of your life stewing in your own juices. You'll go nuts sitting here in your birthday suit, reading the racing forms, and thinking about what your cousin did. It's better to go back and face the music and make sure no further damage gets done to the ones you love."

My brother remained unconvinced. "And if I don't turn myself in, you're going to knock me over my head and toss me in the back of that rental piece of shit you drove down here and drive me back to Vegas to 'face the music'? Some private-eye code of ethics says you've got to turn a person in, never mind you grew up with that person and think he had a right to break the law? Look, Salzman, you gotta do what you gotta do. But unless you take me back with you right now, I'm not going to be here when the feds come looking. You think the authorities are going to go to the trouble to extradite a nobody like me for killing some child-pornographer piece of crud?"

I looked from Ebby to my brother, trying to decide, if this conversation came to blows, whose position I would defend. As much as I loved my brother, and as little as I wanted him to spend even one day in jail, I couldn't bear the thought we would have come all this way, only to return home empty handed. As disloyal as it made me feel, I had little doubt that if push came to shove, I would help Ebby tackle my newly reduced brother, wrap duct tape around his wrists, and carry him to the car.

But Ebby had no such plan. "You've got my intentions all wrong, bro. I was hired to find you, and I found you. I earned the money my client paid. I'm off the hook. The only code of ethics that governs a private investigator is 'Do No Harm.' Now, if it was a matter of preventing you from killing somebody . . . But the harm's been done. Or undone, depending on which way you see it. I'm speaking here as a friend. I'm speaking as a man who knows that a father in jail is better than a father who's on the lam."

"Well, *friend*," my brother said, "that's where we disagree. Personally, I think my kid would be better off if she never sees or hears from her old man again."

If I didn't object, it wasn't because I thought if my brother disappeared, my niece might live with me.

"I hear you," Ebby said. "But this isn't a decision to be made in a snap. What say your sister and I take a little tour of the sights, then we rendezvous back here at thirteen hundred hours?"

I wanted to ask if Ebby actually thought it was a good idea to turn our backs on a fugitive who had just expressed a sincere desire not to be taken alive. Not to mention my brother had left his watch by my cousin's corpse and hadn't seen fit to buy a new one.

"Let's give your brother a chance to consider his alternatives." Ebby cupped my elbow and led me off—if my brother was in no position to resist this big man's will, I was even less so.

"But—" I kept saying, "but—"

He steered me along the beach.

"But, Ebby!" I finally said. "What if he isn't here when we get back!"

A Frisbee fell at Ebby's feet. He picked it up. A teenage boy stood waiting a few yards off, naked from head to toe.

"Hey, man, thanks." Ebby flipped the Frisbee. The boy snatched it and dashed back in the surf, where he was joined by another boy and four spectacularly winsome girls who had risen from the sea like nymphs. We knew it wasn't proper etiquette to stare, but neither of us was able to avert our eyes. We had been so absorbed in my brother's plight we hadn't noticed what was going on around us. Now, like some anti-Adam and anti-Eve, we looked around and saw that we were fully clothed and no one else could say the same.

I know naturists believe God meant us to enjoy the sun and wind on our naked skin. And watching those nubile young people skim their Frisbee above the waves, I might have believed this. But as Ebby and I kept walking, we came upon the middle-aged adults who constituted the main clientele of Playa Naturalista, and it struck me that Man had invented clothes not only to keep off the elements but to keep everything he did from being laughed at.

Take the game of volleyball being played by coed teams. The players were nowhere near as young as the Frisbee players, and things that shouldn't have jiggled did, which wouldn't have been so bad except when someone spiked a ball and an opposing player missed, he or she got hit on such a sensitive portion of the anatomy it made me wince. A little farther on, we passed a group of men playing horseshoes, and I couldn't help but picture the players hanging their horseshoes you-know-where. I won't describe the image that went through my mind when we saw a bunch of well-endowed guys standing beside a barbeque on which sausages were being grilled. And what could be more comic than a man equipped in a mask and fins but nothing else? Or an otherwise naked woman wearing a fanny pack and a visor, walking heel-toe, heel-toe, listening to a Walkman? It reminded me of the joke about the doctor who puts his ears to his patient's breasts and apologizes because he isn't able to hear the music her husband hears when he puts *his* ears to the woman's breasts, to which the woman says, "Of course you can't hear the music, doctor. You aren't plugged in like he is!"

Nor do I believe nudity is the great social leveler. If anything, the absence of clothing emphasizes the smallest differences, there being no way to cover up the inequalities between the haves and have-nots. I wasn't even sure the guests wanted to be equal. Why else would they sport gold chains around their necks and heavy gold rings in places I would rather not see rings at all? All of which reminded me this was not some primitive island upon which Ebby and I had washed up, but an expensive, well-run resort. A person needed to be rich to afford the privacy in which to take off his or her clothes. My brother must have been carrying more than his passport and Pickles Pinkowski's forty thousand dollars when he hitchhiked to Tijuana.

Ebby, no doubt lost in similar meditations, indicated a thatched awning under which four older men in sunglasses and not much else sat playing a game with cards and chips.

I had to laugh. "Why isn't Potsie out there playing? Do you think they figured out he's a pro?"

"Maybe. If he won too much, some guy might get pissed off and turn him in."

We heard a terrific splash and turned to see a man my brother's size—or rather, the size my brother used to be—surface in the pool.

"I wish I could say this helps," Ebby said. "But these people don't seem wholesome. *Nothing* seems wholesome anymore."

I was beginning to feel the same way. If I stayed a minute longer at Playa Naturalista, I might never have sex again.

Ebby looked at his watch and said we better be getting back. We wanted to give my brother enough time to change his mind and return with us to Vegas, but not enough time so he could change his mind a second time and chicken out. Rather than retrace our steps along the beach, we took a shaded path that wound past the main buildings. Many of the guests were clothed, and we thought we were home free, until we came upon a thatched roof beneath which children sat weaving potholders, building jewelry boxes out of Popsicle sticks, and weaving lanyard key-chains. It might have been the camp at my parents' hotel, except that the kids were nude. Part of me thought I was seeing the most beautiful sight I had ever seen; the other part wanted to be sick.

Ebby tugged my arm.

"What?" I said. "Oh." The counselors were staring at us as if we were the same kind of perverts as my cousin Perry.

When we got back to my brother's cottage, he was wearing the shorts he had been wearing before we left, but he'd put on a pair of huarache sandals and a short-sleeve shirt. I was so surprised to see him wearing anything but a Yankees jersey I couldn't help but think that George Steinbrenner had drummed him off the team.

"Let's go," Potsie said. "I can't do to my kid what Perry's parents did to him. He was a fucking pain in the butt. But think what it must have been like to know that his mom and dad preferred a needle full of heroin to him. No offense, I'm not about to leave my daughter to be raised by her aunt."

Despite his puny warning that I not take offense, I did. Then again, how could my brother know how much I loved his daughter? Or that I considered myself a better mother than Amy/ValZorah or Janis/Sunshine?

"I just don't want my daughter to grow up thinking her father preferred saving his own skin to looking out for hers." He tossed a bunch of fancifully colored bills on the table for the maid. "I was planning on bringing her here to live. I mean, not *here* here. I'm not that much of a nut job. I mean Mexico here. Or Costa Rica. But that would have been a shitty thing to do, wouldn't it, uproot her and make her miss senior year? And what about when she's in college? She and her friends fly down to Cancun for spring break, and Meryl says, 'Hey, guys, I gotta take a little side-trip to see my fucked-up fugitive of a dad.'"

Ebby started to disagree—not about my brother going back, but about what a fuckup Potsie was.

"Nah," Potsie said. "I see where you're going with that, but I let my daughter down, and I let my sister down. Times used to get rough, I would think, 'Potsie, you may be a worthless sack of shit, but your daughter loves you, and your kid sister still puts up with you,' and if the two smartest, nicest women in the world still loved me, I couldn't be that much of a schmuck. But it turns out I was."

I knew my brother was fishing for my forgiveness, but some wave of love washed over me and I didn't mind being caught. I threw my arms around him—I was surprised at how far those arms now reached—and I smelled that familiar Potsie smell, which took me back to our ride on that horse at Woodstock. He smelled like a horse himself, except he also smelled sweet from all the candy bars he ate, with a slightly artificial odor from the saccharine he now ingested instead of sugar. And I knew that no matter what, I could never give up loving him.

He didn't need long to pack. He had arrived at Playa Naturalista wearing nothing but a shirt and shorts, and it wasn't as if he had needed to go out and buy an extensive wardrobe to fit in with the other guests. But he wasn't in a hurry to get back home. As we drove south along the coast, my brother gave off such a reluctant presence I could have sworn the rear end of the car was dragging. We bought him a ticket for the plane, and although he rarely drank, he ordered a Bloody Mary, which he gulped in one big gulp, after which he made his way to the restroom and was gone so long I worried he might have jumped.

We landed and were whisked through customs, then walked straight out in the heat, where we climbed in Ebby's Silverado and drove to my brother's house. Potsie sat in back, shaking his head and cursing. At one point, he whispered, "Oh shit" and ducked. Apparently, he'd had to leave town more quickly than he intended and left some of his biggest clients in the lurch, which meant there were more disgruntled gamblers on the streets than Pickles Pinkowski.

But it was Meryl who truly scared him. When we drove up to La Mancha Estates, Potsie began shaking so badly I could feel the front seat vibrate. He remained sitting in the truck after Ebby shut off the motor. Then he couldn't bring himself to go inside.

"Daddy!" Meryl ran out to meet us. "I knew you would come back!"

Watching my brother and his daughter hug brought tears to my eyes. How could I not feel proud I had accomplished their reunion? But my happiness was tinged with grief that nothing I ever did would make my niece this overjoyed to see me.

Then again, no one would be this angry at me, either.

"Someone shot Donnie!" Meryl pounded her father's chest. "Right in our yard! With all the other dogs watching! It was your fault! You're such an idiot! It was some scumbag who bet on a horse and you didn't pay him so he killed my dog!" She kept hitting him as hard as a girl that age could hit. My brother could have grabbed her fists and stopped her, but he chose to take the blows. "You're so *stupid!* You just ran away and left me! How could you! How could you!" She stopped hitting him long enough to drag him around the house to see the grave Ebby had dug for Donner.

"Pinkowski did this?" Potsie pulled Ebby close. "I'll kill the fucker. Shooting my daughter's dog . . . I've got plenty of money stashed away. But that fucking dog-killer doesn't get another fucking cent."

"I hate to say this, you're not in a position to call the shots. I gave the man my word. I can understand you want to hang on to what cash you have. But you can see the man's point. A person loses as much as Pickles Pinkowski has lost over the past few decades, and then, through no fault of his own, he backs the right horse . . . A person like that gets stiffed, it could drive him to all sorts of evil. The dog getting whacked was as much your fault as Pinkowski's."

Potsie nodded. "Yeah," he said. "I hear you." He clapped Ebby on his arm. "And don't think I don't owe you. Watching out for my kid the way you did. Taking care of that pig Pinkowski." Then my brother shocked us both by squatting at Ebby's feet. I was afraid he had lost his head. Then I realized he was begging pardon of the *dogs*. He rubbed noses with Prancer and roughed up Vixen. "Sorry," he said. "Guess old Potsie let you down."

Dogs being dogs, they accepted his apology. Eventually, the rest of us would do the same. We always find excuses for the people we love, as long as we are sure they love us, too.

To celebrate my brother's return to the living, Ebby and I cooked a feast. All of us—Miranda, Kalindi, Saffron, Meryl, Nate, and Leo—ate at the table in the dining room, with the dogs begging for scraps and pats. Ebby was uncomfortable around Kalindi, but my brother took her on his lap, where she snuggled against his chest and let him pet her. He tickled her feet and played piggy with her toes and promised that even after her mother got a job and they found their own place to live, she could swim in his pool and play with the dogs any time she liked.

"I don't get it," Kalindi said. "How come everybody's so nice to me all of a sudden?"

It occurred to me she was right. Why hadn't anyone cared that Kalindi and her mother were living in a van? While I hardly blamed myself for what my cousin had done to Kalindi and the other strippers' daughters, if I hadn't kept my childhood secret to myself, none of this would have happened. My brothers and father would have beaten Perry to a pulp. But he might have gotten help. Kalindi and the other girls wouldn't have ended up on the Web, and Perry might not have died.

Miranda saw no validity to this point of view. She regarded me as Kalindi's savior. And she treated Potsie like a god for having smashed a computer monitor over the head of the man who had filmed her daughter.

My niece was overjoyed to have her father home. But she seemed even happier to have her boyfriend back from an archaeological site so remote he hadn't been able to call or send an e-mail. He apologized for his failure to bring her a shard of Anasazi pottery, but removing anything from Chaco Canyon was forbidden, and Nate was not a boy to overlook such a rule. Instead, he had painted a stone with the pictograph they had climbed the cliff to see. Later, when Meryl and I were in the kitchen, she whispered excitedly that Nate had said he hoped they could keep up their relationship after he went off to school.

"He used that word! He said 'relationship'!"

I didn't have the heart to say that most long-distance relationships do not survive. For all I knew, a boy so scrupulous about treating his girlfriend as a Thou would be less likely to replace her with an It. Sitting beside her as we ate, Nate paid Meryl so much attention that her father began to stare, although after the trouble he had caused, he was in no position to interfere. At one point, Ebby, who was serving the pot roast Leo had cooked for us, stopped behind me and rubbed my back. Potsie's eyebrows shot halfway up his skull. But if he wanted to voice a complaint, he must have thought better of his right to do so.

For dessert, we ate a pastry Leo had prepared. He hadn't worn an apron, and his shirt was specked with flour. "Sorry it's not a strudel," Leo said, "but Hania never did manage to teach me how to get the layers flaky and thin, like she does."

The image of Hania teaching Leo to bake a strudel struck me as surreal. "Leo," I said, "after so many years of Hania resisting your advances, maybe you should take the hint."

From the way his face fell, I wished I could take back my unkind comment. "For your information," he used his imaginary cigar to jab home his point, "the lady reciprocates my affections. Problem is, right before the war, Hania married this Polish bigwig whose mother was a German. The Nazis marched into town, and the son of a bitch threw in with them. A few of us at this table have done things we are none too proud of. A few of us, we have blood on our hands. But that's a different matter from wading in the substance up to your fuggin' neck." He made a motion to show the blood rising to his chin. "So this husband of hers goes one way—namely, trailing after Hitler—and Hania and her family go another way. Yadda yadda, long story short, the Russkis come in, Hania and her family emigrate to America. Believe me, she was not exactly sad to lose track of that no-good Nazi. But these Catholic broads, the husband is still alive, even in Argentina, in the eyes of the pope the two of you are as married as if you're lying in bed, screwing every night."

Leo got a knife and jabbed it in the *placek* he had baked, sliced the first piece, and, using two forks, lifted it on a plate. He handed it to Ebby's daughter. "A few nights ago, Hania gets a call informing her the SOB finally kicked the bucket." Leo laughed and licked his fingers. "Guess my ship finally came in. Just like that nut Pinkowski! The *SS Hania Hasse* finally came in to port! Except, pretty soon, she's going to be renamed the *Hania Bialik*! Can you believe that? Old Leo has been baching it for eighty-three years, and he's finally getting hitched!"

After we got over our shock, we burst out in applause, whooping and wishing Leo and Hania *mazel.* Then we celebrated Nate's imminent departure for college and Miranda's new job as bookkeeper for a company that supplied linens to the casinos. My jubilation was tempered only by the fact that Ira, Mike, and Howie weren't there to enjoy the feast, and Kalindi and who-knew-how-many other children had been damaged for life, and my brother would need to spend time in jail.

This last possibility made me sick. Looking at my brother, I saw him in an orange jumpsuit, shuffling along a cafeteria line, getting lumps of meat and scoops of mashed potatoes on a tray, then slouching off to eat at a table heavy with tattooed brutes whose murders hadn't been committed accidentally. My brother had palled around with shady characters his entire life. He was a shady character himself. But to me, he was still the overweight boy who had learned to gamble so he could win the Mars bars to which he had become addicted, as any kid whose mother is a bookie and whose grandfather owns a candy shop might come to be. Surely no jury would convict him for killing a child pornographer in a rage that rose from seeing his little sister in a film. And how many months in jail could anyone get for scheming to defraud his wife? Couldn't Ebby testify as to the services my brother had rendered in keeping the police informed as to the business dealings of the Mafia? If the lawyers allowed me to take the stand in Potsie's defense, I would give the performance of my life. Not to mention his daughter would testify as to the damage that would be caused by her only remaining parent being jailed.

When the last few crumbs of Leo's *placek* had disappeared and Saffron and Kalindi had run upstairs to play, Potsie pushed back from the table and stood as slowly as is possible for a person to stand. Well, he said, he might as well get it over with.

"What?" I said. "You're going to turn yourself in?"

"No," he said. "It's time to call Mom and Dad."

He picked up a phone and dialed, although after he had said, "Hi, Ma," he didn't get the chance to say much else. Even after he had said, "Goodbye, Ma," Potsie stood stunned into silence. Finally, he asked, "How could anyone say she loves me and curse me the way she did?"

"Oh come on," I said. "You always were her favorite. Mike was Dad's favorite, and you were Mom's."

"It wasn't Ira?"

"Nah. You're the kid who's most like her. Maybe every mother loves the screwup best. Maybe if I had screwed up more, she and Dad would have loved me better."

"Mom and Dad love you plenty. It's just, you were nothing like the rest of us. It's like what Leo said. The rest of us, even when we didn't have blood on our hands, we had blood on our hands."

"Blood?" I said. "Or cherry juice? Or maybe Hawaiian Punch?"

It took Potsie a while to get my drift. "Just for the record, it was NyQuil mixed with strawberry Kool-Aid. Perry took great pains to find the right combination."

I had no trouble imagining our cousin mixing vats of bright red drinks and cackling. But why did I think that from now on, Perry would take the blame for every misguided deed my brother did?

"What I mean is, we didn't want to touch you with those hands. It was like that show on TV. The one where the father was Frankenstein and Grandpa was, like, a vampire?" He seemed pleased with this comparison. "Yeah. You were the normal kid on *The Munsters,* and we didn't want to, you know, corrupt you."

I was about to say that in their efforts to spare me from such corruption, they had left me in the hands of my cousin Perry. But Potsie read my thoughts.

"What can I say? Things don't always work out the way you plan." He looked at his daughter. "I really let you down, kiddo. I wouldn't blame you if you didn't want anything to do with me."

Meryl started to speak but couldn't. She got up and hugged her dad. Anyone could see she intended to hold on to him forever. But after a good long while, her father kissed her on her head and peeled her off.

"Okay, Salzman, might as well take me in. Nothing the DA says or does could make me feel any guiltier than I already am."

12.

THERE ISN'T MUCH more to tell. Given that my brother already had skipped the country once, the best his lawyer could do was get him confined to his house with one of those homing devices around his leg. But he got the better end of the deal than I did: while Potsie had Meryl, Kalindi, Miranda, and the dogs to keep him company, Ebby, Leo, and I were called upon to escort my cousin Perry home.

Why did we take him back? Someone had to bury him. And my parents were next of kin. They were appalled at what Perry did, but they couldn't bear to think of my father's cousin's child being tossed in some potter's field with an unmarked stone. Not to mention the best way to convince our friends that our family hadn't suffered an unspeakable disgrace was to bury him with a proper service in the Weinrach plot.

My mother hadn't left the hotel grounds in years. She barely had left our house. But if she didn't attend the funeral, people would gossip even more. Hania helped her dress—none of Totie's muumuus were black, so she had to make do with white—after which I escorted her to the car. Ebby lifted my father into the back seat while Leo folded the wheelchair into the trunk. Knowing what I knew, I couldn't help but think of the other bodies he must have folded in a similar way and laid in other trunks. But already the shock of Leo's history was wearing off. I could see myself incorporating his career into a routine about my lovably wayward family and their ties to Murder Inc.

Leo drove us to the cemetery, where we were met by a funeral director who consoled us for a grief none of us could pretend to feel. The midpriced casket my parents had bought for Perry—we didn't want to appear cheap, but neither did we want to pay a fortune to bury such accursed bones—lay reflecting the morning sun as if the body inside were no different from any other corpse, which, at that point, it wasn't. Each of us stood lost in thought. There lay my grandpa Joe and grandma Marcia, and, beside them, Ira and Mike, and, at Mike's feet, Morty. I couldn't stop hearing that line from Isaac Singer's story, the line Morty helped Singer write. It's the part where Gimpel's wife comes back from the grave to say, "Gimpel, just because *I* was false, is *everything* false? I never deceived anyone but myself. I'm paying for it all. Here in hell they spare you nothing."

Oh, Morty! I thought. *I hope you suffer nothing on my account! Despite your crimes and misdemeanors, I will ask to be buried here beside you. Although I have to admit, I hope I will be lying with a new husband on the other side.*

My mother collapsed to her knees, sobbing my brothers' names and kissing each chiseled letter on their stones. "Ira! My baby! How could anyone as strong and brave as you have died so young? And Mike! My handsome sweet young Mike!"

I patted her on the back and tried to comfort her. When she wouldn't be consoled, I contented myself with taking out a Kleenex and wiping the tears from my father's cheeks. *Oh, Mom,* I thought. *Oh, Pop. My heart is breaking for you both.* But I also wanted to shake them. How many lies can one family stand? Ira ran off to Israel because he wanted to get away from any reminder of the busboy who had been paralyzed for life because the poor kid was stupid enough to climb into Ira's sports car when Ira was too drunk to drive.

And Mike. Yes, he was a handsome, funny, bright. His death was a tragic waste. I miss Mike all the time. But his life and death were no nobler for having been associated with Donald Trump than they would have been if he had worked at the five-and-dime. My brother died to make a fabulously rich man richer. And now here we were, burying my child-pornographer of a cousin as if he were a hero, too.

Oh, Mom, I thought. *Oh, Pop. Illusion begets illusion. A lack of reality begets the same.*

As if to prove my point, the rabbi came up and asked when "Mr. Weinrach" had expired. Not wanting to say "two months ago," my mother told him that we were holding the funeral "at the earliest possible opportunity." I needed to bite my tongue to keep from adding that if my cousin didn't get into heaven, it wouldn't be because we hadn't gotten him into the ground within twenty-four hours of his demise.

The rabbi was old and bent—so few Jews were left in the Catskills that one semiretired rabbi served the needs of several towns. We barely knew the man—my father had donated money to the shul, but it wasn't as if any of us had attended services. "Please," the rabbi pleaded, "how can I compose a eulogy if you won't give me even a few crumbs of information about the deceased?"

"We don't need a fancy eulogy," my mother said. "Just the basics."

Which meant the poor man was reduced to extolling my cousin with the sorts of boilerplate phrases every rabbi uses: *Perry Weinrach tried to live a good Jewish life. He tried to make the world a better place for the next generation of Jewish children.*

As much as this made us squirm, we weren't about to stop the service and correct him. He said a few more prayers, then motioned the two men who had dug the grave to help Leo, Ebby, and the funeral director lower Perry into the ground. As dictated by Jewish custom, the rabbi turned the first shovel of dirt on my cousin's box, then tried passing the shovel to my mother. Apparently, I was the only member of the family able to muster some compassion for a man who had been abandoned by his parents, suffered a miserable death in a seamy room behind an even seamier strip club, then been abandoned a second time, this time in the desert, by the closest thing he'd had to a brother.

I ladled a few clods of dirt. Then I shoveled faster. A good Jewish life! A man who tried to make the world a better place for Jewish children! I must have gotten back my sense of humor, because what the rabbi had said seemed the funniest joke I had ever heard.

That was just this morning. If Ebby and I hadn't stopped off at my apartment to pick up my mail and toss out that rotten cantaloupe, I would have forgotten I was supposed to meet the chair of the Department of Popular Culture at Columbia University this very afternoon so he and a representative of the Mel Brooks Archive of Ribald Americana could cart away my late husband's papers and objets d'art.

Which leads me to the subject of how I intend to spend the considerable amount of money I am being paid for my late husband's smut. As you might have read in the *Times*, the governor nixed the plan to legalize gambling in the Catskills. The deal to turn our old hotel into a casino fell through. The bulldozers retreated, and whatever hoary secrets lie at the bottom of Cuyahoga Lake will continue to rest there undisturbed. Leo and Hania plan to live in my parents' house as caretakers while my parents move to Vegas, where they will look after my brother's house—which, in name, they own. Maybe my mother will be more inclined to leave her room once she no longer lives amid so many reminders of what she's lost. Also, she seems to believe that whatever catastrophe she feared would strike my brother instead has struck my cousin. After Potsie serves whatever time the judge sees fit to mete, he will return and live with them, at which point, no doubt, my mother will help him get his bookmaking operation back up on its feet. Potsie's few remaining assets are certain to be eaten up by lawyers. You can imagine how outraged my sister-in-law was to learn that my brother engineered his own abduction. Although she would have fought harder for her share of his worldly goods if I hadn't found the letters that Innocenzio Incognito was so anxious to have returned. I doubt my sister-in-law would be embarrassed if the correspondence merely had revealed she committed adultery with her neighbor. But the letters also describe—in detail—her predilection for playing X-rated games involving Nazis, whips, and Jews.

As for Ebby and me, we intend to sublet Morty's flat and use a sizeable share of the check the university paid for Morty's archives to buy a house in Vegas large enough to provide a room for Ebby's daughter, Nate, and Nate's iguanas, and a studio in which Ebby can pursue his art. Meryl will spend most of her time with her grandparents, but we will see plenty of her here, especially when Nate comes home from school. That said, Ebby and I will need a house large enough to accommodate whatever other waifs and runaways need a place to stay.

Because that's what we intend to do. If Janis can rescue dogs, why can't Ebby and I rescue teenage girls? I find it difficult to forgive my husband for denying me children of my own to care for. But Morty reached back from the grave to provide me with the means for caring for other people's kids. I think Morty would approve. Plus, I intend to keep searching for his daughter. The girl must be in her thirties. But that doesn't mean she's too old to be informed that her father tried his best to find her, or to be offered the chance to live somewhere better than the dump she lives in now.

So I want to use this opportunity to express my thanks to Columbia University, not to mention the Mel Brooks Archive, for their generous support of Ketzel Weinrach's Home for Teenage Runaways, as well as Eberhard Salzman's artistic career and my plans to take my niece and stepchildren on an archaeological tour of the Middle East. By the time the check runs out, perhaps my agent will have called to say that I have been cast as the ditzy neighbor on Larry David's newest show. Now that I have regained my sense of humor, I might go back to doing stand-up. Although I would only tell jokes I would not be ashamed for my niece to hear. Perhaps I will ask Harvey Blatt to rent a hall and sell tickets to a slightly shorter performance of this story I've been telling you. Morty would disapprove. But there are worse things than observing the details of your own life, laughing at what deserves to be laughed at, and getting angry at the rest.

I don't mean to get too personal, but I thought you might also be pleased to learn that in addition to my regaining my sense of humor, Ebby has regained his pleasure in making love. This happened while we were staying at our old hotel. He hadn't been back in years. Naturally, he was sad to see the site of his earliest triumphs reduced to a wasteland. He was moved to tears by the still-visible baselines in the field where he earned his first accolades pitching and hitting, the rusted rim of the basketball hoop, and the fifty-hole Monster golf course, which, though it showed signs of wear his father never would have allowed, was still in use.

As sad as this was, we found a certain satisfaction in touring those ruins together. Ebby pointed to a twisted wood ramp poking up like a mammoth's spine. "Wasn't that the toboggan run? Geez, it sure seemed a lot taller when we were kids. I guess it's good to go back and see that the scary things weren't all that scary. Or the things you thought were out of reach weren't so far away."

I don't regret a single year I spent with Morty. But how could I feel anything but grateful for the opportunity to go back and begin again, this time with a man who, when I reminisced about my childhood, didn't pull out a pen and take notes? We ate dinner with my parents, then walked to the lake, which, even with all the algae, looked inviting. The air was stifling, and Ebby tore off his shirt and shorts and waded in.

"Come on," he said, "let's swim to the raft." When I shook my head no, he shrugged, put his arms above his head and dove beneath the scum. I wanted to be out there with him. But—call me squeamish—I did not find it appealing to swim in a lake in which so many men had met their end. Then again, sometimes you need to take a deep breath and plunge in over your head in your family's history before you can step out again on dry land, dripping with scum but clean.

"Wait," I called. "I'm coming, too!" At which I remembered the little boy in Morty's joke, the one who was afraid of being left behind to pay the mortgage. I sensed Morty urging me to jump in and swim. *Go on,* he said. *After everything we had together, would I want you to live the rest of your life without a man? You won't get stuck holding the mortgage again, I promise.*

I caught up with Ebby at the raft, which was slick and soft with rot, and we hung on while we rested. In the moonlight, I saw him grin. Then he ducked underwater and swam back to shore. By the time I had crawled up on the beach, he wasn't there. "Ebby?" I said. "Where are you?" At which he sprang out and startled me, and though I pretended to dodge and run, his years of professional training allowed him to tackle me to the sand.

And no, I won't describe what happened next, except to say a man needn't have written a book about making love to be able to please a woman. By the time the sun came up over Cuyahoga Lake, Ebby had regained his ability to appreciate the unclothed female form to such an extent he didn't want to stop appreciating it, and we needed to scramble to put on proper clothes for my cousin's funeral, which in my case consisted of a dress I'd had the presence of mind to borrow from my sister-in-law's closet before we left Vegas.

And now, I don't mean to be impolite, but I really do need to go. I hear Ebby on the stairs. And, as much as I loved my husband, I need to start worrying about my life instead of his. I hope you have enjoyed my story. I couldn't have asked for a more intelligent or attentive audience. But goodbye now! God bless! Good night!

CAVEATS AND ACKNOWLEDGMENTS

Although this novel is meant as a work of fiction, my references to the life and work of Morty Tittelman are in large part derived from the life and work of Gershon Legman. The reader interested in learning more about Legman is urged to consult Mikita Brottman's *Funny Peculiar: Gershon Legman and the Psychopathology of Humor* and Jim Holt's essay "Punch Line" about Legman in the April 19 & 26, 2004, double issue of the *New Yorker*. The quote from Morty Tittelman's *Bible of Dirty Jokes* on p. 54 of this book is a tribute to Legman and is taken from pp. 28–29 of his crazy masterpiece *The Rationale of the Dirty Joke*.

For some of the details related to Potsie's disappearance and Perry's murder, I am indebted to Clifford Linedecker's *Blood in the Sand*. Although no resemblance is intended between anyone in my novel and any real person, living or dead, my sympathies go out to the families of Bruce Weinstein and Mark Grossinger Etess.

Much of my knowledge about the activities of Murder Inc. and the history of gambling and bootlegging in the Catskills comes from my father's stories, supplemented by the more verifiable accounts to be found in *Tough Jews* by Rich Cohen; *Murder, Inc.* by Burton Turkus and Sid Feder; and *Retrospect: An Anecdotal History of Sullivan County, New York* by John Conway. Readers interested in Catskill legends and lore also might want to consult *It Happened in the Catskills* by Myrna Katz Frommer and Harvey Frommer; *To the Mountains by Rail* by Manville Wakefield; and *Catskill Culture* by Phil Brown. For my knowledge of the ins and outs of the business of comedy in Las Vegas, I am indebted to an article by Richard Abowitz in the August 5, 2004, issue of *Las Vegas Weekly*. The routine by the black female comic at Nips is a tribute to Tess Drake, a real stand-up comic.

My *undying* thanks to John Fudenberg, Gary Telgenhoff, and the rest of the strangely happy crew at the Clark County coroner's office. Thanks, too, to Officer Jose Montoya of the Las Vegas Metropolitan Police Department and the officers and staff of the Missing Persons Detail, as well as Peter Psarouthakis of the Michigan Council of Professional Investigators.

For stories, facts, encouragement, and advice, my thanks to Joanna

Edelson, Julie Halpert, Marcie Hershman, Arlene Keizer, Joan Pollack Warren, Noah Glaser, and my mother and father (the latter even as he lay dying). For editorial suggestions: Maxine Rodburg, Suzanne Berne, Adam Schwartz, Josh Lambert, Steve Stern, David Galef, Maria Massie, and Laura Kasischke. My deepest gratitude to my agent, Jenni Ferrari-Adler, and to Martha Rhodes, Vesna Neskow, Ryan Murphy, Sally Ball, Martha Carlson-Bradley, Lytton Smith, and everyone else connected to my beloved Four Way Books. Most of all, thanks to Marian Krzyzowski and Therese Stanton, without whom this book would not exist.

Publication of this book was made possible by grants and donations. We are also grateful to those individuals who participated in our 2017 Build a Book Program:

Anonymous (6), Evan Archer, Sally Ball, Jan Bender-Zanoni, Zeke Berman, Kristina Bicher, Laurel Blossom, Carol Blum, Betsy Bonner, Mary Brancaccio, Lee Briccetti, Deirdre Brill, Anthony Cappo, Carla & Steven Carlson, Caroline Carlson, Stephanie Chang, Tina Chang, Liza Charlesworth, Maxwell Dana, Machi Davis, Marjorie Deninger, Lukas Fauset, Monica Ferrell, Emily Flitter, Jennifer Franklin, Martha Webster & Robert Fuentes, Chuck Gillett, Dorothy Goldman, Dr. Lauri Grossman, Naomi Guttman & Jonathan Mead, Steven Haas, Mary Heilner, Hermann Hesse, Deming Holleran, Nathaniel Hutner, Janet Jackson, Christopher Kempf, David Lee, Jen Levitt, Howard Levy, Owen Lewis, Paul Lisicky, Sara London & Dean Albarelli, David Long, Katie Longofono, Cynthia Lowen, Ralph & Mary Ann Lowen, Donna Masini, Louise Mathias, Catherine McArthur, Nathan McClain, Gregory McDonald, Britt Melewski, Kamilah Moon, Carolyn Murdoch, Rebecca & Daniel Okrent, Tracey Orick, Zachary Pace, Gregory Pardlo, Allyson Paty, Marcia & Chris Pelletiere, Taylor Pitts, Barbara Preminger, Kevin Prufer, Vinode Ramgopal, Martha Rhodes, Peter & Jill Schireson, Roni & Richard Schotter, Soraya Shalforoosh, Peggy Shinner, James Snyder & Krista Fragos, Megan Staffel, Alice St. Claire-Long, Robin Taylor, Marjorie & Lew Tesser, Boris Thomas, Judith Thurman, Susan Walton, Calvin Wei, Abby Wender, Bill Wenthe, Allison Benis White, Elizabeth Whittlesey, Hao Wu, Monica Youn, and Leah Zander.